Her lashes dusted her cheeks, and Tor reached over to push aside strands of her hair from those thick lashes.

She suddenly looked up, and the glint in her eyes lured him closer. Without thinking, he leaned in and nudged his nose aside her cheek, drawing in her perfume, a tantalizing mix of lemon and lavender. He felt her shiver.

When he tilted his head, his mouth grazed her cheek and her lips parted. He brushed them lightly, closing his eyes because the moment demanded he focus on their closeness, the warmth of her skin, the tickle of her hair against his fingers, the scent of her. It all combined with the herbs hanging overhead and the sulfur still lingering from the snuffed candles. A sweet dream. He had never kissed a client before...

Tor pulled a few inches away from Mel's mouth. She gaped at him.

THIS STRANGE WITCHERY
&
TAMED BY THE SHE-WOLF

USA TODAY BESTSELLING AUTHOR

MICHELE HAUF

AND

KRISTAL HOLLIS

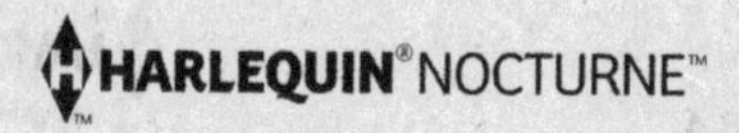

ISBN-13: 978-1-335-22000-4

This Strange Witchery & Tamed by the She-Wolf

This edition published by arrangement with Harlequin Books S.A.

For questions and comments about the quality of this book, please contact us at CustomerService@Harlequin.com.

Printed in U.S.A.

CONTENTS

Michele Hauf is a *USA TODAY* bestselling author who has been writing romance, action-adventure and fantasy stories for more than twenty years. France, musketeers, vampires and faeries usually feature in her stories. And if Michele followed the adage "write what you know," all her stories would have snow in them. Fortunately, she steps beyond her comfort zone and writes about countries and creatures she has never seen. Find her on Facebook, Twitter and at michelehauf.com.

Books by Michele Hauf

Harlequin Nocturne

The Witch's Quest
The Witch and the Werewolf
An American Witch in Paris
The Billionaire Werewolf's Princess
Tempting the Dark
This Strange Witchery

The Saint-Pierre Series

The Dark's Mistress
Ghost Wolf
Moonlight and Diamonds
The Vampire's Fall
Enchanted by the Wolf

In the Company of Vampires

Beautiful Danger
The Vampire Hunter
Beyond the Moon

Visit the Author Profile page at Harlequin.com for more titles.

THIS STRANGE WITCHERY

Michele Hauf

Here's to you, Weirdo.

Chapter 1

The key to disposing of a werewolf body was to get the flames burning quickly, yet to keep them as contained as possible. Torsten Rindle had been doing cleaner work for close to ten years. When a call came in about a dead paranormal found or deposited somewhere in Paris, he moved swiftly. Discreet cleanup was one of his many trades. Media spin was a talent he'd mastered for whenever he was too late to clean up and a human had stumbled upon the dead werewolf. He also dallied with protection work and the occasional vampire hunt.

It was good for a man to keep his business options fluid and to always expand his skills list. And if he had to choose a title for what he did, he'd go with *Secret Keeper*.

But some days…

Tor shook his head as the blue-red flames burned the furry body to ash before him. The use of eucalyptus in the mix masked the smell of burning dog. For the most part.

The creature had been rabid, eluding the slayer until it had gotten trapped down a narrow alleyway that had ended in a brick wall. The slayer had taken it out not twenty minutes earlier, and then had immediately called Tor.

Those in the know carried Tor's number. He was always the first choice when it came to keeping secrets from humans.

Thankful this had been an old wolf—werewolves shifted back to human form after death; the older ones took much longer, sometimes hours—so he hadn't needed to deal with it in human form, Tor swiped a rubber-gloved hand over an itch on his cheek. Then he remembered the werewolf blood he'd touched.

Bollocks.

He was getting tired of this routine: receive a frantic call from someone in the know regarding a rabid werewolf who may be seen by humans. Dash to the scene. Assess the situation. Clean up the mess (if extinguishing the problem was essential), or talk to the police and/or media using one of his many alter-ego names and titles, such as Ichabod Sneed from the Fire Department's Personal Relations. Then return home to his empty loft.

Eat. Crash. Repeat.

Tor knew… He knew too much. Monsters existed. Vampires, werewolves, witches, faeries, harpies, mermaids. They all existed. And yes, dragons were known to be real assholes if you could find one of them. A regular human guy like him shouldn't have such knowledge. That was why, over the years, he had striven to keep such information from the public. Because knowing so much? It fucked with a man's mental state.

And then there were some days he wanted to walk away from it all. Like today.

This morning he'd been woken and called to assist with media contacts while a minor graveyard at the edge of the city had been blocked off from public access. Routine cosmetic repairs, he'd explained to the news reporters. The truth? A demonic ritual had roused a cavalcade of vicious entities from Daemonia. Slayers had taken care of the immediate threat, but that had left the graveyard covered in black tar-like demon blood. And the stench!

Tor had spent the better part of this afternoon arguing with a group of muses about their need to "come out" to the public regarding their oppressive attraction to angels who only wanted to impregnate them. Something to do with the #metoo movement. Sexual harassment or not, the public wasn't ready for the truth about fallen angels and their muses. But, being a feminist himself, he had directed the muses to the Council, who had recently put together a Morals and Ethics Committee.

"I want normal," he muttered. He grabbed the fire extinguisher to douse the flames. He refilled the canister at the local fire station monthly. "It's time I had it."

It took ten minutes to clean up the sludgy ash pile and shovel it into a medium black body bag. Fortunately, this werewolf had been tracked to the edge of the 13th arrondissement not far from the ring road that circled Paris. It was a tight little neighborhood, mostly industry that had closed during regular business hours, leaving the streets abandoned and the dusty windows dark. Tor hadn't noticed anyone nearby, nor had he worried about discovery as he made haste cleaning up the evidence. His van was parked down the street.

He hefted the body bag over a shoulder, picked up the extinguisher and his toolbox filled with all the accoutrements a guy like him should ever need on a job like this, and wandered down the street. His rubber boots made squidgy noises on the tarmac. After dousing the flames, he'd rolled down the white polyethylene hazmat suit to his hips. With shirtsleeves rolled up, his tweed vest still neatly buttoned, yet tie slightly loosened, he could breathe now.

"Normal," he repeated.

He'd scheduled a Skype interview early tomorrow afternoon. The job he had applied for was assistant to Human Relations and Resources at an up-and-coming accounting firm in *la Defense* district. About as mundane and normal as a man could hope for. He'd never actually worked a regular "human" job.

It was about time he gave it a go.

The olive green van, which had seen so many better days, sat thirty feet down from a streetlight that flickered and put out an annoying buzz. Humming a Sinatra tune, Tor opened the back of the van and tossed in the supplies. He'd dump the body bag at a landfill on the way home. He'd done his research; that landfill was plowed monthly and shipped directly to China for incineration.

"That's my life," he sang, altering the lyrics to suit him.

Sinatra was a swanky idol to him. Singing his songs put him in a different place from the weird one he usually occupied. Call it a sanity check. The Sultan of Swoon relaxed him in ways he could appreciate.

He peeled off the sweaty hazmat suit, hung it on a hanger and placed that on a hook near the van ceiling. At his belt hung a heavy quartz crystal fixed into a steel mount that clipped with a D ring onto a loop. He never went anywhere without the bespelled talisman. Another necessity for sanity. The rubber boots were placed in a tray on the van floor. He pulled out his bespoke Italian leather shoes from a cloth bag and slipped those on.

"Ahhh..." Almost better than a shower. But he couldn't wait to wash off the werewolf blood. Odds were he had it in more places than the smear across his cheek.

Closing the back doors, he punched a code on the digital lock to secure it. While he sorted through his trouser pocket for the van key, he whistled the chorus to the song that demanded he accept life as it was...*that's life.*

Maybe... No. Life didn't have to be this way for him. He was all-in for a change of scenery.

Before he slid the key in the lock, he saw the driver's door was unlocked. Had he forgotten? That wasn't like him. He was always on top of the situation. Which only further contributed to his need to run from this life as if a flaming werewolf were chasing his ass.

Tor slid into the driver's seat and fired up the engine. Another crazy midnight job. His final one. He would stand firm on that decision. And after getting a whiff of the dead werewolf's rangy scent—someone please show him the way to his new office cubicle.

Adjusting the radio to a forties' swing station, he palmed the stick shift.

When the person in the passenger seat spoke, he startled. "Whoa!"

"Hey! Oops. Sorry." The woman let out a bubbly nervous giggle. "Didn't mean to surprise you. I've been waiting. And watching. You've quite the talent, you know that?"

"Who in bloody—" He squinted in the darkness of the cab, but could only see glints in her eyes and—above her eyes? Hmm... Must be some kind of sparkly makeup. "How did you...?"

"The door wasn't locked. You really should lock your doors in this neighborhood. Anyone could steal your van. Not that it's very steal-worthy. Kinda old, and there's more rust than actual paint. But I'm guessing you have important stuff in the back. Like a dead werewolf!" she announced with more cheer than anyone ever should.

His eyes adjusting to the darkness, Tor could make out that she had long brown hair and big eyes. She smiled. A lot. He didn't get a sense about her—was she paranormal or human? But then, he didn't have any special means of determining whether a person was paranormal or not. Sometimes he didn't know until it was too late. But he did pick up an overtly incautious happiness about her.

Without letting down his guard, he reached across the console to offer his hand. "Torsten Rindle."

"I know!" She shook his hand eagerly. "I've been looking for you. And now I've found you."

If she knew who he was, then she probably knew what he did for a living. Which still didn't solve the issue of *what* she was. Humans hired him all the time to protect them from paranormals. But to find him, they had to be in the know, and also know someone who knew someone who knew him. Who, in turn, had his phone number.

He pulled back his hand and leaned an elbow on the steering wheel, keeping his body open, prepared to move to either defend or restrain. "Who are you, and why are you in my van?"

"It's a rather beat-up old van, isn't it?"

"So you've said."

"Doesn't really jibe with you in your fancy vest and trousers and designer watch."

The watch in question showed it was well past midnight. This had been a hell of a long day.

"I don't need to draw attention by driving a sports car," Tor offered. "And the van is as utility as it gets. A requirement in my line of work. Now. Your name? And why are you sitting in my van?"

"Melissande Jones." She fluttered her lashes as she pressed her fingers to her chest, where frilly red flowers made up the neckline of her blouse. "My friends call me Lissa, as does my family. I'm not sure I like the nickname, but I hate to argue with people. I'm a people pleaser. Sad, but true. And I'm here because I need your help. Your protection, actually."

Tor played her name over in his brain. The last name was familiar. And in Paris, it wasn't so common as, say, in the United States or London. He made it a point to know who all the paranormal families in the city were, and had good knowledge of most across the world. Blame it on his penchant for getting lost in research. And for needing to know everything.

Recall brought to mind a local family of witches. The two elders were twin brothers. And he knew the one brother had twin sons, so that left the other…

"Thoroughly Jones's daughter? A dark witch?"

"Yes, and mostly." She turned on the seat so her body faced him. Her bright red lipstick caught the pale glow from the distant streetlight. Her lips were shaped like a bow. And combined with those big doe eyes and lush feathery lashes? "Can you help me?"

"I, uh…" Shaking himself out of his sudden admiration for her sensual assets, Tor assumed his usual emotionless facade, the one he wore for the public. "I'm not sure what you've heard about me, but I'm no longer in the business of providing personal protection."

"You're a cleaner." She gestured toward the fire truck that was pulling up down the street where the werewolf had been burned. Someone must have witnessed the fire after all. "You also do spin for The Order of the Stake."

Two things that most might know about him. If they were paranormal. And again, knew someone who knew someone who—

"And you own the Agency," she said, interrupting his disturbed thoughts. "A group that protects us paranormals."

That knowledge was more hush-hush. And not correct.

"Not exactly. The Agency seeks to put their hands to

weapons, ephemera, and other objects that might fall into human hands and lead them to believe in you paranormals."

"You paranormals," she said mockingly and gestured with a flutter of her hand that made Tor suddenly nervous. A bloke never knew what witches could do with but a flick of finger or sweep of hand. "You're human, right?"

"That I am."

And she was a witch. A dark witch. Mostly? He had no idea what that meant. And…he wasn't interested in finding out.

"Like I've said, I don't do protection. And I've handed off the Agency reins to someone located in the States. But of most importance is, I really do not want to get involved with anyone from the Jones family. I respect your father and his brother. They are a pair of badass dark witches most would do well to walk a wide circle around." He'd come *this close* to stepping into that dangerous circle a few years back. And he wasn't a stupid man. Lesson learned. "If you need someone—"

"But your Agency protects paranormal objects, yes?"

"It does. The Agency always will, but I'm not doing that sort of—"

"Then you can help me." She bent over and reached into a big flowered purse on the floor and pulled out something that blinded Tor with its brilliance. "I have a paranormal object."

Tor put up a hand to block the pulsating red glow. It was so bright. Like the sun but in a shade of red. He couldn't see the shape or the size, yet knew that she held it with one hand. "Put that away! What the hell is that?"

She set the thing on her lap and placed a palm over it, which quieted the glow to a smoldering simmer. "It's Hecate's heart."

Tor didn't recognize it as a volatile object from any lists he had read or compiled, but that didn't mean anything.

There were so many weapons, objects, tools, even creatures that were considered a danger to humans and paranormals alike. The most dangerous had to be contained, or Very Bad Things could happen in the mortal realm.

"What does it do besides blind a man?" he asked.

"Hecate was the first witch."

"I know that. But she's long dead. Is that her actual heart?"

"Yes." Melissande patted it gently. The object pulsed with each touch. "It's said that should her heart ever stop beating, all the witches' hearts in this realm would suddenly cease to beat. Ominous, right?" The red glow softened her features and gave them an enchanting cast. Her lashes were so thick, they granted her eyes a glamorous come-and-touch-me appeal. "But it's pretty indestructible. I dropped it earlier. Got a little dirt on it. No big deal. Though it looks like glass, it's not. It's sort of a solid gel substance."

"You dropped it? Wait." Tor took a moment to inhale and center himself. And to remember his goal: normal. "I'm not doing this. I'm no longer in the protection business."

Melissande's jaw dropped open. And those eyes. Why couldn't he stop staring at those gorgeous eyes? Was it the sparkly makeup that made them glitter, or did they really twinkle like stars? Maybe she'd cast an attraction spell on herself before finding him. Witches were sneaky like that. And how had she found him? Tor prided himself on his ability to blend in, to be the classic everyman. That she had been able to track him down without a phone call…

He wasn't going to worry about this. He'd made his decision. Normal it was.

"I need to get on the road and dispose of the remains," he said, turning on the seat and gripping the steering wheel. "You can leave now."

"I'm not going anywhere. Did you decide *just now* you're not doing the protection thing anymore?"

"No, I—"

"Or is it me? I get that my dad and his brother are a couple of big scary witches. Woo-woo dark witch stuff *is* imposing. But I'm not asking you to work with them."

"I've been considering this decision for weeks. Months," Tor protested. "And it's final—"

"Oh, come on. One more job? I need your help, Tor. I'm just one tiny witch who has an ominous magical artifact stuffed in her purse that seems to attract strange things to it. In proof, on the way to finding you, I gave a zombie the slip."

"Zombies do not exist," Tor said sharply. "Revenants do. But the walking dead are a false assumption. It's impossible to have a dead person walking around, decaying, and actually surviving more than a few minutes."

"Is that so? That's good to know. Still not sure I believe you. But revenants..." She cast her gaze out the passenger window.

And Tor couldn't help but wonder what it was about revenants that gave her pause. Damn it! He didn't care. He could not care. If he were going to make the transition to normal, he had to get rid of this annoyingly cute witch.

Yet the glow from the heart, seeping between her fingers, did intrigue him. Something like that should be under lock and key, kept far and safely away from humans. And should it fall into the hands of the Archives, whom her uncle Certainly Jones headed? The Archives wasn't as beneficent as they were touted to be. The things they stored weren't always left to sit and get dusty. Tor didn't even want to think about all the nasty happenings that occurred because something the Archives had obtained had been used.

Yeah, so maybe he had stepped into that circle of danger with one of the Jones brothers. Whew! He knew far too much about the ominous power of dark magic. And yet he had lived to breathe another day.

"You want me to protect you and that thing?" he asked. "You know the Agency would take that heart in hand and put it under lock and key? In fact, if you want to hand it over, I guess I could take it right now—"

"No." She lifted the heart possessively to her chest. Tor squinted at the maddening glow. "Can't do that. I need it for a spell that I can't invoke until the night of the full moon."

Which was less than a week from now. Tor always kept the moon cycles in his head. It wasn't wise to walk into any situation without knowing what phase the moon was in. Had tonight been a full moon? That werewolf would not have gone down so easily for the slayer. And burning it would have roused every bloody wolf in the city to howls.

Tor rubbed two fingers over his temple, sensing he wasn't going to be rid of her as easily as he wished. "Why me? What or who directed you toward me and suggested I might want to help you?"

"If I tell you, you'll think I'm weird."

"I already think you're weird. I don't think a person can get much weirder than stealing a dead witch's beating heart and then breaking into a stranger's van to beg for his help."

"What makes you think I stole this?"

"I—I don't know. Is it a family heirloom you dug out of a chest in the attic? Something dear old Granny bequeathed to you on her deathbed?"

"No." She hugged it tightly to her chest. Guilty of theft, as he could only suspect. And he *had* locked the van doors. He never forgot.

"People only find me because someone has given them

my name," he said. "And I always know when someone is coming for me, because that's how it works. I want to know how you learned about me."

"Fine. This evening, after I'd gotten home with the heart and sat out on the patio to have a cup of tea—I like peppermint, by the way."

"I'm an Earl Grey man, myself." The woman did go off on tangents. And he had just followed her along on one! "You were saying what it was that led you to me?"

"Right. As I was sipping my tea, a cicada landed on my plate. It was blue."

Now intensely interested, Tor lifted his gaze to hers.

"Cicadas always look like they're wearing armor. Don't you think? Anyway, I didn't hear it speak to me," she said. "Not out loud. More like in my head. I sensed what it had come to tell me. And that was to give me your name. Torsten Rindle. I'd heard the name before. My dad and uncle have mentioned you in conversation. Cautiously, of course. I know you stand in opposition to them. And they know it, too. But they also have a certain respect for you. Anyway, I knew you could help me."

A cicada had told a witch to seek him out for help?

Tor's sleeves were still rolled to the elbows. Had the light been brighter, it would reveal the tattoo of a cicada on his inner forearm. The insect meant something to him. Something personal and so private he'd never spoken about it to anyone.

"How did you know—"

A thump on the driver's side window made Tor spin around on the seat. A bloody hand smeared the glass.

"That's the zombie," Melissande stated calmly. "The one you told me didn't exist."

Chapter 2

Melissande observed as Tor swung out of the driver's seat and darted into the back of the van. Heavy metal objects clinked. The man swore. His British accent was more pronounced than her barely-there one. He again emerged in the cab with a wicked-looking weapon. Actually, she recognized that hand-sized titanium column as one of those fancy stakes the knights in The Order of the Stake used to slay vampires. Was that supposed to work with zombies, as well?

"Stay here," he ordered. Tor exited through the driver's door, slamming it behind him.

Crossing her arms and settling onto the seat, Melissande decided she was perfectly fine with staying inside the nice safe van while the hero fought the creepy thing outside. Zombies didn't exist? The man obviously knew nothing about the dark arts.

A hand slapped the driver's window, followed by the

smeared, slimy face of something that could only be zombie. One eyeball was missing. From behind, Tor grabbed it by the collar and swung it away from the vehicle.

Melissande let out her breath in a gasp, then tucked the heart she still held into her bag on the floor. Growing up in a household with a dark witch for a dad and a cat-shifting familiar for a mom, she should be prepared for unusual situations like this, but it never got easier to witness. Dark magic was challenging. And sometimes downright gross. She was surprised she'd accomplished her task today, securing Hecate's heart. But she hadn't expected it to attract the unsavory sort like the one battling Tor right now. Earlier, that same creature had growled at her and swiped, but she'd been too fast, and had slipped down the street away from the thing in her quest to locate the one man she knew could help her.

Anticipating the dangers of possessing the heart, she had known she might need protection. She couldn't ask her dad, or her uncle. And should she ask her cousins—the twins Laith and Vlas—they would have laughed at her, saying how she'd gotten herself into another wacky fix.

She did have a knack for the weird and wacky. It seemed to follow her around like a stray cat with a bent tail. She didn't hate cats, but she'd never keep one as a pet or familiar. When one's mother was a cat-shifter, a girl learned to respect felines and to never take them for granted.

The not-zombie's shoulders slammed against the vehicle's dented hood. Melissande leaned forward in time to watch Tor slam the stake against its chest. The zombie didn't so much release ash as dechunk, falling apart in clumps, accompanied by a glugging protrusion of sludgy gray stuff from its core. Gross, but also interesting. She'd never witnessed a zombie death.

With a sweep of his arm, Tor brushed some chunks

from the hood. He tucked the stake in a vest pocket, then smoothed out the tweed vest he wore. Shirtsleeves rolled to his elbows revealed a tattoo on his forearm, but she couldn't make out what it was in the darkness.

He was a smart dresser, and much sexier than she'd expected for a jack-of-all-trades human—because she had expected something rather brute, stocky and plain. Probably even scarred and with a gimpy eye. Tor's short dark hair was neatly styled (save for the blood smeared at his temple and into his hairline). Thick, dark brows topped serious eyes that now scanned the area for further danger. With every movement, a muscle, or twelve, flexed under his fitted white shirt, advertising his hard, honed physique. And those fingers wrapped about the stake…so long and graceful, yet skilled and determined…

Melissande's heart thundered, and it wasn't from fear of a vile creature. The man did things to her better judgment, like make her wonder why she had never dated a human before. Maybe it was time to stretch her potential boyfriend qualifications beyond their boundaries.

"Did you get him?" she yelled through the windshield.

Tor's eyebrow lifted and he gave her a wonky head wobble, as if to say, *Did you not see me battle that heinous creature then defeat it?*

She offered him a double thumbs-up.

He strolled around the side of the van. The back doors opened, and he pulled out something, then came back to the front. A shovel proved convenient for scooping dead zombie into a body bag. He was certainly well prepared.

After the quick cleanup, he again walked to the back of the van. Melissande glanced over the seats into the van's interior. When he tossed in the bag and slammed the door, she cringed. The driver's door opened, and Tor slid inside. She noticed the blood at his neck that seeped onto his starched white collar. It looked like a scratch on his skin. If that thing had originally been a vampire, it could be bite marks. Tor slammed the door and turned on the ignition.

Melissande leaned over to touch his neck. He reacted, lifting an elbow to block her. But she did not relent, pressing her fingers against his neck. "I'm not going to bite," she said. "I want to make sure *you* didn't get bitten."

"It's just a scratch. The thing didn't get close enough to nosh on my neck. Sit down and buckle up." He pulled away from the curb as she tugged the seat belt across her torso.

"Was it a vampire?" she asked.

"I'm not sure. Hard to determine with all the decay."

"Zombie," she declared.

"Not going to have that argument again. Probably a revenant vamp."

"I've heard they're rare. And don't live in the city."

"Dead vampires who live in coffins and have no heartbeat? Most definitely not common. And generally not found in any large city, including Paris." He dusted off some debris from his forearm. "Though I didn't notice fangs. And usually decapitation is required. Whatever it was, it's dead now."

"You're driving with me in your van," Melissande remarked cheerfully. "Does that mean you're going to protect me?"

"No. That means I'm going to take you home and send you off with a pat on your head and well wishes. Where do you live?"

Pouting, she muttered, "The 6th."

In the flash of a streetlight, he cast her a look. It admonished while also judged. Such a look made him fall a notch on her attraction-level meter.

"You're not very nice," she offered.

Tor turned his attention back to the street, shaking his head.

"I'll pay you," she tried. "I would never expect you to work for free."

"What's the address?" he asked.

Obstinate bit of…sexy. If he weren't so handsome, she would ask him to stop and she'd catch a cab. She was not a woman to hang around where she wasn't wanted.

After a reluctant sigh, Melissande gave him the street address and muddled over how to convince him to protect her. She didn't know who else to contact. She'd overheard her dad and his brother one evening talking about the various humans in the city whom they trusted. The list had been short. And while they'd both agreed that Torsten Rindle was definitely not on their side, they'd also agreed that he was a man of honor and integrity who could get the job done, and who had a concern for keeping all things paranormal hush-hush without resorting to senseless violence or assuming all nonhumans walked around with a target on their foreheads.

At the time, Melissande had known if she'd ever need help, he was her man. And then, when the whole conversation earlier with the cicada had occurred—well. She never overlooked a chat with a bug.

She hadn't told her dad, Thoroughly Jones, this part of the plan, though he did know her ultimate goal. She'd agreed to take on this task because she knew how much of an emotional toll it would take on her father. And she intended to handle every detail on her own, so he could focus on taking care of her mother, Star, when she really needed the attention.

Poor Mom—she had only just been reborn a few weeks ago after a fall from a sixth-floor rooftop, and this life was not treating her well.

Melissande's neighborhood was quiet and quaint and filled with old buildings that had stood for centuries. The Montparnasse Cemetery wasn't far away, and often tourists wandered down her street, but were always respectful of the private gates and entrances. She loved it because she had a decent-sized yard behind the house, fenced in with black wrought iron, in which she grew herbs and medicinal flowers. It served her earth magic. Her two-story Victorian, painted a deep, dusty violet, held memories of ages past. But no ghosts. Which bummed her out a little, because she wouldn't mind a ghost or two, so long as they were friendly.

Tor parked the van before her property. The front gate and fence boasted a healthy climbing vine with night-blooming white moonflowers. Opening the van door, she breathed in the flowers' intoxicating scent. "Blessed goddess Luna." Soon the moon would reach fullness. And then Melissande would be faced with her greatest challenge.

Tor swung around the front of the van before she'd even gotten her first foot on the ground. "I'll walk you up," he said as he rolled down his sleeves.

She dashed her finger over the cut on his neck and was satisfied it was just a nick.

"I'll live." He offered her his arm.

Startled by such a chivalrous move, Melissande linked her arm with his, and with a push of her hand forward and a focus of her magic, she opened the gate before them without touching it.

She'd been born with kinetic magic. Sometimes the things she needed moved did so before she even had the thought.

"Witches," Tor muttered as he witnessed the motion.

"What about witches?" she challenged. The narrow sidewalk forced them to walk closely, and she did not release his arm when she felt his tug to make her step a little faster. "You got a problem with witches?"

"I have little problem with any person who occupies this realm. Unless they intend, or actually do, harm to others. Then that person will not like me very much."

"I know your reputation. It's why I came to you. But you're not a vampire slayer, so why the stake to fight the zombie?"

"Revenant." They stopped before the stoop, and she allowed him back his arm. Tor pushed his hands into his trouser pockets. "I like to keep my arsenal varied. The stake was a gift from an Order knight. I also carry a silent chain saw and a variety of pistols equipped with wood, iron and UV bullets. And at any given moment I might also be wielding a machete. Gotta mix it up. Keep things fresh."

"You don't use spells, do you?"

"Not with any luck."

"Good. That's my expertise. Do you want to come in for some tea before you abandon me to be attacked by all the vile denizens that seek the heart?"

"No, I'm good." He winked.

Melissande's heart performed a shiver and then a squeezing hug. Surely the heat rising in her neck was a blush, but she couldn't remember a time when she'd blushed before.

"I'm beat," Tor said. "It's been a long day. Had to talk down a couple muses from going public with their life stories before that werewolf cleanup. Started the day with a demon mess. And capping it off with a revenant slaying put me over the edge as far as social contact." He held out his hand for her to shake. "Good luck finding the person you need for protection."

Melissande stared at his hand for a few seconds, deciding it was the sexiest hand she'd ever seen. Wide and sure, and the fingers were long and strong. She'd like to feel them handle her as smoothly and as confidently as he had the stake.

As she reluctantly lifted her hand in a send-off to her last best hope, she remembered something. "I forgot my bag in your van. It's got the heart in it."

"I'll get it for you—"

They both turned when a growl in the vicinity of the van curdled the night air. Looming before the vehicle was a skeletal conglomeration of bones and smoke with a toothy maw.

"Really?" Tor said. "A wraith demon? What the hell is up with that heart?"

"I have no idea," Melissande offered as she grabbed him by the arm and clung out of fear.

"Go inside," he ordered. "I'll handle this."

"Good plan. I'll start tea." As Tor strode toward the growling demon, unafraid and shoulders back, Melissande called, "Don't forget my bag!"

Tor's strides took him right up to the wraith demon. The thing slashed its talons at him and hissed, "You have something I want, human." It dragged its obsidian talons across the passenger door, cutting through the faded green paint to reveal the steel beneath.

"If it's a wish for a new paint job, you're right, bloke," Tor said.

Not giving the thing a moment to think, he swung out and landed a solid right hook on the side of its head, just below the horn. That was a touchy spot where no bone covered whatever tender innards were contained within the thing. The demon howled in pain.

Not wanting to wake the neighbors, Tor acted quickly. Taking out the stake from his pocket, he plunged it against the demon's chest and compressed the paddles to release the spring-loaded pointed shaft. It wasn't the first line of defense against demons, but it did slow them down just long enough.

From his belt, he unhooked the vial of black Egyptian salt—that he purchased in bulk—and broke the glass outward so the contents sprayed the demon's face. *"Deus benedicat!"* The *god bless you* wasn't necessary for the kill, but he liked to toss that in. Those were the last words a demon wanted to hear as its face stretched wide in a dying scream.

"Bastard!" the thing shouted before its horns dropped off. The wraith demon disintegrated to a pile of floaty black ash at Tor's feet.

Glancing over his shoulder, Tor scanned the neighborhood. No lights on in any nearby houses. And the altercation had occurred on the side of the van facing the witch's house, so he'd been partially concealed. But he waited anyway.

Curiosity always tended to come out in moments of fear. If any humans had witnessed this, he'd know about it soon.

Checking his watch, he verified it was nearing 2:00 a.m. Too late. And like he'd told the witch: he'd had a day.

"Normal," he muttered, and shook the ash from the toe of his leather shoe.

Sure the demon slaying had gone unnoticed, Tor opened the passenger door and grabbed the floral tapestry purse. It was so heavy he wondered if rocks were inside it, and red fringes dangled from the bottom. Girl stuff always gave him pause for a moment of genuine wonder. What was the purpose of so many fringes? And what did women put in their purses that made them heavier than an army rucksack? He'd like to take a look inside, but he knew that a wise man did not poke about in a witch's personal things.

He turned toward the house, then paused. He should take out Hecate's heart and toss the purse on the step. That would solve a lot of problems he didn't want to have. Namely, revenants and crazed demons.

The purse had a zipper. He touched the metal pull—

"Didn't your mother teach you it's not nice to snoop in a woman's bag?" Melissande called from the threshold.

Tor rubbed the tattoo under his sleeve. No, his mother had not.

With a resigned sigh, he strode up to the witch's stoop and handed her the curious receptacle filled with marvels untold.

"Tea?" she asked sweetly. As if he'd not just polished off a wraith demon in her front yard, and wasn't wearing werewolf blood on his face like some kind of Scottish warrior.

"Why not." With weary resolution, Tor stepped up. Pressing his palms to the door frame and leaning forward, but not crossing the threshold, he asked, "Wards?"

"None for you, but as soon as you step inside, I'll reactivate them. Come on. I won't bite, unlike some people."

Tor's chuckle was unstoppable. He stepped inside and closed the door, then followed the witch down a hallway papered in cutout purple and gray velvet damask and into the kitchen, which smelled of candle wax and dried herbs.

Two cups of tea sat on a serving tray, which she picked up before leading him into a living room filled with so much fringe, velvet and glitter, Tor closed his eyes against the overwhelming bling as he sat on the couch. And settled deep into the plushest, most comfortable piece of furniture his body had ever known.

"Right?" Melissande offered in response to his satisfied groan. "I like to become one with my furniture. That's my favorite spot. If you relax, you'll be asleep in two sips."

Tor took a sip of the sweet tea. Not Earl Grey, but it was palatable. "I never sleep on the job."

The witch sat on an ottoman before him, which was upholstered in bright red velvet. "On the job? Does that mean…?"

That meant that Tor had just fended off two crazed creatures who had wanted to get to the heart in the witch's mysterious purse. There was something wrong with that. He couldn't ignore that she was in some kind of trouble. Whether dire or merely mediocre, it didn't matter. When bad things came at you, a person needed to defend themselves. And she didn't seem like someone who knew how to protect herself, even if she did possess magic.

He took another sip of the tea, and his eyelids fluttered. This was good stuff. He'd had a long day. And combined with his growing nerves for tomorrow's interview, his body was shot. His tight muscles wanted to release and…

Tor's teacup clinked as it hit the saucer. He didn't see the witch extend her magical influence to steady the porcelain set in midair, because sleep hit him like a troll's fist to the skull.

Chapter 3

Melissande leaned over Tor, who was slowly coming awake on the couch. He was so cute. Not a high-school-crush-with-long-bangs-and-a-quirky-smile kind of cute (though there was nothing wrong with that), but rather in a grown-up male I-will-save-you-from-all-that-frightens-you manner. His glossy hair was cut short above his ears, growing to tousle-length at the top of his head. She restrained herself from dipping her fingers into those tempting strands. Didn't want to freak him out and send him running when he'd only just agreed to help her.

His face shape was somewhere between an oval and a rectangle, and essentially perfect. Even the remaining smudges of blood at his temple did little to mar his handsome angles. His nose was long yet not too wide or flat. A shadow of stubble darkened his jaw, but she suspected he was a morning shaver and liked to keep as tidy as his knotted tie. The zombie debris smudged on his white shirtsleeves must be driving him batty.

Her gaze traveled to his mouth, while she traced her upper lip with her tongue. The man's lips were firm, and sprinkled with a burgeoning mustache on the skin above. That indent between nose and upper lip was something she wanted to press her finger to. It was called a philtrum, if she recalled her explorations in anatomy (for spellcraft, of course). Maybe, if she was really sneaky…

Tor startled and Melissande quickly stood, tucking the offending finger behind her back. "Good morning!"

She waited for him to fully register wakefulness. He shook his head, stretched out his arms and curled his fingers. Then he patted his chest as if to reassure himself of a heartbeat. His next move was grasping for the large crystal hooked at his belt—she figured it was a kind of talisman.

The man looked around the living room, brightly lit by the duck-fluff sunshine beaming through the patio-door windows—and groaned. "What the hell did you put in that tea, witch?"

"Chamomile and lavender. You had a long and trying day. And you said you were tired, so I knew those specific herbs would help you along."

"Help me along? To where? Oblivion? That stuff was hexed. It knocked me out like a prizefighter's punch. It's morning? Bloody hell. I have business—"

"It's only eleven."

"Eleven?" He stood and ran his fingers through his hair. "I've slept half the day."

"I've made breakfast. You have time to eat and get a grasp on the day."

He winced. The man really did have a hard time coming out of a chamomile-tea sleep. Sans spell. She hadn't added anything to the tea leaves. Honest.

"Appointment's at—" he checked his watch "—one."

"Good, then you've time. This way!"

She skipped into the kitchen, which gleamed from a cleaning with lemon juice and vinegar. It was the coziest place Melissande could imagine to create. The kitchen was a large circle that hugged the front corner of the house. A pepper-pot turret capped the room two stories up, giving it an airy, yet still cozy vibe. Everywhere hung tools of her trade such as dried herbs twisted into powerful protection sigils, a bucket of coal (all-purpose magical uses), abundance and peace spells carved into the wooden windowsills, and charm bags hung with bird feet, anise stars and such. Drying fruits and herbs hung before the windows and from the ceiling. Crystals suspended from thin red string dazzled in all the windows. And the curved, velvet-cushioned settee that hugged the front of the house and looked out on the yard glinted from the tangerine quartz that danced as if it were a fringe along the upper row of curtains.

On the stretch of kitchen counter sat the fruit bowl she'd prepared while listening to Tor's soft and infrequent snores. She had already eaten, because who can prepare a meal without tasting? And really, she'd risen with the sun to collect fading peony petals for a tincture.

Stretching out his arms in a flex that bulged his muscles beneath the fitted shirt, Tor wandered into the kitchen and cast his gaze about. He took in the herbs hanging above and the sun catchers glinting in the windows, and then his eyes landed on the frog immediately to his left, at eye level.

He jumped at the sight of the curious amphibian. "What the bloody—? A floating frog?"

Melissande shooed the frog into the dining area where the table mimicked the curve of the windows and wall. The fat, squat amphibian slowly made its way forward, but not without a protesting croak. He did not care to be ordered about. "That's Bruce, my familiar. And he does not float."

"Looks like it's floating to me." Tor sat before the counter, checking Bruce with another assessing glance.

"He's a levitating frog," Melissande provided with authority.

"I don't think I understand the difference."

"Anyone, or any creature, can float. And a floater just, well...floats. But a frog who levitates? That implies he's doing it of his free will. Not many can do that. Am I right?"

Tor's brow lifted in weird acceptance. He tugged at his tie.

"I hope you like smoothie bowls." She pushed the bowl of breakfast toward him and held up a spoon.

Tor took the spoon, but his attention was all over the bowl of pureed kiwi and pear spotted with dragon fruit cut in the shape of stars and sprinkles of cacao and coconut. "It's...blue?"

"The algae powder makes it blue. Lots of good minerals in that. Do you like hemp seeds?"

"I...don't know." He prodded a small pear sphere that she had cut out and added to the bowl arranged to look like a night sky filled with stars. "It's so...decorative. I'm not sure I can eat it."

"Of course you can. Dig in. It's super healthy, and the dragon fruit is only in season for a short time. I already ate. I have a tendency to graze more than sit down for official meals. When you're finished we can discuss your payment plan."

"My payment plan?" He scooped a helping of the smoothie and tasted it. With an approving nod, he ate more.

"You did say you were on the job last night. I took that to mean you were going to protect me."

She fluttered her eyelashes, knowing she had abnormally long lashes. The action was one of her well-honed man-catcher moves. Well, she hadn't actually field-tested it as a kinetic magic, but surely it had some power.

Tor sighed, and the spoon clinked the side of the bowl. "Really? Using the ole bat-your-lashes move on me?"

"Did it work?" she asked gleefully.

He shook his head and snickered. "I am impervious."

Standing on the opposite side of the counter from him, Melissande leaned onto her elbows and gave him another devastating flutter. "That's very sad that a man has to make himself impervious to a harmless little thing like me."

"You, I suspect, are far from harmless." He plucked out a star of white dragon fruit speckled with tiny black seeds and downed it. Stabbing the air in her direction with the spoon, he said, "I'm not buying the tea story. There was something in that brew. And you *are* a witch."

"Wow, you got that on the first guess."

"Don't patronize me. I know my paranormals. All ilks, from shapeshifters to alchemists, to the feral and the half-breeds. And I know..." He set down the spoon and looked her straight in the eyes.

And Melissande's heart did a giddy dance as his brown irises glinted with such a promise she didn't know how to describe it, only it made her know—just *know*—that he had been the right choice. In more ways than she could fully realize.

"Fine." He looked away from her gaze, clutching for the knot in his tie to ease at it self-consciously.

"Fine?"

He conceded with a headshake that was neither a yes nor a no. At least, he was trying hard not to make it an all-out yes. "To judge from the events that have taken place since we've met, it is obvious you need protection from—whatever that *thing* you have in your purse is attracting. And I would never refuse to defend anyone in need."

Melissande clasped her hands together.

"But I would prefer you simply hand over the heart and let me place it in safekeeping."

"Can't do that, because I know you won't give it back."

"You are correct. The Agency takes containment and security very seriously. Once we obtain an item, there is no way in hell—or Beneath—we'll let that thing out of hand or sight."

"Then that's a big *no way* on the safekeeping suggestion. And I know you can't take it from me because that would be stealing, and that'll have magical repercussions."

"Yeah? Did *you* steal the heart?"

"I..." She walked her fingers along the counter toward the dish towel and grabbed it, then turned to dust the front of the fridge.

"As suspected. Guess that means I'm on the clock for the next handful of days, eh?"

Melissande tossed the towel to the sink and clapped gleefully. "Oh, thank you! You won't regret it. I won't be trouble. I promise."

"That promise has already been broken. Twice over." He scooped in more of the smoothie. "But this ornamental fruit thingy makes up for some of it." He twisted his wrist to check his watch. "I didn't expect to take on a protection job. I do have other plans, and an online appointment I need to make in less than two hours. I have to go home to clean up and prepare."

"Then you'll come back?"

He finished off the smoothie bowl and stood. "You're coming with me. From this moment, I won't let you out of my sight. Not until our contract is complete."

"We have a contract?"

He held out his hand to shake, and Melissande slapped her palm against his. His wide, strong hand held hers firmly. And if she hadn't been so excited for his acceptance, she would have swooned in utter bliss. Maybe she did a little of it anyway, but she gripped the counter to keep her knees from bending and sinking too far into the silly reaction.

"Yes, now we have a gentleman's contract," he said. "Grab whatever you need for the day. We'll discuss details and logistics later, after I've finished with the appointment. Do you think you can stay out of my hair while I do that?"

"Of course. Although, you've some very nice hair. I almost ran my fingers through it while I was watching you sleep."

"You were watch—" Tor put up a palm. "Don't want to know. Let's head out."

"I'll get my things!"

"Uh..." Tor glanced toward the dining table. "The frog stays here."

"Of course he does," Melissande said. With a snap of her fingers, the door leading out to the narrow side yard opened a few inches. "He'll be going out for his noontime bug hunt, anyway!"

This was not how he'd intended his day to go.

Tor liked to keep to a schedule, which could be significantly different from day to day. But that he planned in advance for the following day's events was key. He was always prepared, even for surprises.

Most surprises, anyway. A cute witch sitting in his van with a strange, glowing heart in her purse? That had been an unexpected one.

He walked into his apartment, followed by the witch, who carried two big bags of—whatever it was witches felt the need to carry with them. *Please, do not let it be rank and slithery spell supplies.* He didn't mind the creepy stuff, so long as it was on his terms.

"I've but an hour before the interview," he said with a glance at his watch. "This is the kitchen. There are food and drinks in the fridge. I'm going to shower and shave. Please, don't touch anything that looks like it shouldn't be touched."

"So that means everything?" Melissande dropped her bags to either side of her feet.

Tor winced as he heard something hard *clunk* against the marble floor. "Exactly. You did bring the heart along?"

"Of course."

"I assume you've hexed it well to prevent those we don't want sensing it from…sensing it?"

"Hexes are dark magic. Of which I am learning. Fast. Although protection requires a ward instead of a hex." She bent and dug out a container from the tapestry bag and held it up. It was a clear plastic container, of the sort women used to store food, which they then placed in their pantries.

"That's…" Tor winced. Really? "Is that a plastic food container?"

She nodded enthusiastically. "I store all my spell stuff in these. They're sturdy, and I have the whole pink set. And it's got a stay-fresh seal on the cover."

First it was a floating frog—make that a levitating frog—and now flimsy plastic kitchenware to protect a foul and officious artifact that seemed to attract the denizens of evil. And he'd yet to learn if that black line that curled out at the corner of each of Melissande's eyes into a swish was intentional or a slip of the wrist.

His initial assessment of the witch was spot-on: weird.

"Ward it," Tor said as he turned to stride down the hallway. He couldn't stand before the woman any longer and not wring her neck. Or try to shake her to see what common sense might tumble out from those gorgeous curly black locks that spilled over her cheeks so softly— "Do it outside on the deck so you don't make a mess in the house!"

"Oh, you have a fabulous deck. So big for Paris. Okay, sure! You take care of your manscaping. I'll be good. Don't worry about me!"

He was beyond worried about the woman who seemed lucky to be alive. And her father was the dark witch Thoroughly Jones? The awesome, fear-inducing magic he knew that man possessed hadn't seemed to have been passed down the family tree, at least not concerning the malevolent confidence dark witches tended to possess. Melissande Jones was a fluff of flowers, glitter and star-shaped fruit who didn't seem capable of wielding a crystal wand, let alone handling and controlling a volatile heart.

"Not going to think about it right now," Tor muttered.

He pulled off his vest, made note of the blood on it and set it aside for the maid to bring to the cleaners. The shirt was a loss. Blood never did come out from cotton. He had a standing order from the tailor and received two new shirts every month. Might he have to change that with a desk job? He looked forward to saving on his clothing bill.

But he'd never see that savings if he didn't get ready for the big interview. Pre-interview, that was. The Skype meeting would allow him to speak to a representative from Human Resources, and they'd likely question his skills and qualifications before granting him the ultimate in-person interview with the CEO. He was ready. Or he would be after a shave.

Removing the rest of his clothes, he wandered into the bathroom and flicked on the shower with a wave of his hand over the electronic control panel by the door. The room was big, and the freestanding shower was positioned in the middle of the concrete floor. Simple and sleek, a U-shaped pipe that he stood under sprayed out water from all angles and heights. No curtain or glass doors. The shower area was sloped slightly so the water never ran onto the main floor. He never liked to be enclosed if he could prevent it.

A glance in the mirror found he looked, if still tousled and smeared with blood and ash, rested. A surprise. Had the witch's tea done that for him? He wasn't buying that it had simply been herbs in that tea. He'd slept until eleven. He rarely slept beyond eight.

"Drop it," he admonished himself.

Because he wasn't the kind of guy who worried. Worry kept a man fixed and stifled. He took action. And sure, he'd been set on leaving his current profession behind and leaping forward into a new, normal life with the grand step of the interview today.

But the witch did need his help. And there was nothing wrong with holding down a job until he found a new one. Not that he needed the money. Nope. He was very well-off, thank you very much. But he was a self-confessed type A, and he knew after a day or two of doing essentially nothing, he'd be jonesing for action. His leisure hobbies were few. So work it would have to be.

"Just don't let it suck you back in completely," he said as he stepped under the hot water. *Ahh...*

Whistling Sinatra's "I Get a Kick Out of You" made him smile. His thoughts went to the frog. Which levitated. Wonders never ceased.

Twenty minutes later, he was shaven, his hair styled with a bit of pomade (he liked it a little spiky but also soft enough to move) and the barest slap of aftershave applied to his cheeks. This stuff had been a gift from the young mother who lived on the ground floor of his building. She sold handmade products online. It smelled like black-cherry tobacco. It was different. As was he.

Now he stood in his long walk-in closet before the dress shirts. They were all white, Zegna, with French cuffs, but the one he touched now had a nice crisp collar. And the buttons down the front were pearl—not too flashy, and small. An excellent choice.

He slipped on the shirt, then pulled out the accessories drawer to peruse the cuff links. A pair of silver cicadas was his favorite. He pocketed them until he'd put them on, which would be right before the interview. Usually, he liked to roll up his sleeves if he wasn't going to be talking to the media or trying to impress an interviewer.

He'd wear the black trousers with the gray pinstripes because they were comfortable for sitting, and he didn't expect to battle vampires or to have to clean up a crime scene, so he needn't worry they would pick up lint and dirt like a magnet. A gray tweed vest and a smart black tie speckled with white fleurs-de-lis completed the ensemble.

As he began to roll up his sleeves, Tor thought he heard something like…

Screaming?

He remembered his house guest.

"Can she not go one hour without attracting trouble?"

Before leaving the closet, Tor pushed the button that spun the wall of color-coded ties inward. The entrance to his armory was revealed. Dashing inside, he grabbed an iron-headed club carved with a variety of repulsion sigils, and then raced out of the closet and down the long hallway into the living room.

Chapter 4

The witch wasn't in the living room.

A flutter of something outside on the deck that stretched the length of his apartment caught Tor's attention.

"What is that?" It hovered in the air above his guest. Long black wings spanned ten feet. Talons curled into claws. "Is that a—? Harpie? I have never—"

There was no time to marvel. Tor pulled aside the sliding glass door and lunged to slash the club toward the harpie currently pecking at Melissande's hair. He noted out of the corner of his eye a salt circle with the plastic box sitting in the center. "Grab the heart and get inside!"

"I have things under control!" Melissande called as she tugged her hair away from the harpie's talons.

The half bird/half woman squawked in Tor's ear, momentarily disorienting him. Her whine pinged inside his brain from ear to ear. A guttural shout cleared his senses, and he twisted to the right and swung up the club, catching the bird in the chest, which sent her reeling backward.

"Inside!" he shouted to the witch.

Melissande gathered up the plastic container and scrambled inside. From within, he heard her begin a witchy chant.

"Curse it to Faery!" he called. That was where such things resided. Usually. Unless this one had come through a portal.

The harpie swooped toward him. Tor dove to the ground, flattening his body and spreading out his arms. The cut of her wings parted his hair from neck to crown.

"*Divestia* Faery!" Melissande called.

The harpie, in midair, suddenly began to wheel and tumble in the sky. And then she exploded into a cloud of black feathers.

"Oh, shoot! I don't think I expelled it to Faery."

Indeed, the thing had disintegrated. But it worked for Tor.

Melissande ran out and stood over him. "Are you okay? Are you hurt?"

"Bloody hell!" Tor pushed up and out of the clutter of black feathers. He eyed the neighboring building, where he knew a very curious cryptozoologist happened to live. The shades were drawn. Which didn't mean much. That kid had a way of seeing things he wasn't supposed to see.

"You've a smudge of black salt here. Pity your vest got torn."

Tor charged past Melissande and into the house. Checking his watch, he abandoned his intent to head out the front door and over to the next building. No time to check on the neighbor. The interview was soon!

He marched down the hallway—then abruptly turned and stomped up to the witch. "Do not move. Do not go outside. Do not even blink. And where is that bedamned heart?"

She meekly pointed toward the kitchen counter.

"Did you have a chance to ward it?"

She nodded. "I used a new dark magic spell."

"Fine." He tugged at the torn tweed vest. Not the first impression he wanted to make to a prospective employer. "I'm going to change. Again. Stay right here."

He turned and stalked off.

"But—"

"Nope!" he called back to her. "Not even!"

The man had changed into a midnight blue vest, combed his hair and now led Melissande back toward his bedroom. This was an exciting turn of events! But she didn't read any sexy, playful vibes coming off him. More like stern frustration as he stretched out an arm to indicate the room they entered.

"I need an hour," he said. "With no distractions. No witches getting attacked on my deck. Not even a peep from that little box of yours."

She clutched the plastic container to her chest. He'd hastily grabbed both her bags and now set them on the end of the bed. This was certainly not sexy or playful, being consigned to the metaphorical time-out corner.

"You can stay in here while I'm online. It's a very important interview. So please, please, be quiet. There's the TV on the wall to entertain you. Keep the volume low. And I've got some books on the shelf."

She noted the books were organized by color of their spines, and they were all in a gradient order, from white to gray to black. Did the man not understand color? Fun? Simple civility?

"Can you do that?"

She met his patronizing glare and huffed. "Fine. The teacher wants to put me in detention for an hour."

"It's not that, Mel—" He sighed. "I just...need this interview to go well. I promise as soon as it's over, you have me at your beck and call."

"What's the interview for?"

"New job. Accounting stuff." He checked his watch and shook his head. "I only have five minutes. I've got to sign in to Skype. I'll come get you when I'm done. Do not come out to check if I've finished. Promise?"

"Fine!" she called as he closed the door behind him.

Melissande plopped onto the bed and crossed her arms. A pout felt necessary. Seriously? He was going to treat her like a naughty five-year-old? She hadn't expected the harpie to come swooping out of the sky, wings flapping and bared yet feathered breasts shocking.

"This heart attracts some strange energy." She tapped the container. "Good thing I had Tor to fight off the bird chick."

Because in the moment out on the deck and under attack, she hadn't been able to summon any deflecting magic. She could do that. With ease. A mere flick of her wrist and a few words of intention would make others walk a wide circle around her, or even push back a potential attacker. But she'd panicked. And in such a state, her magic was useless. Only when she'd gotten inside and knew she was out of the harpie's path had she been able to focus.

Now she gave her kinetic magic a try. A twist of her wrist slid the books on the shelf from one end to the other. "Just so. I seriously have to learn to relax during terrifying moments."

Yet despite her faults, she had managed to obliterate the harpie. And that made her sad. She hadn't wanted to kill the thing, just consign it back to Faery. Truly, this strange new magic she sought was going to take some getting used to.

With a nod, she decided she would concede to Tor's request. The man had a life, and he had agreed to help her. Which meant she had to understand that he must have engagements and things to take care of. He wouldn't be able to stand as her guardian 24-7. And she didn't expect that. Should she?

She was getting nervous that the next few days could prove more harrowing than she was prepared for.

Her only chance to acquire the heart had come yesterday afternoon while searching the Archives for the proper spell. A spell she'd already had, thanks to one of her father's grimoires. However, she'd told her uncle Certainly she hadn't the full version, so he had allowed her to search the stacks.

The Book of All Spells contained every spell designed, conjured and/or invoked by every witch who ever existed (and some by witches who were yet to exist). It was constantly updated as new spells were spoken. She'd browsed that massive volume without intent to copy anything out. Never was an item allowed out from the Archives—it was first and foremost a storage facility—but she'd often copied out spells or spent an afternoon studying an incantation to enhance her magic.

Having already studied the spell, she'd gone into the Archives knowing exactly what ingredient was required to make the spell successful: Hecate's heart. And after a lot of digging and sorting through dusty books, old wooden boxes and piles of unidentifiable artifacts, she'd found it wrapped in faded red silk, tucked between a book on crystal alchemy and a steel box that had rattled when she'd brushed it with the back of her hand. She had absconded with it while Uncle CJ had been talking on the phone.

With a wave and a *merci, Uncle!*, she'd told him she'd see him soon.

Fingers crossed that her uncle didn't notice it missing from the Archives. It wasn't as though he did a thorough inventory. He very likely had no idea exactly where the hundreds of thousands of items were at any given moment. Melissande had but to perform the spell and free her mother from the haunting, and then she could return the heart. And in the process of invoking dark magic, she could prove to her dad she had what it took to be a dark witch. Just like him and his twin brother and her twin cousins, Laith and Vlas. Even CJ's wife, who had once been a light witch, was now half-and-half.

The practice of dark magic was a Jones family tradition.

"Whoopee." Melissande sighed.

Was dark magic all it was cracked up to be? Try as she might, over the years she'd never been able to bring herself to pull off so much as a hex. Hexes were strictly dark magic. They fed off negative energies and sometimes required demonic familiars. Bruce was about as far from demonic as a familiar got. That amphibian was light, all the way.

Of course, she was aware that without dark magic, light magic could not exist. It was how the universe functioned. No good without bad. No peace without war. No heaven without hell (if you were a human). No Beneath without Above (for the paranormals). No yin without yang. No black without white. No glitter without ash. Someone had to practice dark magic. And in the hands of her dad and his brother, it was handled with grace, respect and kick-ass power.

Her sister, Amaranthe, had possessed that kick-ass skill. She had once been able to stand between CJ and their dad, TJ, and hold her own. Melissande missed her. But lately it was difficult to feel compassion toward her younger sibling for the havoc and utter terror she currently held against their mother.

And if a nudge from Amaranthe was required to push Melissande toward the dark in order to save her mother's sanity, then so be it.

She glanced to the big-screen TV that hung on a black wall. She shook her head. She wasn't much for mindless entertainment. And the books…

"The 7 Habits of Highly Effective People." She read one of the spines. "The man is uptight. But a cute uptight. And what a swing he's got."

Watching him wield the club against the harpie had almost distracted Melissande from the spell. Well, actually it *had* distracted her. Otherwise, the harpie would have been banished to Faery, and not…dead.

"She deserved it," Melissande muttered. "Can't have harpies flying about Paris all willy-nilly."

Bouncing up to her feet, she ran her fingers along the wall opposite the bed, then opened a door, which she assumed was the closet. A press of the light switch at shoulder level flicked on an overhead row of fluorescent bulbs. She leaned in and peered down the long stretch of closet, which was a small room lined on both sides with immaculate shelves and clothing hung and spaced precisely. Everything was neat as a pin. And all in blacks, grays and whites.

A hint of cherries and tobacco tickled her nose. Mmm… he smelled so good.

Unable to resist the adventurous call to explore, she ventured inside.

Tor thanked the interviewer for his time and ensured him he was on call for an in-person follow-up.

"We'll call you soon if interested, Monsieur Rindle."

"You've got my number. *Merci*."

Tor signed off from Skype and sat back, clasping his fingers behind his head. A smile was irrepressible. He'd aced it. He could win this job—if the in-person interview went well. Which it would. He was experienced in human relations, having worked spin for The Order of the Stake. The only difference was he'd be talking about human issues to humans. He could do that. He had no doubts about his qualifications, and had successfully bluffed his way through the real-world applications parts.

As was necessary to any sort of spin job, he knew how to take rotten lemons and make spectacular lemonade.

Closing the laptop, he hummed a few bars from "They Can't Take That Away From Me" and performed a side-to-side then forward swanky dance step into the kitchen. He opened the fridge and pulled out a bottle of Perrier. He drank half and set it on the counter. The day had taken a turn. It hadn't started out all that swell, with a tea hangover and the harpie attack. All because of the—

"The witch." He'd forgotten about the witch in his bedroom.

Loosening his tie and humming his way down the hallway, Tor felt a new enthusiasm for this unexpected protection job. The witch needed his help. He was the man who could help her. It would be his last hurrah before entering the corporate realm of humans and all things mundane.

Opening the bedroom door, he stepped inside to find… no witch.

"Hmm…" To his left, the closet door was open. Had he forgotten to tell her not to touch anything? He never overlooked the details most important to him.

Tor stepped into the closet. "I'm finished—"

The witch, who stood at the end of the closet, turned abruptly, her smile exaggerated and her shoulders to her ears. She wore one of his vests over her red blouse. One of his black silk ties hung loosely about her neck. And in her hand was one of his fedora hats.

"Oops," she managed.

Aghast, Tor took a moment to settle his sudden need to shout an oath. He put up a hand. "I don't even want to know." He truly did not.

He had to force himself to leave the closet, but— "Okay, wait." Turning to face the witch, he planted his feet and crossed his arms. "I really do need to know."

Melissande carefully placed his hat back on the shelf and made a point of aligning it as neatly as it had originally been placed.

"Why are you in here?" he persisted. "Wearing my things? Are you…mentally unbalanced?"

She gaped at him. "I got bored. I don't do TV, and I wasn't interested in your literary choices. And I figured if I worked some magic, it could get noisy. And you did reprimand me to be quiet."

"I don't reprimand—"

"Oh, it was definitely a reprimand."

"So you decided to try on some of my things as a means to…?"

"I'm a curious person," she defended herself. "And your clothes smell good. Cherry and tobacco. Like you, I presume. But I can't imagine that you smoke. That's not very attractive. Speaking of, you are much more attractive than I'd expected."

"Than expected?" He had to ask. She had a way of teasing out his curiosity.

"Sure. I thought you'd have a gimp eye or, at the very least, a scar. You know, with the kind of work you do."

He really did not know, and if he thought about it too hard, he might go down the path she followed. And that scared him more than a raging demon or a squawking harpie.

Melissande tugged the tie from her neck, and he rushed to grab it.

"I'll take that." He carefully folded it and placed it in the open tie drawer. A few adjustments to the other ties she'd obviously touched and moved out of order were necessary. "I'm sorry. The interview went long. The rest of the day I'm all yours. In fact, we need to sit down and discuss a game plan."

"Good idea. But I'm hungry."

"Of course you are, you harpie-banishing, vest-wearing witch. Let's just get that vest off you…"

He helped her slip off the vest, and as he did so, Tor drew in the lush scent of her dark hair. Like lemons, but sweeter, almost candy. It was surprising how the scent attracted him. When she turned to give him an inquiring look, for a moment their faces were but inches apart. Exceedingly intimate. And…he had but to move his hand an inch to touch her hair…

"Right." Tor backed away and hung the vest to distract his straying thoughts. Why was he so confused about whether to reprimand or kiss her? "I keep some prepared meals in the freezer. You might like the poached salmon mousse."

"Sounds futuristically unappealing, but I'm in." She marched out of the closet, leaving him in her lemon-scented wake.

She was a handful of kooky and strange, and she annoyed him in virtually every way. Trying on his clothes? He closed the tie drawer carefully. And yet he couldn't think of a single reason to push her out the door and wash his hands of her crazy. So for now, he'd play along.

At the very least, she was entertaining.

Chapter 5

"If that was a job interview," Mel said while prodding at her microwaved dinner, "I'm guessing it's not your usual protection and cleanup work?"

"It's a one-eighty turn from what I usually do. A job in an accounting firm. Completely normal." Tor had finished his meal and was cleaning the plastic bowl for the recycle bin beneath the counter he'd pointed out to her.

"Huh. But you do what you do so well. I don't understand why you'd want another job."

"I need normal. And let's leave it at that. Deal?"

"If that's the way you want to play it. Do I have to stay here while you're protecting me?" The meal he'd taken from the freezer and reheated in the microwave was supposed to be some kind of wild-caught fish-mousse thingy with lemon sauce on green beans but—ugh. "Don't you ever eat fresh food?"

"That's fresh. The chef delivers it frozen. No time to cook, and I eat out a lot. Lots of fresh choices that way."

"Depends on where you eat. I need to go home this evening and pack some stuff if you expect me to stay here. Not to mention bring along half my fridge. A witch can't survive on tough beans and rubber fish."

She shoved the food tray forward, finished. Hey, she'd given it a shot at least.

Tor took it and, using a brush, began the same meticulous cleaning under the running sink water. "As protector, I follow you," he said. "If you need to go home, that's where I will go. I'll be the one who packs some things. And once you're home, you can add a cloaking spell to that thing." He nodded to the plastic container sitting at the end of the counter. "Apparently whatever ward you put on it—"

"I only had time for a quickie ward before the harpie flew in."

The heart didn't glow now. Through the pink plastic, it merely looked like a hunk of meat. Which was odd to Melissande. The artifact was the real heart taken from Hecate's chest. But when she touched and held it, it felt like glass, save for its rubbery texture. If it needed cold storage and might get stale on her, she had better not only cloak the thing but perhaps also keep it on ice.

She sniffed the air, but didn't notice a rancid smell. "That's a good idea. A cloaking spell will enhance a ward. But I'll need Bruce's help since I'm still new to dark magic. Such skills are a lifetime endeavor. It's always a learning process, no matter the magic a witch practices."

"Does the floating—er, *levitating* frog help with your spells?"

"Of course. He is my familiar," she stated as if he should know better.

She slid off the stool and grabbed the heart. "Let's head out. I'm hungry, and I've got some fruit salad at home with my name on it."

"Let me grab a few things before we leave. Won't be but a few minutes."

The man strolled down the hallway back to his bedroom, whistling as he did so. He had a long, easy stride that spoke of confidence. Something Melissande was always unsure she possessed. And that was the paradox of it, wasn't it? If you weren't sure you had it, then of course you didn't.

Hugging the plastic box to her chest, she wandered down the hallway, cringing only a little that earlier he'd found her wearing his clothes. Everything had smelled like cherry tobacco. It was a deep, heady scent that had lured her to sniff his clothing. And wearing him on her had allowed her to submerse herself in his world. To feel, for a moment, what it must be like to be Torsten Rindle, stylish protector against all means of evil. She bet not a lot of slayers or cleanup professionals could work the bespoke suit like he did *and* still manage to take out the enemy with such skill.

Tor must have plenty of enemies. She hoped he didn't consider witches enemies. A man like him must work for all breeds and species, so hopefully he didn't discriminate. Yet if he did not, that could also imply he didn't discriminate when it came to slaying one.

Peeking into his bedroom, she spied him zipping up a small bag. He startled at the sight of her. "Oh. Uh..." He glanced to the open closet door.

That man's closet was a fashionista's wet dream.

"I, uh...was thinking I should arm myself with a few extra weapons before leaving."

"Sounds like a plan." She remained in the doorway.

Tor stayed by the bed, peering into the closet.

"So?" she prompted.

He pointed toward the closet, then smoothed a hand down his tie.

"You keep weapons in your closet?" she guessed. "I didn't see any when I was—well, you know."

"My closet is a sort of personal stronghold to me."

"Where you keep all things most important to you."

He winced. "It's not so much that—give me another few minutes." He strode into the closet.

And Melissande followed.

"I said to give me a few," he insisted as he spun to stand before a small panel on the wall he'd opened. She hadn't noticed that when she'd been in here earlier.

"You have a secret weapon stash?" She slipped around him and studied the panel, which consisted of a few round buttons. "What does the red one do? Sound the alarm? Send out the hounds? Alert the dragons?"

Tor sighed and gripped the little door that had concealed the buttons. "It reboots the system should an electrical failure occur due to lightning or power outage."

"Oh." Melissande dropped her shoulders. Sounded a lot like her place. It was an old house in desperate need of new wiring. There wasn't a storm that occurred that did not leave her sitting in the dark, from a few minutes to hours. Not that she minded. Candles were always better than electric lighting. "So show me. Oh, come on—it's not like I don't already know your secret identity."

"My secret—" Shaking his head, Tor pressed the topmost button, and the panel that displayed his ties in neat rows swung open. Inner fluorescent lights flashed on to brightly illuminate another room. He waggled an admonishing finger at her. "No touching."

She sighed dramatically, then conceded with a nod and followed him inside.

This secret closet was as big as the clothes closet. The longest walls, parallel to one another, were covered with a mosaic of weapons. Melissande's jaw dropped as she swept her gaze over pistols, rifles and semiautomatic weapons in all sizes and calibers. The knife section boasted the smallest pocketknife to a machete the size of a man's arm. Garrotes were neatly coiled and hung with precision on the gray microfoam-padded wall. Dozens of wooden stakes were neatly stacked on the marble counter. An entire section featured vials of what she assumed were either spells or vile concoctions designed to injure or even kill. The vials with crosses etched onto the glass must be holy water.

Behind her, Tor took down a handgun and checked the bullet cartridge. "You will not tell anyone what you've seen in here."

"Of course not." She ran her fingers over the smooth matte-black finish of something that resembled a rifle but could also be a crossbow. She wouldn't have the first notion what to call all these weapons, let alone gossip about them.

But thinking about gossip…she really needed to get together with the girls and tell them about her studly new protector. Tuesday was living with the handsome vampire Ethan Pierce. And Zoe had been shacking up with the gorgeous slayer Kaspar Rothstein for years. It was high time Melissande got to brag about a sexy man.

But first she needed a better reason to brag than that she was paying him.

"Can you not touch?"

"Of course I can. I mean, cannot." She pulled back her hand and watched as Tor fit a knife in the inside pocket of his suit coat. A box of shells and another Order-of-the-Stake-issue stake were grabbed and tucked away in various pockets or loops on his attire. "What is everything for, exactly?"

"Vampires, werewolves, demons."

"Mermaids?"

"I have a suffocating lariat should I encounter a vicious mermaid."

He ran his fingers over a small iron sphere that had spikes coming out of it.

"What's that for?" she wondered aloud.

"Dragons. They need to swallow it, and it'll explode in their gut. Messy."

Wow. Melissande had never seen a dragon. He lived an exciting life. Gossip-worthy, even.

"Faeries," he recited as he moved his gaze over various weapons. "Reptilian-shifter. Angel. Kitsune."

"What about ghosts?" Melissande tried.

Tor turned his gaze directly on her. "I don't do ghosts."

"Oh, but—"

"No ghosts," he repeated firmly. And he brushed his fingers over the crystal talisman hanging from his belt. She was about to ask what it was for when he said, "Ghosts are just… No. Now come on. And don't touch that!" he called as he filed out of the room.

Melissande made a point of gliding her fingers along a bayonet-like weapon after he'd called out the warning. She barely slipped out into the fore-closet as the door swung shut. Tor gestured for her to vacate the room, and she felt like she was being directed around like a child. She wouldn't have ruined a thing in that room. How could she, a tiny witch, manage to do that?

"You have trust issues," she concluded as she followed him down the hallway and into the living area and kitchen.

"And you are far too trusting," he countered. "Where's the heart?"

She caught herself before saying *oops*. Holding up a staying finger, she then dashed down the hallway, grabbed the plastic container from the end of his bed—took one more moment to inhale his uniquely sexy scent—then rushed back out to the man who waited by the open front door.

"Don't worry," she said as they exited his place with her bags in hand. "We'll sync onto one another's wavelength. I'm already dialed into yours."

"Is that so? Right."

She turned right as they walked outside and remembered he'd parked in that direction.

"Yes," she said. "You're controlling, precise and closed. I might be able to work with that."

They arrived at his van, and he opened the passenger door for her. "You don't need to work with anything. Just be you. Cloak and ward the heart. Go about your normal—whatever it is you do. And let me do my job. Deal?"

As she slid up onto the seat, Melissande turned and stuck out a foot to prevent him from closing the door on her. "How much is all this going to cost me?"

"We'll come to an agreeable arrangement." He shoved her foot inside and closed the door on her.

The man could be intolerable. But that made her smile. He was a tough one. She would enjoy peeling away his layers to get to the soft mushy stuff in the middle. Because everyone had that mush. Some even wore it on their outermost layer.

She did. And she knew she had to toughen up for the unavoidable trial that would arrive in a few days. She could do this. Her mother needed her. And her father would be so proud.

"Maybe I can learn to toughen up from Tor," she muttered. Behind her, he deposited his supplies in the back of the van and closed the door. "Time to step up, Jones. Your family needs you."

She smiled when Tor got in and fired up the engine. She had made the right choice in choosing her protector. But no ghosts, eh?

That could prove to be an issue.

Chapter 6

Carrots, celery and an onion." Melissande set the vegetables on the counter before the cutting board and handed Tor a knife. "When you're finished, I'll get the mirepoix simmering for soup. Meanwhile, I'm going to the spell room with Bruce to put that cloaking spell on the heart."

"Please do." Tor grabbed a carrot. "Peeler?"

"Nope, I leave the skin on. It's better for you. Nutrients and all that."

He gave an indecisive tilt of the head at that statement. "What is it that you do, anyway?"

"What do you mean?"

"Earlier, when I said you should go about doing what you do. I— Do you have a job? Will I be guarding you while at work? Or are you just…a witch?"

"Oh, I work! I mean, most of the time. I'm a bit of a jack-of-all-trades, like you. I worked at Shakespeare and Company for a few months. Then I got a gig at the ice-cream shop around the corner. I loved that place. They didn't love me giving out free samples. Oh, and just last month I was taking tickets at the d'Orsay, but the manager fired me for letting in tourists on expired city passes. I'm sort of between jobs right now. Which is a good thing. I'll be focusing my attention on perfecting the spell this week and making sure I've got it ready to go. Which means we'll be spending a lot of time together! Come on, Bruce!"

The witch scurried out of the kitchen on a sweep of fluttering black hair. Tor paused before touching the knife to the first carrot.

Bruce floated through the kitchen, passing eye level with Tor. The frog delivered a judgmental croak. Then he floated out. Or levitated. But wait—wasn't levitation more a nontraveling action? It was floating that moved a person—or frog—from one place to the next. Levitation merely moved an entity up and down. Maybe? He wouldn't argue with the witch about it. She was just weird enough to have a completely rational explanation for it.

And he was just curious enough about her to want to engage in such a chat.

"Right, then."

They'd be spending a lot of time together. Tor wasn't sure how he felt about that. While she was definitely pretty to look at, and wasn't at all a threat to him, he wasn't sure her wackiness could be endured for more than short bursts at a time. He did value his privacy and alone time. He had his…ways. And he didn't like when they were disturbed. Like finding his silk tie hanging about her neck. Even if she had been the cutest thing ever—

Well, she had been.

Tor remembered the time he'd had to protect a celebrity singer from the vampire she'd attracted by mistakenly answering a text she had thought was a tease to drink her blood. That woman had clearly defined high-maintenance to Tor. He would never live down the trips to the beauty salon for seaweed wraps if anyone learned he'd had to accompany her there.

He should be thankful Mel was seemingly self-sufficient and didn't seek the spotlight or have too many friends. He liked to keep what he did a secret. It was a necessity.

He turned back to the task. Chop vegetables? Not a problem. He eyed the length of carrot, took a moment to calculate his slices, then began. She hadn't told him how many carrots to chop. There were at least ten in the bag. And as much celery.

As he chopped, he decided this activity was a weirdly soothing task that occupied his brain in a way that allowed him to focus. So often, he had a dozen things going on at once in his temporal lobe. Where was the dangerous creature? How many? Was he surrounded? Where were the escape routes? Had he loaded enough ammunition? What chemical was required to clean up sticky, tar-like demon blood? And would he get a call for the second interview?

He felt the Skype interview this morning had gone well. And hoped to hear back within a few days for another in-person interview. He'd doctored his résumé as best he could, leaving out the parts where he did spin for a group that slayed vampires and, in turn, spinning his skills to show that he worked with the local news outlets and reported on current events that could impact the residents. Spin was making the unordinary sound ordinary. Vampires? Get real! It's just a bunch of satanic idiots.

And while the accounting firm employed number crunchers, someone in the human resources department didn't require such skills. So he was safe there. And he could make nice with humans and paranormals alike. Changing a man's mind after he'd witnessed a werewolf tromping through his gardenias in the backyard? Not a problem. Did he know that gardenias gave off an intoxicating scent that was actually studied and determined could alter a person's thoughts and give them illusions? No? Well, it was true.

Fake science worked every time.

Tor took pride in what he did. Every single thing he did. He pushed aside the growing pile of orange carrot cubes and eyed the bag of celery.

Everything.

Half an hour later, he set down the knife after a round of near-tears with the onions.

Mel bounded into the kitchen and set the container with the heart on the counter. When she eyed Tor's work, her jaw dropped.

Behind her, Bruce floated over to levitate above her shoulder. The reptile croaked in the most judgmental enunciation Tor had ever heard.

"That's a lot of vegetables," Melissande declared at the sight of the piles that Tor had heaped onto the countertop on a piece of waxed paper. She noted the empty plastic bags that the carrots and celery had been in. "You chopped them all."

"You didn't say not to."

"True. And..." She bent to study the meticulously chopped bits of orange, green and white. All remarkably uniform. "Did you use a ruler?"

"I have very good spatial awareness. I like things in order."

"I guess you do, Monsieur OCD. It looks like a machine did this."

"Thank you."

Mel didn't really care what she was going to do with

a shit ton of veggies all chopped into perfect half-inch squares. This was too wonderful. The man was a marvelous freak. And she could fall in love with him right now if he wasn't holding the cutting knife like he intended to defend himself against her.

"You trying to decide whether or not to stab me with that thing?" she asked carefully.

"Huh?" Tor noted the knife he held, blade facing outward and arm pulled back as if to stab. He quickly set it on the cutting board. "Sorry. Force of habit."

"Right." She pulled a big soup pan out of the cupboard, and with a swish of her fingers, she swept a third of the vegetables into the pot. "Thanks to you, I'll have mirepoix for weeks! I should invite you over more often."

"Always happy to help. What sort of soup are you making?"

"Whatever strikes my fancy. I'll get the veggies simmering then toss in whatever is on hand. I've some gnocchi and chicken stock. Toss in some spices and spinach and there you go."

The man straightened his tie, watching as she went about the motions of adding oil to the pot along with the veggies and a good helping of butter, because life wasn't worth living without lots of butter. She and her family bought all their dairy products from a witch who lived an hour outside Paris. She milked her cows by hand and churned butter and made her own cheese. It was heavenly.

Meanwhile, she handed Tor a couple of plastic freezer bags. "Hold those open for me, will you?" He did so, and she again swept the chopped veggies into the containers with but a few magical gestures.

"Handy," he said, sealing the lockable bags.

"It's just…me," she decided. "Kinetic magic. Never known any other way of life. We witches got it going on."

"I'll say. Makes normal look so…"

"Normal?" She leaned a hip against the stove. "How long have you been in the know with us paranormals?"

"Most of my life. Like you, I haven't known much different. But I feel like it can be better away from all this… supernatural insanity. It's hard to explain. It's something I need to do."

Unconvinced, Mel shrugged. "I'll have you know I'm the normal one in my family."

Tor's eyebrow lifted in question.

"It's all about perspective. Family full of dark witches? Then there's little ole sparkly me." She winked at him, knowing her purple glitter eye shadow caught the sunlight. "Do you know what it's like to be the odd witch out?"

"I actually do. Which, again, is reason for me to want to pursue this job."

"I suppose I can understand that. You need to see if the grass is greener. Trust me. It's not." She turned and stirred the pot. "Too bad for us paranormals. Not having you to have our backs."

"Someone else will take up the reins."

"How will that happen? How did you take up the reins?"

"Monsieur Jacques taught me after I moved to Paris. Well, uh…hmm…it's not important."

He hadn't thought about passing along his knowledge to anyone? Mel felt sure he hadn't thought through the whole idea of normal either. But who was she to overexplain something the man had to learn for himself?

"Did you get the heart cloaked?" Tor asked.

"Yep."

He bent to study the container she'd set at the edge of the counter, cracking open the lid to peer inside. "It looks…like a real heart. Wasn't it more glassy when you first showed it to me?"

"It was. And it's not glowing as much either." She seasoned the ingredients with pepper and her favorite smoked black sea salt. "But it doesn't smell, so I think I'm okay."

"That's your determination of an efficacious cloaking?"

She shrugged. "Doesn't it work for you?"

"Well—okay, I can agree with you on that one. Not like I know much about hearts left over from long-dead witches. What, exactly, is this spell you plan to invoke on the night of the full moon?"

"The full *blood* moon," she said.

"Really? Ominous."

"Right? There's a lunar eclipse on the night of the full moon, which will make it appear reddish-orange. The blood moon portends the closing of struggles and new beginnings. Couldn't be more perfect timing for such a spell, if you ask me."

Placing the bamboo spoon across the top of the pot to keep the brew from boiling over, Mel turned her back to the stove to face Tor. The setting sun beamed through the front window in a cozy orange glow and backlit him in the most delicious manner. He looked less uptight this evening. More amiable. And she still wanted to run her fingers through his hair.

It was easy enough for her to reveal a few things to him. As a means to gaining his trust. Because he still wasn't completely on board with her beyond this merely being a job she would pay him for.

"My mother needs protection," she started, then cautioned herself from saying *from a ghost*. The man didn't do ghosts? What did that mean, exactly? "And since she's only recently died—again—my dad is busy getting her back up to speed with life, so I offered to do the spell and take that worry off his hands."

Tor put up a palm to stop her. "So many questions."

"You know my dad," she offered. "Thoroughly Jones, dark witch, husband to a cat-shifting familiar."

"Yes, and your mother is Star. And she's recently died?"

"Fell from the top of my parents' building. She was…" Couldn't tell him Star had been spooked. "Doesn't matter how it happened. Only that she didn't land on her feet. That's a myth about cats. Anyway. You know how it is with familiars?"

"I do. Mostly. I'm not sure about frogs." He looked about the kitchen, but Bruce was nowhere in sight. "I do know that cat-shifters have nine lives. If they die, they come back to life the same age at which they died."

"Exactly. But they never come back with memories of their former life."

"Oh. That's— I didn't know that detail. Wow, that's gotta be tough. For the familiar and for her family."

"Tell me about it. In my lifetime, my mother has died four times. With each death, she forgets I'm her daughter. That she had two daughters, actually. She died after giving birth to me. Poor Dad had to take care of a newborn *and* a newly reborn wife who couldn't remember him or that she'd had a baby. My sister's birth was event free, thankfully. Mom made it through that one like a breeze."

"You have a sister?"

"Had."

"Oh. Sorry." He splayed his hands before him. "Isn't there a life history of some sort you could record to help get your mom up to speed?"

"Dad does keep a video journal for her. It helps a lot. But it's never easy. Poor Mom."

"And you said she needs protection?"

Mel nodded. "It's a private family matter. I hope you can respect that. But suffice it to say, the spell I intend to invoke should bring an end to her worries."

"Is she aware you are trying to help her?"

A sigh felt necessary. Over the years, Mel had struggled to develop a relationship with her mother. It wasn't easy when she died every five or six years. But she did love and respect her, and knew she was kind and so loving. They had baking and listening to loud music in common. And Dad always said she'd gotten her mom's whimsical nature, even though it had been a long time since he'd seen that in his wife.

"She's getting used to the idea of having a husband and a daughter. Again. It always takes a few months to get her back up to speed," she said, and turned to check the pot. The savory aroma of the sautéed veggies perfumed the room.

"I'm sorry," Tor offered. "I'll make sure you're able to perform the spell. I promise."

"Thank you," she said quietly, unwilling to look at him now.

It was tough talking about her family. They were odd, when most already considered them two shades to the left. In the realm of the paranormal, dark witches were the creepy characters that most feared and walked a wide circle around. Add to that a feline shapeshifter and a family history that had seen centuries of persecution and more than a lot of dabbling with the demonic, angelic and the alchemical arts, and—well, it was hard to fit in with human society, let alone attend a party filled with the usual suspects like vampires, werewolves and, yes, even the glitter-crazed faeries. Mel wanted to prove to her dad that she had what it took to master the dark arts and fit in with the Jones family norm. And she would.

Because it was expected of her.

"It's starting to rain," Tor noted. "You want me to close the door in the living room?"

"Just pull closed the screen," she said. She liked to keep the door open a crack for her familiar. "Make sure Bruce is out first. He loves the rain!"

Tor walked into the living room and she heard him mutter, "Hurry up," then the screen door slid closed on its metal track. The smell of the rain mingled with the soup, and she whispered a blessing.

"Bring hope and peace to the Jones family. Free my mother from her persecution." With a sprinkle of thyme over the surface, she infused the blessing with a snap of her fingers and a blink of hope.

"Mind if I turn on some music?" Tor called from the other room.

"Go for it!"

She heard the radio switch between stations, and finally Frank Sinatra crooned softly. At least, Mel guessed it was the singer; she wasn't up on the Rat Pack, but it sounded like a song from that era. And accompanying him was a man she'd thought hadn't the capacity to relax and let loose.

Mel crept over to the doorway separating the rooms and peered around the frame. Tor stood before the radio, singing softly and…he snapped his fingers and nodded his head in time to the music. His voice was deep and resonant, in sync with the music.

Feeling as if she was witnessing a private side of him, she remained by the door frame, ready to whip back out of sight but unwilling to leave, for this new glimpse into the man was incredible. Tor's voice was deep and mellow, and when he performed a dip to the side, he tipped an invisible hat from his head, before sliding back up and turning—

Mel swung back into the kitchen. A grin stretched her mouth, and she pressed her fingers to her lips.

Now that was an interesting man.

Chapter 7

That was the best meal Tor had eaten in a while.

Now he stepped out of the shower adjacent to Melissande's bedroom and grabbed a bright pink towel to wrap around his hips. He used another pink towel to dry his hair. The witch's bathroom had white walls and white floorboards, yet the ceiling was hung with fragrant herbs tied with bright ribbons—same as the long streams of bright ribbons and spangles he'd had to pass through to enter her bedroom. Seemed to be the theme around here: sparkle witch.

Yet the bedroom he'd walked through to get in here had offered unexpected nonquirky decor. The bare pine floorboards had stretched to the wall facing the backyard, which featured a gorgeous, tall, four-paned window that was topped with a half-circle window. Only the bed, a nightstand and a big plush violet lounge chair furnished the room. Richly colored velvets covered the bed. Candles of all colors, heights and thicknesses littered the floors by the window. A witch necessity, he figured.

But the lack of adornment did surprise him. He'd expected fluff and froof, and maybe even pink and purple on her bed.

Whistling one of Sinatra's tunes about *doing it my way* that had played earlier while they'd shared soup and baguettes, he pulled a toothbrush out of his bag and cursed forgetting toothpaste. He opened the medicine cabinet, which revealed an apothecary's buffet. Not a single brand-name product. Everything was in glass vials or stout little pots with handwritten labels.

He read a label. "Belladonna." It was a volatile herb; he knew that much. "Wonder what she uses that for?"

He didn't want to know, because he knew the herb could be deadly.

"Charcoal." He decided that must be the tooth powder and took down the jar. It was messy, but he managed the job and had to follow with a thorough cleaning of the marble vanity. The black powder had gotten everywhere.

When he looked over the pink towel covered with charcoal, he shook his head. "What kind of houseguest am I?"

Realizing he'd left his clothes bag out in the living room, Tor resigned himself to walking down the hallway with nothing but the pink towel wrapped about his waist. He smelled the intense petrichor, an after-rain scent, as he entered the living room and spied Melissande standing in the open patio door, her back to him.

"Duck!" she yelled.

Tor ducked, dodging a look toward his bag, where he knew a handy switchblade was tucked.

But a sudden giggle had him straightening and assessing the situation. From the backyard came waddling through the patio doorway a—

"That's a duck," he said.

"Got that one on the first try. But I did give you a hint. Did you actually…?"

He put a hand to his hip and stretched back his shoulders. "No."

"Oh, yes, you did. You were taking cover."

"You did tell me to duck."

"That's her name." The witch patted the wet fowl on her white head. "She's my Duck."

"You have a pet duck named Duck?"

She nodded cheerfully. "Though she's not really my pet. I'm more hers. She stops in and checks on me daily." Her eyes lowered to Tor's abdomen, where he hadn't yet dried all the water from his six-pack, and he was feeling a warmth rise in his loins standing before her greedy gaze.

"What's that black stuff?" She bent to study his abs closer.

"Charcoal." He stepped back and placed a palm over the smear. "I forgot toothpaste."

"No problem. You can use anything in the house that you need. Except I suggest you avoid the belladonna."

"Not going to be an issue. I shouldn't ask but…"

"It's for girl stuff," she quickly answered. "You know, for when the moon is full and our cycles are raging?"

Tor put up a palm. "Good enough. I should have never asked."

"Does the fact that we women have periods freak you out, Tor?"

"Nope. Just makes you stronger than you all appear. If I bled for days every month, I'm sure I'd be dead."

"Just so." She wiggled her shoulders in triumph. "I'm going to let Duck sleep inside tonight. She's got a nest over in the corner."

Tor noted the wooden box stuffed with wood chips and feathers. Cozy.

"As for you..." She tapped her lips as she gave it some thought. "I have a cot folded up in the storage room that I might need help getting down from the rafters."

"I can sleep on the couch. Done it once already. It's a comfy couch. Though I'm still not sure that was because of the comfort, or that I was under the influence of some kind of sleeping spell."

"Oh, darling, if I were going to put a spell on you, you would know. I'll grab you some blankets and a pillow. Uh..." Her gaze again fell to his abs and even lower. "Do you sleep in the buff?"

Generally? Yes.

"I left my stuff by the front door." Tor spun to leave the room. "I'll put something on while you get the blankets."

"Don't get dressed on my account!" she called after his departing figure.

Smiling as he grabbed his bag and headed back toward the bathroom, Tor replayed that hungry look she'd given him in the living room. So he worked out and had muscles to show for it. It was necessary when he sported the kind of résumé he did. But if it caught a woman's eye? Bonus points.

On the other hand, did he want to attract a witch's attentions?

"Maybe?" he muttered to himself. A smile was irrepressible. He wouldn't deny she was attractive, and he did like being around her. And below those bright sparkly eyes were a pair of lush, red lips that did entice him to wonder...

He'd never kissed a witch. Nor had he kissed a client.

Right, then. Back to the real world. Now, what to wear beyond the shirts and silk ties he'd packed?

When he returned to the living room in boxer shorts and a longer dress shirt with unbuttoned cuffs, Melissande gave him a nod of approval and then handed him a cup of tea.

"Uh..." He winced and sniffed at the brew.

She sipped her tea, then offered it to him. "I got you covered tonight. It's not bespelled. And to prove it, you can drink mine. I just took a sip. It's safe."

He accepted the mug, then sat on the couch. Mel settled onto the floor before the ottoman, and the duck waddled over to sit on her lap. The tea tasted different and sweeter. Maybe he trusted it. Maybe not. But it was a great way to end the night. A quiet evening after a day fraught with craziness.

"An evening without trouble," he commented.

"I was thinking the same," she said. "My cloaking spell must have worked."

"Must have? You never seem very sure of your magic."

"Lately it has a strange tendency to not last long," she confessed. "It has no sticking power. That's what my sister used to always say when her spells didn't take. I'm not sure why. Some stuff sticks. The stuff that comes easy and right from my heart."

"Maybe the magic you're not completely enthused about feels that lack of enthusiasm and so...?"

"I've not heard it explained quite that way. It is possible. But I hate to consider it the truth. I mean, I'm not overexcited about the full moon spell. If what you say is true..."

"It'll work." Tor set down the cup and clasped her hand. She startled, but then gave his hand a squeeze. He'd meant it as a simple gesture of kindness, but now that they sat there a few moments, in the quiet darkness, it grew to a deeper connection. More intimate.

And he liked it.

"You know dark magic takes a witch's lifetime to master," she said.

"And you think a few days will be just what you need to perform the full moon spell?"

"No, but..." She sighed. Probably unsure, and maybe even worried.

He could relate. For as psyched as he was to start a new job in the normal world, could he really do it?

He shouldn't go there, to that place of doubt. And he didn't want Mel to see him falter. Besides being unprofessional, it was just too…personal.

"You'll do fine," he said. "I know you will."

And he pulled up her hand to kiss it. For a moment he lingered there, with his lips against her warm skin that smelled like soup and spices and lemons. Kind of a crazy moment. He felt as if the world did not exist. As if it were just the two of them. Alike in the most bizarre manner. And yet so different. Worlds apart.

Normal—according to her strange definition—and wanting to be normal. Could they coexist?

Sunlight beamed through the patio doors and shocked Tor awake. He didn't do bright light in the mornings. That wasn't a weird vampire thing. It was common sense. Any sane human needed to cling to the few rare hours he did manage to sleep.

He swung his legs off the couch, and his bare feet landed on a furry rug before the coffee table, his toes sinking deep into the soft texture. It was fake *something*, with long white nap that felt good beneath his wriggling toes. But he still winced at the sunlight.

Standing, he padded over to the patio door, gripped the gauzy white curtains in preparation to pull them closed—at least until he could gather his wits about him—when he noticed something moving in the yard. It was small and—there was more than one. It couldn't be the duck called Duck.

Tor narrowed his gaze. Frogs didn't move like that either.

Chapter 8

Something crouched near what looked like an iron cauldron under a chestnut tree. Tor started to wonder about the big black pot—how cliché could a witch get?—but his attention quickly returned to the moving thing.

"What the hell? Is that…? No. Really?"

Dashing for his pack, he pulled out the pistol loaded with salt rounds, then spun and pulled aside the patio door. Stepping outside in his shirt and boxer briefs, he wandered across the concrete patio crowded with wicker chairs and potted plants and right up to the edge, where long grass blades hugged the concrete.

The things growled at him. And revealed fangs. And then an ear dropped off one that resembled a dog. Not a normal dog either. This one was big and—half its fur was missing, and the two front legs were bones.

"Zombie dogs?" Tor muttered. "What the…? That's

impossible. Zombies don't—" Gulping back the denial, he crouched into defense mode.

There were five of them, in all sizes ranging from a dachshund to what must have been a former wolfhound. They tromped toward him with maws opened to reveal fangs and black ooze dripping to the grass.

Taking aim, Tor fired at the wolfhound as it leaped for him. The salt round pierced the creature's mouth and exited the back of its head, spraying bone in the too-bright air. That alerted the other beasts—and they all charged.

"Holy crap!" a voice called out from behind Tor.

"Stay inside! Close the door!"

Firing at the smallest one that crept along the ground, Tor was startled when Mel touched his back and joined his side. "I said to stay inside!"

"What are those creatures? They're…dead? Oh mercy, the heart."

"I thought you put a cloaking spell on that thing?"

Another zombie leaped toward Tor, but midair, the body fell apart and a crumble of bones landed on the grass.

"I did, but I opened the container this morning to check that it was all right. That must have broken the spell. I wasn't thinking. Like I told you, the dark magic I've been studying never lasts for long. That one is going after Bruce!"

Tor twisted and aimed for the creature that had its jaws open less than a foot away from the slowly fleeing levitating frog. He pulled the trigger. Bones scattered.

"One left," Mel narrated. "I could toss a fireball at that one."

Tor caught her arm just as she was ready to fling whatever magic she thought might help. "Let me handle this. Go inside! And take your frog with you!"

"Fine. But I hardly think zombie dogs are a threat."

At that moment, the final creature scrambled across the grass and nipped at Mel's ankle, which, thankfully, was encased in leather from the knee-high boots she wore.

"Not a threat, eh?" Tor kicked at the thing, and yet it clung to her boot with tenacious fangs.

"Shoot it!"

He was out of salt rounds. So instead, Tor clobbered the thing over the head with the pistol barrel. That released its hold so he could shove Mel toward the open patio door. The zombie dog followed close on her heels. The patio door slid closed. The dog got its head inside and—

—the torso and legs of the dog fell to the ground as it was decapitated.

Tor gave a cursory glance about the yard. No more threats. And now he spied the holes in the garden, from where the dogs must have risen. Former pets buried in a pet cemetery? No doubt about it. But the witch didn't strike him as a dog person.

A white-headed duck popped its head out from behind the cauldron and quietly quacked.

"All clear, Duck," Tor offered. He made to shove the pistol in the holster, which should have been under his arm, then remembered he had just risen and wasn't suited for this kind of adventure.

"The witch needs more protection from herself than anything." He glanced to the patio door, behind which Mel, clutching the frog to her chest, stood staring at the dead dog's skull. "The full moon can't come soon enough."

Melissande set a smoothie bowl on the counter and a spoon beside it. She heard Tor come back inside, swear as he stepped over the slimy remains of the beheaded zombie and wander into the kitchen.

"Breakfast," she announced cheerily.

"I'll clean up the yard dogs first."

"Zombies," she corrected.

He lifted a finger in preparation to argue her point, but then did not.

Standing before the counter, he inspected the smoothie. It was made with blueberries, chia, dragon-fruit stars, pomegranate arils and a touch of magic. It made the whole dish sweeter, but didn't alter or bespell the eater.

Mel didn't notice the smoothie so much as the man and what he was not wearing. She'd been too frightened when standing out on the patio to notice his attire, but now… His legs were long and muscular and dusted with dark hairs. Powerful thigh muscles flexed with his movement. Even his feet were cute.

"What?" he asked, then dipped a finger into the blueberry concoction.

"You're not wearing pants." She stated the obvious, and then quickly wondered if she should have pointed that out. "But that's fine by me."

"Same thing I had on last night. I don't normally sleep in—I'll be right back."

"Don't get dressed on my account!" she called as he slipped into the living room.

Darn. Why did she keep telling the man to put on clothes? The last time she'd had an opportunity to admire eye candy had been… Mel sighed and shook her head. Just because her dating life was awkward and random at best didn't mean she didn't have some great experiences. But lately she'd been too focused on her family to consider her own needs and desires.

Desires being a key word on the list of overlooked things required to make a person happy. She had a half-naked man in her home right now whom she'd just told to put on pants.

"I didn't tell him that," she whispered back at her conscious. "I would never."

"What's that?" Tor glided back in, now wearing pants and buttoning up his shirt to hide those incredible abs. Of which she'd not taken the time to do a proper ridge count. Stupid. He scooped a serving of smoothie into his mouth, followed by a few more. "I'm going to clean up the mess quickly. I'll finish this decorative meal—" two more scoops "—when I get back in. I'm assuming those were all former pets of yours?"

"No! I don't do dogs. Why would you guess that?"

"They were revenants."

"I thought you said zombies don't exist?"

"They don't. And yet..." Tor shook his head. "You've got me thinking down new tracks lately. Maybe they were zombies. I honestly don't know. Haven't had experience with zombies. But they did climb up from graves in the garden."

"Oh, gross. The former owners must have had dogs. I've only lived in this house five years. I do recall I had to do a major cleaning job to remove all the dog scent and hair from the walls and floors. Smudged this place for days to get out the smell."

"That heart." Tor pointed to the container on the counter next to his smoothie bowl. "Needs to be cloaked, chained up and—I don't know—buried until the full moon."

"I'll recloak it right after you finish breakfast. I'll need a triad to invoke a stronger spell this time. You'll serve as one of the threesome."

"Whatever you need." He scooped in more smoothie, then grabbed the bowl and the spoon and wandered into the living room to clean up the mess.

Twenty minutes later, Tor returned with an empty bowl, dirt smudges on his face and a grin that popped in the dimples on his cheeks. She hadn't noticed those impressions in his cheeks before. Never thought something like that could appeal to her, but—wow. The dimples seemed to only draw attention to his sparkling eyes. Laughter hid in his irises, but it wasn't something he let loose too often. And that gave his whole cute-guy vibe a hint of stoicism that brewed it all into an irresistible facade.

It was hard not to grab him for a hug so… Mel did just that.

"Thank you," she said, pressing her cheek against his shoulder. He smelled so freaking good. Overripe cherries and sharp tobacco-infused leather. Mmm…

"Just because I buried them doesn't mean they'll stay put," he offered. "I'm fresh out of chlorinated lime to dissolve the bones. If you know a spell that'll fix them in the earth, I'd suggest you perform one."

"I'll look one up in my father's grimoire. I own a copy. You've some dirt on your chin."

She licked her thumb and made to dash it over his chin, but he caught her by the wrist. For a moment, she suspected his stoic need to always be the strong one took flight and was replaced by sudden desire. They stared at one another for what felt so long, but could have only been two seconds. And just when she felt herself go up on her tiptoes—

The doorbell rang. Tor's musculature tightened and he gripped her wrist painfully. Her startled gasp shook him out of warrior mode, and he released his grip.

"Sorry. You expecting company?" he asked.

"No. No one ever visits little ole me."

"Then stay put." He swung around the corner into the living room and reappeared with the salt-round pistol.

Impressed by his ability to switch from cleanup guy to alpha protector, Mel felt her heart thump double time. She'd not asked for a hero, but somehow one had dropped into her life. Everything he did fired all the desire receptors in her body. But she knew now was no time for another hug. Even if a kiss had been *so close* to happening. Not when he was responding to his need to protect.

She peered around the corner, following Tor's strides as he walked up to the front door. He opened the door, pointed the pistol barrel into the forehead of the man waiting on the front stoop and—

"Dad!" Melissande yelled.

She heard Tor mutter, "Ah, shit," and then witnessed her father's remarkable magic fling her protector against the wall and pin him there, feet dangling a foot above the floor.

Chapter 9

The dark witch's grip about Tor's throat cut off his air. But he wasn't going to struggle. Or argue with the man. He had been the idiot to point a gun at his head, thinking it might have been a dangerous intruder intent on harming Mel.

His mistake.

Now he'd pay.

"Who are you?" Thoroughly Jones demanded in a deep and slightly malevolent voice. "Why are you in my daughter's home? And how dare you…" He squeezed his fingers so Tor actually squeaked. The silver rings the witch wore cut into Tor's larynx. "…challenge me?"

Tor could but blink. And hope he'd survive to fight more backyard-garden dogs, should that be what the universe tossed his way.

An aura of sweet darkness surrounded the man with onyx hair who wore velvet and leather and whose blue eyes held wicked secrets that Tor didn't want to know. Ever.

"Dad, don't hurt him! He was only trying to protect me."

"From your own father? Insolent—wait." The witch's eyes narrowed as they took in Tor's face. Tor didn't want to look into them. A witch could read a man's soul. "I know you. You're the shill for The Order of the Stake."

Not a shill, Tor wanted to mutter. *A master of spin, actually.* But he'd best remain silent. Not that he could utter more than a garbled plea. His feet still dangled, and his spine was lengthening. That was not a pleasant feeling.

Thoroughly released him and stepped back, yet Tor remained magically pinned to the wall. The dark witch snickered at his helplessness. His expression was menace mixed with a daring mischief.

"I hired him to protect me," Mel insisted.

Her father glanced to her and assessed her truth, then with a nod, turned back to Tor. With a hissed magical word and a slash of his hand, he released Tor from his exile pinned to the wall. Tor dropped, but managed to catch himself and not go all the way down. But he did drop the pistol on the hardwood floor. He'd leave it there. Witches were tricky, and he knew well this dark witch was not someone he wanted to anger any more than he already had. For he could tap into Daemonia, summon demons and exorcise all sorts of strange creatures.

"Why are you in need of protection, Lissa?" Thoroughly asked while he maintained an icy stare on Tor.

"It's the spell I promised you I'd do for Mom. It required an ingredient that is volatile. I felt the need to take extra precautions for the next few days until—you know."

"I can protect you," TJ insisted. His sneer at Tor indicated his unspoken words: *a hell of a lot better than this idiot.*

"You're busy with Mom. Dad, don't worry about it. I got this. Okay?"

Tor sensed the witch release his breath and saw his

shoulders drop as he took another step back and nodded, relenting to his daughter's gentle persuasion. "Right. We did talk about this. You can handle it. I know you can." He offered his hand to Tor. "No hard feelings?"

Tor slapped his palm against the witch's and shook. Their squeeze pressed the heavy silver rings into his skin, and Tor wondered if his bones would take on the impressions. "If you can forgive my rashness, I'll forgive yours."

"Done. I know your reputation. Torsten Rindle, correct?"

Tor nodded.

The man sighed heavily, but with a positive resignation. "You and my brother had a row a few years back. He tends to be impulsive and dangerous with his magic. But… I know your integrity is unwavering. I trust you to protect my daughter."

Melissande embraced her dad from the side and laid her head against his shoulder. He was a tall, dark one, but Tor's gaze was level with his eyes.

"Now that we're all buddies, let's go have some tea and you can tell me why you stopped by," she said. "You never visit, Dad. I sometimes wonder why not."

"You know it's your mother." He wrapped an arm around his daughter's shoulder, and the twosome strolled toward the kitchen. "She's…a handful."

Tor remained by the wall, tugging at his tie, which constricted him more than usual. He felt suddenly unwelcome. It would probably be best to give the two some space. Besides, his throat ached, and he wasn't eager to see what further torture the witch could offer if angered.

"I'm going to do a perimeter check!" he called, and picked up the pistol and stepped outside.

Closing the door behind him, only then did he release his breath. He'd almost had his larynx crushed by *the* Thoroughly Jones. One half of the notorious Jones twins who were Paris's most infamous dark witches. If you were in the know about witches, you knew of them. And a wise man walked a wide circle around their air.

Why had he agreed to protect his daughter? Oh right, because she'd batted her lashes at him, and those big doe eyes had stolen away a smart refusal.

Never before had he allowed himself to be swayed by pretty eyes. And a sexy smile. Not to mention, she sparkled. And she was so seemingly unaware of her cuteness. Or that she was a bit inept with her magic. And the frog and duck. What was it about her menagerie? It was all endearing. And appealing. And…

"What the hell have you gotten yourself into, Rindle?"

Was he starting to have feelings for the wacky witch? That wasn't his MO. He didn't notice women while on an assignment. It had never been a focus for him when his job, and the lives of others, depended on him staying in control.

And yet their proximity was teaching him a different perspective on how to handle client relations. Mel demanded a closer, yet more casual approach. She insisted he let down his guard while also maintaining it. It was a weird dichotomy that made him shake his head.

And he'd held her hand last night. Hadn't wanted it to end.

Was he in over his head?

"Never. I can handle one little witch. Even a sparkly one."

He stepped around to the backyard and decided poking about to ensure there were no more pet graves on the property would be a wise move.

Five minutes of searching confirmed his suspicions that any buried dead thing had already risen. Tor stood at the back of the yard beneath a fall of lush pink flowers that smelled like women's perfume. No more revenants. Or zombies. Hell, really? Was he going there?

It was possible that zombies did, indeed, exist.

Sliding a hand over the crystal talisman hanging from his belt, he smiled as a pair of squirrels chittered and scampered up the trunk of an ancient chestnut tree that mastered the back corner of the yard. And there was that cauldron capped by a round wooden cover. Dare he peek inside?

The hairs on the back of his neck tightened. And it wasn't from thoughts of what could be inside the iron cauldron.

Tor didn't turn around. He didn't want to. He felt the man's presence as a clutch about his throat. Again. But this time he wasn't pinned against the wall.

"Rindle."

Tor winced as Thoroughly Jones joined his side. The air had changed and felt heavy on his shoulders. And he had the foreboding thought that if he swallowed, it would use up the last of his saliva. The witch tapped a pink bloom, and the stamen released a fall of bright yellow pollen. Much more than was normal.

Witches, Tor thought. Too freaky for his peace of mind. Yet he remained calm. Cool was his forte.

"More than being surprised by having a gun pointed in my face at my daughter's front door," TJ said, "finding you in her home, alone with her, puts up my hackles."

Was the man really going to play the part of threatening father to his daughter, who was a grown woman? She had to be midtwenties, at least. An independent woman who lived on her own and had to be long out of her father's care.

"She found me," Tor said. "She hired me. I'm doing a job."

"Uh-huh."

Tor winced as something tightened about his neck. The man hadn't moved to touch him, but he was working some sort of subtle magic on him.

"Protecting your daughter requires 24-7 guarding," Tor said. "I slept on the couch, if that's what's sticking in your craw."

"Lissa is a big girl. I don't interfere in her love life."

"This is not a—" Tor shook his head.

"Exactly. Even you don't know what this is. I can see the stars in my daughter's eyes when she speaks your name. She's always been flighty and walks a few inches above the earth. *Whimsical* is what my wife calls her."

Tor sensed the dark witch hadn't a clue how to grasp the concept of that word. How Mel had turned out so completely opposite her father was a wonder to him. *Whimsical*, indeed.

"You will ensure no harm comes to my daughter."

"That's sort of how it works, me being a protector."

"Sort of?" TJ turned and lifted a brow. The menace had returned to his gaze. He didn't fit in this garden of sweetness and wonder. Unless you factored in the zombie dogs.

"She's safe with me. I guarantee it."

"You are a mere human."

"I've been around the block. I know things. And I take precautions."

"Yes, your reputation is solid." The witch's gaze dropped to the quartz talisman at Tor's hip. "But why ghosts?"

Unwilling to get into that conversation, Tor crossed his arms high across his chest. "Listen, if you don't trust me—"

"I do. I… I came out here to apologize. I was too hasty at the front door. But self-preservation is ingrained in us all. I've seen things, Rindle."

"I imagine the entire Jones family has. Of course, Melissande is—she's a light witch." Tor stated the obvious, but he wasn't sure how to approach his curiosity with her father. He wasn't going to come right out and state he thought she was doing something to prove herself to her father.

"She'll come around," TJ said breezily. Now he splayed out his hand before him and the flower canopy shuddered, dropping a storm of pollen onto the grass. "You allergic, Rindle?"

Only to dark witches. "No. Why do you ask?"

"Ghosts," TJ muttered. A quirk of his brow pondered the word, but he didn't say more.

Tor wasn't going to give him anything. Especially not about ghosts.

"I'll foot your bill," TJ suddenly said. "Don't bother Lissa about that."

"Of course."

"You going to be here 24-7?"

"That's how—"

"—it works. Right. My daughter is beautiful."

"That she is. And if you think intimidation is necessary here, I don't really understand. Like I said—"

"Just doing your job." TJ chuckled. "The results of your cooperation with my daughter will surprise us all. Know that whatever you expect to happen? Will not." The witch turned to him completely and held his hand before him, then slowly clenched his fingers into a C shape. And as he did so, Tor felt the grip about his throat again, not touching, but warning. "Don't fuck this up, Rindle."

The grip released and Tor breathed in quietly. But instead of nodding like a chastised little boy, as the witch turned to leave, Tor gripped him by the arm, stopping him. TJ's look could have maimed, and it probably would have if Tor held on any longer, but he wasn't about to back down to magical grandstanding.

"She's doing this for *your* family," Tor said. "Don't let whatever this is between us become a war you don't need to fight."

The witch lifted a brow. Smirked. Then with a nod, he tugged his arm from Tor's grip and strolled out of the garden and around the side of the house.

Tor nodded. "Damn bloody straight."

* * *

Mel kissed her dad on the cheek and walked him to the front door. She'd understood immediately when he'd confessed that her mother was a handful. It had been three weeks since Star had died. She'd taken a leap from the top of the building in an attempt to make the neighboring building. It hadn't gone well.

TJ was suspicious of that leap. As was Mel. Could her sister have been responsible?

Of course she had been.

That made invoking the spell under the full moon even more urgent. To once and for all end Star's torment and to put her father's mind at peace. It always took a few months for her dad to ease Star back into the life she had once led. That involved showing her videos of her family, walking her around the house and telling her stories of all the adventures they had had. It was trying and hard on Thoroughly.

The fact that Vika, Melissande's aunt, had offered to spend the afternoon with Star and give Thoroughly a few hours off had been gratefully appreciated. He'd only wanted a few hours to relax, breathe, and sit and hold his daughter's hand. They had both watched Tor poke around in the backyard garden. The bright pink clematis had tickled his skin, and purple foxgloves had brushed his ankles as he'd poked and prodded the soil. At one point, he'd fired his weapon into the ground and a sift of dark ash had spumed up. Taking care of any remaining potential zombies, she'd decided.

"He's a strange one," her dad had said. And then they'd both looked at each other and laughed.

Because really, they knew, in the world of strange, their family ranked right up there. Yes, even in the paranormal realm.

At the front door, her dad pulled her into one of his generous hugs and they stood there for a long time. Mel loved it when his hair covered her face and she nuzzled her nose against his chest, drawing in his earthy dark scent. Most would question his motivations to the dark and the acts he had committed over the decades in the name of his magic. He had done some bad things. Yet just as many good things. He was perfect to her. And she would never let him down.

"What does the protector mean to you?" he suddenly asked.

Mel bowed her head and shrugged. "He's doing a job, protecting me."

TJ lifted her chin with a finger. She couldn't look into his eyes for long without a sigh. "I like him, Dad. He's… different. Like me. I've always been the weird one in the family."

"The black sheep," TJ provided, as they'd labeled her more than a few times over the years. "Be cautious, Lissa. But remember I love you. No matter what you are. Weird or normal. And promise me you'll not get in too deep," he asked of her. "Dark magic must be approached with caution."

"I've watched you over the years, Dad. I know what I'm doing." Mostly. Too late to beg leave of the task now. "Don't worry about me. I'll take care of the problem. Then our family can finally breathe a sigh of relief. Give Mom a kiss for me, will you? I'll stop by after the full moon. I don't want to run into Amaranthe, if at all possible."

"She had your mother shivering under the sink all last night. Your sister seems impervious to my magic. I can't expel her from the house. And I have expelled many a spirit in my lifetime."

"This spell will work," she reassured him. "Its efficacy is

increased by blood invocation. And my blood is my sister's, so..." She kissed him again on the cheek and opened the front door. Tor walked around the side of the house. "Thanks for taking care of that last zombie," she called to him.

"Zombies don't—uh...huh," Tor said as he again shook Thoroughly's hand. "Monsieur Jones."

"Do not let any harm come to my daughter," Thoroughly said firmly.

"Absolutely not. She's in good hands. But then, you know that."

TJ eyed Tor up and down and then kissed his first two fingers and drew a sigil in the air between him and Tor. The movement left a brief violet illumination in its wake. He turned and gave Mel a kiss on the cheek, then strode down the sidewalk to the street, where his car waited.

"He's intimidating," Tor commented as they watched the car roll away down the street.

"Tell me about it."

Tor touched his forehead. "Did he just curse me?"

"No, that was a blessing."

"I'm not sure a blessing from a dark witch is such a good thing."

"Oh, it's good. And rare. He trusts you. And that's remarkable coming from my dad."

Tor exhaled deeply. "Then I'll take it for what it was."

Mel tugged Tor inside. "Let's perform the cloaking spell. And this time hope it sticks. We don't need another zombie invasion."

"Zombies don't—"

"Yeah, yeah, whatever." She tugged his hand, cutting off his protest. "Come on, Bruce! Meet us in the bedroom for the invocation!"

Chapter 10

Tor pushed aside the silly bunch of multicolored ribbons and spangles and wandered into Mel's bedroom, a little unsure, but a lot more curious. Whistling a tune about witchy women, he took in everything. The room's atmosphere, with its natural wood and rich scent of herbs and spices, wrapped him with a welcome calmness. The ceiling was scattered with dried flower bouquets of sorts he hadn't names for, though he suspected all had come from her garden. It smelled great. The curved window on the far wall looked out on the lush junglelike backyard. And that plush violet chaise across the room looked like something he could settle into with a book and lose the afternoon soaking in the sunlight.

If a guy did things like that. But Tor did not. He hadn't time for relaxation. He—well, he was leaving his current profession, but that didn't make him any less busy. He expected a call for a follow-up interview soon. And then he'd be back to the grind. He liked to stay busy. It kept him from…

Thinking about things he'd best not consider. Like mistakes and hopes and dreams. Some people were put on this earth to do the creative stuff like make art, build empires, dance and share their feelings. And practice witchcraft.

Others—like him—had to balance that out with hard work and a go-getter attitude that had never served him wrong. He had no definition for vacation. Life demanded. He answered. With a gun in one hand, a machete in the other and…a Sinatra tune tossed in for sanity.

A man couldn't be so hard that he didn't allow in a creative trickle. The songs he sang kept him from jumping over the edge. Singing improved his mood, so he allowed in that bit of creativity whenever possible.

The witch who lived in this house was as creative as they came. And wild and exotic and weird and quirky. And…beautiful. He wondered if her bedroom was reflective of her soul, peaceful and serene, while the rest of the house and the backyard mimicked her outer quirks.

Startled by the frog who floated past his shoulder, Tor stepped aside and watched as it hovered over where Mel was laying items outside a circle that appeared to have been poured out of black salt onto the hardwood floor.

"Come sit over here," she directed. "This is awesome to have a triad. That's probably why the first few cloaking spells didn't stick. I've never done one before. Well, of the dark sort. Live and learn."

"Right, because, you know, there's nothing like fighting revenant dogs in a person's backyard because the spell didn't work."

"I need more practice with this dark stuff. It'll be perfect on the night of the full moon." She closed her eyes.

Briefly, Tor wondered if she were praying her words

would come true. He certainly hoped they did. For her sake. And for her family's sake. It was a tough deal they had going on. And if he could help in some small way, he would.

He stood outside the circle where she'd pointed out and observed her collection of items. A crystal knife, a feather, a couple potion bottles of which he really didn't want to know the contents. Three black candles were placed around the circle, nestled into the black salt. And a few crystals in shades of purple, blue and red were scattered beside her leg.

On her head sat the most remarkable tiara. It wasn't a fancy diamond concoction. It looked cobbled together with wire and different-sized clear quartz points.

"You're a princess then today?" he commented.

"Huh? Oh." She tapped the tiara. "It's my spell-casting crown. I made it from Lemurian quartz. It focuses my magic. What? You think it's too haughty?"

"Nope. I like it on you a lot. You could do the princess thing."

She waved off the comment with a dismissive gesture. "I don't think so. Too much fanciness and fuss for me. But you really like it?" She blushed, which pinked her cheeks as if with makeup. So pretty.

"It suits you. But you don't do fancy and fuss? I thought you were the glitter queen."

"Oh, for sure!" She drew a fingertip under her eye, then followed the curve of black sparkly liner that Tor thought gave her an Egyptian flair. "But you know, *fancy* as in *haughty* and *fuss* as in *high maintenance*."

"Ah. Nope, you're not that. Not when you have a cauldron in your backyard. You know that's a bit..."

"Cliché? It is, but I make soap in it and I like to do that

outside because of the fumes. And Duck naps in it. Sit," she said. "Bruce is ready and so am I."

Tor sat, awkwardly finding a position that worked with crossed legs. A bloke didn't sit on floors all that often.

He eyed the frog, who levitated across the circle from him. As far as backyard frogs went, the critter was large. More like a bullfrog. Should he hold the thing, it would cover his palm. Not that he had any intention of doing that. Something about a floating frog creeped him out a hell of a lot more than an attacking harpie or long-dead dogs risen from the garden.

"How does Bruce figure in as a third hand?" he asked.

"Oh, Bruce is my secondhand man. You're the third." Mel placed the plastic container with the heart in the center of the circle. "As my familiar, Bruce helps with all my spells."

He didn't want to know. Really, he did not. And yet… "Is he a magical frog?"

She tilted such a look at him, Tor swallowed. And then he said, "Of course he's magical. He can levitate. My mistake. Sorry, Bruce. No offense. Can he…? Understand what I'm saying?"

"The question is, does he *want* to?" Mel hid a smirk behind a brush of her hand across her face as she straightened the crystal tiara. So beautiful. "Are you ready?"

"I'm all in." Tor rubbed his palms together. "Just tell me what you need me to do so we can get this show on the road."

"Why? Are you in a hurry?"

"No, but if I hear another knock on the front door, we've ruled out your father, so it can only bode danger."

"I get it. There is a need to keep whatever is picking up on the heart's vibration from feeling that and coming after it."

"Seems like it attracts dead things."

"That makes sense since it's going to bring a dead thing back." Mel spread her palms over the circle and spoke a Latin word that lit the candles. Sulfur briefly tainted the air.

But Tor was still stuck on what she'd said. "This heart is going to bring a dead thing back? Wait. Necromancy?" He put up a firm yet protesting palm. "I didn't get the memo on that particular activity. I thought this was going to be a spell to—well..." He made a thinking noise as he got stuck on pondering this new development. Really, he didn't have any information. And since when had he so blindly stepped into the fray?

Right. When the one leading the charge batted her glittery lashes at him. And she was no less attractive now that she had shown him how dark and desperate her family and lifestyle was. Damn.

"No time for discussion," Mel rushed out. Closing her eyes, she waggled her ringed fingers over the circle. "I've already tapped into the heart's aura. The spell has begun."

She cocked one eyelid open. She had the same deep blue irises as her father. And almost the same chastising look. Though she hadn't mastered the evil, I-can-hurt-you-with-a-snap-of-my-fingers look. She was the furthest thing from evil.

As far as he knew.

Tor swallowed and decided he would get an answer to his question later. And he would. Because bringing back the dead did not sound like a day at the beach.

"Should I close my eyes?" he whispered.

"Whatever makes you happy," the witch answered. "Uh, but...hmm."

"What?" Tor opened his eyes.

"That crystal on your belt. That might interfere with the spell. What's it for?"

He clutched the heavy quartz. "Just protection. It's focused only for me. It won't cause problems with other magics. I know that."

She considered it while he hoped she wouldn't question him further. It was too personal. And he never went anywhere without this talisman.

"Fine. You'll tell me about it when you're ready."

He would never be ready.

"Here we go."

Mel quickly slipped into a fast and focused whisper that streamed words into the atmosphere Tor did not recognize. Her hands moved over the plastic container, sweeping, drawing sigils. Or so he supposed. Her movements did not leave a trail of illumination as her father's had. She used the feather to draw around the entire circle as her chants grew rhythmic. The flames flickered higher and thinner until they were as narrow and tall as each of the candles.

Tor did not necessarily oppose magic. When it was used for good. And while he'd been witness to its use on many occasions, he still could never shake the prickle of unease that rose at the back of his neck when it occurred. Witches could summon power from out of thin air, using elements and familiars. And it was freaky.

"All right," she announced. "Now we all join hands and I'll complete the cloaking."

Tor reached to clasp her hand. It was warm and felt small and delicate in his grasp. The connection ignited a sudden want in him, not so much sexual as sensual. He liked being near her. She surrounded him with a unique air. Soft yet playful. She teased at his staunch need to remain, well, staunch.

When he reached to the left, he realized her request wasn't possible. "Frogs don't have hands."

Melissande sighed. "Do what I'm doing," she instructed.

He saw she had extended her forefinger so the amphibian's front paw or foot—whatever the hell it was—curled over it. Right, then. Tor reached out and the frog slapped his webbed footpads over the tip of his finger. Weird. Just…

He wasn't going to overthink this one.

The witch recited three final words. The candle flames flickered out. Bruce ribbited. And Tor felt a strange and warm jolt shiver through his system. He retracted his finger from the frog, who had hopped onto the box in the middle of the salt circle.

"Complete," Mel announced. She sat back with a sigh, catching her palms behind her. Stretching her feet through the salt circle, she toggled the container on which the frog sat. "No one should be able to see this now."

"I can see it," Tor stated the obvious.

"Yeah, but you can't *feel* it, can you?"

He wrinkled a brow. He supposed those creatures that had risen to seek the heart had felt it as opposed to actually having a visual on it. In some strange manner, it was sending off supernatural vibrations and now… "No, I can't. But I never did. I mean, I'm not— Fine. Let's hope this one sticks. Now what?"

"I'll have to vacuum up the salt, but I'm in no rush. You have any appointments you need to make today?"

"No, but I should run home and pack some casual clothing."

"You have casual clothing?" Her shock didn't sound mocking, but he wasn't sure.

"I do. It's not me though."

"I should think not, Monsieur Proper-British-and-Uptight."

"I'm not uptight."

And to prove his point, he leaned back, but his crossed legs set him off-balance, and he wobbled as he tried to untangle his legs. He managed a graceless sway to the side and caught an elbow on the floor and his hand against the side of his head.

"I've never seen a more uncomfortable relaxed man in all my life," she declared. She leaned to the side, putting their faces close. "What do you do to relax, Tor? Count the ties in your closet? Organize the shirts? Wait. You space the hangers using a ruler, right?"

She was…not wrong. But hearing it spoken with the faintest tone of mockery cut at him. It shouldn't. It had never bothered him what others thought of him. He didn't need to please anyone. So he had some OCD tendencies. Didn't everyone? But for some reason, he wanted her approval.

"Relaxation, eh? I like to sing," he offered.

"I noticed that. You whistle while you work, as well. I had no idea it relaxed you."

"It does. A little Sinatra. Some Sammy Davis Jr., Dean Martin."

"The Rat Pack, eh?" She turned onto her stomach to give him her complete attention. A man could get lost in those big bright eyes for sure. "Have you ever sung karaoke? Do you know they have karaoke parties down by the Seine all summer long?"

"I do know that. In the 5th. I've gone to one or two."

"To sing?"

"What else does a person do at a karaoke party?"

"You do surprise me. I find it hard to believe that you'd let down your guard to sing in front of others."

"You don't know a lot about me," he said.

"I don't. But I like what I'm learning. Singing is so intimate."

"You think?"

"It is for the singer." Her big blue eyes sought his. "Isn't it?"

"I suppose. And the song choice makes it even more intimate."

"What does Sinatra mean to you?"

He shrugged. "Teenage memories."

"Such memories must give you confidence."

"They…taught me that being myself was okay."

"Nice." Mel toyed with the salt grains. "Can we go to the riverside karaoke party sometime?"

"I, uh…"

Was that a date request? Because he wasn't sure how to actually do dates. Not like he'd ever taken the time to woo a woman before. The few times he had stopped by the party near the river had been on the way home from a job, and he'd surrendered to the need for mindless engagement. "Maybe?"

"There's my uptight guy returning to his roots. I can accept a maybe. Thanks for helping me with the spell. Your energy is off the charts, you know."

"Probably because it's nervous energy."

"No, you were initially nervous when forced to hold Bruce's hand, but I could see beyond that small annoyance. You are confident and bold. You may appear to be the average Joe to others, but I can feel all that you are inside."

"Is that so?" Now he rolled onto his stomach to face her. Sunlight glinted in the crystals crowning her hair. Her violet eye shadow sparkled, as did her irises. Sparkle witch. A guy had to love it. "How do you know all that about me? Did you perform some kind of witchy gaze into my soul?"

"I'm not that talented. That's my dad's forte. It's just a feeling I have about you. Kind of like a knowing. You're a good one," she said, then dipped her head. "I have to tell you something. Please don't laugh."

Intrigued, Tor caught his chin in his hand and waited for her to speak.

"It's important I prove myself to my father," she said.

"I had wondered about that after talking to him."

"I've never strived to practice dark magic. That was always my sister's calling. And through the years, I noticed that she and Dad got on much better than I did with him. And now…well, now's my chance to show him that I've got what it takes."

Tor suspected that even if she had what it took to invoke dark magic, she didn't want to. But proving oneself to another, especially a parent, was a strong motivator. He couldn't imagine what it must be like to seek approval from a parent. Though maybe it was similar to seeking approval from a mentor. He'd jumped into some wild situations to learn his various trades. All because Monsieur Jacques, his mentor, had asked him to meet some extreme challenges. A werewolf cleanup here, a trip to a vampire lair there. And how many times had he been handed a book on chemicals and told to learn it? He'd won approval from Monsieur Jacques and moved on to become the man he now was.

"We all do what we have to," he said. "I would never judge you, Mel. Much as dark magic freaks me out, it is a necessity to balance out—"

"—the good," she finished for him. "That's what I always heard growing up. My mom would whisper it as Dad and Amaranthe would go off to bind a hex or communicate with the demonic realm."

"You haven't told me about your sister."

Mel sighed. "Nope. And I'm not going to either. Not

unless you want to start coughing up details about your secrets and personal stuff. Can we agree to not share that which makes us most uncomfortable?"

Most definitely. "Agreed."

Her lashes dusted her cheeks, and Tor reached over to push aside strands of her hair from those thick lashes. She suddenly looked up, and the glint in her eyes lured him closer. Without thinking, he leaned in and nudged his nose aside her cheek, drawing in her perfume, a tantalizing mix of lemon and lavender. He felt her shiver.

When he tilted his head, his mouth grazed her cheek and her lips parted. He brushed them lightly, closing his eyes because the moment demanded he focus on their closeness, the warmth of her skin, the tickle of her hair against his fingers, the scent of her. It all combined with the herbs hanging overhead and the sulfur still lingering from the snuffed candles. A sweet dream. He had never kissed a client before…

Tor pulled a few inches away from Mel's mouth. She gaped at him.

"I'm working for you," he said, not entirely behind the statement, but it was a truth, no matter how conflicted he felt. Why had he made such a move?

Because he'd not been able to resist her soft and compelling allure. Or her crystal glitter eyes.

"Oh right." She glanced aside. A wisp of her hair fell across his forehead. "I suppose."

The moment felt wrong. Like he'd just stepped on a ladybug, crushing her delicate shell. Yet Tor could not deny his curiosity for her, so…he would not.

He slid his hand along her jaw and smoothed his fingers into her hair, gliding over the combs that fastened the crystal crown. He tilted her face up to meet his. The connection of their mouths shocked a fiery heat through his system. It was the weirdest thing, and at the same time, the most incredible experience. He wanted to burn himself on her surprising fire, so he pushed away the ridiculous worry that clients were not to be kissed.

And if he even started to consider the fact that her father was a powerful dark witch—

"No," Tor mumbled against her mouth, but he didn't stop the kiss. She tasted too good, and he wanted too much. It was easier to relate to her without words.

He slid closer, nudging across the salt barrier, and slipped his hand down her back to pull her to him. When she tickled his mouth open with her tongue, he groaned as the intensity of her heat flooded into him. All thoughts grew singular. Want. Need. Desire. Heat. Take. Give. Lush.

The curve of her hip undulated under his palm, and he clutched at her, keeping her there, hugging his thigh. Against his chest, the teasing connection of her breasts alerted him how hard her nipples were. He moved his hand beneath her breast, gently cupping the perfect handful. He was moving quickly and…

"Not right?" Tor managed as he took a breath against her mouth.

"Very right."

With her consenting nod, he pulled her back and dashed his tongue across her teeth. Now her body swayed against his, and he felt her weight push into him, so he relented and rolled onto his back. Her breasts hugged his chest. She straddled him with her knees, and not once did their lips part.

Had he been bewitched? Cajoled by a practitioner of magic into succumbing to base passion? What was wrong with acting on his desires? He could kiss a woman when he wanted to. If she was in agreement. And this woman agreed with every move he made.

His elbow nudged something, and he felt a warmth slide up against his shirt. The candle had toppled and the wax spilled onto the fabric of his dress shirt. Another candle was knocked over by his shoulder.

"Mel," he whispered.

"What? Don't say *no* again. I like kissing you." She gave him a quick kiss. "This is awesome."

"Just… Mel," he muttered. He received another kiss that this time made him smile widely against her lips.

Wrapping an arm across her back, he turned them on the floor until she lay beneath him. Clasping one of her hands with his, he then bowed his head to kiss down her chin and neck. She smelled sweet there, like lavender and spice and the blueberries from breakfast. He nuzzled his face against the top of her breasts, drawing her in, sensing his hard-on was striving for maximum steel. He hadn't put all his weight on top of her. He wouldn't be so forward. This was their first kiss. He wasn't that guy.

Most of the time.

Mel giggled and said, "Is that a talisman on your belt or are you just happy to see me?"

He snickered, but then closed his eyes and bowed his head against her neck. Adjusting his stance, he moved so the heavy quartz talisman nestled against her upper thigh and was not more centered, as it had been. "Slower," he said.

"Why?" she asked on a whisper.

"Because I want it that way." He hadn't thought that answer through; he'd spoken from his heart. It felt right. It needed to go slow between them, if anything was going to happen. And he hoped it would. "Okay?"

"Well, I wasn't about to let you jump my bones, if that was what you were hoping for."

Tor chuckled and then kissed her quickly. "I wasn't,

despite what a certain part of my anatomy might make you believe."

"Oh, so it wasn't just a big chunk of quartz." She tapped him on the nose. "I know you fellas have difficulty controlling your second brain."

"My second—?" Tor rolled off her to lie on his back and laughed. "If that's the way you want to play it."

His cell phone rang, and he tugged it out of his trousers pocket and answered. The caller was Rook from The Order of the Stake, an organization he hadn't worked with for months.

"I'm setting that part of my business aside," Tor said to the man's insistent request. "Really?" Tor blew out a breath. "In the 8th? I can stop by in an hour. But for future jobs, find someone else to do your cleanup work." He hung up and turned to lean on an elbow.

"What's that about?" Mel asked.

"There's a media alert that needs immediate attention. A woman was bitten by a vampire last night, and she's been texting pictures of the bite mark. Local news stations have been calling her for interviews. Rook wants me to nip it in the bud."

"That's what you do, isn't it? Make things all better."

"I help people to believe that what they saw wasn't actually what they saw. Vampires? Come on. What a bunch of malarkey."

"I kind of like occasional bouts of malarkey."

He kissed her quickly. Too quickly. "I favor some good nonsense talk myself."

She beamed up at him. And Tor's heart performed an acrobatic flip.

"Can I come along?" she asked.

"You'll have to. I'm not letting you out of my sight until after the full moon. Grab the heart. We've got a job to do."

Chapter 11

Practically flying behind Tor as he walked down the narrow aisle leading to the inner courtyard of a tony 8th arrondissement building, Mel licked her lips and didn't hide her smile. He hummed a tune she recognized: "Witchcraft" by Sinatra. It was about a man seduced by a woman.

Interesting. And points for her.

After she'd performed the cloaking spell, he'd kissed her. It had been a perfect moment, the two of them sprawled over the extinguished spell. She still had some salt grain marks on her knees, but it was all good.

The man's kiss had been electric. Unexpected. The complete opposite of his outer appearance. It had been hot and uncontrolled. And it was not something she wanted to go too long without getting another one of. And another. What luck that the man she had hired to protect her could also kiss like a charm? She'd suspected a softer inner side to him after hearing him sing and agreeing to hold Bruce's hand during the invocation. Was she invading his stronghold? Tearing down his stalwart defenses? How exciting to even try!

She abruptly ran into the man's back as he stopped before a door. His humming ceased. The gentle squeeze of his hand on her shoulder to keep her from spilling forward into his arms reminded her that he was on a business mission right now. And she didn't want to screw things up for him, so she would remain on her best behavior. Keep thoughts of kissing him longer, deeper and harder out of her brain.

This was going to be more difficult than invoking a dark hex.

"Where's the heart?" he asked.

She patted her tapestry bag.

He pushed the hair from her eyes and over her ear, then looked her up and down. She'd changed into a violet velvet minidress that featured a splash of red spangles at the hem. The dress matched the minuscule red sparkly stars dotting her violet eye shadow. White go-go boots had seemed an appropriate pairing.

"That color suits you," he observed.

"Why, thank you. Your choice of ties is always spot-on."

He tugged at the simple gray tie, which was knotted in a complicated triple layer that impressed the heck out of her.

"Why the sudden assessment of my wardrobe?" she asked.

"If I'm going to keep you within eyesight, you'll have to assume a role once we step behind this door. I work hard to wear a facade. Play a role. It's integral to my work. You're going to have to play my assistant. Take notes. Make it look good. Can you do that?"

"I don't have any paper."

"Where's your phone?"

"I rarely carry it on me. The EMF energy messes with my magic."

Tor nodded. "I get that. Take mine for now." He pulled a fancy gold iPhone out of an inner vest pocket and, punching in the passcode, handed it to her. "Make it look official. But don't mess with anything."

"Like don't touch anything?"

He rolled his eyes. "Thanks for that reminder. You're going to mess with things, aren't you?"

"I promise to stay on my best behavior. I will be quiet and make it look like I'm taking notes on the phone."

"Good. Should I refer to you at any moment, just play along. Deal?"

"Deal. If I do well, can I get another kiss?"

"I—er." He paused from knocking on the door.

"Sorry," she said. "You don't mix business and pleasure. I get that about you. A big no-no to combine the two. But—well, we did kiss. You remember that, right? When the world sort of tilted...just a little." She looked for some sign of agreement but only got a tightened jaw from him. "Okay...business. Forget I asked. We'll discuss it later. Right now, you're on."

"Thank you." He knocked on the door, and a full minute later the door finally creaked open to reveal wary blue eyes beneath a tousle of blond hair. "Mademoiselle deStrand, I am Inspector Jean-Pierre Cassel. Paris Police. I'm from the human relations department."

"I already spoke to the police. They laughed at me. Loudly." Her face pulled away from the crack between the door and wall.

Tor stuck his toe over the threshold, preventing her from closing the door. "I never laugh at someone who has been victimized, *mademoiselle*. I simply want to ensure you are well and safe. The incident last night with the viral outbreak…" He paused and looked to Mel.

"Viral outbreak?" The woman inside opened the door a bit wider. "No, it was a vamp—"

"Oh, I understand, *mademoiselle.* And I accept your previous statement given to the officers who met with you for truth and one hundred percent validity. That was obviously a separate incident. But as I was reviewing the dossiers this morning, I noticed you were in the vicinity of the hot zone during your attack. The Parc Monceau. Not far from here?"

"Yes, it was just off the bike trail. I met a man who lives directly on the park and has twenty-four-hour access— A hot zone? What does that mean?"

"You met a resident? That wasn't listed on the police report."

"It wasn't? But I gave it all."

"Might I come inside? There's some information I need to record such as your exact location, possible contaminant exposure and inhalation of toxins. It's all to ensure your safety."

"My safety?"

"The virus acts quickly, *mademoiselle.* Have you a will prepared?"

"A will? *Mon Dieu...*" The door closed and the chain slid across the wood.

Tor flashed Mel a dimpled smile.

Mel smiled so widely her cheeks hurt. But when the door opened, she resumed a calm demeanor. She couldn't wait to see Tor work his form of fast-talking magic on this woman.

"Come in," Mademoiselle deStrand said. "I don't know what you are talking about, Monsieur Cassel. As I reported to the police last night, I was bitten by a vampire. He lives in a house on the park. I know you won't believe me—"

"Of course I believe you." Tor pointed to the woman's neck. "I can see that by the marks on your neck. The evidence is clear." He followed her inside to a dark living room, and Mel stayed close behind. The television was tuned to an evening serial. "Oh, this is my assistant. She'll be taking notes for the database."

"The database?" the woman asked, and glanced to Mel. She waved the phone, then started to type random letters into the text program which, if sent, would go to her own phone. "They keep a database on vampire bites? You really believe me?"

"Whether or not I believe in creatures with fangs who crave human blood is not the issue right now, *mademoiselle.* What is—are you feeling well? You look pale."

"I've had my curtains drawn. I don't want to turn into a vampire and I know sunshine is not good—I've been feeling poorly all day. You think I'm pale?" She pressed a shaking hand to her neck.

"It's one of the first signs of the virus. Isn't that correct, Madame Jones?"

"Huh? Oh, yes. First sign. Pale skin. Fear of the light."

The woman gaped. "The virus?"

"There was a leak last night in the park," Tor explained. "A medical transfer vehicle crashed, and a container holding a dangerously virulent biotoxin was crushed. The virus went airborne. And from our canvass reports of the immediate area, you seem to be the only one who was outside at the time."

"But the vampire was…"

"Yes, the vampire." Tor turned to Mel. An elegant arch of his eyebrow didn't so much convey doubt but rather a sort of astute knowledge. He was talking babble as far as Mel could determine, but it did sound feasible. He focused his attention fiercely on the woman. “Are you sure the person you say assaulted you wasn’t instead trying to infect you with the virus? Did he take you into his house?”

“No, he, uh…pointed out his mansion as we were strolling in the park.”

“Alone?”

“Yes, of course—it was after midnight. The park was closed. Do you think he was trying to infect me?”

She swiped a hand down her throat, covering the obvious bite marks. Mel thought whomever had bitten her had been sloppy. Most vamps lick the wound following the bite, and their saliva would cause it to heal within twenty-four hours, leaving no visible sign they’d punctured flesh. That wound looked torn and ragged. Infected, even.

“A virus?” the woman repeated slowly.

“It can be delivered in many ways,” Tor offered. “Through saliva with a cough or sneeze, airborne release such as the crash, direct injection with a needle, exposure while trekking through an infected country. Even a sloppy puncture and then touching the bloodstream with an infected item, such as, say, a set of fanged dentiture.”

“That sounds like an elaborate method of doing something so harmful. And if you say there was a crash—”

“Staged, yet contained, we believe. A skillful ploy carried out to spread the virus as a means to test its virulence. But you shouldn’t tell anyone I gave you that information. This has not been released to the public. The area has been cleared and decontaminated. All are safe. Except those who were there last night between eleven and one a.m.”

“I was leaving the nightclub and having a walk home when I met the man. He was so charming. A walk in the park sounded perfect. It was just after midnight. Why didn’t the officers I spoke to last night mention the crash?”

"This is an active investigation, *mademoiselle*. The few facts we had at that time were not confirmed until early this afternoon. Has anyone come to you with a request for testing?"

"Testing? No."

"Good. Such a request could only be a ploy from the people who released the virus. And they are not the good guys. You should sit down. You look—" Tor glanced to Mel. "Don't you think she looks unwell?"

"Most definitely." And Mel made a show of putting her hand over her nose and mouth and taking a step backward.

"I have been feeling woozy." Mademoiselle deStrand sat on the couch.

Tor rushed to sit beside her. He took her hand, and the woman gazed at him with desperation.

And Mel could only be impressed.

"What was the viral incubation rate?" Tor asked her suddenly.

"The what?" Mel asked.

Tor nodded insistently. "You know…"

"Oh! Oh right, the virile incubation rate." She made a show of clicking away at his phone, but it had already gone back to the password screen and the time blinked at her. "The data says a thirty-two-hour window from time of release into the air." She winked then, because she'd impressed herself with that speedy reply.

"Thirty-two hours?" The woman clutched Tor's thigh. "What does that mean? I thought it was a vampire…"

"I would never question what you believe happened, *mademoiselle*, but you must know there are types who like to use the persona of such a creature to disguise their disgusting crimes. If you've been infected, you need emergency care. Stat."

"Stat," she whispered, lost and swallowing.

"Are you sure you saw fangs?" Tor pressed. "There is a perp we've been after who wears fake fangs. He bites the person before rubbing a vile compound into their skin. It's a weird cult. Science gone wrong. We had a death a month ago."

"Death?" The woman stood and gripped her throat. "No, I don't want to die."

"But if you insist that it was merely a vampire…" Tor started.

"No, I—I *thought* it was. He was so handsome. And when I saw he was going to kiss me, he— I saw his fangs."

"Handsome." Tor again glanced to Mel.

She returned an authoritative nod. "The usual MO."

The woman gasped. "I can't believe it."

"Vampires don't exist," Tor said. He smoothed his palm over her hand reassuringly. "You're a smart woman, *mademoiselle*. You've been traumatized. And with the virus exposure, you've not been in your right mind. I'm so sorry. You've been manipulated on a diabolical level. But as I've said, I know you are smart."

The woman nodded.

"Vampires do not exist," Tor repeated. And once more he said softly, as he stroked the back of the woman's hand, "Vampires do not exist."

"Of course they don't," the woman replied.

Mel tucked the phone in her pocket. Mission accomplished.

"I'm going to order a car to pick you up and transfer you directly to Emergency Care. Perhaps I should call an ambulance." Tor stood and reached inside his vest, then looked to Mel. She walked up to him and slyly slipped him the phone.

"No ambulance," the woman on the couch ordered. "I can't afford that bill. You really think I should go in?"

"It is imperative. You've been exposed."

"But you're not wearing a mask, and neither is she. Aren't you afraid of being near me?"

"Not at all. It is a blood infection. Once it gets in your system, you can't infect another person without direct exchange of fluids. You're not going to spit on me, are you?"

She shook her head, obviously baffled. Her shoulders dropped as she sank into the realization she had been a victim of something much worse than a mere bite.

"My team can be here within the hour," Tor said. "You'll need blood tests, and an antidote."

"And that will save me?" The woman clutched his arm.

"Of course. But I'll ask you to keep this hush-hush with the media. We are close to tracking the perp's hideout. If the right information got out to the wrong person… it could ruin the work we've accomplished on this case. When you feel better, we'd appreciate your cooperation. I'm sure you'll have all the evidence that will lead us directly to him. Your help will prove invaluable."

"Really? You're such a nice man. Why didn't you show last night when I was being interviewed by the other officers? They were so rude to me."

"I was out on the perp's trail. So sorry. Sometimes our personnel feel they can handle an issue that is far above their expertise. But I'm here now. And I'm going to take care of you."

"Oh, *merci*." The woman hugged Tor and he patted her shoulder.

He winked at Mel.

A flush of warmth to her neck and cheeks stirred up thoughts of kissing him again. The man could lie his way into her heart any day.

After a car had arrived and whisked away the woman to the ER, Tor made the required phone calls to the major media outlets to inform them the victim had been off her meds and had been transferred to Sainte Anne's for psychiatric care. *No vampires here, people.* They bought it.

They always did.

He'd call Rook back, too. A vampire living in the Parc Monceau? Possible. But more likely, the asshole had told deStrand he lived in one of those fancy houses when he did not. The Order of the Stake would further the investigation.

He started the van and turned onto the main road. Mel, on the passenger seat, practically bounced with enthusiasm.

"You were amazing! But where are they really taking her?"

"First stop is the ER at the Hôtel-Dieu. I have a man on the inside. He'll take her blood and make it look official to Mademoiselle deStrand. He'll give her some directions for rest and what to watch for regarding contracting the virus, like sudden death." He chuckled. "I love that rogue-virus routine. It works every time. And no one dares speak about it because they've been such a help to the Paris Police Department."

"That was crazy."

"The crazy part was the vamp who left the evidence. Did you see that wound? Idiot. I don't have any intel on vamps in that area. And if there were, they'd be elite, very cautious of their actions."

"It is a ritzy part of town. Which could be why the vamp led her there? To throw suspicions off his tracks?"

"It's a possibility. Look at you, thinking all procedural."

She wiggled with pride on the seat. "But the woman…"

"She'll be fine in a few days, after the bite marks go away and the placebo she's been given miraculously keeps her from dying."

"But if the wound wasn't sealed correctly, she could transform."

"She'll get a vamp saliva antidote. Works like a charm."

"I've never heard of such a thing."

"It was developed by The Order of the Stake. New technology."

"Cool. You are a valuable asset to our world, you know that?"

"What? Doing spin to cover the idiocy of stupid vampires?" Tor shrugged. "Anyone can do it."

"But has anyone been doing it as long as you have? Does anyone have all the knowledge you have of the paranormal species that live in the mortal realm? Very few humans are in the know and aware that having such knowledge must be kept hush-hush. You're special, Tor. I can't believe you want to walk away from this."

"I'm not special. I might even be the unfortunate one who had this knowledge dumped on me. Doesn't matter. My mind is made up."

"I think you should reconsider. What happens when you're not around to reassure an obvious victim of a vampire bite that she was instead exposed to a dangerous virus?"

Tor chuckled again. "I bloody love that spin." The sun was setting and he was hungry. "You want to stop for something to eat?"

"I'd like that. Can we call it a date?"

"I, uh..." He stepped on the brake at a stop sign.

A date was something he couldn't manage while on the job. Should he have kissed her back at her place? Obviously it had given her ideas about what could conspire between the two of them. And much as he'd considered it...

"Can we just call it getting something to eat?"

"Oh sure." Disappointment was evident in her voice. "I'm up for whatever."

Tor drove on, but he noticed out of the corner of his eye that Mel seemed let down. She wasn't bubbly anymore. He didn't want her to take things the wrong way. And what was wrong with making her feel good and being nice to her? Kissing her didn't mean he had to have sex with her. He'd been in the moment. Had reacted and…

Yet he wondered now what that might be like. Kissing her again. Taking it further. Just…letting whatever they wanted to happen happen.

She was beautiful. If weird. And smart. If kooky. And she needed his protection. If only for a few more days.

And then what?

If he stepped into the normal, he'd have to leave the world of the paranormal behind. And with that, Melissande Jones.

Chapter 12

At her suggestion to check out one of the more touristy places to eat in the 5th, they now walked side by side as they both nursed ice cream in cups. He had chosen vanilla. No surprise there. And she had picked her favorite, cherry and chocolate. Before that, they'd eaten a meal of roast chicken and carrots at a little outdoor restaurant.

Now they strolled past the famous Shakespeare and Company bookstore that she had worked in for all of three weeks. They stocked some esoteric books on the occult and magic, of which she would occasionally find a gem. Of course, while working, she'd tended to get lost in the books and ignore the customers. A person always thinks a bookstore would be a great place to work, but really, it's the biggest candy shop in the world. And who wants to be interrupted by customers?

The evening was still young, though the streetlights had flickered to life, competing with the alluring shades of twilight and the flash of passing headlights. As they walked toward the river, the scents of roasted meats and vegetables gave way to a bitter perfume of tarmac and motor oil.

Tor stopped and leaned his elbows on the concrete balustrade. Below, the river was calm until an oncoming bateau mouche filled with tourists disturbed the water. He set his empty ice-cream cup on the balustrade and turned around, facing away from the river, rolled up his shirtsleeves and then propped his elbows behind him.

“I don’t get you and your family,” he said, his gaze strolling down her miniskirt and to the go-go boots. “I know there are some things that you don’t want to talk about. I’m cool with that. I have my own secrets.”

“Secrets are your thing.”

“That they are. I proudly wear the title of *Secret Keeper.* But help me explain how someone like you can exist in a family that practices dark magic. *You’re* the weird one?”

Mel shrugged. “That I am.” Half her ice cream remained, and she scooped for a big chunk of cherry.

“But your dad is all dark and demonic, and you did mention something about your sister practicing dark magic. And yet from what I’ve gleaned about you, you sway more toward the light and…”

“Unicorns and glitter?”

He chuckled. “Unicorns are vicious.”

“How do you know that? Have you ever—have you seriously seen a unicorn?”

His dimples popped into his cheeks as he bowed his head, but then looked up at her with a telling smirk. “Maybe.”

“No way! I would kill to see a unicorn. I mean, well, not kill an animal. Maybe a cabbage. Anyway, what was it like? Where in this realm did you see a unicorn?”

“I can’t say. It’s a trust thing.”

"Secrets."

"Exactly. And it may or may not have been…free."

"Oh no." She caught a palm against her thundering heartbeats. "Was it captive? Please tell me it wasn't in chains."

"Can't say. My clients' secrets are my own."

"Now I'm going to worry about that poor unicorn."

"No one should ever worry about a unicorn. They're tough. And they possess some incredible magic. It's ineffable. But back to the light witch, who makes masterpieces out of fruit, collects an odd menagerie of pets and likes all things that sparkle." He pointed to her eyes.

Mel's glittery eye shadow had given her away. She turned and leaned against the balustrade next to him. Cars passed by slowly, their drivers taking in the sights. A double-decker bus with passengers on the top open level snapping pics parked across the street to let on new travelers. "Believe it or not, I'm actually the black sheep of the family. Isn't that crazy? Of course, I don't mind being the weird one."

"You are weird."

"Why, thank you. You've a touch of the weird about you yourself. What about you? Do you have family? How did you ever develop this relationship with our world of the weird and strange?"

"I…don't have a family."

"Tor, that's so sad. But everyone has a family. Parents, at the very least. Did something terrible happen to them?"

He exhaled, winced, then said, "My mom died after giving birth to me. She was only seventeen. I wasn't put up for adoption and ended up in a home for boys just south of London. Grew up there."

"That means the people in the home were your family."

"Not really. I never developed a close relationship with

any of the boys. And the nuns and staff were—well, you've heard rumors, I'm sure. They were a tough bunch. Though Miss Thunder had her moments."

"Miss Thunder?"

"She was the Science and Physical Education instructor. She was also the barracks chief and general hard-ass. But…every Sunday afternoon when the nuns were praying and singing and doing all that religious stuff, Miss Thunder would sit outside her window, listening to old Rat Pack tunes spinning on an ancient record player inside her room. Smoking a joint."

"And how do you know that?"

Tor smirked. "She taught me how to inhale properly."

"Wow. And that's how you developed your love for the old songs?"

"Most definitely. I'd sit there for a couple hours with Thunder. She wouldn't say much except that I was an odd boy. Very odd. Then she'd hand me the doobie and I'd take a toke and laugh. The nuns never found out. I always marveled at that. But then, they tended to walk a wide circle around me."

"Because you were odd?" Mel asked.

"Because I would point out the presence of…" Tor exhaled and shook his head. His thumb stroked the quartz hanging from a belt loop. He dismissed something she wanted to hear, Mel felt sure. "Anyway, I left when I was fourteen. Moved to Paris when I was twenty. Been doing fine ever since."

"Have you always been interested in the paranormal?"

"I wouldn't call it an interest, initially. More like it was always around me, so I simply didn't know anything else. And… I don't want to talk about this. It's too…"

"Sorry. Secrets. We'll change the subject." Not what she wanted to do, but she respected his need for privacy about his personal life. "Did my dad give you the don't-touch-my-daughter speech?"

Tor turned a half grin on her. "Basically."

"Are you going to do as he asks?" She fluttered her lashes at him.

"Should I?"

She shook her head. "He's all bluster. Trust me."

"I'm not so sure of that. My throat still aches. You know your dad could take me out without even touching me."

"He could. But he won't. He would never do something that would upset his daughter."

"What if his daughter had an issue with the guy?"

"Well then," Mel said dramatically. Then she shook her head. "I would never ask such a thing of my dad."

"Yeah, I'm sorry. I know you wouldn't. That's not you. You're not a dark witch."

"Just like you're not a normal man. If you insist on seeking a job in the normal world, you're trying to be something you're not, Tor."

"Just like you, eh? Miss Light Witch going for the dark?"

He had her there. And, like him clamming up about personal issues, she didn't want to talk about it. Or she did, but she didn't know how. Wasn't sure he was ready to hear it all. She didn't want to scare him off, having already dodged the necromancy concern he'd brought up earlier.

"I'm just trying to do my best," she offered.

"I can relate. I've never been one to follow the rules or listen to what's best for me. I live in the moment. And right now, the moment calls to me." He held out his hand and she clasped it. "I think there's something you should see. Come on."

Curiosity giving her a giddy shiver, Mel walked alongside Tor. They strolled on, hand in hand.

"You got the heart?" he asked.

She patted the bag she'd slung over her shoulder. Good thing the heart wasn't heavy. But it wasn't light either. The guy could offer to carry it for her. Then again, she wanted to keep it close, and she wasn't sure she trusted he could handle the magical energy attached to the thing.

"Know what's ahead?" he asked, as he took her empty ice-cream cup and spoon and tossed them into a bin as they passed.

Mel didn't—but then she heard the music. "Really? Is that the karaoke party?"

Tor spread out his palms before him in invitation, and a dimple popped into his cheek. "All work and no play…"

"Your name's not Jack, and for that I'm glad." She picked up her pace toward the stairway that descended to a wide cobblestoned patio that edged the river below. "This is so awesome!"

The riverfront was alive with people dancing to the sounds of a remarkable trio singing to a famous pop song. The party stretched along the cobblestones. Mel bounced on her heels.

"I just remembered this place," Tor said. "And you did say you like karaoke."

"I love it! Can we dance, too? This song is so catchy."

"My lady." Tor offered his hand and then led her into the fray. The twosome immediately picked up the beat and joined in the crowd as they sang the chorus to cheers and encouragement from the singers with the microphone.

Mel didn't know any official dance steps, but she didn't need to. Just to follow the music and let her body react is what her father had taught her when they'd go to the rooftop and blast some music in the summertime. Her sister had never been interested. And it was one of the rare times Mel had actually garnered her father's undivided attention.

Tor spun her in a circle as her laughter spilled out. He had some moves. His hips and shoulders were loose, which was surprising for his muscular build. He was sinuous and graceful, with a touch of funky. What a treat to see him let loose like this!

Pumping her fists up and down, Mel guessed she was doing an approximation of the "mashed potato." Hey, she was in the zone.

When Tor suddenly pulled her close to him, their eyes fixed on one another's. Mel sighed. If he kissed her, that would make the night perfect. It didn't matter that they were surrounded by so many others. She just wanted…

The song ended with a raucous cheer from the crowd. Someone tapped Tor on the shoulder. "Your turn, *monsieur*?"

"You're on, Sultan of Swoon," Mel said.

"I guess I am." He kissed her quickly on the cheek, then took the microphone and stepped over to the karaoke machine to select a song. The time period plunged back to the mid-twentieth century, and a saxophone led Tor into a croon. The crowd took on the vibe, and a few swayed in pairs as Mel stepped to the edge of the dancers to watch her protector work his human magic.

She snapped her fingers and nodded to the beat as Tor performed a soft-shoe step and twirled and crooned to her.

Sinatra had nothing over Tor's cool dimpled smile and ease of the moment. He was in his element. Confident and sure.

And Mel wondered if a woman could fall in love faster than taking a trip down the sidewalk. How silly was that? She wasn't in love with the man. He'd only kissed her once. Twice, if she counted the cheek kiss just now. And she did. But she certainly had tripped into something weird and spectacular, and utterly enchanting.

At the end of the song, Tor leaped into the crowd and tagged another, who went on to select a slow tune that demanded couples pair up. Tor bowed to Mel and again offered his hand. She took it and he pulled her to him.

"You have an amazing voice," she said.

"Thank you. It makes me happy to sing."

"Memories of Miss Thunder?"

"You bet."

"It makes me happy to watch you sing."

"An intimate glimpse into the weirdness of me. I'm glad we came here. In the middle of this crazy, anxiety-ridden week, I needed this."

He hugged her closer and turned her to sway on the cobblestones amongst the others. Tor moved with a sensual ease that enticed her to match him, to follow him, to fall into him. And she did, plunging into his scent and his hard chest and his direct way of guiding her deeper into that experience.

Was she a fool to tease the possibilities? They were so close, she never wanted to part from him. The singer's words grew fainter as their connection pulsed in her ears and throat and heart. He had her; she had him. Together they alchemized an intriguing match. Mel didn't want to lose a moment of this remarkable experience, dancing with a human who was protecting her from the denizens who would seek the heart in her bag…

The bag.

She'd set it down by a stone step when he'd taken her hand and led her into the dance. The next turn around, Mel searched the steps and—yes, there it sat. Her red tapestry bag with a dead witch's heart inside, sealed within a plastic container and warded and cloaked to the nines. With the cloaking spell at work, no one should sense what was inside. She hoped. Her dark magic was anything but exacting or lasting. *Please, let it improve, and quickly.*

When the next song began, in yet another slow and sensual beat, Tor leaned in. "Another?"

"Yes, please."

If they closed the place down dancing, Mel could not be happier. And experiencing Tor's entire demeanor change from ultrastiff and always on, to the relaxed, smiling charmer who held her as if only they two existed was a dream.

This was natural magic at its most intoxicating. Gladly, she surrendered to the spell.

When the dancers clapped at the end of the song and the new singer launched into a rap beat, Tor tugged Mel toward the steps and they sat. He tilted his head onto her shoulder. "I like dancing with you. We seem to pick up each other's intentions easily."

"I was thinking the same thing." And snuggling next to him was not something she would trade even for a whacked-out heart that could save her mother. He was just so…much. Manly and handsome, and charming. Sighing, she wrapped a hand about his arm and nestled closer.

"I forget about the real world while singing," he said. "It's been a while since I've had such a good time."

That she could be the one to give him this experience set her heart to a pace even faster than it was already beating. Turning to face him, she asked, "You said you live for the moments. What does this moment beg of you?"

"Focus," he answered. A pulse of his jaw muscle made her wonder if he'd slipped back into protector mode. But his smile discouraged that worry. "On you."

Dimples rising in what she was beginning to note was an indication of his playful side, he leaned toward her and she met his kiss. Clutching her shoulder, Tor deepened the kiss and pulled her close. He invaded her with a delicious intent. The world slipped away. The only time passing was marked by the flutter of her heartbeats. He mastered her with his gentle hold and his seeking mouth.

Don't let this end, she thought. And then it did as he bowed his forehead to hers and they gasped in one another's joy.

"Will you sing another song?" she asked.

"If they'll let me."

Mel turned to grab her bag and—it wasn't there. She dipped to peer around the side of the stairway, but there stood a garbage bin and no sign of the red tapestry bag. Had they sat on a different stairway? She glanced across the crowd of dancers and toward where the singer bounced to his funky rap. Another stone stairway was close to the bridge, but they hadn't come down that one.

She gasped. "It's gone."

"Right?" Tor said. "What a way to get rid of the stress. We should do this again soon."

"No, the bag." She clutched his hand. "My bag with the heart in it is missing. I set it right there."

"Ah, hell." Tor's body stiffened, instantly moving from relaxed to alert. His eyes took in the crowd and then traced along the riverfront. "It was red with big flowers?"

"Yes. I wonder if the cloaking spell dissipated? Or maybe it was a thief taking advantage of an unwatched bag."

"There!" Tor pointed up toward the street level.

Mel sighted a man walking swiftly, her bag slung over his shoulder.

"Let's go!"

Chapter 13

Tor grabbed Mel's hand and they soared up the stairway to street level. Here at the edge of the 5th the traffic was lighter, but the streetlights were also spaced farther apart, darkening their path. Half a block ahead, they saw the dark-haired man turn a corner.

"I've got this!"

Tor took off, leaving Mel to follow. She reached the corner and saw Tor take another right into what must be an alleyway. She heard shouts and what could only be described as a fist meeting flesh and bone. Creeping toward the turn, she snuck a look around the side.

Tor struggled with a man who snarled and lashed out with deadly knives in each hand. But what was most deadly were the fangs jutting from his mouth.

"Vampire?" Mel muttered. "But how could he know what was in the bag?" Had her cloaking spell been—again—ineffective? What was up with her magic lately?

The tapestry bag sat on the ground ten feet away from the men's struggle. Mel slipped around the corner and crept over. When her fingers glanced onto the wooden bag handle, she saw the glow from within. She picked up the bag and peered inside. "Why is it doing that?"

She hadn't a clue how the thing worked, only that it was necessary for her spell. It hadn't glowed since the night she'd stolen—*borrowed*—it from the Archives. When the dead things had risen from her backyard, it hadn't been glowing.

Curious.

"Watch out, Mel!"

Dodging the oncoming vampire body, Mel stepped to the side and pressed her back to the brick building. Tor lunged and grabbed the creature by the shirt. He wielded a stake high in the air. Just as he swept down his arm to stake the vamp, his opponent kicked him in the shin, setting Tor's trajectory off course and felling him to one knee with a painful groan.

The vampire dove for Mel and gripped her by the shoulders. She clutched the bag to her chest. She wasn't afraid of a vampire. Even if he did flash his fangs—one of which was chipped.

"Divertia!" Her repulsion spell sent the vamp flying away from her. His shoulders hit the wall and he slapped his palms to it.

"A witch, eh?"

"How do you know about the heart?" Mel demanded.

"Heart?"

Tor stepped before Mel. "That's enough chatting. You like to steal things, flesh pricker?"

The vampire snarled. "There's something in that bag I need."

"But you didn't know what that something was?" Mel

called from behind Tor. She bounced on her toes but couldn't see over his broad shoulders.

"I know now that it's a heart." The vampire stood and curled his fingers into claws. "It called to me. And I take what I want."

"It can't call to you," Mel muttered from behind Tor. "It's warded. And cloaked!"

"Oh, it called." Fangs bared, the vampire again lunged for Tor.

Tor bent, plunging the stake upward. Mel saw the vampire's fangs graze Tor's neck, drawing blood, and then the vamp shoved him to the ground as it stumbled backward. The stake had found a place in its heart. Yet the creature didn't turn to ash as it should.

"Heh, heh." The vamp pulled the stake from its heart and tossed it to the ground. "This is not over!" He took off.

Tor, falling to one knee before her, slapped a palm to the brick wall to catch his breath.

"Aren't you going after him?"

He stood and gripped the bag she held. "This is not warded."

"Yeah, I get that. Sorry. Vampire getting away? And why didn't he ash?"

"Because it's a bloody revenant. And—hell." Tor stood and marched down the alleyway. "Let's go home. It's been a long day."

After a shower, Tor walked out of the bathroom to find Mel asleep on his bed and snoring. Her white vinyl boots were strewn on the floor. The flowered bag was hugged tight against her chest, her knees tucked up and her mouth open. He hoped she didn't drool on his Egyptian-cotton pillowcase. Then again, he did have a maid.

Smiling at her easy fall into slumber, he snuck into the

closet and pulled down an extra pillow and blanket for himself. Wandering down the hallway in boxers and bare feet, under his breath he sang a lullaby he knew Sinatra had once performed. "Lay thee down, now and rest, may thy slumber be blessed."

In the living room he eyed the leather sofa. It did not look at all inviting. He'd purchased the boxy, hard item because it went with his masculine, streamlined decor. And his decorator had suggested it suited his personality. In the four years he'd lived here, he'd probably sat on it half a dozen times.

With a sigh, he lay down and confirmed the utter hardness of his night's rest. As a consolation, the cushy pillow provided a saving grace.

He hadn't gone after the vampire because it wouldn't have proven fruitful. The creature had been revenant. Not even a stake could kill an already-dead thing. That particular breed of vamp needed to be beheaded in order to be ashed. And he hadn't been packing a machete.

And the key question remained: Hadn't the cloaking and ward worked? How had the vampire been attracted to the heart? Tor had held a frog's hand for that spell.

Mel's spells seemed to work, for the most part. But so far none of her wards had lasted for long. Was it because she wasn't an expert with dark magic? How would she accomplish the greater spell under the full moon if even a small warding wasn't effective for her? The woman had very big plans for that night.

"Necromancy," he muttered. The word sank into his gut like a spiked iron ball. He'd forgotten to ask her more about that unsavory development. Had he known that was part of the plan, would he still have taken the job? "Probably."

Because lush lashes and big doe eyes. Sometimes a man

couldn't resist. And maybe, just maybe, she possessed a sort of lash magic. Anything was possible with witches.

Tugging the blanket over his face, he dropped into sleep almost immediately.

When the phone rang, Tor startled upright, winced at the pull in his back muscles and slapped around for his cell phone. Dragging himself up with a groan, he spied the phone over on the kitchen counter. The daylight beaming in through the deck windows shocked him completely awake as he wandered to the kitchen. It was morning? He noted the time of eight thirty as he answered.

The man on the phone sounded pleased. It was the very same one who had interviewed him via Skype a few days earlier. "You're one of three final candidates for the job, Monsieur Rindle. We'd like you to come in for a face-to-face on Monday at 8:00 a.m."

"I'll be there," Tor confirmed. He pumped a triumphant fist. *"Merci, monsieur."*

Hanging up, he again pumped the air and then moaned as his shoulder muscles screamed in protest. "Damn couch. Whew!" He sat on a stool and leaned forward, catching his palms against his temples.

He'd gotten a second interview. Of course, he hadn't doubted he'd aced the first interview. He was excellent at the verbal volley. And face-to-face? He was even more confident in that.

"What's the hubbub?"

A tousle-haired witch wandered into the living room, yawning and stretching her arms above her head. She still wore the violet dress she'd had on yesterday. She walked over to the kitchen counter, and Tor noticed her smile grew to a teasing smirk.

"What?" he asked.

"You're not much for pants, are you?"

He'd forgotten his lacking night wear. Boxers were comfy to sleep in. The woman should be lucky he wasn't naked, as was his usual sleeping mode. On the other hand, maybe he should label that unlucky?

"Not for sleeping in," he commented. "And the hubbub is that I got an in-person interview on Monday."

"Hey, that's awesome." She leaned forward, catching her elbows on the counter. Her eyes glinted with morning sunshine. Unicorns and sparkle? Or lash magic? "The day after the full moon."

"The day after the—ah, hell. Really?" Tor rubbed a hand through his hair. "I wasn't thinking about that."

"That's okay. On Sunday night I'll invoke the spell. All will be well. Your employment with me will be complete. And you won't have to deal with me, or the Jones family, anymore. Monday morning comes around and you get to step into the normal human world of mundane and boring office work."

"That's life," he said.

Sunday night he'd escort the witch to whatever spell-invocation ritual she required, stand guard and make it happen. Monday morning he'd arrive at the accounting office ready to slay the interview.

The only part that didn't sound ideal was the not-dealing-with-Mel part. She'd grown on him. Sort of like a fungus. But still, he liked her close.

"I might need another shower this morning," he muttered. "That couch was like sleeping on a rock."

"None of your furniture appears conducive to comfort. You must have hired a designer."

"How do you know?"

"They tend to make a man's place look manly but never consider that our bodies like soft, comfy things as opposed to leather and wood." Mel shuddered. "But your bed is a dream to sleep in. And it smells good, too."

"It…smells?"

She leaned across the counter and whispered into his ear, "Like you. All manly and macho. Are you sure you don't smoke a pipe?"

"Positive. It's my soap."

"Well, I love it. Delicious. Want me to make some breakfast while you shower with lots more of that soap? I might be able to find something edible in your cupboards."

"You won't. The stocks are low. Grocery delivery isn't until Saturday. I'll shower quick and then bring you home. Then maybe…you can make us some smoothie bowls?"

"Love to."

Tor wandered down the hallway. His cell phone rang, and he stopped in the doorway to his bedroom. It was his contact at the Hôtel-Dieu ER, where he'd had the vampire victim sent.

"What's up, Jean-Paul?"

"That woman I did the usual runaround on yesterday?"

"Thanks for that. You know I'll pay you."

"Of course you will. It's not easy making up a blood test and disposing of the evidence without some asshole in administration getting onto my ass."

"I know. It's a fine line, but you walk it well. So why the call?"

"There's been a strange complication."

Mel noticed when Tor pounded his head against the door frame leading into the bedroom. Whomever he was on the phone with had not given him good news. Closing the fridge door, she wandered down the hallway to find he had entered his closet and was selecting a shirt and tie.

"No shower?"

"Change of plans."

"Emergency?"

"Of a sort. The woman bitten by a vampire? My contact at the ER did the usual blood work on her and let her believe she'd received an antidote against a vampire bite—which it was not."

"But it was."

He pulled on his shirt and paused, giving her a good view of his abs. "You're missing the point, Mel."

She liked when he called her that. Everyone else called her Lissa. Mel felt more personal.

"I didn't miss it. I know the story. We want her to believe there are no vampires. So what's the sort-of problem?"

He flipped up his collar and threaded a tie around his neck. She stepped up and took command of the silk tie, and he let her.

"The sort-of problem is that Jean-Paul checked the blood. It actually showed a rare strain in her system that only Jean-Paul would have recognized because he's an expert on vampire DNA and bodily fluids. She was bitten by a revenant."

"The same kind of vamp you staked and set free last night?"

"Yes, and I did not set him free. I didn't have a means to slay him. You need to behead those bastards."

Mel stuck out her tongue in disgust and twisted the silk around a length that hung to his chest.

"And since the antidote vampire saliva that Jean-Paul usually injects at the bite sight isn't effective against revenants—because they're dead vampires, and there's no way to inoculate against death—we've got a potential transformation on our hands. Not cool."

"Which means you're getting all prettied up to go slay a potential vampire."

"I wouldn't call this pretty."

"I would." She fluttered her lashes up at him. He brushed the hair from her face, and she realized she'd crawled right out of bed and wandered in for breakfast. "And look at me. This hair hasn't seen a comb and I desperately need a toothbrush."

He leaned down and kissed her forehead. "You are beautiful, Mel. The more tousled the better."

"Really?"

"Really. Is it good?" He patted his tie and frowned.

She shrugged and gave up on the mess she'd created. "I have no idea how to tie a tie."

He patted at the bow she'd formed as if wrapping a package. "Apparently." With a few flips and tugs, he produced a tight square knot. Then he grabbed a pair of pants and nodded toward the control panel. "I need a machete."

"Doesn't sound like a picnic." Mel punched the top button and the door swung open. "I thought you weren't a slayer?"

"I'm not." Tor entered the weapons closet and she strolled in, gliding her fingers along a sword boasting a decorative hilt that gleamed gold. "I'll give Rook a call on the way there. This should be his target. Damned Order of the Stake needs to learn how to clean up their own messes. Hand me that stiletto. I like that one."

He took the blade from her, flipped it and caught it expertly. "You'll have to come along."

"Does that mean I get a weapon?"

He winced. "Don't you have magic in your arsenal?"

"Oh. Right. Of course I do. When it sticks."

"About that—"

"No time! You're in a hurry."

Tor grabbed a wicked machete and led her out into adventure.

Chapter 14

Mel did as she was told, and waited in the van while Tor walked through the courtyard toward the victim's home. He shook hands with a man wearing a black leather duster coat who had been waiting for him. Must be Rook from The Order of the Stake. One of her good friends, Zoe Guillebeaux, was in a long-term relationship with a knight recruited by the Order. She knew the Order was a bunch of human men who had taken vows to defend other humans from vicious vampires. Supposedly they were discriminating and only went after the bad vamps, but Mel had her suspicions that when in the heat of the moment, any mortal man might plunge a stake through the heart first before asking questions or determining benevolence.

She winced to think that Tor was going inside to, in all likelihood, stake the woman she had met yesterday. Mademoiselle deStrand had been an innocent victim, bitten in an attack. And to top that off, the police had laughed at her, and then later she'd been manipulated by Tor to believe that what she'd thought was true had not been so. It wasn't right.

On the other hand, the sensible, protecting-the-masses side of things, this matter could not be ignored. If the human had been bitten by a revenant, she would not develop like a normal vampire, one who could blend in with society and exist alongside humans. She would become feral and, well…dead.

"The poor woman." The clutch Mel had on the door handle was turning her knuckles white. It was so difficult not to run out and stand up for the woman's rights. She whispered, "Just stay put." Tor knew what he was doing. This was his turf.

Her determination lasted four seconds. The urge to help another was so strong, she pushed open the door and dashed out. She got halfway up the walk to the courtyard and stopped abruptly, turning back to the van. "Forgot the heart!" Rushing back to the vehicle, she grabbed the bag.

What would be a good spell to hold back two vampire slayers while she determined if the woman had transformed to vampire and was indeed a threat? She had a motionlessness spell that could fix a person in place for a few seconds. That required nothing more than a few words of invocation and… "Charcoal dust," she muttered. "Left my spell supplies at home. Shoot!"

Locating the door to the woman's home and seeing it was open, Mel rushed up and peered inside. The room was hazy due to the drawn shades. She could hear voices around the corner. An agitated woman who…snarled?

Mel rushed down a hallway, bag banging the wall as she did, which alerted Tor. He stepped out from a room and grabbed her by the shoulders. "I told you to stay in the van."

"She didn't ask to be bitten," Mel argued. "You have to hear her out. Maybe she won't transform."

Tor's jaw pulsed. Then, without a word, he turned her toward the open doorway and, hands still on her shoulders, pushed her forward to stand in the threshold. The bedroom was decorated in blue and white chinoiserie. The knight, with a bladed collar glinting at his neck, held a stake high above the creature who cowered against a dressmaker's dummy, clutching at the torn fabric stomach.

The woman Mel had seen yesterday was no longer. She had changed to a snarling, fanged thing who drooled blood and spat at the knight. Her eyes were…white.

"She must have died last night or early this morning," Tor stated over her shoulder. "She's a revenant vampire now. You still want us to keep her alive to live such a life?"

Mel swallowed. She was too late. Or not. Was there some way to save the woman? She did not know of a way to reverse vampirism. But she didn't know everything. There could be something in one of the books at the Archives. Yet if she had died…

This whole nightmare of dead things coming back to life was enough to break Mel's heart. Was the woman's condition because of the heart she carried in her bag?

She shoved backward and pushed around Tor. "Do it," she muttered, and then ran down the hallway and out into the courtyard, where she gasped in fresh air.

From inside the apartment, she didn't hear any sounds of struggle, but she knew. Her entire body cringed when she suspected the woman had taken a stake to her heart and… Tor hadn't brought along a machete for no reason.

When the man she respected and trusted brushed quickly by her, she didn't speak. He was in a hurry, headed to his van, and she wasn't going to interfere this time. A minute later he returned to the courtyard, unfolding a black body bag. His eyes met hers. His jaw pulsed. Stern and focused. No whistled tunes this time.

She closed her eyes, wrapped her arms across her chest and wandered back to the van, where she tossed in the tapestry bag and climbed up onto the passenger seat. Five minutes later, Tor returned, hefting the body bag, folded in half, over a shoulder. She shuddered.

The knight cruised out behind him, looking not at all disturbed. Just another day at the office.

Which it was to him.

How could they be so utterly unfeeling?

Mel clutched herself tighter. Two days would bring the full moon. And an immense challenge to her tender heart. Could she accomplish such a vile task?

Tor slid into the driver's seat and fired up the engine. Mel sat on the passenger seat, legs bent and arms wrapped around them, head bowed to her knees. He had tried to warn her to remain in the vehicle. Women. They never listened when it was important.

Yet he couldn't disregard the heavy emotional vibes emanating from her right now.

"Sorry," he offered as he backed out and navigated the traffic on a route toward the river.

"You were doing your job."

"She was beyond hope, Mel."

She nodded and turned her head to face the passing cars outside.

"I'll take you home. I need to run some errands alone."

"I do need to shower and change. I'll be good for a couple hours."

"I know you will. But you'll stay in close contact with me on your phone, yes?"

"I don't know where it is. I have one, but I never use it."

Not a surprise, coming from the natural witch who grew her own herbs and spell concoctions outside on the patio, and whose familiar was a frog, and who also claimed to be owned by a duck.

"There's something that bothers me about all this," he said. Because much as he should not prod at her sensitivities, this needed discussion. "The cloaking spell we did on that heart. It seems to have not worked. The vampire last night and—"

"The heart didn't attract that vampire to the woman. And it wasn't the same vampire who stole my bag last night. I don't think. I didn't see the vamp who attacked the woman, but the one last night had a chipped tooth. But that's besides the matter." She tilted her head against the seat and declared "I don't know why my spells are not working. I was calm. Not nervous. There must be something wrong with me."

"I don't— I can't speak to your magical skills, but I also suspect the woman's attack had nothing to do with the heart. Yet the vamp that stole it was called to it, even though it wasn't sure what it was stealing. You say he had a chipped tooth?"

Mel nodded, then hugged the bag to her chest. "What do you want me to say? I'm baffled by this."

"We've got to figure this out, Mel. Tell me everything," he said. "Especially the part about you needing to raise the dead. We never did discuss that. Please?"

With a heavy sigh, she turned on the seat and tilted her head against the headrest. She'd slipped off her boots and looked beautiful with her tousled hair, rumpled clothing and rosy cheeks. He wanted to kiss her, but he didn't want to drive through any traffic lights. But man, a kiss would make him feel much better right now.

And when had he decided thinking with his heart instead of his brain was acceptable? He had to stop doing that, or something would go wrong.

"The spell requires I raise the dead in order to protect my mother," she explained. "It's complicated and..." She shook her head. "All you need to know is that there will be a dead...entity on the night of the full moon."

"Why does your mother need protection again?"

"She's being tormented by...someone."

"What aren't you telling me, Mel?"

"I'm telling you as much as I can. Mom's in trouble. It's the reason she died a few weeks ago. She was so frightened she ran off the rooftop. Dad wants me to believe it was a miscalculation on her part, but I know better. Something spooked her. Dad picked up her little kitty body from the ground and took her home to recover."

Tor couldn't imagine living such a life. Being married to a woman who could change to a cat, but then who could also die and come back to life? How many times had Thoroughly Jones witnessed his wife's death? And Mel? She must have experienced her mother's repeated deaths through the years.

"What if your mom died and...no one found her?"

"She'd come back to life and have no clue about her former life. Would probably wander about lost for days. Naked. Maybe longer if we couldn't find her. Dad had her tattoo his phone number and address onto her ankle after death number three. She's had to use it once, but it took her a couple days to figure out it was a number to call. He made her go back and tattoo *call for family* on there, as well."

"That must be tough for the entire family. But necromancy? How is that supposed to help your mom?"

"It's dark magic," she said, as if that was the norm. "Listen, I know it's freaky to you, but not to me. You have to understand, practicing dark magic carries a certain weight in our family. Both my dad and his brother are dark witches. And CJ's twin sons—my cousins—are dark, as well. Vika was light, but she's come over to the dark side."

"Vika is CJ's wife," Tor stated, recalling the family trees of the Paris witches. "I know something about her having a sticky soul?"

"Her soul attracts lost souls that are unable or unwilling to cross over." She sighed and looked aside. "Most of them, anyway. But not all."

"Victorie Saint-Charles is her full name," Tor said, referring to his mental database of the local paranormal families. "And doesn't she have a sister or two who are also witches?"

"Libby and Eternitie are both light. Libby is married to a former angel."

"That must be interesting."

"Reichardt is cool. He's no longer angel. He got his soul back when he found his halo and now—well, he's kind of like you."

"Like me?"

"In the know, but human. Yet not afraid to step into the fray and fight for what's right."

Tor turned left, but also tilted his head so she wouldn't see his frown. Stepping into the fray was everything he was not about lately. Or at least, he was striving for that out-of-the-fray lifestyle. "You know I have the interview on Monday."

"Right. Because you're going to try to be something you're not."

"Maybe it's something I need to be."

"It's not," she said with confidence. "But you'll never know until you give it a try. Too bad though. Paris really needs a guy like you, stepping into the fray and all. You're a good man, Tor. As upset as I am about that woman's fate, I think you did her a favor by staking her. There was no hope for her."

"There wasn't, and *I* didn't stake her."

"No, I suppose the knight did that part." She sighed.

She'd seen him carry in the machete. Tor had been the one to decapitate the revenant. That was the only way he could get through such an act, by calling her a revenant and not a human. There had been no humanity left in her. She'd been a creature, a dead thing destined only to vile and evil acts, end of story.

"Rook's looking into the local vamp scene for me today. Also checking out the Parc Monceau, where the woman's attacker claimed to live. I'm not sure I believe that. This is the Order's concern, but since I've stuck my fingers in it, I want to stay in the loop and learn what Rook learns."

"Rook was the guy in the leather coat," Mel stated. "I've heard about his girlfriend, Verity. She knows Zoe, who is a good friend of mine."

"Zoe and Kaz," Tor said. "Kaspar is a friend of mine."

"Really?"

Tor nodded. "I connected him with the Order when he was a teen. Made sure he found his way when he needed some guidance."

"Well, look at you, all helpful and kind."

Tor smirked. "Introducing the guy to the world of vampires and slaying? Not sure that was kind. But he's a good man. We're here."

He pulled up and parked before Mel's home. He would watch until she got to the door and then leave to dispose of the body.

"Ah, nuts. I'm going to really need your protection now," Mel said.

"What? Why?"

She nodded toward her front stoop. On it stood a man with long dark hair and a serious glint to his eye.

"Your dad's back again? What does he want? To finish me off?"

"That's not my dad." Mel got out of the van, dragging the tapestry bag along with her.

Tor swore and turned off the engine. This was even worse than the dad. Certainly Jones, of the twin brothers, was the stronger and darker of them. And he and Tor had once already gone to heads.

"Protection," he muttered. "But for whom?"

Chapter 15

Mel's uncle marched down the steps and grabbed her by the shoulders. She didn't have to see the anger in his eyes; she had sensed it when stepping onto the sidewalk. The concrete hummed with his dark energy. And while that was normal, the anger tingeing that darkness was not.

"Monsieur." She felt Tor's hand go to CJ's on her shoulder. "If you don't mind, I'll ask you to take your hands off this woman."

CJ reared at that statement but did take his hands off her, slamming them to his hips. "Who the hell are you? And—wait. I know you. You're the bastard spin doctor who fucked up my spell against tribe Monserrat."

Mel managed to step before her uncle as he lunged. She wasn't about to repel him with magic, because that would bounce right back at her. Painfully. His body was covered with tattooed wards and repulsion sigils for just such a purpose. But neither was she willing to let the big boys battle it out in full view of the entire neighborhood.

"Uncle CJ, what a nice surprise. What are you doing here? You never visit." Though she didn't want him to answer. *Please, don't answer.*

"You know damn well why I'm here, Lissa."

"Maybe if you'd just tell her," Tor said. "She's had a rough morning."

"Is that so?" CJ crossed his arms and eyed her with the searching gaze she knew could read her like a book. It didn't take him more than a few seconds to pull out one of her secrets. "Revenants? Since when are revenants in Paris?"

"I don't know," Tor offered. "But The Order of the Stake is on it, as well as myself."

Mel felt Tor's confident hand on her shoulder while his other hand gripped the handle of her bag. She let him have it. Now to get inside and away from her uncle.

When she took a step toward the house, CJ moved quicker, blocking her. "Where is it?" he asked.

Tor slung the bag over a shoulder and took a step to place him immediately in front of Mel. "Where is what?"

"She stole Hecate's heart from me," CJ announced sternly.

"You—stole it?" Tor narrowed a condemning look at her. "I knew it."

"I borrowed it," she corrected. "And I only need it for another two days, Uncle CJ. I promise I'll bring it right back as soon as I'm done with it."

"What reason do you have for needing such a volatile artifact?" CJ defied her with his intensity.

Mel glanced to Tor. She hadn't given him all the details. And she wasn't about to. "Can we talk, CJ? Alone?" She nodded to indicate that Tor should take the bag with him. "Why don't you go check the garden out back for… you know."

"Sounds like a plan." Tor bowed to CJ. "Monsieur Jones. I'll have my ears open for trouble. Your niece is my client. I've been charged to protect her—from whomever should mean her harm."

CJ mocked the man as he took off around the side of the house with the heart in the bag. And Mel blew out a breath, thankful to, at the very least, have that out of the way. Though surely CJ must sense the heart. Maybe?

"Come inside," she said to her uncle. "Didn't my dad tell you what I have to do?"

"He did, but he didn't mention any of the items required to complete the spell." CJ followed her inside and closed the door. "Why the bodyguard? Oh. Mercy. Of course. That's what it does. Is the heart attracting the undead?"

"Depends on your definition of *undead*. They seem pretty alive when they come rushing toward me with claws or spittle drooling from their mouths."

"Lissa, Lissa, Lissa."

"Yes, I know. I should have asked, but you never would have allowed me to take the heart out of the Archives."

"No, I would not have."

"Even if it meant helping my mom? It's required for the spell. I can't complete it without the heart. It brings up the dead, CJ. You know that's very necessary. And I had to take it days ago when I was visiting you because—well, I saw an opportunity. I didn't want to keep it so long. And I really did not expect it to attract…things. But there you go."

"Where is it now?"

"I'm not going to tell you that."

"The spin doctor has it, doesn't he?" CJ strode down the hallway, and Mel hustled after him.

In the living room, he peered out the patio door at Tor, who leaned against a support beam under the trellis, his back to them, bag in hand.

"It's in that bag," CJ declared. He gripped the door pull.

Mel slapped her hand over his. "CJ, you have to let me complete that spell. My mother's life depends on it. Your brother would never forgive you—"

He put up a palm to stop her tirade. "Don't try that with me, young lady. I've been around far too long and been to too many dark places of the soul to allow anyone to pull fast-talking on me. I know the situation. I…" He blew out a sigh. "This is magic at its darkest, Lissa. You're not accomplished enough to control it."

"Yes, I am. My dad believes it, too. And I'm going to prove it." She hoped. When would her dark magic decide to kick in and prove effective? "I couldn't let him do this. He's got enough to worry about what with Mom coming back into her new life and my sister hanging around."

"Your sister," CJ hissed in a whisper. "Vika did try her hardest to get her soul to stick to hers."

Vika was her uncle's significant other. They'd been together a long time without the marriage certificate; a piece of paper wasn't important to them.

"The family appreciates her trying," Mel said, "but there's only one way to fix this, and that requires the spell and subsequent release. You know that."

"One of your father's specialties. Release. It's kind of you to take this on for him. He is always in a tough place following your mother's deaths. I'm sorry. But if the heart is attracting dead things, you should cloak it."

"I have. A few times. It never seems to stick." Mel winced and didn't meet her uncle's gaze. "It's dark magic I've used for the cloaks and wards. I'm still getting a handle on it."

"It shouldn't require getting a handle—ah." He ran his fingers back through his hair. "You've never practiced dark magic before."

"Well, of course not. But don't think I'm not capable."

"I'm sure you are."

She wasn't too sure he was being honest.

"But, Lissa, the only way dark magic will answer to your beckoning is with a sacrifice. Hell, didn't TJ warn you about that?"

"A sacrifice?"

"It's the reason your cloaking spells haven't been effective. The dark magic you put out slips off things as if they were greased. If you want it to stick, you need to sacrifice to—well, Hecate would be fine—to prove your worthiness of the dark."

Mel gaped at him. She'd never heard of such a thing. Her father had done such? And Amaranthe? She couldn't recall her sister ever—oh, wait. That one time when they'd been eleven. Amaranthe had eaten her familiar's heart. Still beating.

"The salamander heart," Mel whispered.

"Your sister." CJ nodded. "I remember that. It doesn't have to be a grand sacrifice. But it must prove your willingness to be open to the dark arts. Where's that familiar of yours?"

"Bruce? No." Mel couldn't keep the tremble from her voice. If Bruce were in the vicinity, she hoped he took cover. Because if CJ got a look at him, he'd surely bind the amphibian and hand him over to her for a snack. "He's my familiar. I would never betray his trust that way."

"Then you have to find another means of sacrifice. And quickly. The blood moon is soon upon us." He crossed his arms and turned to study Tor, who still stood outside, back to them, observing Duck waddle about the yard. "And the day after the full moon, the heart gets returned to the Archives."

"If there's anything left of it. I mean—" Mel avoided his questioning gaze. "Yes. Promise." She crossed her heart, a binding that all witches took very seriously. "And Tor is protecting me, so everything is good."

"That man is not an ally."

"Nor is he a foe."

CJ lifted a brow. "True enough. But he got in my way a few years back—"

"He's helping the Jones family now. Accept that."

"Very well. But he is merely human. I'd be much more accepting if you had someone with actual skills or magic to protect you."

"Tor has skills. He knows his way around a weapon and how to keep his clients safe. You know that well. He protected that vampire tribe from your dark magic."

"Indeed." CJ rubbed his jaw. He'd lost to Tor, but he should have never taken on the entire tribe in the first place. Her uncle wasn't always kind or benevolent. In fact, his magic was often malevolent.

"I looked in your eyes outside on the steps. I saw the new female revenant," CJ said. "Is that about the heart, as well?"

"The revenant vampires are a different situation Tor has been dealing with. A human woman was bitten and—she had to be slain. We're not sure those vamps' presence in Paris are related to Hecate's heart."

She was pretty sure they were. But Mel had a hard time assigning blame to the innocent woman who'd been victimized.

"I don't like this. It's too sketchy. Maybe I should do the spell."

"I can do this, Uncle CJ. I have to do this. I know Amaranthe the best." She splayed her palm so he could see the scar on it. "We had a bond like no one else in this family."

He nodded. The man was a twin to her father, and his sons were twins. They each had a bond that was inexplicable. Though she and Amaranthe were not twins, they had formed an equal bond through a blood ritual when they were little. A cut on each palm, some magic words and the desire to never be apart and to always have one another's back. Was such a bond unbreakable? Death had broken her physical bond to Amaranthe. And spiritually, she had not been able to communicate with her ghost. It seemed only her mother could see and hear Amaranthe.

But she would do what she must to reaffirm their bond. Even if it killed one of them. Again.

CJ peered out the patio windows. "What is he doing out there?"

Tor was now prodding the toe of his shoe at the edge of the garden where the dirt had been pushed up. "Uh, I had an issue with zombie dogs."

"There's no such thing as zombies, Lissa."

"You see? You and Tor do have a common bond. You both have the same belief. But trust me, when the dead rise from their dirt beds, I call it like I see it. Zombies."

CJ scratched his head. "Disturbing. I'm going to look into that. And I'm going to have a few words with the man digging through your clematis."

Mel caught her uncle by the arm as he headed toward the patio doors. "Just chill, all right? He's helping me. He didn't want to, but he is. Don't do anything to piss him off."

"We'll see." He shrugged out of her grasp and headed outside.

Not a day ago, Tor had stood in this same spot and had felt the same creep of dread crawl up his neck as the other half of the notorious Jones twins had come out to the yard to give him a piece of his mind.

He'd expected a conversation with the dark witch. The time a few years back when he had successfully defended a tribe of vampires against CJ's dark magic, Tor had not spoken personally to the man about it. The witch had been so enraged, he'd charged off before Tor could offer his side of the story. He'd been hired to protect clients. He did his job well. Even if they were vampires.

Vampires were not inherently evil. Most humans would not be able to pick them out of a lineup, and some might even have vampire friends without knowing it. They blended in, and they insinuated themselves into the mortal realm because they chose to do so. They did not need to kill for blood to survive; a drink every few weeks sustained them. And transforming a human to vampire was not a requirement to get that sustaining blood.

Tor straightened his tie as the witch approached him from behind. A glance to the house confirmed the bag he'd tucked behind a wicker chair was barely visible.

"Listen, bloke," Tor started. "Your niece hired me to protect her, and I'm going to do that."

"Lissa is *paying* you?"

Tor nodded.

"Don't take any money from her. Send me your bill. Got that?"

"Of course. Thank you." And her dad had offered the same. He'd sort it out later. "I promise you I will be the first to make sure that annoying heart is back in your hands on Monday morning after the spell is completed."

"Funny, I would have thought you'd keep it for your Agency."

"I'm not head of that organization anymore. Dez Merovech has taken it over, and as it is, the Agency has its hands full. Hecate's heart belongs in the Archives. That's where it will be returned."

"I appreciate that. The Archives is a repository for dark magic. Your Agency is still so young, untested with handling such vile objects."

"We fare very well. You'd be surprised the objects we have in storage. And apparently, under much better security and surveillance than in the Archives."

The witch lifted his chin at that dig. It had been deserved. Tor was tiring of being confronted by pissed-off dark witches. He wasn't working for them. Mel was his client. And he would defend her against her own family if he had to.

"Lissa is no expert on handling such magic," CJ said. "I don't want to stand back and let her do this alone, but I respect her decision to take it over when it might have been left in my brother's hands."

"She knows what she's doing. And if she doesn't, I'll be there to pick up the pieces."

"Yes, well, we've figured out why her cloaking spells have not been effective. In order to access dark magic, a witch must show it she means business."

"And how does Mel go about that?"

"That's for her to figure out." CJ narrowed his gaze on Tor. "Do you really know what you've gotten into, Rindle?"

"Of course. I've handled it all, from vamps and weres, to harpies and unicorns. And now mother-freakin' zombies. Trust me, I've got this one covered."

"Yeah?" The witch's gaze averted to the talisman at Tor's hip. "What about ghosts?"

Chapter 16

Seething from what Certainly Jones had told him, Tor marched around the side of Mel's house, stomped on a climbing vine that tried to trip him up, and took the front steps in a leap. Once through the front door, he stalked down the hallway to find her standing before the fridge holding a bunch of celery.

"What part about *I don't do ghosts* did you not understand?" he asked.

Mel's jaw dropped open. The celery hit the counter, and she clasped her hands before her. "Tor, I couldn't tell you that part."

"Why? Because you're keeping secrets? Because you have to do something weird and strange to make your dark magic take hold? What else haven't you told me?"

"I've told you everything. At least, everything that I could. I didn't think it was important to mention the part about my sister being a ghost because, well, first, I thought you'd figure it out. And second, if you didn't, it wasn't important because you wouldn't ever have to deal with her, anyway. And I don't know what your deal with ghosts is. You only said *I don't do ghosts*. How's a girl supposed to interpret that vague statement?"

"Vague?" Tor resisted fisting his fingers, but it was a struggle.

The nerve of her to keep important information from him. And he had generously agreed to help her, even after he'd decided against doing protection work.

When she started to speak again, he put up a palm between them. "Enough. Let me state this one more time, loudly and clearly. I. Don't. Do. Ghosts."

"I got that, but—"

He shook his finger at her. "No. No more *but*s. If you can't be truthful with me and respect my one small caveat, then I'm out of here."

He swung around and sailed down the hallway. Expecting her to rush after him, he fled out the front door and slammed it behind him.

He marched out to the van without turning around to see if she'd be peeking out the window at him or yelling for his return.

She had broken a rule that he had adhered to for years. And he couldn't conceive of relenting now.

Mel turned toward the counter and caught her head in her hands. Tor had every right to charge out all angry and alpha. Which is why she hadn't run after him. She'd wanted to. But her only excuse would have been because she felt desperate and had lied to keep him on the job.

She hadn't lied to him; she just hadn't divulged all the details.

He wasn't going to protect her anymore?

She glanced to the plastic container sitting next to the celery on the counter. Ugly things had surfaced, attracted to that heart.

"What if they come for me?" she whispered.

Jerking her gaze to all the windows, she looked for moving shadows in the grayness caused by the setting sun. She might like to think she was strong. She might even think she could invoke the dark magic required to save her mother's life. But she wasn't brave. And any courage she had had just marched out the front door.

Bruce came into view, hovering near her left shoulder.

"What are we going to do, Bruce? He left. I don't have a big, strong man with weapons to protect me should something evil and dead charge through my front door. The doors! We've got to batten down the hatches."

Bruce moved over to the chair in the dining room.

"Right!" After slapping her palms together, Mel began to move furniture. A few magical words and gestures lifted the heavy chairs, which were carried down the hallway to park before the front door. And…she'd have to blockade the kitchen door and the patio, as well as the spell room. "We've got our work cut out for us, Bruce."

Tor tossed the body bag with the revenant body into the incinerator and then kicked the machine's on button that burned the contents to ash. A brand-new revenant didn't ash, remaining in human form with death. Rather, a second death, since the person actually died as they transformed to vampire.

The majority of vampires—a good ninety-five percent of them—were alive. They did not die when bitten and then transform to vampire. The vampire taint was passed to the victim and then, with a massive blood exchange, they also became vamp.

No death. Hearts still beat. Blood still flowed.

Revenants were literally a dying breed amongst the species. Because it was difficult for anything that had already died to maintain life for long after death. But they could, and they did manage to blend in with humans surprisingly well. Save the obvious smell of decay and their voracious hunger for blood—that hunger being the only thing that kept them resembling aliveness and able to stand upright instead of falling apart like…

"A zombie," he muttered as the flames flared before him.

Two different things, revenants and zombies. And he'd never believed zombies were real until he'd seen the dogs in Mel's backyard. They existed. And he didn't like it one bit.

The dead witch's heart possessed some vile energy. He should have taken it from Mel that first night and been done with it. And now? Now the whole world had become a shit storm of dead things.

He walked out of the salvage yard, punched in the digital code to lock the gates and met the knight waiting at the back of his van with arms crossed. "You know all the spots, don't you?" Rook asked.

"For disposal? That I do." Such knowledge would never afford him a real job. A normal job. But a bloke didn't need such expertise to sit behind a desk in a cubicle. He couldn't wait for that to happen.

"This was a tribe," Rook said as Tor went about removing the hazmat suit, hanging it up in the van and replacing his shoes. The usual after-disposal routine. "And I'm not sure we got them all."

Rook had called Tor an hour earlier. He had been fighting revenants in the 18th. Tor had made it there in record time and had joined the knight. They'd slain eight vampires in a dark warehouse. Tor was confident no one had witnessed their actions. But he wasn't sure the vampires had actually been nesting in the warehouse or if they'd just been trapped by the UV lights set up in a stand outside the building. Some local-artist exhibit was photographing graffiti on a time control, and the lights had been left on all night without supervision.

"What's up with revenants in Paris?" Tor asked. "Aren't they rare? And don't they prefer unpopulated areas? Those things were wild, bloke. As close to animal as a vamp is going to get."

"Yeah, I don't know." Rook winced. "The knights haven't seen any revenant activity in over a decade. And those we just took out were all drones." He closed one side of the van doors at Tor's gesture. "No leaders present that I could determine. Mindless, yet hungry. Something is directing them. And I'm not sure I buy that it's an old witch's heart in a box."

"Why not?"

"It doesn't fit with the woman attacked the other day. That was purposeful. She was lured to the park and bitten."

"Might have been the leader, creating new blood. That last one I burned was new, unable to ash with second death."

"We can be thankful the older ones do ash. I don't understand revenants," Rook said. "They don't survive long in a city. They are monsters. But they don't decay like a zombie and can live undead for a long time. Years, even. To risk coming into the city was stunning."

"Can they procreate?"

"No. It wouldn't have made sense for them to change the woman with hopes of her birthing vampire children. Revenants don't work that way. They all begin as humans, who then die and are brought back to life with the blood exchange. But to be safe, maybe we could get that heart under lock and key?"

"It's needed for a full moon spell. Then it's back to storage."

"So the next day will be spent tracking dead things. Joy. The Order ranks in Paris are currently me, Kaz and Lark. And at the moment, both Kaz and Lark are on a business trip to Romania."

Business trip? Such a euphemism was something Tor would use in his own fast-talking spiels. "Seriously? Romania? That's about as cliché as it gets when it comes to vamps and slaying."

"I don't write it—I just slay what needs slaying."

"So it's just you and King in Paris right now?"

"King is..."

Tor didn't need an explanation. The elusive founder of The Order of the Stake had recently been discovered to be vampire. Really. A vampire had founded the Order that slayed his own kind. King had been lying low. Though his knights had stood by him. Hell, he really was a former king of France, and despite his questionable authority, his Order did do a good job at slaying the vamps who needed slaying.

"I'll help when I can," Tor offered, "but I'm quitting the business."

"Quitting?" Rook laughed. "That's like me saying I'm going to pull on some yoga pants and start teaching classes outside in the park."

Not a stretch for the knight who had been practicing yoga for centuries and was a yoga master.

"I'm serious," Tor said. "I've had enough of this crazy shit. I want..."

"You'll never have normal, Tor. Trust me on that one. The things you've seen, known and done cannot be unseen, unknown or undone. There's not a talisman big enough in this realm to make that happen."

Tor clasped the quartz that hung from his belt. Rook knew what it did for him because he was the man who had introduced him to the witch who'd charmed it for him.

"Don't we pay you enough?" Rook asked.

"It's not the money. I have more than I'll ever need. It's…peace of mind."

"Protecting innocent humans from the weird shit doesn't give you peace?"

Tor sighed. It should. It did.

And it did not.

"If not this, then what the hell are you going to do with yourself?" Rook asked.

"I have an interview in a few days. Office stuff. Normal human cubicle stuff."

Rook grasped his throat, mocking a choking motion, and stuck out his tongue.

"Have you ever tried the normal?" Tor challenged.

His cohort shrugged. "I'm no longer immortal. Gotta beware the vamp fangs as much as the next human. As for normal? What's so great about that? If you ask me, I'd much prefer knowing than not knowing. And like I said, it's too late to put that genie back in the bottle. Not unless you have a memory-loss spell. Which I'd highly recommend if you're serious about this career change. Because you can give normal a try. But you'll always know what's out there."

Again, Tor touched the crystal, its heavy weight reassuring. It had taken away his ability to see ghosts. A memory-loss spell? It was a good suggestion.

"I guess a man has to do what he has to do," Rook conceded. "It'll be tough not having you to call on when we need you."

"You'll find someone to replace me. I haven't been doing much work for the Order the past few years anyway."

"Sure, but whatever you do, be careful. You can walk away from this life, but I'm pretty sure this life won't allow you to walk away without keeping one eye over your shoulder."

Which was another fact Tor knew. Would he always be running away from that which he had once so freely run toward? *Could* he do normal?

"Will you at least consult with me on this revenant issue?" Rook asked.

"Of course. I won't leave you a lone slayer standing amidst a bunch of wild vampires. It's just this witch who hired me to protect her—"

"Now I get it. You've got a pretty little witch to protect, eh?"

"She hired me, Rook. It's a business deal. Which..." How quickly he forgot. "...I ended earlier today."

"Uh-huh. You don't sound pleased about that decision. You want my advice when it comes to pretty witches?"

The man's girlfriend was a witch. A very pretty witch.

"I'm not sure."

"Doesn't matter, I'm giving it to you. If she makes you smile, then don't ignore that. It isn't often guys like us get to simply smile, is it?"

Tor considered the strangeness of an easy smile, and before he could agree, Rook said, "She means something to you."

"She's kind and beautiful and—"

"Sexy?"

"Weird."

Rook chuckled. "Those are the best kind."

He hadn't expected that agreement, but now Tor smiled broadly and turned his head down to hide it from the man he had only ever been serious with, or stood alongside to slay vampires, or worked out a game plan with for media spin with the Order.

"So should I destroy your phone number?" Rook asked.

"Not until after the full moon."

He should get back to Mel—ah, right. He'd stormed out on her. Had given her his walking papers after learning she'd not told him a ghost was involved in the job.

He slid a hand over the talisman, clutching it.

"You want coffee?" Rook asked. "I'll buy."

The two men got into the van cab, and Tor navigated toward the city center near the river. He'd handled things wrong with Mel. He shouldn't have stormed out on her. He shouldn't have been so mean. He should have explained himself.

He should have. He should have. He should have.

Now what was done was done. And he had not ended it properly. Not in a way that sat well with his morals or his soul.

Stopping at a light, he swiped a palm over his face, leaned back against the seat and closed his eyes. His fingers tapped impatiently on the steering wheel.

He'd never quit a job before. Even when he'd faced insurmountable odds, such as the cover-up of a werewolf gaming den where they'd pitted tortured vampires against one another to the death. There had been dozens of crazed vampires left behind in a warehouse located in the center of the city. It had to be cleaned out and sanitized, and he'd had to field more than a few calls from the local police, fire department, news stations and even the EU-OSHA.

Not to mention the werewolf pack that had returned to challenge him. He'd stood before them all, shown them his mettle and talked down the pack from angry retaliation, as well as handled all the city agencies with a flair that sometimes even impressed him. He walked away cut, bruised and sometimes near death, but he always survived.

To do it again and again. And always because he knew if he didn't do it, no one else would.

So why couldn't he allow himself to even be close to a woman who may or may not have an instance where he would be in the vicinity of a ghost? The ghost incident that had pushed him over the edge had been years ago. He'd moved on. There was no way to change what had happened. He should fear nothing.

"Tor?"

"Huh?" He pulled across the intersection, driving toward the Rue de Rivoli, where Rook said a late-night coffee shop was located. "Sorry, man."

"You're distracted. Is it the pretty witch?"

"She's a client. Was a client."

"Was?"

"I…don't work with ghosts. You know that."

"Uh-huh. Who's protecting her now?"

Tor cast the man a glance. He knew the answer to that one.

"Ghosts are assholes," Rook offered. "But I've never known you to back down from a challenge. You surprise me, Rindle."

"You shouldn't be. I'm over it all. The life. The weirdness—"

"This side of normal is a hell of a lot more interesting than the one you think will change your life. Pull over. I'll run in and grab us a couple."

Tor did so, and Rook got out, closing the door behind him.

"This side of normal," Tor muttered.

He clenched the steering wheel. Normal. Normal, normal, normal. Why was it proving such a hard concept to grasp? And when had he backed away from a challenge? That wasn't him. While he'd avoided anything that reminded him of that horrible night, he—well, he could avoid it forever. But that would be…

"A lie," he whispered.

He couldn't run away from his truths. Because to hide was like being haunted all over again. A constant haunting that would always cling to him, and never relent. He'd seen ghosts since he was a child. Had never feared them, even thought they had intrinsically guided his life to exactly where he stood this day. He'd never seen his mother in ghostly form but had always sensed when she was near, with the presence of a cicada that would show up in the most unexpected times and places.

A few winters ago, he'd found a cicada in an old house, tucked between two books. It had peered at him with wise eyes. And the books had been titled *Always with You* and *I Love You to the Moon and Back.*

His mother's way of saying she had his back. She had never left him.

And now Mel and her family were being tormented by a ghost in such a personal way. A family member sought to harm Star? That was terrible. He could imagine the grief and pain associated with it.

And that was the part that tore at him. He knew that emotional pain.

Rook opened the door and handed him a coffee that warmed Tor's fingers when he wrapped them about the cup. He noticed the elaborate artwork on the paper cup and realized it was a floral line drawing featuring flowers and one very prominent…cicada.

The knight put up a boot on the dash and leaned back. "You think about what I said?"

"Yes," Tor muttered, knowing the man had ulterior motives. He tapped the cicada.

"Good. Then drop me off and head back to the witch's home."

Chapter 17

At the sound of a knock on her front door, Mel startled awake and sat up from the floor. She'd fallen asleep? It was dark in the house. Down the hall, in the kitchen, a candle flickered softly. Bruce levitated before her. She peered at him through her goggles.

Another knock. The frog tensed.

Gripping the crystal athame in her left hand and the carrot shredder in her right, she turned onto her knees to face the door. "Who is it?" she called out cautiously.

No response.

Bruce ribbited.

"I *did* ask," she shot back at the amphibian.

Another croak in response.

"Not loud enough? Do zombies *have* ears? They could have fallen off."

She clutched the shredder against her chest and peered around the side of the inverted easy chair. Her heartbeats thundered. Something lurked on her front step. And yet, would zombies have the courtesy to knock?

Calling louder, she said, "Who's there?"

"It's Tor. I'm sorry, Mel! Can I come in?"

"Tor? Oh yes!" She pulled at the huge easy chair before her, but it didn't budge. "Hang on! I'll be right there!"

Using the kinetic magic she'd employed to stack the chairs before the doorway, she now managed to shift the barricade as a tangled mass about a foot away from the door.

The door opened, and Tor popped his head inside. "I know it's late but—what the bloody mess?"

"You can slip through!" she called. "Climb over the furniture."

He did so, and stepped awkwardly onto a wooden kitchen chair, finessing the obstacle course until he landed on the easy chair before her. Seated, he bent before her—she was still on her knees—and tapped the plastic goggles she normally wore when cutting onions.

"I'm afraid to ask," he said.

Tugging down the goggles and tossing the grater aside, Mel felt her fears evaporate. Yet in the process, her anxiety gushed to the surface, and she began to cry anew. She didn't want to, yet it was impossible not to.

Tor slid off the chair to kneel and pulled her into a hug. He kissed her head and wrapped his arms about her. "I'm sorry. I shouldn't have walked out on you like that."

"I thought I was alone," she said between sniffles. "And you don't know how I attract the weird stuff to me. I was afraid something would get through to attack. And I'm not sure if zombies would knock or just crash through the windows. I did the best I could. But I'm not very brave. Oh!"

He pulled her up with him as he sat on the chair, and Mel bent her legs and snuggled against him. Hugging his hard chest, she clung and sniffled. Her anxiety lessened as she focused on the slide of his hand across her back, a soothing move. She was safe in his arms. Her protector had returned.

"So you barricaded yourself inside?" he asked.

"Bruce helped me. But I don't have many weapons. I'm not into guns and garrotes like you. And when I'm upset, my magic always malfunctions. That's why I couldn't clear the chairs away now."

"I'll put them back for you. It was wrong for me to walk out on a job. But more so? It wasn't right to leave you alone when I know you need support. I'm here now. To protect you."

She looked up at his face. Minute stubble darkened his jaw. His hair was tousled. He looked as though he'd had a tough day. Yet truth glinted in his eyes. She believed him. He'd needed an escape, some time to work out his apparent issues with ghosts.

Ghosts. No avoiding that topic any longer.

"If you stick around to the end, I can't promise there won't be ghosts," she said. "At the very least, one."

"I wish you would have told me about that from the get-go. But that's neither here nor there now. If there's a ghost, I'll have to deal."

She nuzzled her head against his firm bicep, drawing his warmth into her bare arms and legs. She hadn't realized how cold and small she'd felt barricaded on the floor. Now she could relax. "Tell me about you and ghosts. Did you say you could see them?"

Tor hooked a hand along her thigh as he pulled her closer. He tilted his head back and exhaled. His heartbeat was steady. Fierce. A warrior in suit and tie. Mercy, but she adored him.

"I can see ghosts," he finally confessed. "I have been

able to see them forever. At least, since I was about five or six and started to realize that the imaginary friend I would talk to wasn't so imaginary, and it was like those spirits the little boy saw in that movie, *The Sixth Sense*. Only then did I realize I saw dead people, too."

He tilted his head forward, and his lips pressed the crown of her head. She sensed that he wasn't keen on revealing this information, but he wanted to. In his way. So she didn't barge in with all the questions bouncing inside her brain.

"I never thought it was a problem until it did become a problem. I grew up believing there were always extra people around the dinner table that the other kids in the boys' home couldn't see."

"That must have been startling for you."

"Yes, well, the first few times, when I mentioned the extra guests and wanted to know why they didn't get served, the nuns were having none of that crazy talk. And Miss Thunder was never there at the dinner table with a joint to relax my apprehensions. I learned to keep that information to myself if I wanted to eat."

"It makes me sad that you were an orphan. How old did you say your mother was?"

"Seventeen when I was born. She died in the hospital a day later."

Mel's heart tugged. "I'm sorry."

Tor stretched out his arm and rolled up his sleeve to reveal the tattoo on his inner forearm. The candlelight from the kitchen glowed softly into the hallway, and for the first time Mel saw what it was. She traced the intricate artwork. The wings were so finely crafted, it appeared as if the insect might lift off and fly away.

"Most cicadas have a seventeen-year life cycle," he said. "They come out of hibernation for a short time. Bring new life into the world. Then die. I got this in memory of my mother."

"It was a cicada who told me to look for you," she recalled. "That's the universe at work."

"I believe that. My mother has always been in my life in the form of cicada sightings. Once I even saw one in the wintertime."

"Wow. She's a very strong spirit."

"But I've never actually seen her ghost. Not that I would recognize her if I did. I was never given a photo or description of her. It's something that has always bothered me. Did I get my brown eyes from my mother? And who was my father?"

"I'm sorry that you never got to know your parents, Tor."

"I've never known anything else, so that's my normal. There are times I feel I'm being directed by an unseen force. And… I like to think it's her. It's never pushed me in the wrong direction. It's what made me return to you now. Earlier, I saw another cicada. On a coffee cup, of all things."

"Some souls lost in this realm are very powerful. Too powerful," she said with a sigh.

"So." He sighed heavily. "That's the story on me and ghosts. And why I'm a freak about working with them." He tapped the quartz crystal at his belt, and Mel was almost going to touch it when she pulled back. A talisman was a personal thing. Only if invited would she touch it.

"When I was in my early twenties and had moved to Paris from London, I met a woman who also saw ghosts. She'd been from mental institution to mental institution, and was living on her own, but barely clinging to sanity. She was haunted by some vicious entities for reasons, I believe, that had to do with her growing up as the daughter of a murderer. Anyway, she wasn't crazy. Too much. And I understood her. We became friends. Never dated. It wasn't like that. Charlotte was more a sister than someone I'd want to date. Then she had to move. Whenever the media got too hot regarding her father, she'd pack up and change addresses.

"Five years ago we met again after not seeing each other for some time." Again he tapped the crystal. "She spoke of the voices that wanted her to kill herself."

Mel clasped his hand. She could feel his pain as a shiver wrapping her spine. The Jones family had been dealing with their own ghost issues. It was not easy. And it was real, as strange as that was for most to believe. Ghosts were not friendly little white blobs. Or sheet-covered spooks. Some could be vicious, homicidal, and could even influence a living person's mind.

"I was supposed to meet her one night for supper," Tor said, "but by that time I was working for The Order of the Stake. I got called to a job, so I was late by four hours. I went immediately to her place because she'd texted me a dozen times. I hadn't paid attention to the texts. It was a particularly busy night talking to the media about—I forget. Probably vampires. I'd turned off my phone to focus."

He drew her closer and gripped her tightly. Clinging as she so wanted to cling to him. A minute shiver traced his torso, and the reverberations hurt her heart desperately.

"Anyway, when I got to her house…" He tensed. "I found her in the bathtub, her wrists slashed. She'd been dead an hour. If I hadn't been late, she might still be alive. It was my fault."

"No, it wasn't. You couldn't be there for her all the time. And ghosts can be nasty. Evil. Malevolent… Oh."

Now she realized how hard it had been for him to return this evening. His issue with ghosts *and* not being there to protect the girl? It was happening all over again for him. And she had dragged him into this.

Oh, Mel, what have you done?

"After that night I made a strict no-ghosts rule. I went out the next day and found a witch to charm this talisman so I couldn't see ghosts. And so they could not make contact with me. They're still around me, I'm sure, I just can't see or sense them. And since then, my life has been going as well as it can."

"Until I dragged you back into it all." She sat up on his lap. "What kind of a person am I? I can't ask any more of you."

"But you have to. That's why I returned. *Had* to return. This has become more than a job, Mel. I care about you. You can ask anything of me. And you should. I want you to. I want you to—well, I like you. Those kisses we've shared? I want it to be a beginning."

"You don't know how much I'd like that, too. But if that happens, I'll be stirring up all your issues."

"Maybe they needed a good stir." He kissed the crown of her head again.

"But you were ready to walk away from this part of your life. And look what I've done. I feel terrible."

"Don't ever feel bad for coming into my life. I'm a better man for it. And for now? This is what I do. I protect others from harm. And if I can't stand up to one little ghost—hell, you said there might not even be ghosts."

"Amaranthe, my sister, has only been haunting my mom. She's in my parents' home. Mom can see her, but Dad and I cannot. Though we can both sense her. Yet we see when Mom is being tormented, both in human and cat form. I don't think Amaranthe's ghost will show tomorrow night at the crossroads when I need to do the spell. Because I'll be raising her dead body, not her ghost. Right?"

"You're asking me?"

"Well, if I give it a good think, I suspect I'll actually be summoning a zombie."

"Zombies—" Mel touched a finger to his mouth to stop him from what she knew he was going to say, but Tor took her hand away and finished "—do exist."

"Since when did you have a change of heart?"

"Since I had to fight the zombie dogs in your backyard. They were not revenants. Revenants are solid and don't suddenly drop off body parts. I am now officially on the zombie bandwagon. But really? You're going to raise your sister as a zombie? That wasn't in the initial instructions to me. Of course, you gave me no details. So why should I be surprised?"

"It's what's required for the spell. And now can you understand why I volunteered to do this instead of allowing my dad? Can you imagine if he had to raise his own daughter from the grave?"

Tor blew out a breath. "But you're her sister. It's going to affect you just as much as it would your father. Can't you have your uncle CJ do this?"

She shook her head. "I've got a connection to Amaranthe that no one else has. See here." She opened her palm and he traced the scar. "Amaranthe and I performed a blood-bond spell when we were little. If anyone is going to raise her from the dead, it has to be me. Of course, now that Uncle CJ said I have to make a sacrifice, I'm not sure what that should be."

"A sacrifice?"

"It's the reason my cloaking spells haven't been taking hold. When a witch wants to perform dark magic, he or she makes a sacrifice to prove their commitment to the art. I remember Amaranthe ate a salamander heart when we were tweens. Poor thing was her familiar. I don't know what my dad did, and I'm not sure I want to know. It doesn't have to be like killing a sacrificial lamb. I have to sacrifice something important to me. And I need to do it soon so I can get the mojo I need to work the dark magic."

"What's important to you?"

At that moment Bruce levitated down the hallway, and both paused to watch him pass into the kitchen.

"I'm not sacrificing Bruce," Mel said. "Or Duck. Or any living being. That's not my style. I'm not sure what would work. A lot of things are important to me. My house, my life, my light magic, my love for nature. Heck, even my love for karaoke. But I don't think promising never to sing karaoke again would fit the bill."

"Probably not." Tor stroked the back of his forefinger along her jaw. "I'll help you. Just tell me what you need, and it's done."

"You're so good to me. I will tell you if I need help. But first, I have to figure out what's most important to me."

"And fast."

"And fast." She pressed a palm over his chest. Now his heartbeats were calm and reassuring. Lost in his steady brown eyes, but searching for an anchor, she said, "Tell me you're out and I'll understand."

"I'm in. And you can't change my mind."

"Thank you." She kissed him. "I owe you a lot for this."

"Actually, your dad and your uncle are now footing the bill. Both told me I wasn't allowed to take money from you."

"Oh really? I'm not going to argue with that."

"So are we good?" he asked. "I mean, beyond the work situation. I know I hurt you—us—by walking away. I was…"

"Dealing with your own stuff. I get that. And yes, we are good. But we'll be even better if you can help me move this furniture back into place. Bruce is no help at all when it comes to heavy lifting!" she called into the kitchen.

"Got it. You stand out of the way, and I'll do it all. Where is the heart, by the way?"

"I put it in the fridge." She shrugged in answer to his lifted brow. "Wasn't sure if spoilage would be an issue, though I doubt it. It wasn't in cold storage at the Archives. Don't worry. I performed another cloak and ward on it, just to be safe."

"The same cloak and ward that had an efficacy of about three hours?" he asked with a dimpled grin.

"The very same. I'll figure out my sacrifice before morning. I have to. Just think—tomorrow night this will all be over. And then Monday morning you can start your new life."

He stood from the chair and slipped his hands down her shoulders as their gazes locked. "A new life," he said. "I want that. But what if I want to keep some of the old in the new?"

"Like what old stuff would that be?"

"Well, she's not exactly old."

"She?" Mel wriggled when she realized he was talking about her. "I'd love to stay in your life. If you could manage a witch in your normal world."

"I don't think I'll ever be completely free from the paranormal world I've grown up in. It will be a challenge to keep it apart from the normal stuff, but I think it'll be worth it."

"If you think so."

"I...have been told I should employ a memory-loss spell."

"A—what for?"

"Rook suggested it. It'll make me forget things. If I'm going to enter the normal world, I can't know what I know now."

"That seems drastic."

"Extreme measures. For my sanity."

He'd obviously considered it, and the man was usually very sure about his decisions. She shouldn't say anything. She wouldn't.

"Of course," she offered as calmly as possible. "It's your life. You do what you have to do."

She kissed him again, quickly, and bounced into the kitchen to put away the grater and goggles. If she'd told him the truth, that she would be lost along with his abandonment of all things paranormal, she might lose his newly given trust.

But really, that man could only exist in her world. *His* world. She knew that. Would he come to realize it? Before he decided to forget it all?

Chapter 18

"Did you have any furniture stacked up in the back of the house you want me to put back in place?" Tor asked Mel as she walked down the hallway.

"I didn't blockade my spell room."

"I've seen that side of the house from outside. Isn't it all windows? Like a conservatory? Anything could have broken through—" Tor decided that stating the obvious wasn't going to help matters. He was here now. He could protect Mel.

And he wouldn't run away from that responsibility again.

"I know. Not very efficient at battening down the hatches. But I ran out of furniture. Come on—I'll show you."

As they entered the spell room, which was a long conservatory attached to the side of the house, Tor fell into a state of wonder. With a snap of her fingers, Mel lit a few candles placed in sconces along the walls. Above them, centered over a stretch of stone table, a candelabra was lit, giving the room a soft, cozy glow. Vines grew all over the windows from the outside, so the night sky was blocked in most places, but the moon shone through, high above, full and round.

Tomorrow night would see the moon's apex. *Showtime*, Tor thought. And he was going to stand by while Mel raised the dead. That would be interesting, for sure. Out of his comfort zone? Nothing doing. But still, it was going to try his bravery.

It would be worth it to help Mel.

The room smelled fresh and summery. Plants in terracotta pots were positioned all along the tiled floor. One wall was lined with shelves and vanities that were stocked with vials, bottles, jars, candles, rocks, more plants, books and—well, everything witchy Tor could imagine.

He smoothed a hand over a massive pink stone table that stood as high as his thigh. The top surface was about four feet square, and it had no legs; it was a solid chunk of rock. He jumped up to sit on it. "Must have taken a crane to get this piece in here."

"I'm not sure," Mel said. She tapped a bit of dried flower that hung from a copper rack over the pockmarked wood table that abutted against the pink stone. Must be her main spellcrafting table. "It's rose quartz. It was here, in that exact spot, when I moved in."

"A witch lived here before you?"

"I think it was a geologist. The whole house, when I did a walk-through before buying, was filled from floor to rafters with pretty stones and crystals. I suppose the owner decided that piece was too big to move. Must have cost a fortune. It feels great, doesn't it?"

Tor pressed his palms to the cool stone and shrugged. "It's a rock."

"Oh, dear, no." She moved to stand before him, and Tor spread his legs wider so she could step right up to him.

Mel slid her fingers along the pink stone, and then with those same fingers, she tapped his heart. He clasped a hand over hers. "Rose quartz is a stone of the heart. It's filled with love and compassion. Self-worth and confidence reside in this stone. And passion."

He wasn't sure about all that, but he was on board with the passion bit. And the way her lashes lowered when she said that, dusting her candlelit, glitter-covered skin, was devastating to his desires. Lash magic. He was bewitched.

Tor bent to kiss Mel. Her mouth was soft and giving, so lush. The moment felt right. Maybe? After today's argument, he wasn't sure. "Is this all right?"

"Why would you ask such a thing? Of course it is."

"Less than an hour ago you were barricaded in your house because you thought I'd abandoned you. I'm sorry."

"I forgive you."

Croak.

Tor startled at Bruce's interjection. He'd not noticed the familiar had levitated so close to them and now hovered but a foot from their heads.

"That did not sound approving," Tor said. "Would you give me a break, Bruce? You can trust me. I like your witch. And I promise you I will protect her and never do anything to harm her."

The frog stared at him a moment. And Tor could only hope he'd get an approving ribbit or whatever was the amphibious offering of acceptance. Instead, Bruce turned and floated off.

"What was that?" he asked Mel.

"I'm not sure. But I'm inclined not to overthink it. Now kiss me and show me just how much you're on my team."

"Team Mel?"

"I like when you call me that."

"I can call you whatever you want me to."

"I like Mel because it's what you want to call me." She pushed up onto the stone table and landed each knee beside his thighs.

Tor slid his hands up her back as her kiss forced him downward to lie across the smooth quartz. Her kisses were passionate and searching, and for a moment he simply lay there, allowing her to do as she wished. Her body hugged his as she snuggled against him. Her hair spilled over his face and neck, and he breathed in lemons and lavender.

Attempting to loosen his tie, she cursed. "Your knots are thwarting my lusty desires. How did you get it like this?"

"It's an Eldredge knot. One of the more complicated knots, but it makes me happy to accomplish it."

"You are a man who likes a good challenge."

"Always. And I would never purposely thwart you. Promise." He gave the tie a shuffle, which loosened it, and then he pulled it free with more than a few twists and tugs.

"I think you practice knot magic," she said.

"Is there such a thing?"

"There's a magic for everything. Tasseomancy, aleuromancy, crystal divination, pyromancy. I'll have to show you my lithoboly skills sometime. Freaks out Bruce."

"I'm not sure I want to know."

"Some things are better left to the imagination. But it does involve rocks raining down from the sky." She slid a hand down to his belt.

"Your talisman against ghosts," she affirmed.

"Lillian Devereaux spelled it for me years ago. You know her?"

"I don't, but I've heard of her. Pretty sure that witch has been around for centuries."

"She's quite the flirt."

"Is that so?"

"I never kiss and tell. Hey, she did me a favor. I can't see or sense ghosts when I've got this on me. And they can't touch me. I never take it off."

"But you know it doesn't repel them. Just makes it so you can't see them."

"That works for me. Are we going to discuss the miraculous powers of my…talisman…" He pumped his hips against her thighs playfully. "Or are we going to make out?"

"I vote for making out." Mel unbuttoned his shirt and her lips landed on his bare skin, following with kisses as each button was released. "This hot, hard chest of yours. Mmm…"

Her tongue traced his nipple, and Tor hissed at the sudden and remarkable shock of pleasure. He gripped her hair, his fingers getting lost in lush, soft curls, and pulled her up to kiss her deeply. He needed to taste her want and desire. And he wanted her to know the flavor of his.

The intense need to become as close to her as possible had him pulling her tight against him. Their tongues danced. Sighs mingled. The tickle of her lashes against his skin felt like the best kind of magic.

"I want to do more than kiss you," she said.

"Me, too," he said on a wanting groan. "Mel, you don't make it easy to resist you."

"Why resist?" She pushed up from him, her soft hair dangling onto his bared chest. She was on top and in control, and he didn't mind that at all. "I can make you do as I say." A waggle of her brow combined with her lash magic to completely enchant him.

"With witchcraft? I have no doubt. But you don't have to resort to sneaky tactics. I'm on board with whatever happens next."

"Good." Her eyes twinkled. She tugged his shirt out from his pants. "Because I have plans."

She bowed her head and kissed a trail down from his neck to his nipples, and took her time with the sweet torture of sucking them, then licking and lashing at them.

Tor sucked in a gasp. Her mouth on his skin did not allow for clear thought.

Above him, the chandelier glinted with golden candle flame. The air swirled sweetly with herb and flower scents. Briefly, he wondered if the vines climbing outside the windows concealed their tête-à-tête from the neighbors' view. The shrubbery was probably high enough.

Mel unzipped the fly of his trousers, and her hand slipped inside to caress his hard-on. The contact worked like a torch to his desires. Tor groaned with soul-deep pleasure.

"You know, I never use a wand," she commented, and kissed him below the belly button. "But this one I'd like to get my hands on for a test drive."

"Nothing magical there," he commented with an intake of breath as her next kiss was placed on his briefs, right there, on the swollen head of his cock. Though now that he considered it, something magical might happen if she continued her efforts. And he wouldn't be able to contain the results, that was for sure.

"Are you comfortable?" she asked, and then snapped the elastic band of his briefs.

"I...was." He winced, wondering if she intended to snap him again.

"I mean, this rock you're lying on."

"I thought it was a passion rock? Isn't it going to make this all glowy and magical?"

"I don't think we'll glow." She tugged down his pants and boxers. "But magic will happen. I can promise you that."

"Yep…that's…nice grip, witch."

She chuckled and ended it with a lash of her hot tongue over the crown of his cock. Tor closed his eyes. Something hot stung his chest and he winced, but he didn't think on it too long as the wicked, wet heat of Mel's tongue traveled the length of him, slowly, firmly and oh, so…

Another hot sting splashed his shoulder, and now he realized what was happening. The candle wax was dripping from above. And…he almost asked Mel to stop so they could move, but now she sucked him deeply and—fuck, that was good.

He grasped a hank of her hair and didn't push or cajole, but merely anchored himself to her as she expertly lured his body to a rigid, trembling frenzy. He was going to come. And she was still completely dressed.

Wax fell in torturous droplets from above. And…none of it mattered as he saw vivid colors behind his closed eyelids, and the tension in his groin burst. His hips bucked on the pink stone. Mel's hands slid up his abdomen.

And the witch whispered, "Now that was magical."

Crouched over her protector on the rose-quartz table, Mel had never felt more powerful, more in her body and so in touch with her feminine core. Her entire body tingled with the pleasure that she had just given Tor. And she wanted to feel it as viscerally and with such an abandoned thrill as he just had.

But her knees were killing her.

Sliding off the rock table, she tugged up Tor's pants, and

he—still breathing heavily and in a sex daze—clutched them at his waist and followed as she grabbed his free hand and led him down the hallway.

"The big pink rock was fun," she said as she entered the bedroom. "But now we're going to do it the comfortable way."

"I'm all for that." Tor dropped his trousers, stepped out of them and flung himself onto the bed. The thick, fluffy comforter slapped over his face and he pulled the blanket about him. "Man, this is soft! It's like a nest in here! You girls get all the good stuff."

Mel leaned over and tapped his erection, which had softened a bit, but was still a mighty wand. "We most certainly do get to play with the good stuff." She kissed his abs and moved up to his chest where— "What's this?"

"Wax." He pulled her up to kiss him. "The candles were dripping on me, but I didn't want to move because what you were doing..."

He kissed her deeply and rolled her to her back, effectively wrapping them into a blanket burrito.

Another drop of wax on his shoulder alerted her. "You should have told me you were in pain."

"It was a good pain."

"You like a little *Fifty Shades*, eh?"

"I don't know what that means. Suffice it to say, I'm not going to lie still if you think dripping candle wax all over me is a good time, but like I said—whew! Now it's my turn." He bowed to kiss her breast through her top. "Okay if I help you out of some of these clothes?"

"Please do."

He untangled them from the blanket and helped her off with the blouse, and when he saw her bra, he bent to study the side embroidery on the yellow and black mesh concoction. "Bees?"

"I love bees."

"Even bees on your boobs?"

Mel giggled as he nuzzled a kiss along the cusp of the lacy cup. A flick of his fingers released the front clasp, and her breasts were freed from their confinement.

"I can still see an impression of the bee here," he said. A kiss to the side of her boob lingered and gave her a good shiver. "You women and your fancy underthings. Who sees them but you?"

"You're seeing them now."

"True. And I do appreciate the effort."

"And if we're going to talk obsessive clothing choices, I know a guy with an OCD closet that'd give a psychologist a wet dream."

"Speaking of wet…" Tor slid his tongue from one breast to the other, forging a slick, heated trail on her skin. When he suckled at her nipple, Mel dipped her head back into the pillow and closed her eyes. She grasped for the sheets, but her fingers only caressed air. It felt so good, and surrendering to the sensation was all she wanted to do.

Wiggling her hips as his hands moved down her skirt, she wrapped her legs about him and pulled his body against hers. Her silky panties slid against his briefs.

"You're so hot and wiggly," Tor said. He suddenly put a hand along her jaw and held her there. She peered into his eyes. "You need to know there's a battle going on inside me right now."

"I know, I know. It's the one where the guy in the suit wielding the stake says this guy right here with the tousled hair and hard-on shouldn't be getting it on with a client."

"You read my mind. Must be a witch thing."

"Trust me, it's a woman thing. I wish I had a spell that would put you in your heart and not your brain, but I don't." Mel sighed and spread her arms out across the mattress in frustration. "I want this, Tor. It doesn't have to be forever. Or even any commitment. Let's have fun. We're both adults. We can have sex with one another if we want to. Do you want to have sex with me?"

"I do. And you're right. I need to get out of my brain."

"I know how to make that happen without magic." She reached down and found a firm hold on him. The man moaned and bowed his head to her chest. He nodded and made a few positive groaning noises, and she knew she had won the battle.

"And don't worry about protection either," she added. "I've got a birth-control spell activated, and it's very effective under the full moon."

"I'll take your word for it." He slid her panties over her hips. "Right now, I want to fall into your lush world of softness and girlie sighs."

Mel sighed for him. "Then come inside me, lover. Come inside."

He kissed each of her breasts. At first he moved slowly, reverently, as if worshipping her skin, her heat, her very being. Then his tongue dashed faster and more firmly, twirling about her nipples, and his lips suckled her to wanting moans.

When he reached for his cock, Mel kept a grip on it, and together they guided him inside her. Tor's body shuddered above hers. Mel's core tightened and shivered as his fingers slicked in her wetness and moved up to circle slowly about her aching, swollen clitoris. As he pumped deeply inside her, the man matched that rhythm with his finger. It was a heady touch that surprised her with its sudden and exacting intensity. He knew just where to touch her to raise up every shivering, delicious, humming thread of pleasure. Her thighs began to shake and her breaths came as gasps.

And when she could no longer cling to the delicious

distraction of being almost there, Mel released and her body pulsed upward against Tor's. Together they came in a clutch of panting moans and cries of triumph. Heartbeats racing one another, they shared the high until Tor collapsed beside her and reached for her hand. He lifted it to his mouth and kissed the palm.

Mel turned and nuzzled up against his impossibly fiery warmth. Seeking all of his heat, she stretched a leg across his and tilted her hip closer to make their bodies snug tight against each other.

"That was good," she said in a whisper.

"It's only the beginning." His chest heaved from exertion, and Mel spread her fingers across it. His heart thundered beneath her fingers. "You make me hungry for more, Mel."

"You can have as much of me as you want."

"Good." He turned her onto her back and glided a hand down to between her legs. "I'm going to kiss you right here..." He swirled his finger about her aching clit. "... until you come again."

Chapter 19

While the shower pattered in the next room, Mel lingered between the sheets. Tor had jumped out of bed ready for the day. And when he'd encouraged her to join him, she had made the tough decision to remain in bed. It was only 7:00 a.m. Who even opened their eyes before eight?

Now she spread her hand over the spot where he had lain next to her through the night. She nuzzled her face against the pillow where his black-cherry-tobacco scent had imbued into the fibers. That had been some good sex. Awesome sex. The kind you wanted to do again and again and again. Which they had. She was blissfully exhausted.

How could the man even think to leave her alone and wash her off in the shower?

"His brain must kick in with the sunrise," she muttered, then smiled to herself.

She figured waking up in a woman's bed, not in the comfort of his ultra-tidy and organized home, had to be a challenge in and of itself. How could he even function without a stroll through his closet and a pressed shirt and tie? He'd have to wear the same clothes today, until he found a moment to run home and recharge his OCD uniform.

Again, she smiled. She liked him exactly as uptight and methodical as he could be. Because she'd seen his lighter, loose side. Singing and dancing. And oh, his kisses. Everywhere on her. Her mouth, her breasts, her pussy. Mmm…

And she would have to give that up. Because right now, she realized what sacrifice she could offer to make her dark magic effective.

Tor.

She swore and buried her face against the pillow. It wasn't fair. And yet it was. A sacrifice wasn't that unless it was great and it hurt and the person sacrificing would feel the effects for long after. She hadn't known Tor long, but excising him from her life would feel as though she were cutting out an organ and tossing it aside.

And she knew exactly how to do it. He'd mentioned something about a memory spell. She would give him that. She'd mix it up this morning and then try her hand at dark magic again. If it worked, she would know her sacrifice had been acceptable.

But until that spell was mixed, she intended to indulge in the man. To make memories that she never intended to dispel. So she returned her thoughts to his kisses skating over her skin. His lips brushing her gently and then firmly, followed by the hot lash of his tongue.

She could feel him glide down her belly and dash his tongue against her clit. Pushing her fingers through her curls and between her thighs, she found that swollen bud humming with want. She gasped as a hint of orgasm teased. She could come with a few strokes, and so…

Mel curled down her head under the sheet as her body shivered minutely and the tingles of a soft, sweet orgasm scurried through her being. She heard someone enter the room and ask what she was up to. With a giggle, she tugged down the sheet and crooked her finger at the man who wore but a towel about his hips.

"Yeah?" Tor's big brown eyes glinted. His hair, still wet and tousled this way and that with droplets of water, shone in the ridiculously bright morning sunlight. He released the towel and dropped it to reveal a sizable interest in her suggestion.

When Mel lifted the sheet to invite him into bed, her phone, which lay on the nightstand, suddenly rang. She pouted and patted the bed. "Just ignore it."

"Sure, but..." He leaned over to read the screen. "It's from your dad. Way to kill a good hard-on."

"Oh shoot." She grabbed the phone and before answering gestured for Tor to put the towel back on. "Or it will distract me," she whispered dramatically, then answered, "Hey, Dad. What's up?"

Her dad's voice was frantic, gasping in between his rushed words. Mel immediately understood what he was asking from her. "I'll be right there. Twenty minutes, tops."

Tearing away the sheets, she flew out of bed and grabbed the first piece of clothing she saw, which was a pair of gray leggings flung over a chair.

"What's up?" Tor picked up his shirt from the floor.

"My dad needs me. My sister is going at Mom like crazy, and Dad is desperately trying to get her out of the house and away from her. But in cat form, Mom tends to hide under the couch or in places that are hard to reach. I have to distract Amaranthe so he can get her. Can you give me a ride?"

"You bet I can." He grabbed his pants and shimmied

into them. Threading his arms through the shirt, he picked up his tie. "Let's go."

"I love you for this." Mel pulled on a flouncy red shirt and grabbed her bag of magical supplies.

She caught his hesitation and decided a kiss was necessary. Tor held her fiercely as she took a moment to find her place in the kiss and reassure him that all would be well.

"You're my protector," she said. "And I am my mother's protector. Or I'm helping my dad as best I can. Night of the full moon today! We've got a busy day ahead of us. There's lots to do. Sacrifices to make, on both our parts."

"You figure out what you're going to sacrifice?"

"I did."

"You going to share?"

"Nope. I think it'll lessen the efficacy of the dark magic if I do."

"Fair enough. But both of us? What do I have to sacrifice?"

"Well, you *are* bringing me to my parents' home. You know what waits there."

"Right." His brows furrowed together.

"Don't think about it too much."

Grabbing his hand, she led him down the hallway. Bruce hovered near the door and when Mel paused before her familiar, he dropped a small round piece of jet onto her palm. A stone to protect against evil, and help one accomplish goals. It also worked well to connect one to the spirit world.

"Thanks, Bruce. Now I'm ready."

Mel clasped Tor's hand and led him toward her parents' building. They lived on the entire top floor of a six-story structure in the 16th arrondissement that had been remodeled by Haussmann in the nineteenth century. It was old but sturdy, and she loved the open style and the industrial furnishings. Massive iron beams and support structures framed all the exposed ductwork and piping high above. Add a touch of dark magic, and the place had always felt like home to her.

Until Amaranthe had begun to haunt her mother, Star.

The accident that had taken her sister's life had happened two years ago. The first year following, Amaranthe's ghost had been weak. The family hadn't realized the knocks and sudden window closings were ghostly activity. Until Star had dreamed one night about the incident for which she would forever blame herself. An accident she had not purposefully made happen. It had been just that—an accident.

In cat form, Star had been fleeing the neighbor's rottweiler, which had chased her into the street. An oncoming car, driven by Amaranthe, speeding at a reckless forty miles an hour, had swerved and crashed into a street pole. The pole had sliced down the middle of the car as if it were a knife halving a sandwich. Amaranthe, the doctors had reported, had died upon impact.

But Star had learned differently in her dream. Her daughter had lived for twenty minutes following the accident, trapped in a broken and dying body, unable to scream for help, yet fully aware of the black cat who had paced on the wreckage of the car's hood as the emergency team had pried the woman's body out from the vehicle.

Star had not died the morning of the accident. But the rottweiler had not relented. Later that evening, Star had gone out to run off the intense sadness that had consumed her after losing her daughter and, blinded with grief, had also become victim of a car's overwhelming power. She'd been struck and tossed thirty feet through the air to land against a brick wall, dropping dead to the ground before the confused rottweiler.

Thoroughly and Mel had mourned two family members that day. Only Star had come back to life, unaware of the family she'd been a part of, a family she had helped to create. It had been trying times for both Mel and her father.

But her father had gone through Star's death many times previously. Thoroughly Jones knew the routine. However, it was not something with which he'd ever grown accustomed to or, in any way, at ease with. It had been different that time, with the added grief of having lost one of his daughters. He had been inconsolable, yet quietly strong in reassuring Star. Mel had volunteered to plan her sister's funeral. Together they had buried her at a crossroads near some family land in hopes she would rest in peace.

Not so. This spring was when Amaranthe's ghost had started to gain strength, and—for reasons Mel could only guess were that she assumed Star had purposely run in front of the car—her sister now haunted their mother with a misplaced death wish.

Star, having recently died three weeks earlier after the fall from the roof, was still having difficulty gaining back memories of her family, her loving husband and one remaining daughter. But to add to that the haunting by an angry ghost? To say the fragile familiar was nearing a complete breakdown was not far off.

Now Mel clutched Tor's hand as she stopped before the building and stretched her gaze up to the rooftop.

He kissed her hand and brushed the hair from her cheek. "Want me to go up?"

She shook her head. "I need to go in alone. If Amaranthe knows who you are or senses anything about you, terrible things could happen. I just need to distract her long enough so Dad can get Mom out of the loft."

“I’ll stand guard down here. If you need me, call out. I’ll be at your side in seconds.”

“I know you will.”

She took a step onto the first of three stairs leading up to the entrance. Clutching her fingers into fists, she closed her eyes and exhaled. She’d avoided her parents’ home these past several days because she didn’t want Amaranthe to get a read on her, to learn that something was up. Not that that particular *something* was going at all well. When would she find time to concoct the memory spell? She had to do that. Today. But she needed vervain. And courage. This whole situation had gotten so out of hand.

“Mel?”

Tor called her back to the moment with his sure, calm voice. And back into the reality that hurt her heart. “I’m not sure I can do this, Tor.”

“Of course you can.” From behind her, he slid his hands down her arms. Nuzzling his cheek aside hers, he pulled her into a hug. All his crazy hard lines and muscles worked in tandem to comfort her. He was a wall of strength to her wobbly, weird jumble of hope, fear and utter panic.

She shifted a hip against his, and the talisman nudged against her. She slid her fingers over the warm, crystal clear quartz.

“I wonder if it can protect you?” he said.

She shook her head. “Probably not. Talismans are very personal.”

“Still. It might give you the strength you require to cross the threshold and face what lies beyond the door.” He unhooked the crystal from the D ring at his belt and placed it on her palm. “Take it.”

“But…you never go anywhere without it. This is…it’s personal to you, Tor.”

"I'll get it back from you as soon as you come down. Think of it as my way of being close to you."

"Okay." She tucked the talisman in her pocket, and the heavy weight against her hip felt right. Yes, he could accompany her in this way. "You'll wait down here in the lobby?"

"I will. But I can follow you up and wait outside the loft."

"No." She opened the building door and, feeling the strong wards her father placed on the entrance shiver through her veins, sucked in a gasp and stepped across the threshold. "I have to do this."

And she marched onward, up the first flight of stairs, not turning back to say anything more to Tor. With his fear of ghosts, she knew argument wasn't necessary to keep him at a distance. And she didn't need him—well, maybe a little—but she truly did fear the consequences should she attempt to bring him along with her. Sliding her hand in the pocket, she curled her fingers about the talisman. It was his magic, and she did feel his presence as a repeat of that reassuring hug he'd just given her.

The stairs were creaky, and yet she never took the elevator. No magical reason, just the remembered fear of being trapped in the tiny one-person box for five hours that one summer when a lightning storm had taken out the building's power.

On the sixth floor, she stood in the vast harlequin-checked foyer before the Jones residence and sucked in a breath. A tear spilled from her eye. She missed her sister. Everything about this situation sucked, big-time. And tonight—if she thought now was difficult, tonight would only prove insurmountable.

Could she do this?

Glancing down the stairs, she wished to see Tor standing there on the landing, his kind brown eyes offering her strength. But he had his own ghosts with which to deal. Another stroke of her fingers over the talisman reassured her. Mel sucked in a breath and walked up to knock on the door.

Her dad answered immediately. He held the handle of an empty plastic cat carrier in one hand. With his other arm, he swept it around her shoulder and pulled her in for a hug. "Thank you for coming, Lissa. This has gotten out of hand. None of my repulsive magic is effective either. She's getting stronger."

"It's not your fault, Dad." She hugged him tightly. Melting into his arms had always felt so good. But now she felt him tremble and could feel the sad energy leaking out of him. "Where's Mom?"

"Under the couch. She knows what I'm trying to do, but she won't put out more than a paw."

"Where's Amaranthe?"

"Somewhere near the couch. I think." He glanced over his shoulder. The couch was across the vast loft, pushed up against the windowed wall. "You know I've no magic to ward off my own blood. Ghost or not. If you could just call her to you."

Mel nodded. "I've got this. You focus on Mom. Soon as you have her, run out of here."

"I intend to." He gave her another quick hug. "We can do this. Tonight it will be over."

"Yes." Mel sucked in a deep inhale.

Tonight would bring peace to the Jones family. If she got her act together. And sacrificed the one really great thing that had happened in her life.

Wandering in behind her dad, Mel searched the air, knowing she wouldn't see her sister's ghost. Amaranthe had never apported into corporeal form. But she could sense her presence by a coolness to the air—there.

The side of her neck prickled, and it felt as if an ice cube had sluiced down her shoulder and to her elbow. She gripped Tor's talisman. It helped him to *not* see ghosts? If only she *could* see her sister's ghost. Still, the inspiring sense that Tor was close, perhaps just behind her, bolstered her courage.

She could do this.

"Amaranthe?" Mel whispered. She closed her eyes. Focusing her senses beyond her body, she tapped into the air about her. "I miss you, sister."

Wavery whispers that she could not interpret slid over her scalp and tickled her ears. It was a faraway call, a fleeting scream for help. But since Amaranthe's death, they'd never been able to communicate with words. Unfortunately.

Not wanting to call attention to her parents, Mel turned the opposite way from the couch and walked over to the window. There, she breathed on the glass and then quickly traced a heart in the condensation. A sudden slash marked the fading heart, startling Mel at the power her sister possessed. Yet behind her, she was aware of her father moving swiftly toward the door, the cat carrier clutched to his chest, and inside was the hissing cat she called Mom.

Cold air chilled Mel's cheek as she felt her sister's ghost rush toward the closing front door. The door slammed, and the light fixtures rattled angrily. Her dad had successfully escaped.

Now to face her sister's wrath.

Tor paced the lobby's marble floor, arms swinging wide and meeting before him with a fist to his palm. Back and forth, slap. Back and forth, slap. When the man in dark clothing carrying a cat carrier descended the stairs in a flurry and stopped before him, Tor swallowed.

"She did it?" he asked, knowing it was a stupid question as soon as he'd opened his mouth.

TJ nodded. "Why aren't you up there with her?"

"I, uh..." Because there was a ghost. And— "Mel asked me to stay down here."

"I thought you were protecting my daughter?"

"I am, but..."

TJ shook his head, disapproving.

"Is she still in the apartment? Alone? With the..."

"I'm not sure what Amaranthe will do. She's dangerous. I can't believe someone who calls himself a protector would allow a woman to walk in on a volatile situation. Alone."

"She said it wasn't wise—" Argument was stupid. And not fair to the family. "You're right. She needs me. I'll take care of your daughter, Monsieur Jones. I promise. How's your, uh...wife?"

The cat in the cage hissed at Tor.

"Frightened. I'm taking her to my brother's for the night until Lissa can invoke the spell. You will accompany her for that?"

"Of course. That's what she hired me to do." Tor took off toward the stairs. "I'll keep her safe!"

"You will," TJ called, "or you will know the Jones family's wrath!"

That was more than enough motivation to quicken Tor's pace. He took the stairs two at a time, not sure why Mel had not taken the elevator. While waiting, he'd seen a man with a briefcase exit it, but—well, magic and elevators. There was something to that combination that he didn't want to test.

While pacing in the lobby, he had struggled with his

fear of ghosts and why he hadn't insisted on accompanying Mel upstairs. And yet she had been firm, and he hadn't wanted to cause problems with the ghost. But now he realized she needed him no matter what.

At the front door, he lifted his hand to knock, then paused. He leaned in close and listened, and heard...crying. Opening the door quietly, he stuck in his head and searched the chilly air in the loft, which was two stories high and open to the rafters. He wasn't sure what he expected to see—well, yes, he was. He would see specters. Ghosts. Haunts.

Nothing.

Had the sister fled after TJ had escaped with Star? Or was she standing over Mel right now, tormenting her? He saw Mel, sitting on the floor, back to him. Her head was bowed and she was sobbing.

Rushing inside, Tor plunged to the floor beside Mel. Before taking her in his arms, he checked her expression. She didn't appear to be frightened or tormented, but she was crying. Perhaps she was not haunted right now. He took her in his arms and pulled her into a hug.

"Tell me what you need me to do," he said.

She shivered against him and sniffled. "She's here."

And he did know that. The instant he'd run inside, he'd felt the cold air, the knowing presence of another.

"Where?"

"Not sure. She won't speak to me. I can feel her anger. Why is she so angry? Why won't she believe that Mom had nothing to do with her death?"

Her mother had not purposely sought to harm her daughter, but fact remained, she had run in front of the car. Perhaps the ghost could not get beyond that. She might only carry the knowledge she had from the moment of the accident, which had been that the cat had run before the car. And when she died, she could have never learned that it had been an accident. Maybe?

Tor didn't want to have a conversation with the entity to learn why.

"Your dad has left the building and your mom is safe," he said. "Let's get you out of here."

She nodded and, with his help, stood. Wrapping an arm about her shoulder, Tor realized she felt smaller, more delicate and so cold. When they neared the open door, it suddenly slammed shut and a gush of icy wind raked through his hair.

"You need to get out of here now," he said, fully planning to follow her out. He gripped the doorknob. The icy metal stung and he hissed, but he managed to pull open the door. "Go!"

"Wait!" Mel paused on the threshold. "I need vervain. I'm out, and Dad said he had some."

"I'll get it." Another gust of wind pushed on the door, and Tor struggled to hold it open. "Where is it?"

"With Dad's spell stuff around the corner."

"Go!" Tor yelled, just as the door slipped from his white-knuckle grasp and slammed shut.

Turning and facing the open space of the loft, Tor darted his gaze about the room. A trickle of cold air brushed his eyelids, yet it wasn't as threatening as the door slamming had been.

"Vervain," he whispered.

Around the corner? He located a kitchen and found what looked like an ancient apothecary's desk and cabinet heaped with vials and bottles and candles and potions. A massive handcrafted book sat splayed open on the center of a wood table carved with ancient sigils that caused the hairs on Tor's arms to stand upright.

He swallowed. "A dark witch's grimoire. Not going to touch that thing."

Tor scrambled over to the shelf and studied the conglomeration of vials and bottles and boxes. Everything was dusty and arranged chaotically—did no one have a sense of order in this family?

"Vervain. What does vervain look like?"

"It's in the jar labeled Vervain."

"Thanks." Tor grabbed the small jar, then swallowed roughly. "Ah, shit." He spun to face a blonde woman who looked a lot like Mel, save her eyes, which were rimmed with dark shadows. And her lips were bloodred. "Amaranthe?"

"You can see me?" The entity floated toward him.

Tor nodded, clutching the vervain to his chest. He slid his other hand down to his hip where the talisman—was not there.

When the ghost raked an icy hand through his hair, he dropped the glass jar, which she caught in a wispy hand that morphed from foggy smoke to a fully formed corporeal hand.

"This," she said, "is going to be fun."

Chapter 20

The room was so cold Tor's breath fogged before him as he breathed, ever so shallowly, and took a step back from the ghost. She had assumed corporeal shape. Flesh-and-blood real. And she looked so much like Mel, except with blond hair. The same big blue doe eyes.

Bollocks. He'd seen far too many ghosts in his lifetime, but never had one been so solidly formed.

"You see me," Amaranthe said, "because the veil between you and my world is nonexistent."

"State the obvious, will you?" he tried.

"Are you mocking me, mortal man? Who are you? Why does a common human enter my parents' home and look about for things that he should not have reason to use?"

"The vervain is for..." He wouldn't give the ghost any more fuel. He had to keep her calm. And get the hell out of here before his insecurity paralyzed him.

"Vervain is for releasing things from the heart and the

soul. Hmm…" The ghost tapped a finger on her lips. "For whom? My father? My mother? Or…" Her brow arched in evil triumph. "My sister. You and Lissa are lovers. My sister is fucking a human."

He would not reply. Must not look at her overlong. She was beginning to lose the darkness around her eyes, the only thing that gave her a skeletal appearance, and her hair was changing to brown and growing even darker. Her bright blue eyes widened. Just like Mel's. Impossible. But nothing was impossible in the paranormal realm. Tor knew a specter could assume the guise of another with little effort.

"She just needed some vervain," he tried. "Silly spell stuff. You know."

"Magic is never silly. Tell me why Lissa gives you the time of day?"

"I, uh… No. I'll just take this…" He grabbed the small glass jar the spirit had set on the desk and stuffed it in his pocket. When he turned back to the ghost, Mel loomed before him, her long hair flowing and her doe eyes beaming at him. There was even glitter on her eyelids. Lemons and lavender filled his senses.

"No," Tor whispered. His jaw tight, he uttered, "You're not Mel. You're not."

"You call her Mel?" The ghost tilted her head. Crimped the edge of her upper lip in disgust. "Strange. Of course, she never did like Lissa. I always called her *twerp.* She's the older one, you know? I have always been younger. More beautiful, yes?" She quickly took on her own persona with the blond hair, and her skin remained young and fresh, not shadowed or dank.

She was beautiful. For a ghost.

"Star did not mean for your death to happen," Tor said.

The ghost snarled and slashed clawed fingers at him.

He didn't feel the cut of her fingernails on his skin, but he could feel the tug to his very being as she connected with him on a metaphysical level. Damn it, he should not have left the talisman with Mel. He'd never allowed anyone to touch it, or worse, borrow it. What had gotten into him?

But he was here now. And he wasn't about to run from a figment, a projection of a former life. The soul caught in this mortal realm was merely wearing a costume of what she'd once been. And that soul was a cruel, violent being who was trying to kill her own mother.

"Amaranthe Jones, why don't you give up and go to the light?" he asked. To use a person's full name had power; it drew them to the moment, crystal clear reality. And the dead never liked to be reminded of their status.

"The light? Ha!" Amaranthe spread out her arms, and at the ends of her fingers green sparks snapped. Ectoplasmic remnants? Or some sort of ghostly magic he did not want to deal with? "You know nothing about me, human."

"I know you're dead. And the dead do not belong in this realm."

"Says the one who has been dallying with nothing but the dead ever since meeting my sister. Oh, I know. I tapped into Melissande's thoughts when she was here. She is enamored with you. And you are of her. It isn't fair!" The ghost cried, clenching her fists. "She gets everything. Mom always did like her better!"

"That…is ridiculous. I've not met your mother but—"

"Which means you don't know anything about her. Star was the reason I will never walk this world in corporeal form. Never again will I know love, or the touch of a man's mouth on my lips."

Her figment hovered before him. Tor veered away, but she leaned in, putting their faces inches from one another. "Would you kiss me, human?"

If he touched her, he would never be the same. Tor had made physical contact with the spirits he'd seen over the years. Not by choice. Each time, he felt the lingering remnants of a soul settle into his skin and deep into his very bones. And one so angry as Amaranthe would surely foul his very being.

"You deserve all that and more," he said, avoiding the deep blue irises that sought to pull him closer, to lure his hands up to caress her hair. As if she were Mel… "You are a soul, Amaranthe. You can live again. But you need to leave this realm first. Do that. Let your soul begin another journey."

"That's death, asshole."

He shrugged, then winced because she was right, and he had never been faced with trying to spin his way into convincing a ghost to leave this realm.

"There is nothing here for you," he tried. "Just…you will be free."

"I go nowhere without my mother's last life!"

He was not appealing to her morals, and he didn't want to make things worse for the family. Tor knew when to cut his losses and run. Slipping quickly around the ghost, he aimed for the front door.

"Your family loves you!" he called.

But as he gripped the icy doorknob, Amaranthe coalesced into form and he ran right into her. The fusion of her death-chilled essence to his warm, living flesh burned him. With a yelp, Tor shoved away from the door. He could feel her essence enter his skin and bite at his nerves.

"You're a conduit. Open to the spirit realm." The ghost stalked toward him. "I could use you."

For what, he didn't want to know. To return from whence she came? He could only hope.

Now her eyes were white and her mouth opened wide

as she yowled a wicked, otherworldly cry that shattered the glass candleholder on a nearby table and broke glasses in the kitchen.

Tor's nerves twanged and his body went rigid. He wanted to swing out in an attempt to push her away, but even as he had the thought, he knew he couldn't allow himself to hurt a woman. Mel's sister, by the gods. And right now, frozen by her wicked essence, he could barely stand, let alone move an arm.

"I won't rest until she stands beside me in this strange Beneath," Amaranthe announced. "My mother murdered me."

"She didn't," he forced out through his tight jaw. The pain was incredible. He yelped, and that utterance worked to release some of the tension in his body. He bent forward, catching his hands on his knees. A shiver seemed to shave off some of her heavy residue. "She was just a cat running away from a dog!"

A slash of Amaranthe's clawed fingers streaked a burn across Tor's cheek. She stood ten feet away from him, but he touched his face and felt the blood. She was gaining strength, a strange power that he was unable to repel without the talisman.

With another unearthly shout, the ghost plunged toward him.

Tor dodged to the floor, rolled onto his back and under the charging ghost, and came up to his feet. He grabbed the doorknob and opened the door. As he crossed the threshold, he tripped on nothing more than air—or more likely, the ghost's aggression. He slid into the foyer, facing the open doorway.

Amaranthe eyed the opening with a glint to her white eyes.

"Shit." Tor lunged to his feet and reached in to grab the

doorknob, and as he pulled it shut, he felt the ghost's iced fingers claw through his hair. He pulled it shut with effort and stepped back, stumbling against the wall and choking at the icy hollow in his throat.

Waiting, peering about him, he sensed she had not escaped the loft. Perhaps bound to the home, perhaps not. But she'd not been able to leave. Yet.

A prickle of hot pain clutched at his system, and he closed his eyes and huffed out breaths, trying to find a calm place instead of surrendering to the tightness the pain coaxed him toward. Panting, he heaved and then turned and caught his palms against the wall, pressing his forehead there. He'd done it. He'd faced down a volatile ghost. And…he was still in one piece. He hoped.

Shaking his arms out at his side flaked off the remaining sludge from the specter. It wasn't tangible, but Tor felt his muscles lighten. Whew!

Patting his pocket to ensure the vervain was still there, he took the stairs rapidly downward and didn't stop until he plunged into Mel's arms outside the building. Inhaling her citrus scent did not reassure him as usual. It only reminded him of what he'd just escaped.

"You're bleeding?" She touched his cheek. "What did she do to you? Oh, Tor, you saw her. The ghost of my sister?"

He nodded. "I'm good."

"I don't believe you." Her eyes pooled with tears.

"Mel, it's okay. Trust me. Just need to walk it off. Get her completely out of my system." He flung out his hand, shaking it, and then, stepping back from Mel, did the same with his other hand. A few jumps shook the lingering tendrils of nerve pain from his body as if sifting out toxins. "I saw her, plain as day. She's beautiful. Like you. But she's very angry."

"You had a conversation with her?"

"She believes your mother murdered her."

"That's wrong."

"I know that, but for some reason she doesn't. You have the talisman?"

"Oh, my mercy. I'm so sorry! You didn't have it on you. No wonder you saw her. And that must be why she was able to touch you. To hurt you."

"I'll survive."

She slapped the heavy crystal into his palm. "I've been clutching it desperately. You have to cleanse it with salt when we get home."

"First thing on my list." He glanced upward, toward the top floor of the building. The ghost had been inside him. He had felt her fingernails claw across his cheek. Her touch had entered his bones. "She can't…get out of the loft, can she?"

"She has when the door has been left open, or a window. But we only have until midnight to make it all stop. I need to go home and practice the spell, and there's the other thing—did you get the vervain?"

He patted his pocket and nodded. "Let's head home."

Mel had asked for a few hours alone in her spell room to go over the spell for tonight. She handed him a pink plastic container of black sea salt for the talisman, so he put it in there to cleanse.

With nothing to do but wait, Tor raided the fridge and found—situated around the plastic tub that held a dead witch's heart—an abundance of fruits and vegetables, which he had no idea how to cook or bake or whatever a person did to make them look fabulous like Mel did. But he was hungry, so he'd figure something out.

He grabbed a few carrots and a kiwi, then found a baguette and some soft cheese. Cutting and slicing, he ate until he was full while he prepared a plate, then set that plate by the entrance to the spell room. Calling out for a delivery, he left before the door could open and headed outside.

After finally shaking off the heebie-jeebies that had been riding him since facing the ghost of Mel's sister at the Joneses' loft, he tightened his tie and wandered up the sidewalk to the van, parked in front of the property. From the back, he pulled out one of the pressure-release titanium stakes that had been designed by Rook for the knights in The Order of the Stake.

He considered it a great sign of trust that Rook had gifted him with a few of these weapons. In preparation for later tonight, he tucked that inside his vest. He always made sure his tailor added special pockets and slip inserts for storing weapons. The man, who worked on Savile Row in London, never asked questions. He was good stock. Yet aging quickly. Who would make his suits in another few years after the old man had passed? Tor didn't want to consider the snappish Parisian tailors.

Shaking his head and laughing because he could actually find something to think about other than impending doom—and it happened to be bespoke suits, of all things—Tor surveyed the van's inventory.

The machete he'd used the other night gleamed. One of his go-to weapons. He gave it some consideration. He shouldn't need it here at Mel's place. As far as he knew, she hadn't made a sacrifice to add efficacy to her dark magic, so he was on guard. He'd reserve the wicked blade for later, when they were on-site. Instead, he took out a pistol loaded with salt rounds and then closed the van doors.

He scanned the neighborhood and took in the small yet idyllic green yards, the brick and limestone house fronts,

terra-cotta chimney pots, and tight boxwood shrubbery that had been tamed to the horticulturist's will. There was old money here in the 6th arrondissement. He assumed Mel had a trust fund, because he was never sure how witches made a living. She had mentioned something about being between jobs. The most enterprising paranormal he'd ever met was a billionaire werewolf who donated all his money to charity. But he'd come by his money through faery magic, not any sort of knuckles-to-the-grindstone work.

The world needed all sorts of workers, craftsmen and handymen. And women. He wouldn't question or argue his place in that hierarchy. He'd done what he knew how to do all his life. And now he was ready for a change, so he'd make that transformation. He could live a normal life. He just had to do it.

And yet tonight he would accompany a witch on a quest to invoke dark magic to raise a person—her own sister—from the dead. There should be something wrong with that. And yet there was nothing whatsoever strange or unusual about it when compared to his usual routine.

And that was the kicker. His normal was severely cocked up. He lived beyond slightly eccentric, or even wild and adventurous. Which was why he didn't have friends. How to have human friends when a man could never engage in conversation about a day at the office but instead about the night out cleaning up dead paranormals? He'd always been a loner, and…it wasn't all it was cracked up to be.

A night at a friend's house tilting back some brews and watching a game? He couldn't imagine it. But he'd like to.

"Yep," he muttered as he strode up the walk to Mel's house. "Ready to leave it all behind."

Mostly. Maybe? Hell, he wasn't sure anymore. Because,

by staying in the thick of things for a few more days, he'd met Melissande Jones and now…

Now he really liked her. He could go so far as to say he had fallen for her. He couldn't imagine not having run into her. His life would have a hole in it without her. How crazy was that?

Mel represented the part he wanted to excise from his life. So what was he thinking? He couldn't have it both ways. Normal life and witch in his life. It just couldn't work.

Rook had been right to suggest he utilize a memory spell. If he couldn't remember ever having met Mel, then he could do this. It was absolutely the only way he could do this.

Tor nodded. It would be tough, but he'd do it. He had to.

Instead of going back inside the house, he decided to patrol around the perimeter. It was sprinkling, and clouds had darkened the sky. Most of his jobs occurred during the night, although the rush jobs were generally because some creature was stalking during the daylight—or had been found dead in a place where any human could stumble onto it.

A job in an accounting office would keep him out of the sun, as well. Tor could do the math. An office job wasn't nine to five, but usually eight to whenever a guy could drag himself away from the desk. He'd miss the physical activity his current profession afforded. He'd have to request the tailor take in his shirts to compensate for muscle loss.

Who was he kidding? He'd up his workout program. He wasn't going to abandon these guns just because he worked in a cubicle.

Would his target skills decrease? And what about his machete-throwing skills? How about his time for cleaning

a dead werewolf? Or his knowledge of which chemicals removed blood and dissolved fur and bones the fastest?

He did possess strange and esoteric knowledge. But he didn't know a thing about the flowers of which he currently strolled beneath. A canopy of soft pink petals dusted his head. They hung from a wrought iron trellis connected to the kitchen side of the house. Tor closed his eyes and drew in the scent. Sweet as Mel's kisses.

A duck's quack startled him, and he stepped out from under the trellis and into the backyard. "Hey, Duck. What's up?"

He'd just said hello to a duck, and…had started a conversation. Without so much as a blink. Tor ran his fingers through his hair. That witch. Did he really want to forget she had been part of his life?

Sitting on the edge of the concrete patio where a patch of moss tried to climb over the stone and take over, he picked a long blade of grass and remembered how when he was a kid he'd used it to whistle. Placing his thumbs together with the grass between them, he managed a screeching yet wobbly whistle. Duck tossed him a wonky look (as wonky an expression as a duck could manage, anyway).

"I'm much better at wolf howls," he said to the fowl. "But I don't want to call any werewolves to the neighborhood."

"Why not?" asked a male voice from under the floral canopy.

Tor jumped to a stand, pulling out the pistol, and aimed it at the smirking werewolf.

Chapter 21

Mel combined the vervain and black salt and the whiskers from a hairless cat. Crushed rose petals soaked in rosemary oil topped the concoction. She whispered the words that would imbue the potion with a spell that would take away memory of which all things a human should not be aware.

It was the worst spell she'd ever concocted. But it had to be done. If Tor intended to walk away from this life, from this world she had always occupied and would continue to live in, then he couldn't know about her. It would be too painful for her if he ever returned and she knew he didn't want to have a relationship with her because of what she was.

Half an hour later, the memory spell settled in the thin glass vial before Mel's disappointed gaze. She was upset because it was complete, and it had proven to serve her what she'd needed: a sacrifice. By concocting the spell with the intent of giving it to Tor so he could take it—to forget about her—she had given the dark forces of magic what they desired most.

And she knew that because the dead ivy currently climbing along the inside of the spell-room window turned greener and more vital with every second. She'd performed a dark magic spell to bring something back to life. And it had worked. Too well. Next, she'd recloak the heart for even more practice.

Which meant tonight she should have control over the dark magic she needed.

But at what cost?

"Him," she whispered, then tucked the vial into her skirt pocket.

"This property is warded," Tor announced. "How the hell?"

The wolf crossed his arms and leaned against the trellis support beam. He was as tall as Tor, yet a wrestler's build beefed up his torso and widened his shoulders beneath a loose T-shirt. Dark brown hair clung close to his scalp, and a nick in his left eyebrow suggested an injury that he might be more proud of than upset about. Wolves rarely scarred, so this had to have been serious. On his neck, a tattoo of two small red spots resembled bite marks and—maybe they were actual bite marks. Because Tor had never met a werewolf who wasted time on tattoos. It wasn't like the ink stayed put on a shapeshifter's skin. Get a tat of *Mom* in the center of a heart? A couple shifts later, friends would question who "Norm" was.

His finger not moving from the trigger, Tor asked, "Who are you?"

The wolf thrust up a placating palm. Tor didn't sense aggression from him, but he wasn't going to let down his guard.

"Name's Christian Hart," he offered. "I was in the neighborhood and got some squicky feelings coming from this house. I like to keep an eye on the old neighborhood. Keep things calm. But I see you're on the job, eh?" One of his nostrils flared as he breathed in the air. "You're just human though."

"And who is Christian Hart?" Tor asked.

"Just a regular guy."

"A werewolf who likes to get bitten by a vampire," Tor guessed, and lowered the pistol, but he wasn't going to tuck it away.

"You think you're so smart?"

"I am. Those are bite marks on your neck."

The wolf shrugged. "Maybe so. My girl's a vamp. No way around it. But you're avoiding the obvious. What's going on here?" He shook out his arms like a prizefighter readying for a fight. "I can feel death creeping up my spine. Feels like I've got it watching me from every which way."

"Got it under control," Tor said. "The hounds can cease and vacate the property."

Hart lunged and gripped Tor by the tie, snarling to reveal his thick canines.

"Settle," Tor said. He slid the barrel of the pistol aside the wolf's hip. "The heart is making you wild. My suggestion is you leave the area, and quick, wolf."

"The heart?" His eyes searched Tor's, but he didn't release him. And Tor felt his growing anger. He could smell it. He shouldn't have used the hound reference. Werewolves were so sensitive about being called dogs. "What is *the heart*?"

"It's a…witch thing."

Hart released him and stepped back. His gaze quickly took in the garden and then the back of the house. Like an animal, he saw it all and probably smelled it all, too. "This is a witch's place?"

Tor nodded.

"I don't like witches." The wolf mock shivered. "They are a nasty bunch."

"Then you should leave. And I won't have to see how well salt rounds work on werewolves." Tor waved the pistol warningly.

"I could take you out with one swipe, human."

"Yes, you probably can. But you won't, because the aggression you're feeling now? It's not you. It's a crazy dried chunk of muscle that once belonged to an ancient witch that's attracting all the dead things to this yard, and—I'm not sure why it attracted you, but like I said, if you leave you'll feel much better. So why don't you slowly back away and get the hell out."

The wolf looked over Tor's shoulder and narrowed his eyes. Tor saw his biceps tighten and his jaw pulse. Just as he sensed he would leap, Tor lifted the pistol. Hart soared toward Tor, but his aim was high and he cleared Tor's head and landed on the vampire who had stalked up behind him.

The wolf scuffled with the vampire, snarling and growling too loudly for Tor's peace of mind. This was a populated neighborhood—though Mel's shrubbery was higher than his head. It had gotten darker, and now the rain threatened to become a downpour. He needed to make whatever this was end. Right now.

Tor pulled out the stake and stalked around the two battling creatures. Apparently, the wolf was on his side. Maybe? He could have let the vamp attack him from behind, so Tor gave him the benefit of the doubt.

Surprisingly, the vampire managed to fling the wolf

off his shoulders and toss him into a nearby shrub pruned in the shape of a cat.

Yes, a cat. Oh, the irony.

But Tor didn't take any more time to snicker over it. Plunging the stake against the vampire's chest, he compressed the paddles, and the titanium stake entered the asshole's heart. Ash formed about the stake's entry point, but the rest of the body merely shivered, convulsing.

"A bloody revenant," Hart said from the ground. He was tangled in the cat's shrubbery tail. "What the hell? How do you kill one of those things?"

"Keep an eye on it!" Tor called as he swung out of the backyard and around the side of the house. Should have grabbed the machete after all. He secured the weapon from the back of the van and sped around to the site where the vampire lay convulsing. The werewolf stood over him, growling.

With one swipe of his arm, Tor brought the machete down. The vamp's head severed from its body. The whole thing finally ashed into a pile of steaming gray flakes. Rain pattered the pile, sluicing it into a sludgy mess on the grass.

"How do you know that one was revenant?" Tor asked.

"Because I can smell its stench." Hart tapped his nose. "Superpowers, don't you know?"

"You know a lot for a wolf."

"Yeah, but what I don't know is, Why was it here? What did you do to attract that thing? Was it that heart you were telling me about?"

"Dead things are attracted to what the witch inside is using for a spell."

"Yeah? Well, I'd like to lodge a protest against dark magic in this neighborhood."

"Good luck with that. Thanks for having my back. Literally."

"No problem. And you are?"

"Torsten Rindle." He made to offer his hand, but the wolf flinched as he raised the machete, so he transferred it to the other hand and then made the offer. The wolf had a good, steady clasp.

"I've heard of you," Hart said. "And it wasn't good. You caged a friend of my girl's a few years back. Domingos LaRoque. Vampire."

"I remember him. Poor guy. But I didn't cage him." That vampire had been tortured by werewolves and now had an extreme aversion to sunlight. Not necessarily a bad thing for vamps. But, as well, he was not always there in the head. *Crazy* was putting his condition gently. "I helped him after his escape from the pack who had tortured him."

And that was all he'd say about that. Client confidentiality was key.

"I should get going," Hart said. He tossed his head sharply, flicking the rain from his face. "You're right. The vibes coming from this house are beyond wicked. But how long will it last?"

Tor tilted the dull side of the blade against his shoulder. "Should be over by morning. Full moon tonight—" He glanced skyward. Rain spattered his cheeks. Clouds covered the moon, which would later be shadowed by the earth. "But then, you know that. Which begs the question—what are you doing in the city?"

"I'm headed out to our château later," Hart said. "But I'm sticking around town as long as my growly side will allow it. My girl's due to give birth any day now and has been staying with a healer in the area who's keeping a close eye on her. I want to stay close, as well."

"Congratulations." Tor could hide his wince like a pro. A child born of a vampire and werewolf? Yikes.

A scream from inside the house alerted them both. Tor

ran onto the patio and opened the glass door. Behind him, the werewolf followed close on his heels. "I got this," Tor called as he raced through the living area.

"Yeah, we'll see," the wolf muttered, still following.

Tor ran down the hallway and into the spell room, then stopped abruptly at the sight of the vampire holding Mel against his chest. Fangs glinting, the bastard gripped Mel tight about the neck. And when Hart joined him and hissed a curse, the vampire cracked a bloody grin.

"Keep your distance, *mes amies*," the vampire said. "I want the heart. But if you're not careful, I might have to rip out her carotid and use it to tie the two of you up to keep you out of my way."

"Cocky—"

Tor caught Hart against the chest with an elbow when he felt the wolf try to rush forward. "Chill, man. Let's have a conversation with the nice vampire, all right?"

"Another revenant," Hart said.

Tor eyed the vampire keenly. The wolf was right. The vampire's eyes were red—not like a demon's, but as if a blood vessel had burst, almost obliterating the whites. He also...smelled. Tor could scent earth on him. As if he'd risen from a grave? That he could smell him, above and beyond the herbs and other scents in this room, was remarkable.

"First, I want to know how you were able to enter the witch's home without a proper invite."

Vamps could not cross a private threshold without an invite.

Mel cleared her throat. "Mortal realm rules are not relevant to a dead thing."

The vampire tightened his clutch on her.

"And," she continued, "my wards are down while I, umm…sealed the sacrifice."

Tor winced. He wanted nothing more than to tear Mel away and decapitate the vampire, but he wasn't a fool. And the vamp was closer to Mel than he was. For now.

"Is there a revenant tribe in Paris we don't know about?" Tor asked.

The vampire tilted his head against Mel's. For her part, Mel appeared calm, but Tor kept an eye on the vampire's hand, wrapped under her chin. One quick slash of those long fingernails could end the witch's life.

"I didn't come to chat," the vampire said. "And tribe business is private."

Which confirmed the question about a tribe. Rook had been correct to make such a guess.

"So is the part where I slayed half your number the other day alongside an Order knight also a secret?" Tor volleyed.

The vampire hissed. "You were the one?"

Tor waggled the machete at his side, but not too boldly. The vampire held his girl.

"You won't use that on me unless you also want her head rolling on the floor beside mine," the vampire taunted. "I've been sent for the heart. Where is it?"

If the vamp knew it was a heart, he could have only learned it from another vamp in the know. And that could only have been the one Tor had let go the other night in the alley after he'd stolen Mel's bag. His mistake.

Or was it? He eyed the vamp keenly. Did he have a chipped fang? He couldn't determine in the candlelight.

Tor averted his gaze to the plastic container that sat on a shelf below the massive wood table on which Mel must have been practicing for tonight's invocation. Beside it, a bouquet of dried roses barely hid the object. Did the vamp not sense how close it was?

Of course, there were so many witchy, magical artifacts and spell ingredients in this room. Even he would have had trouble pinpointing it had he not recognized that container. And then he had an idea…

"It's…" Tor hiked a thumb over his shoulder. "In the kitchen."

The vampire narrowed his brows at him.

"Hey, it's a freakin' heart," Tor offered. He swiped a hand over his rain-slick hair, averting the water drops from his face. "You have to store that thing on ice. It's a necessity."

Mel's eyes went wide and she nodded subtly.

"Have the wolf go get it," the vamp said.

"No, I know where it is. You stay here, Hart. Keep an eye on the dead vampire. If he so much as jerks, you take him out."

The vampire chuckled.

"You think I won't sic my dog on you?" Tor challenged.

"Wait." Hart splayed out his hands before him. "Let's get this straight, human. I am not a dog. And most important, I am not *your* dog. I thought we covered this outside?"

"We did, but then that rude vampire interrupted and I had to decapitate him." Tor waggled the machete.

"Right." Hart folded his hands before him, and both men looked to the vampire and the captured witch. "He likes cutting off vamps' heads."

"Get! The fucking! Heart!" the vampire commanded.

"Guys!" Mel yelled. "Would you please give the creepy vampire what he wants?"

Tor smoothed a hand down his tie. It was difficult to move when he was being ordered by an idiot. Who was also dead. And who held a knife on his girl.

Yeah, she was his girl.

"Tor!" Mel insisted, startling him out of a growing

smile. "Seriously. I don't want to get bitten by a dead thing today."

"Tor?" The vampire jerked her up closer against his body. "Are you the one I've heard so much about? The human who likes to spin the truth so the other humans think they've gone wacko? You were the one who fucked up the Monceau job."

"The Monceau job?" Tor crossed his arms. He really didn't like this guy. "Would that be the innocent human woman who was bitten in the park the other night?"

"She wasn't innocent. She had been chosen by our leader to become our queen."

Tor laughed and Hart joined him.

When the vampire dug in one of his sharp fingernails at Mel's neck, drawing blood, Tor stopped. And when Hart kept laughing, Tor elbowed him in the ribs.

"What is it they say?" the vampire asked. "Do not suffer a witch to live?"

Hart growled.

Tor said, "You've hurt her. Now the heart will never be yours."

"Yeah?" The vampire nodded backward toward the windows, which had darkened in the time they'd been inside. It was still raining, and a crack of lightning suddenly lit up the surrounding area.

And in that streak of lightning were illuminated the dozen faces that stood outside the windows looking in.

Revenant vampires.

Chapter 22

"Get the heart out of the kitchen," Mel muttered from behind the vampire's foul grip. The creature smelled, and she was pretty sure it was because he was dead. But if Tor was going to grandstand and waste time joking around with the strange werewolf, she was not having it. "Please, Tor!"

"I'll keep an eye on him," the werewolf said.

Where he had come from was beyond her, but she couldn't worry about that right now. She'd already tried to zap the vamp with repulsive magic, but her nerves made that impossible. She should have recloaked the heart. Fortunately, the vampire couldn't sense it so close because of the dried wild roses hanging overhead. They were a powerful block, and sometimes even repellent to vampires.

"Fine." Tor took a step back, but made a show of taking in the windows.

A dozen sets of eyes, most with white irises, peered in, giving Mel the creeps. She could handle one vampire.

Maybe. Probably not. Her nerves wouldn't allow her to even whisper a repellent spell right now. But she felt safe with Tor and the werewolf close. But if the other vampires got inside? Tor had said he wasn't a slayer. He was just the cleanup guy.

"Hurry," she managed to say.

Tor nodded and slipped around the corner. A whistled tune echoed down the hallway and into the kitchen. How the man could sing at a time like this—then Mel realized it was his fuel. He was whistling a song she recognized: "Call Me Irresponsible," about a man who realized he'd fallen in love.

Damn it, she was probably falling for him, too. Not even probably. She'd fallen hard for the guy who had killer dimples and a soft heart for levitating frogs.

The revenant's grip loosened a bit, and Mel could breathe more easily. She wouldn't move though. She wasn't stupid. But she was—curse her—curious.

"What are you going to do with the heart?" she asked. "Every dead thing in Paris has been after it. I don't understand. What use will it serve you?"

"It gives life to the dead," the vampire said. "Who wouldn't want it?"

"In case you haven't noticed, Monsieur Revenant, you *have* life. And you are dead. What difference is the witch's heart going to make?"

"Don't you understand? With the heart's power, I will be alive, not dead. No longer a revenant."

"Go for it," the wolf encouraged. "That will make you easier to kill. Beheading unnecessary." He crossed his arms high on his chest and kept his gaze to the windows. "Once you're like all the other vamps? Just a stake will do."

"He has a point," Mel said, crimping her brow as she realized she was agreeing with a werewolf. A strange, wet werewolf she had never met before. "Don't you like having the added failsafe your current status of undead provides?"

"Do you like me, witch?" The vampire nudged his nose against her ear. His hot breath wilted across her cheek. His scent resembled earth upon which mushrooms had spoiled and rotted into the ground.

"I generally do not like men who are mean to me, and who threaten to kill me," she said. "So, my answer is *no*. And you smell."

"Not my fault. Death does that to a man. Among other things, like being unable to get it up because some things are just…" He started a sigh but then caught himself as he again tightened his grip about Mel's neck. "You see why I want the heart?"

"Got it!" Tor reentered, wielding a pink plastic container high. He gave it a shake and something inside sloshed around. In his other hand, he had not let go of the machete.

Mel couldn't figure out what he might have put in the container. The real heart was under the table right now. She just hoped the vamp didn't peek inside the decoy container before taking off.

"Give it to me," the vampire commanded.

"Let her go first." Tor held the container before him in a teasing waggle. "She gets to move to the other side of the table, away from you. Then I hand you the heart. That's the only way it's going to work."

The vampire roughly shoved her away. Mel caught her forearms on the spell table, sweeping a spray of black salt to the floor. She quickly sidled around to the opposite side, but when she started toward Tor, the vampire hissed.

"Right there," he commanded. "Until your boyfriend hands over the goods."

Tor tossed the container, and while it was airborne, the vampires outside the windows clawed at the glass and made a hungry ruckus. Mel shivered. She couldn't wait for this night to be over. And this was only the preshow.

The vampire caught the container, then made to open the cover.

"Uh!" Tor put up a finger. "That thing needs to be kept on ice, and you shouldn't expose it to the volatile herbs and chemicals here in this witch's spell room."

The vampire gave the warning some thought.

"Hey." Tor shrugged. "If you want to render the thing useless, by all means, open it and give it a look over. But the heart has been on ice ever since she obtained it."

"Then how am I supposed to use it?" the vamp asked.

Mel looked to Tor for another fast retort, because she had nothing right now.

"That's your problem, thief."

The vampire snarled. The crew outside the window pushed against the windows, and the glass panes creaked.

"Keep it on ice," Tor said as a means to quiet the possible invasion. "And to use it? Just being in its vicinity activates it."

"So right now I'm growing more alive?" The vampire caressed the container greedily. "I *can* feel it."

"I suppose. But it won't last for long." Tor winked at the werewolf.

Mel furrowed her brow. What were they up to?

"It'll last as long as I keep it on ice," the vampire decided. He turned and hefted the container over his head to show his minions.

Outside, cheers rose.

And Mel could only be thankful the neighbors were away on holiday.

"I'll be going, then. I do thank you." The vampire bowed and exited out the back door into the yard.

"Stay right here. Put up a protection ward," Tor ordered Mel.

"Where are you going?"

He brandished the machete boldly before him. "Can you use vampire ash for your spellwork?"

"Always."

"Then Hart and I are going to harvest a batch for you."

The werewolf bumped fists with Tor, and the men headed out the back door.

And with the first vampire's yowl, Mel winced, but then she smiled. With a few spoken wards, she put up a screen of protection around the house and extended it as far into the yard as she could. And then she dipped to look under the table. Hecate's heart was still there, safe, nestled amidst the wild roses and...soon to prove much more harrowing than this experience had been.

She whispered a cloaking spell using her newly acquired dark magic. A shivering hug enveloped her body and she gasped. Dark magic was now hers.

And that made her more fearful than ever.

Tor thanked Hart for his assistance as the werewolf kicked a pile of soggy vampire ash on his way out of the backyard. But Hart paused and turned to count the piles.

"What?" Tor asked.

"I have a suspicion we missed him."

"Who?"

"The head vamp. The one who had your woman in his clutches. There's a dozen piles. We got all the minions, but I don't recall beheading the bastard who stole the heart. Did you?"

"No. Bollocks."

"And where is the heart?"

"It wasn't the real thing. I put a chunk of watermelon

inside a plastic box. Figured it would provide the weight and size of a heart. But you're right. I don't see the container anywhere."

"He's still out there."

"Yes, but hardly dangerous. I'm not sure how deadly a vampire and his box of watermelon will prove."

The werewolf snickered, but then winced. "Still."

"Right." Tor glanced to the patio doors. Mel had been shaken by the vampire. He needed to go to her.

"I'll sniff him out," Hart said. "You take care of your woman. You said this would be over soon?"

"If all goes as planned, midnight will end it."

Hart checked his watch. "Got a few hours to go. There's a lunar eclipse tonight. Blood moon."

"I know. Not like it couldn't have been performed at high noon. You know how witchcraft works."

The werewolf visibly shuddered. "I'd better set to the trail, and check on my sweetie. See you later, man."

"Great to know you, Hart!" Tor called as the wolf left the property.

He had no worries that the man would not track down the rogue vampire. So he strode up to the house and tried to open the patio door—but was forcefully repulsed. His body landed in the wet grass just off the patio. A sludge of vampire ash oozed near his head.

Tor could do nothing but chuckle. "Good going, witch." Her wards were back up.

From inside the living room, Mel shouted, then opened the door. "I'm so sorry! Just wait." She drew a sigil in the air and recited two words. Tor felt the air noticeably change. In fact, his whole body relaxed on the ground.

He'd better enjoy it while he had this opportunity.

"Oh, my. That's a lot of vampire ash. That'll keep the

Jones family in stock for a long time. Even wet, it will prove useful."

"That werewolf has some masterful claws. Hell of a lot easier than my machete to remove a vamp's head. He's a good guy."

"Where did he come from?" Mel stepped out and offered him a hand to help him stand. She brushed off some ash smudges from his vest and shirtsleeves. "I don't know the guy."

"He used to live in the neighborhood and was attracted to the heart. We talked it out. He's on our side. It's been quite the day, hasn't it? I'll be glad when tonight is over. What time is it?"

"Eight."

"When do you want to head to the crossroads? Is it far?"

"It's about an hour out from the city. We should leave a little after ten. I suppose you'll want to change your uniform."

He shrugged. "I'll dry off."

He kissed her then, and it didn't matter that he was covered in ash from revenant vampires or that he'd pulled a muscle in his thigh and it ached with every step. Or that he was even more determined to walk away from this lifestyle. Mel was in his arms. And that made everything better. The world in all its wrongness slipped away. He could hold her always.

"You taste like ash," she said, and then laughed. "But you also taste like Tor." She wrapped her arms about his chest and hugged him fiercely. "Thank you for everything. I need you to know that before tonight's spell."

"Why? Do you expect something to go wrong?"

"No. Maybe? I don't know. You know how my magic seems to have a mind of its own."

"It'll be good. I know it will. This is something you are

determined and focused on. Nothing will go wrong. And I'll be there in case something does."

"And what about after?"

"After?"

"You're heading off to your normal life, right?"

"Uh, right."

She shook her head. "I understand that. I'd like to change your mind, but I am the last person to want to change another's mind. In proof, I, uh…made this for you." She slipped her hand in her skirt pocket and pulled out a vial. Without handing it to him, she instead slid it into his shirt pocket and gave it a gentle pat.

Tor placed a hand over the pocket. "What's that for?"

"It's a memory spell. It'll make you forget everything you know about the paranormal. It's all done by inhalation. Might make things easier."

"Oh. Uh, thanks." He winced and rubbed the shirt pocket. "Do you want me to do that?"

"No." She stepped back, nervously swaying side to side. "Yes. Tor. I… I don't want you to leave my life. But if you have to do it, then I don't ever want to have been in it. It'll be too hard for me."

"Then maybe you're the one who should take the memory potion?"

Her heavy sigh hurt his heart. "It doesn't work on a non-human. Besides, it's… Oh mercy, it's my sacrifice, Tor. I made it for you and now it's done. My dark magic now works. And I know it because I've been able to anoint the heart and do some preparations. And I know the cloaking spell worked this time. So, yeah. That's what I did."

Hell. Him leaving her life was a sacrifice to her? He hadn't realized how much he meant to her. But he could understand, because she meant as much to him.

How was he going to walk away from her? Waltz out of

her life after tonight's big finale? He didn't want to do that. But if he had to, a loss of memory might prove the wisest course. Then he'd never have to regret having known Mel and walking away from her.

Bollocks. This sucked.

"Thank you," he said quietly.

"Thank you for not questioning me or refusing the spell, or for making this harder than it has to be. I've fallen for you, Tor. I had to say that so you would know it. At least for a few more hours, and then you'll forget it all. Oh." She kissed him quickly. "I wish we could have sex."

"We can always have sex." He would prefer a shower before tumbling into bed with her, but if she was in the mood, and they did have time...

"I want to but I also need to store up my energy for the spell. Sex with you would leave me a panting, depleted witch. A very happy witch. But in no shape for spellcraft. Especially the dark stuff."

"Then I probably shouldn't kiss you anymore."

"Oh, no, kisses are great. They activate my root chakra and ground me in my power."

"I'm not sure what you just said, but it works for me."

Lifting her into his arms, Tor carried her into the living room, and with the heel of his shoe, closed the sliding glass door behind him. He set her on the edge of the couch and leaned in to give her another kiss that would activate her root—hell, he just wanted another kiss.

Mel pulled him against her, and together they tumbled onto the couch amidst her giggles. He kissed her quickly, again and again, as if to capture each bright giggling tone. His anger at witnessing the vampire holding her captive fell away. Thankful to have her safe and in his arms, he luxuriated in their connection. It was truly magical, being lost in her strange witchery.

When Mel nudged him to the side and then showed him her palm, covered with vampire sludge from his clothing, Tor sat up and pulled her up to kiss the crown of her head.

"I'm going to take another walk around the yard, make sure we got everything," he said. "You okay in here by yourself?"

"I am."

"Did you have time to go over the spell?"

"I did. I'm as ready as I'll ever be. I'll make us something to eat before we leave, yes?"

"Sounds good." He kissed her again. "Thank you."

"For what?"

"For finding me when you needed help."

She nodded.

I can't imagine my life now without you in it. That's what Tor wanted to say, but instead, he kissed her on the forehead, then headed out to the yard.

While Tor forked up the salad she'd made, Mel left him alone in the kitchen. She told him she wanted to do a last check through her supplies and a once-over on the spell. Inside her bag, she'd packed all the accoutrements required for the big event.

But how to concentrate on the spell when all she really wanted to do was tug him into her bedroom and make love to him and wish it all away? Wish that in the morning they would wake, never having gone to the crossroads. That her mother would never again be haunted by her sister. That Tor could forget his goals of having a normal life.

"Normal." Mel shook her head. "It'll never fit him."

But she couldn't deny him the opportunity to give it a try. Because if she did somehow manage to convince him to remain in her life, he would always wonder what could have been.

She'd never been in love before. Not the sort of love where her toes tingled and her belly swirled and her smile always jumped out before she knew she was happy. But that's how she'd felt the past few days. When Tor was around, she felt silly-happy. Goofy, even. Filled with the possibility of whatever could happen between the two of them.

Who would have thought she could fall so quickly?

It was meant to be.

Best to end that tonight and move forward tomorrow.

Hooking her bag over a shoulder, she flicked off the lights in the spell room and wandered out to the kitchen.

"You packed and ready to go?" Tor cleaned his dishes in the sink, then turned, wiping his hands on a dish towel. He'd changed to dry clothing and now sported a bright red tie with his white business shirt and tweed vest. "What will my role be, exactly, when we get there?"

Mel's thoughts veered to everything she wished could happen. Like the spell being unnecessary and her mom being safe from her sister's wrath. And her falling into her protector's arms and living happily ever after. "Oh, just looking handsome."

"Huh?"

"I mean—" Shoot. That was wrong. This story was not going to give her a happily-ever-after if she wanted to help her family. And she did want that. "Well, you are handsome."

"Handsome isn't going to protect you."

"Seems to be working fine so far. But seriously, I'll need you to be on guard. I'm not sure what is going to happen. Or what creatures will be drawn to the heart while it's in use. I'll have to uncloak it for the spell. The crossroads should repel most, but you might want to load up on weapons."

"Got it. This could be a challenge for both of us."

Most especially the witch, who wasn't sure she wanted this night to end the way it would. Which could only be with Tor walking away from her.

And leaving her with an unhappily-ever-after.

An hour later, Mel sat on the passenger seat, clutching the bag of her spell supplies while Tor navigated the country gravel road. She'd dressed in an ankle-length red dress that tied in the back with black corset ribbons. It reminded her of a Victorian-style dress, but with a touch of Goth to it. It felt…ceremonial. And she needed everything she wore, touched and spoke to set the mood and tone for tonight.

The rain had stopped and clouds had cleared. The moon, blocked by the earth's shadow, was tinged with a red-orange sheen, and sat full and bright in the sky. The blood moon. She could feel the heart pulsing within the bag. It was almost as if it were aware that something momentous was going to occur.

Or something evil. And dark. And so wrong it could never be right.

Don't think like that, she cautioned inwardly. She could do this. She could. She…

"I don't think I can do this!" Mel burst out.

Tor pulled the van over to the shoulder of the road and turned to give her his full attention.

"It's crazy," she said in a panic. "I thought I could. And I really do have to. No one else in the family has the blood bond to Amaranthe like I do. But—oh." She sought Tor's gaze in the shadows. "I don't think I can kill my sister tonight."

Chapter 23

Tor shifted into Park. He turned on the van seat to face Mel. And said, "Wait. What?" He shook his head, knowing perfectly well he'd heard her clearly. "Let me get this straight."

She nodded, her big eyes gleaming in the darkness. Somewhere the full moon hung in the sky, but it didn't light up the cab.

"First, I learn you've stolen a valuable artifact that attracts revenants like the plague."

"Zombies. But yes."

"Zombies." As much as he hated to admit it, zombies did exist. Unfortunately. "Then, you tell me you're going to invoke necromancy. I was cool with that."

"Because you're a cool guy."

He did have that going for him. "But then, you tell me about the ghost. Which I had a very firm rule about not working with. It took me a while to come around, but I did."

"I forgive you for your reluctance."

Tor opened his mouth, but nothing came out. She was so…oblivious sometimes. And yet it was a cute obliviousness that he couldn't seem to resist. Heaven help him; he adored the woman.

And yet.

"But now you tell me not only are we going to raise the dead. And deal with a ghost. But also then…kill her?"

"It's how the spell is designed. Oh, but, Tor!" Mel caught her face in her hands and shook her head. "I can't do that. I can't kill my sister again."

He swallowed and forced himself to pat her on the shoulder. "You're not killing her again. It was an accident the first time. I mean…you haven't killed her before. Unless there's something you haven't told me about?"

"No! I would never raise a hand to my sister. Dead or alive."

"I didn't think so." Exhaling, he leaned to the side, his shoulder nudging the seat. Just when he thought things could not get any weirder, they did. Should he have expected as much? Probably. Mel had a way of keeping him on his toes, like it or not.

And he did like it.

"I think I've done a good job of keeping up with your antics so far, but I have to say, you're losing me here, Mel. Dare I ask why you want to end your sister's life a second time?"

"Don't you get it?"

"If I did, I wouldn't be asking. Explain. Please?"

"I can't let her live! Once the spell is invoked, Amaranthe will come to this realm not as the ghost she's been. I will literally raise her up from the grave. And the number one rule of witchcraft, even dark witchcraft? One should never raise the dead."

"Then why do it?"

"Because that's what the spell requires. I must call forth the wounded party and demand she cease her actions."

"You really think a conversation with your dead sister is going to get her to stop tormenting your mother? She didn't seem very amenable when I spoke to her at your parents' place."

"She will. I'll tell her she has to believe the truth. Oh, but Tor. How can I do this? After we've talked and she's agreed to leave Mom alone, then I have to return her to the grave in the most peaceable manner. And that involves..." She reached into her bag and drew out a crystal blade. "...this."

So much for peaceable.

She shuffled forward and bowed her head to his knees. Sniffles filled the van. And Tor, for once in his life, was without words. He didn't know what to tell her. This job had jumped the cliff that first night he'd found her waiting in the van. And since then they'd been struggling to keep their heads above the current. But now he could only see them going down, down, down a swirling whirlpool to hell. Or Beneath, which the paranormals called it.

This dark magic stuff was not for the weak of heart. And Mel's heart was full and wondrous and pink and fluffy and filled with all things good. If she invoked such magic tonight, she would never again be the same.

He didn't want to lose her to the dark side. *But you're going to lose her anyway when you step over to normal tomorrow. She gave you a freaking memory-loss spell as a sacrifice!* And if he didn't use the spell, would her sacrifice have been in vain? How would it affect her dark magic? For all purposes, it would work tonight. But tomorrow, what foul deeds might be reversed if he didn't drink the spell?

He stroked her hair. Midnight was twenty minutes away. If she didn't invoke the spell, her mother would forever be tormented by her daughter's angry ghost. Or only so long as she was still alive. If Amaranthe had her way, she'd see her mother dead sooner rather than later.

"Maybe we should think about this," he offered. "If your father could keep Star away from your sister's ghost—"

"Seriously? You saw Amaranthe. You know what state she's in. As well, my dad is barely holding it together. He almost strangled you. Tor, this has to be done. Tonight, under the blood moon. Did I tell you? Mom is on her last life."

"The ninth?" Things just got better and better. Not.

So that ruled out a slow and thoughtful approach to the situation. Which Tor felt sure the family had already considered long enough. This was a last-ditch effort to save the mom's life. And to put the sister to rest peacefully.

With a crystal blade.

Thoroughly Jones had warned Tor that whatever he'd expected to happen with Mel would not. He never could have foreseen this job ending in the witch needing to kill her sister. Dark magic or not, it was not a task he wished upon Mel.

He gripped Mel's wrist and she lifted her head. "I'll do it," he offered. "You speak the spell, then I'll plunge the knife through your sister's heart. You don't have to take that darkness into you. I've done it enough. Another—"

Mel lunged forward and kissed him. Deeply, lusciously. And for a while he forgot about the foreboding situation that faced them. He'd found a good one. Rather, she had found him. And he did not want to walk away from her. To...forget her.

How to make things different?

When she pulled away from the kiss, tears in the corners of her eyes glinted due to the sparkles that dotted the black liner curling out from each eye. She forced a smile. "You're my hero. But you can't do it." She held her palm up to show him the scar. "I'm the one with the connection to Amaranthe. And the spell maker has to be the one to do it."

"I'll speak the spell. You just tell me what to do."

"You can't enter the consecrated circle with me. And I need you to stand guard for whatever zombies or revenants come crawling up to get their hands on the heart. It's uncloaked right now."

"But, Mel, I don't want you to get hurt. Or get your hands dirty with this dark magic. You're not sure of yourself. I know that."

"I'm not. I know I don't want to be a dark witch. I'm perfectly happy with unicorns and sparkles. But it needs to be done. And I've made the sacrifice, so I don't want that to be in vain. And… I love my mom. And my sister. I want Amaranthe to rest peacefully. If I can give her that, I will." She blew out a breath. "I guess that means I'm doing it. Whew! I might need a drink after this is over."

"I've got a bottle of vodka in the back."

She quirked a brow.

"It's a good flame starter when I need to burn evidence. Also, I have been known to need a shot or two before a job. And after."

"You do the things no one else will do," she said. "And yet you remain a kind and generous man. So maybe I can do this thing tonight and the dark won't harm me too much?"

"Turning dark or remaining light at heart—I believe it's always a choice. If I didn't keep a good attitude about things, my heart would have turned black years ago. Hell,

I wouldn't be alive today, I know. It's a strange balancing act."

"I can learn so much from you. The world will have lost a great protector when you walk away from it."

"Tomorrow," he said, "isn't here yet."

"Right. Do you have the memory spell on you?"

He patted an inner vest pocket.

She bowed her forehead to his. "I don't want you to take it, but I don't want to be the one to make that decision for you. I'm giving you the option, like it or not. I… Tor, you mean a lot to me. I know we've only known each other a few days, but… I think I love you. I've fallen for you."

"I know exactly how you feel."

"You do?"

He kissed her then. Slowly, lingering in the warmth of her mouth. He felt right here. With her. Sitting in the center of a world teeming with danger. This strange witchery had lured him to the edge. Now, to step over it or cringe and turn away from it all?

"We'll take it one minute at a time," he said, and tucked the vial into the change holder by the driver's seat. "Yes?"

She nodded. "Let's get this show on the road."

He clasped her hand and bowed his forehead to hers. "You look so beautiful this evening. I'm a lucky man. And I don't want you to worry. I'll be close to you always. If you need anything, you call out. Got it?"

"If I call out…?"

"I'll come running. Promise."

Mel hefted her spell bag over a shoulder and followed Tor toward the crossroads where, two years earlier, she and her family had buried her sister. They'd chosen the crossroads because her death had been violent. They had hoped—with a spell designed by her father—to keep her at peace and buried.

That hadn't happened.

So now she would rectify that. Even though her heart was crumbling inside her rib cage right now. Someone had to do it. And it couldn't be Tor. Though she loved him for offering. If there had been a way for her to hand over the reins and let him do the dirty work, she would have done so. But magic didn't work that way. He wasn't a witch. Nonwitches could perform a few simple housewitch spells, but the real magic could only be innate, and soul deep.

Gravel crunched under their footsteps. Long grass sprang up along the edges of the old road. It smelled green and lushly fertile. Tor gestured for her to stay put while he walked the next ten feet and stood in the center of the crossroads. Two old gravel roads intersected here in the valley not far from Versailles, but far enough out that this was actually a private area that rarely saw humans. It was on land owned by Mel's dad and uncle. Someday the family may build here. She would love to live out in the country.

Tor hefted an altered rifle over one shoulder, having explained to her that it shot salt rounds, regular bullets (silver encased) and even flames. In his other hand, he wielded the machete. At his hip he wore a belt with knives and other weapons attached to it. The crystal talisman caught the moonlight. He looked like a warrior—in a three-piece suit. He'd removed the coat, and the tweed vest was dark gray. His red tie was neat, and his shirtsleeves were rolled to his elbows. He looked all business.

If a man's business were kick-assery.

Which it was.

Mel felt his intensity as a visceral warmth in her muscles. Something about a man in a suit ready for battle really did it for her. But now? Whew! If she wasn't preparing to raise the dead, she'd go after that sexy man and have her way with him.

With luck, all would go well and they could head home early and spend the rest of the night making love.

After pacing two full turns and scanning the area, Tor gestured for her to approach the center point where the barely used road formed a cross of grassy tufts between the tire ruts.

"You ready for this?" he asked.

Never! "Yes. I can do this. You think we're safe?"

"No. But I'll make sure nothing approaches while you invoke the spell. What's just beyond that forest?"

"It's an old family graveyard—oh."

Both met each other's gaze with the intense knowing that caused a sinking feeling in their guts.

"Really?" Tor asked, with all the frustration of the past few days punctuating that one word. "A graveyard. Bloody perfect."

Just the right breeding ground for more zombies. Bloody perfect, indeed. Not.

"Will you make it snappy?" he asked.

"I will work as speedily as the threat of a zombie invasion will allow."

"You going to lay down a protection circle?"

"Yes, I'll get that ready and I'll ward it so you, and nothing else, will be able to enter it while I'm invoking the spell."

"Good. Make it ironclad. I'm going to wander toward the graveyard to check out that potential nightmare. Don't worry, I'll keep you in my eyesight."

"I'm not worried," she lied. "You'll have my back. It's what you do best."

"For another few hours, anyway," he muttered.

Right. And then he'd drink a memory-loss spell and walk away from her forever.

"I'm going to take this off." He unhooked the talisman from his belt and handed it to her. "Best I see whatever comes our way."

"Are you sure?"

"Positive. Just because I can't see the danger doesn't mean it's not there. It's about time I faced up to that which most disturbs me. I'll never be able to begin a new life if I don't do that."

He had gotten wise about that. Unfortunately. Mel tucked the talisman into her skirt pocket, and before she could argue, Tor turned and wandered off.

She wished he would have kissed her before striding away. Standing beneath the moonlight at the center of the crossroads, she suddenly felt so alone. A thin cloud crept across the moon's crimson face. Crickets chirped in the long grass, but she sensed no other animals nearby, not even a squirrel or bird. Tor's footsteps *shushed* through the grass, but he was already out of sight, for the trees shadowed his position.

Midnight would toll in ten minutes. Mel set down her tapestry bag and knelt by it. She had a lot of work to do. First she took out the crystal tiara and placed that on her head. Inhaling and exhaling, she centered herself and cast a thin violet light around her. Nothing too strong. She would need access beyond her physical body.

Next she poured the salt circle about ten feet in diameter. It would provide enough space to work, and…for two people to stand in. As she finished the circle, she said a blessing, then closed her eyes to invoke the protection wards and seal herself inside. Spreading out her arms and tilting back her head, she whispered to the universe to hear her summons and join in her magic this night. It may be dark magic, but she honored all kinds and respected the elements required to make this work.

"And ye harm none; do as thou wilt" was the witch's rede that she respected. Even dark witches.

As she closed the circle, the moonlight seemed to swell and beam down upon her. Everything felt electric, from the air brushing her cheeks and hands to the glitter of moonshine on the grass blades. Mel glanced about to spy Tor walking around the circle thirty paces away, gun over his shoulder, machete swinging in the other hand, alert. When his eyes met hers, he nodded, then gifted her with a dimpled smile.

She had fallen in love with that man. And he had confessed the same to her. But would tonight's events make her lesser in his eyes? The nature of his job required him to do many evil things. Or if not necessarily evil, then bad things that needed to be done to protect the greater good. Vampires had to be slain if they proved harmful to innocents. Same with werewolves, and others. Evil was all in the perspective. So was bad. And dark. Someone had to partake of it.

As she would do now.

Pulling her supplies out of the bag, she set them on the grass. A crystal athame given to her by her father, carved from smoky quartz, had darkened over the years as he had used it in his own magic. She could feel the immense power within it, and had rarely used it herself, for it was dedicated to the dark arts. Beside that she set vials of rosemary, sage and hyssop. Red salt and a black candle. A cloth bag of tiny bones from various animals such as mouse, frog and rat. She'd left Bruce home tonight because she hadn't wanted to risk his life. There was no telling what would occur within this circle. She would invoke a willing elemental to use as a familiar for this spell.

And finally, she drew out the plastic container within which the heart pulsed. It cast a red glow from inside the blurry plastic. Mel peeled back the cover and the thing thumped as if it were inside someone's chest. Hecate, the goddess of magic and witchcraft. And necromancy. How appropriate that her heart was required for this spell.

"I honor you, Great Mother," Mel said as she placed the heart on the grass before her. It continued to beat and grew redder and glowed brighter. After arranging the rest of the items and then lighting the candle with a snap of her fingers, Mel had it all ready to go.

A tug to her dress smoothed out the skirt around her legs. A sweep of her hand brushed the hair from her face. And she felt the clock tick into the witch's hour as a tightening in her muscles and a knowing in her soul.

"All's clear!" Tor called. "Weirdly."

Yes, that was weird. But she wouldn't question a good thing. Everything could change on the turn of a thin gold euro.

Adjusting the crystal tiara on her head, Mel then began the spell with a whisper. She'd memorized the incantation. It was simple. Slowly she found a rhythm. The words were few and Latin, and must be repeated over and over until she reached a crescendo and a beat that thundered in her ears.

Gripping the crystal athame, she stood over the candle and drew the blade across her palm to drip her blood to mingle into the wax. Tilting back her head, she called up the elements of earth and fire to assist her this night of a dark summoning.

Tor altered his attention between the vast darkness that surrounded their little circle in the middle of nowhere, and the center stage where the witch with whom he had become enamored was enacting a vile and repulsive spell.

Hecate's heart glowed like a beacon. He thought, if any paranormal creatures could *not* hear the witch's chants, then surely they would be alerted by that glowing organ.

To think about witches and all the crazy things they used in their spells would make him question his sanity for engaging in such an alliance. So he didn't. Instead he kept one ear cocked for movement in the darkness. One finger on the trigger. And one eye on the beautiful witch in the breathtaking red gown.

Her chants mesmerized. Her body swayed as if with the wind. She created a dance to the sounds of her incantation; her jet hair fluttered in waves about her shoulders and elbows. The athame she waved through the air traced a red line of light that lingered long after. She drew sigils that he did not recognize, but could feel in his soul. For they made him uncomfortable and his mouth dry.

Pausing in his pacing, Tor witnessed the sudden burst of grass being mown flat in the circle center and radiating out up to his feet. Mel stepped aside, nudging the heart over with a toe. The candle flames burst to a length nearly as high as Mel's hip. And with a slash of her athame over the newly broken ground, a hand burst free from beneath.

Tor heard a growl from the darkness behind him. He spun around to face glowing red eyes.

"Bring it," he muttered.

Chapter 24

Aware that Tor had fired at something in the dark, Mel did not take her eyes from the woman who had clawed her way up from the earth to stand before her. Blonde, slender and dressed in her ragged black burial dress, Amaranthe shook off the dirt from her arms and hair. She was Mel's younger sister by eleven months. Looked exactly like her, save for the hair she'd consistently bleached since her teenage years.

Pale dead skin gleamed like moonstone under the blood moon. Even the dirt smudges and bruises discoloring her arms and neck could not alter her beauty. She embodied a tattered glamour. Or, as her father might say, a glamorous evil. Mel's eyes dropped lower. Her sister's hip bone poked out through skin and torn silk fabric.

When she finally looked at Mel, Amaranthe's blue eyes brightened momentarily with recognition. And then she snarled. "What have you done to me?"

In the distance, a creature yowled. Tor's gun echoed a few shots. And—was he whistling Sinatra?

Of course he was.

Mel clutched the glowing athame to her chest. "Amaranthe, I love you."

"Love me? You—you've raised me from the grave! How dare you? Is this the vile punishment you wish to bestow upon me?"

"For tormenting Mom? I should," Mel said defensively. Then she deflected her sudden anger. She'd not come here for a fight. "But I am not so cruel as death has made you."

Amaranthe tilted her head to the side and her neck cracked, leaving it at an unnatural tilt. "Star killed me. And now she will suffer."

"Mom did no such thing. And you know it! She was being chased by that nasty dog from Apartment B on the ground floor. You know how frightened she was of that big ugly beast. She had no idea you were driving down the street."

"Yes, well, I was driving, wasn't I? I was so angry at him!"

Mel swallowed. The reason her sister had left in a huff that evening was to go to her boyfriend's house and ask him if what her family had told her was true. Amaranthe's boyfriend had made a pass at Mel. And when Star had tried to convince Amaranthe that the fledging wizard was no good for her, she'd accused them both of lying to her.

"It was my fault," Mel said. "I never should have told Mom what he did. But he creeped me out. He suggested… things."

Amaranthe snapped up her head and looked down her nose at Mel. "It was true. That bastard had a roving eye for other women. But that doesn't change the fact that I am no longer alive, and it was because of my mother. I can still feel the moment of impact. The metal slicing through my skin and bone. Tore my leg clean off." She slapped her exposed hip bone, and her entire body wobbled as that joint threatened to give free and collapse her. "Damn it! Curse you, witch! I will rip out your heart if you do not restore me to the grave in which you laid me."

"In due time," Mel said as calmly as she could manage.

Her sister was a mess. And truly, she was torturing her by allowing her to exist in such a state. She felt the energy within the circle cringe and quickly redrew the warding sigil in the air. It lingered near Amaranthe's head in a brownish-red light that mimicked the moon's shadowed glow.

"Protection from what?" her sister asked with a sneer at the glowing sigil. "The idiot over there shooting at anything that moves?"

"Tor is protecting me while I perform this spell. It is to put you to rest peacefully, Amaranthe. And to save Mom. She has only one life remaining!"

"I know that. And she is so frightened of my incorporeal spirit. It is comical how easily I can get that feline to shiver."

Mel lifted a hand, prepared to slap her sister, but she refrained.

"Don't want to slap my head clean off?" Amaranthe retorted. "Considerate of you. What are you doing? Practicing dark magic now? Who do you think you are? I was the one following in Dad's footsteps. You and your silly light magic should know your place."

"Seowen," Mel recited.

Red thread sewed shut Amaranthe's mouth.

Mel bit the corner of her lip. She must hurry, or she would faint from utter horror. Indeed, the dark arts were not to her taste.

"Forgive Mom," she commanded. "Admit you loved her when you were alive. She is your mother. You are her daughter. Give her freedom. That woman would never harm a soul. She chases mice and then lets them flee. She loves you so much, Amaranthe."

Her sister scratched away the threads closing her mouth. "She doesn't even remember me. Or you!"

"She does. Dad teaches her and she remembers. I know she does. It is innate in us all to know our family and those whom we love. Please, Amaranthe, I love you. And I forgive you for scaring Mom off the rooftop."

Amaranthe's switchblade smile cracked her mouth open a little too high on one side.

Tor backed toward the circle, gun in hand and a stake in the other. "Almost done?"

Amaranthe turned and looked over him. "You again? I can show you things that'll make your stomach turn—"

Tor stopped and looked down. His shoes almost touched the salt. He shuffled backward.

"It should have been me!" Mel suddenly said.

Amaranthe spun to face Mel. "What did you say?"

"I should have been in the car that day," Mel said. "I know it. You know it. Your beef is with me, not Mom. I should have driven to Jacques's house and told him to leave us both alone. I should have protected you. My little sister."

Amaranthe straightened her neck with difficulty and lifted her chin. "You always did that. Put an arm around me, step in front of me when the bullies showed their might. Jacques was using me. Oh! He confessed it all when I went to him that night. Wanted to blood bond with me to gain my dark magic. He said he'd tried to take some of yours."

"I know that," Mel said quietly. She hadn't intended to tell her sister that. Jacques had chased her and attempted a binding spell on her. She'd only wanted Amaranthe to leave the man, not hate her for his wayward attentions.

"I was so angry," Amaranthe said. "Driving home in such a fit…without paying attention. I'm sorry I didn't believe you about him right away." Amaranthe bowed her head. "We always trusted one another. It's what sisters do."

"Then do one last thing for me," Mel said. "Forgive Mom and set her free. And then I will help you to rest peacefully."

The candles flickered. A cricket chirped somewhere nearby. Yet the air was heavy, as if a storm could crack open the sky at any moment. And over it all, the red moon was witness.

"I miss you," Amaranthe said. "And Dad and Laith and Vlas. We had such fun times with our cousins. And… Mom," she breathed out on a whisper.

"I think of you every day," Mel said. "You are always in my heart. And here." She splayed open her hand.

Amaranthe did the same to reveal the matching scar on her palm. Then she glanced to the glowing heart on the ground. Behind them, Tor spun and rushed to fire at another approaching predator.

"Is that Hecate's heart?"

"It is," Mel offered.

"How did you get that?"

"I stole it from the Archives when Uncle CJ wasn't looking. He's quite angry with me."

"You try so hard to be bad, Lissa. You'll never be a dark witch. You couldn't have made a sacrifice."

"I did." Mel held up her head, trying desperately not to sink into a flood of tears. She'd done what had to be done. "I can invoke dark magic," Mel said, "if it means enough to me. Like you. You mean the world to me, Amaranthe. I wish you were still alive so I could hug you."

Again, Amaranthe glanced behind her to Tor. When she turned to Mel, the look on her face was unreadable.

Her sister nodded over her shoulder. "He calls you Mel?"

"Yes, and I like it. I like him. I might even love him. I never thought a person could fall in love so fast, but it feels real."

"You never dated that often, but when you did, it was with your whole heart. He will hurt your heart, Lissa. Mel."

"That man is incapable of doing such a thing." Unless, of course, he intended to walk into normal the moment they'd finished here. "Tor is a real hero."

"Maybe. Maybe not. You need to know what he is made of before you lose your heart to him."

"He's trustworthy and brave. What more is there to know?"

"He has a secret."

"I know about the woman who killed herself."

"All of it?"

What was she up to?

"Oh, sister." Amaranthe bowed her head on her crooked neck. "I'm tired. I do want to rest. To move on."

"Then do what you must. And I will do what I must."

Amaranthe reached to touch the athame Mel held, and it glowed red when she did so.

"I don't want to do it," Mel said. "I'm pretty freaked about all this, actually. But you know me."

"You couldn't harm a fly. Don't worry. It won't hurt. And you're right, it will give me peace. I'm sorry. I've harmed not only Mom but the entire family."

"Mel!" Tor shouted.

Over her sister's shoulder, Mel sighted a gang of zombies charging toward her protector. They were much more agile than one would expect from the undead. In but moments Tor would be inundated.

No time to waste.

Mel plunged forward to hug her sister, and her hands went right through what she realized was a figment. Not even a zombie. "Do it now," she said. "Say what needs to be put into the universe. Make it real."

"I forgive Star for what I'm not even sure was her fault."

"Amaranthe."

"Very well. It was an accident. Not planned. I was in the wrong place at the right time. Curse that bastard Jacques. I love Mom," Amaranthe said. "I do."

Tor's shout indicated he was not winning, but rather, was in pain. He wasn't holding the machete. In fact, Mel saw it on the ground, far from where the zombies now surrounded him.

"I will give you peace," Mel said to her sister.

"And I will leave you with a parting gift. It has to be done. It will reveal his darkest truth. And then you can determine if he is worthy of your love."

"I don't understand."

"You will. Goodbye, Melissande. I love you. I will see you in our next reincarnation."

"Promise. *Nox restitutio!*" Mel recited, and then plunged the athame into her sister's chest. At the same time, the scar on her palm opened and began to bleed. Tears spilled from her eyes and she cried out. She'd felt the resistance of blade entering muscle. Like her sister was not a ghost but—

"Thank you," Amaranthe said. Her bleeding hand swept over Mel's hair. And then she was nothing. Not even ash or mist. Mel simply stood there holding nothing in her arms.

She sniffed at oncoming tears. Smelled blood in her hair. Squeezed her fingers as the blood dripped onto the ground. At her feet, the heart, spattered with her blood, had settled its glow. It looked rather dark and desiccated. And then she heard Tor's shout again.

Racing out from the salt circle toward the machete abandoned on the ground, she grabbed it. It was so heavy! She needed both hands to lift it.

A zombie snarled at her and pounced.

Mel used her kinetic magic to thrust the blade through the air toward Tor. A zombie leaped for it and missed its target. The machete dropped, landing in Tor's grasp. The growls surrounding him were silenced as the zombies realized who now held the power.

With a flick of his wrist and a spin of his hips, Tor cut the weapon through the multitude of zombies. Howls and yelps accompanied the ones able to run away.

With determination carving his features fiercely, Tor marched toward Mel. Just when she was close enough to hug him, he pushed her behind him with one arm and raised his gun in the other, aiming toward the zombie who crept toward the salt circle—the glowing heart was in its hand.

"No!" Mel pushed Tor's arm, and his aim missed the zombie. "It'll damage the heart! If you destroy it, all the witches in the world will die."

He met her frantic gaze. "Bollocks." Dropping the gun, Tor rushed the zombie and jumped onto its back. The heart wobbled and fell onto the grass.

"Duck!" she heard, and instead of looking for her pet, she did as she was told. A zombie soared over her head.

Tor stomped past her, stake in one hand and the machete in the other. He jumped onto the fallen zombie and staked it in the heart, then drew the blade across its neck.

Stumbling backward, he dropped the stake. His foot landed on uneven ground, toppling him to a sitting position. And for the first time, Mel noticed how torn-up and battered he was. He bled from a cut on the forehead. His shirt was shredded. A long slash down one thigh bled onto the ground.

The beheaded zombie body convulsed on the ground as it dechunked.

"Don't look!" Tor called. He turned and pulled himself up, then caught her and turned her back toward the circle. "You don't need to see that."

Mel nodded. Not like she hadn't seen worse. But his concern bolstered her. And his embrace reassured her like nothing else ever could. In his arms, she was safe. And loved. Now to keep that feeling for their short time that remained.

"Is your sister at peace?" he asked.

He clung to her, and she realized it was for support more than anything. Mel nodded. "She is."

"You did good."

"So did you."

"There's cleanup to do. Gotta bury the remains. I'll need some time."

"You want me to help?"

"Nope. This is what I do. Or did do."

Please, no. She didn't want him to leave his life behind. And her.

But that was not her choice.

"I'll gather my things and wait in the van," she quietly offered.

"Give me twenty minutes."

Mel nodded and started toward the salt circle. But she stopped when the pale woman in a long white tattered dress bent over the salt and picked up the pulsing heart. "Oh mercy. Tor!"

Her protector rushed up behind her.

"There's one left," Mel said.

"Not this," Tor said on a gasp. "Charlotte?"

"Who's Charlotte?" And then Mel remembered. She was the woman who had killed herself because Tor had not been there to rescue her from the ghost haunting her tormented soul.

This was her sister's parting gift.

Chapter 25

Tor swallowed and reached for the crystal talisman—that he'd handed over to Mel because he had thought he was beyond the need for it. And he had been. But he'd not expected to see the one person who had given him reason for the safeguard in the first place.

How could she be here? He'd never seen her before as a ghost. Of course, he'd always worn the talisman.

"Charlotte," he said on a heavy breath.

The specter stood in the salt circle, clutching the pulsing heart to her chest as if it were a wondrous child's toy. Her short red hair flitted about her head and—she didn't look like a decaying zombie, but her skin was blue. Tor could still remember finding her body that cold February morning. He hadn't believed a person's skin could be so blue. And her lips, as well as the bruising under her eyes, were purple black. She'd worn a floaty white dress, one she'd once told him had been her first-communion dress.

The ghost standing in the circle suddenly noticed him, her attention veering from the heart but her fingers clutching deep into the pulsing muscle. "Tor?" Her lips struggled with a smile. "Is that you? What are you—you can see me now?"

He nodded. Behind him, he was aware of Mel's presence, but she stood off to the side. He had slain all the zombies. He hoped.

Not sure what to do, he stepped toward the circle. "Yes, I can see you, Charlotte."

"You've avoided me for so long. You terrible, terrible man. Why did you do that? I've been pleading for your attention. Tearing my hair out to simply get you to notice me. Did I disappoint you when I did as I was told and cut my wrists in the bathtub? Such a peaceful death, that."

"No," he said calmly. He had no desire to fast-talk his way out of this one. He needed to face her. But his knees grew weak and his fingers trembled at his sides. He didn't notice the machete had slipped out of his hand. "I was never disappointed, Charlotte. I loved you."

"You don't anymore?" She crushed the heart, and blood dripped down her white dress.

"If she destroys that heart..." Mel hissed from behind him. "Tor!"

Charlotte took in the witch with a sneer. "I've been watching you with her. You notice her. You love her. Why could you never love me like that, Tor?"

Another squeeze of her fingers against the heart pushed out more blood from the thing. Its pulsing had slowed.

He approached cautiously, fully aware that he should not step into the circle with her. That would give her the ability to connect with him on a visceral level. "Charlotte, you should set down that heart. You don't need it."

"But it will give me life." She hugged the thing tightly. "I can feel it."

Behind him Mel groaned.

Tor turned to look over his shoulder to find Mel had fallen to her knees, and she clutched her throat. Was Charlotte's squeezing the heart taking away Mel's life? The life from all witches?

"Please, Char, you can't have life. You'll never be as you once were. You'll always be like this."

"What's wrong with me, Tor? I'm like all the other ghosts you can see. Are we not your closest friends? Don't you like me now? Am I not pretty enough for you? Why did you never want me as a lover? I was so in love with you."

He'd known that, but he'd only ever felt Charlotte was a friend, and hadn't been in the frame of mind to start a romantic relationship with another screwed-up person who could also see ghosts and who was slightly mad. Yes, he'd had a bit of better sense back then. Unfortunately, he'd never had the courage to tell her that and had allowed her awkward flirtations. A cruel manifestation of his own cowardice.

"You are so beautiful," he offered. "But you must stop squeezing that heart. It's getting your dress all messy. And if you break it, it won't work anymore."

She bowed her head over the fading heart, and a teardrop spilled onto it and dripped off in a bloody splat onto her bare blue foot.

"You can have it." She thrust it toward him.

Tor took a step, but at Mel's groan behind him, he realized his toe touched the salt circle. He wasn't sure if it was keeping Charlotte in, and didn't want to test that theory by breaking the line.

"Toss it to me," he said. "I hurt my leg and it's hard to

walk." It was true. And blood did stain his pants leg. But as Charlotte bent to study his thigh, she clutched the heart to her chest again, keeping it well out of his reach and inside the circle.

Charlotte looked up at him and lifted a haughty chin. "You're protecting her, aren't you?"

"Of course I am. She hired me to do a job. I told you about my work."

"And look how well you are doing that job. She lies on the ground near death. You can't take care of any woman, Torsten Rindle. You fail us every time."

Indeed. And even more reason to step away from the protection business. Who was he to believe he could make a difference by swinging a machete or wielding a stake? Ridiculous. The spirit was right. Mel would be better off without him in her life.

"Failure," Charlotte repeated. "As a friend, a man and even as a protector." The ghost let out a throaty chuckle that tightened Tor's skin and lifted the hairs all over his body.

And with that, Charlotte hoisted the heart high. Blood drooled down her wrist and forearm. A squeeze made it glow brightly, and then she thrust it toward Tor. He leaped to catch the thing in his hands, finding it was difficult to grasp the slippery thing. He stumbled and went down, landing on his back near Mel.

But the growl from inside the circle rolled him to his side. Charlotte's visage changed, her skin brightening to an unreal blue and breaking open to beam out brilliant red light from within. Her eyes glowed white and her mouth opened to snarl with a toothy maw.

Managing to tuck the heart against Mel's chest, he heard her whisper, "You have to sacrifice for the dark magic to take her down."

"Sacrifice? But what? How?"

"She needs to die before the heart does."

"I've never slain a ghost. I'm not sure..."

"Your sacrifice will give her the peace she deserves."

A bone-crunching howl filled the air. Tor scrambled up to a stand, limped toward the machete and grabbed it. In the distance, he saw movement near the graveyard. "More zombies," he muttered. "Can a bloke get a break?"

Charlotte's ghost had increased in bulk and muscle and now stomped the ground outside the circle. The grass browned under her steps. Mel swore and whispered an incantation.

The ghost slapped down a hand on the grass, and it burned a flaming path up to Mel. Her skirt ignited. The witch screamed and scrambled away, leaving the heart lying but inches from the fire. Tor jumped to extinguish the flames.

When Charlotte approached him, he pressed the tip of the machete to her chin. The blade moved through her figment, a useless weapon against an incorporeal specter.

The ghost gripped the sharp blade, and it turned red as an ember. Tor felt the heat of the metal permeate the hilt, and within seconds he was unable to hold the burning weapon. He dropped it.

"Tor!" Mel yelled.

He looked over his shoulder and saw the crystal talisman soaring through the air toward him. He reached to grab it—but at the last second, retracted his hand.

Not seeing Charlotte wasn't going to change anything. And it would only piss her off all the more. It was time he faced his demons.

The crystal talisman hit Charlotte in the chest, and instead of going through her, it lodged there. She yowled and slapped a hand to it, but couldn't get it out of her chest.

Tor wasn't sure what it would do to her. It had only been charmed so he couldn't see ghosts and protect himself from their attack. It symbolized that which had most frightened him. His greatest fear was now standing before him, and…

He stepped up and grabbed Charlotte by the face, one hand to each side of her head. His hands did not go through her figment, but instead he felt her as a solid, cold being radiating with a fiery heat that must be from the crystal.

"I loved you then and I love you still," he offered. "As family. As two souls who needed one another. We both know ghosts have power, Charlotte. And your mind was half in and half out of the two realms. They would have gotten to you sooner or later, no matter if I had been there that night or not."

She struggled against his hold, but he held her firmly. The talisman in her chest beamed brightly and he smelled sulfur, as if the demonic were burning its way out of her.

"Take the peace you deserve," he said. "But if you choose to stay as you are, I will accept that. And I promise you I will never wear that talisman again. I will see you always. I will allow you to haunt me as you see fit."

The ghost's eyes teared up, and now her smile was genuine. "You would do that for me?"

He had to. He would. Tor nodded.

She touched the crystal, and now her whole body glowed a brilliant white. "I can feel you in this. Your kindness. Your strength. Your compassion. It's taking the darkness from me. The spirit that haunted me has been inside me since my death. I haven't been able to get free from it. Tor…you have released me."

"I don't understand."

"Your unselfish ways have helped so many. I love you." She clasped the crystal and pulled it from her chest.

As Tor stepped back, he watched a great spume of black

smoke trill out from Charlotte's chest and dissipate in the air above her head—as if a demon being exorcised.

"It's gone." She dropped the crystal onto the grass, and then her figment flickered and dispersed.

"Charlotte!"

Tor dropped to his knees inside the circle and bent over the glowing crystal. And in that glow, he felt the years of friendship they had shared bubble up like laughter. It felt giddy in his heart and lightened him. And he smiled as he wrapped his arms across his chest.

"Be at peace, Charlotte. I love you."

Who would have thought the one thing he'd carried with him for years could be the thing to set both him and his lost friend free? He picked up the crystal. It felt light, and it sparkled as if dunked in faery dust. Over the years it had taken on the shadows and dark vibrations of all those ghosts he'd not wanted to deal with. And now…it had been cleansed.

He hooked it at his belt and pushed up from the grass. Brushing the salt from his palms, he shook his head and looked up to the moon. It was lighter now, white and bright, no longer red. It was as if the moon had also been cleansed.

He stepped backward, and his foot crushed the machete blade into the ground. Turning to pick it up, he then saw Mel lying on the ground beneath a spindly maple tree, her eyes closed, the red skirts splayed out like blood. The heart beside her did not pulse or glow red.

"Mel!"

Plunging to the ground beside her, he shook her head, but she didn't respond. The hem of her skirt had burned, but he didn't see any damage to her leg. Frantically, h bowed to place an ear over her heart. He could still he her heartbeat, but she felt cold and lifeless.

"No, it can't be like this." He grabbed the heart, w

resembled a hunk of dried meat. He shook it. "It's not broken." He examined it and found there were no cuts or breaks where he'd earlier seen the blood ooze out when Charlotte had squeezed it. "It's fine. It was just a squeeze." There were no burn marks on it from the fire. "Mel?"

The sudden chirring whine of a cicada sounded, and from the tree above dropped an insect that landed on Mel's chest. Tor watched it crawl slowly across the red fabric up to her shoulder, where it paused and seemed to look at him. He swallowed. A smile was irrepressible. Really?

With a spread of its wings, the cicada rose into the air for a few seconds, then landed on the heart he held. Tor lifted the organ to study the insect more closely.

"I wish I could have known you. I have loved you all my life."

In response, he felt an overwhelming warmth flood his chest. The meaning was unmistakable. Tor nodded. "You love me, too? I know you do."

With that, the cicada took to flight, a slow journey that wobbled her over the salt circle and higher into the air until Tor could no longer see her wings glint with moonlight.

"That was freakin' cool."

He turned to the smiling witch beside him. "You're alive?"

"Of course I'm alive. What? Did you think I was dead?"

"Yes. The heart. When Charlotte squeezed it..."

"It felt like my heart was being squeezed. It's possible every witch in the world felt it. But if I'm alive, that means we're all alive." He set the heart on her lap and it began to glow. "You did it, Tor. You saved the world."

"I didn't save anything. You're the witch with the amazing dark magic. You gave your sister peace."

"And you gave Charlotte peace with the sacrifice of your need to be safe from ghosts. We both did all right."

"That we did." He kissed her, then stretched onto his back to lie beside her.

She tilted her head onto his shoulder, one hand gently clasped about the pulsing heart. "I love you. Is that weird to say? We've known each other just a few days, but it feels…real."

"It is real. As real as the cicada that landed on your chest and made me understand that my mom is always watching over me. I love you, too, Mel."

They clasped hands and looked up at the star-speckled sky. It was difficult to see stars when in Paris. One had to travel out to the country, away from the city lights. And tonight dazzled with a thick constellation of starlight, with the moon as the spotlight.

Mel turned and looked at the side of his face while he stared up at the stars. "You know something? I don't feel all that dark right now. I actually feel pretty good that I was able to help my mom and sister. But I couldn't have done it without you."

"And I couldn't have given Charlotte her freedom without your support. And this." He waggled the quartz talisman above them. "It cleansed her of the evil that had been inside her since before her death. Amazing."

"You do know that a talisman is just an object. It's the belief of the owner that provides the real magic."

"I did not know that."

"You did it all by yourself, Tor. With or without a chunk of crystal. It was all you."

It was an interesting concept, and it would take him a while to accept it. Tor hooked the crystal at his belt loop, then took Mel's hand again. "We should date," he said. "We're kind of perfect for one another. You balance out my extreme side."

"You tolerate my goofy side."

"You make amazing smoothie bowls."

"You are a fashion rock star. I've never been so attracted to a man in a tweed vest in my life."

"You have weird pets."

"You have OCD."

"You like to talk to flowers and sing to the sky."

"You have a talent you don't recognize."

"I recognize it. I'm just..." He sighed. Though the vial tucked in his pocket was virtually weightless, he felt it heavily upon his heart now. "There is that goal of mine."

"I know. We both know. And we're ready for it. Like it or not, it's how the universe wants us to be. We should get on the road. It's late. Or rather, early."

Tor checked his watch. "Really? 4:00 a.m.?"

He had four hours before his interview.

As the two stood and turned to the van, Tor picked up the abandoned crystal tiara and put it on Mel's head. "Wear this. Always. Sparkles and unicorns. It's you." He kissed her. "I'm not tired. I think I'll head home for a quick shower and straight on to the interview."

"Sounds like a plan. But we have one problem to take care of before we go anywhere."

"What's that?"

She pointed toward the van, where a werewolf crouched on the top and growled at them.

Chapter 26

Mel had just enough energy to summon a repulsion spell, and combined with the infusion of dark magic she'd worked, she had never felt more powerful. However, when she thrust out her hand toward the werewolf standing on top of the van and opened her mouth to recite the spell—Tor grabbed her wrist and spun her around to face him, effectively obliterating any magical energies that may have zapped the predator.

"Holster it, Mel. I know that wolf."

"You do?" She squinted at the beast now crouched and peering at them with big gold eyes. How could a person determine one werewolf from another? They were all hairy and ugly, and their heads were wolflike while their bodies were sort of still human, except übermuscly and—so much hair!

"That's Christian Hart. You met him earlier."

"Oh." She put down her casting hand. "You sure?"

"Hart!" Tor waved to the beast.

The werewolf jumped from the van, landed in a crouch, then stood. As he strode toward them, he shifted in a matter of seconds. His head grew smaller and human shaped, and arms and legs conformed to the normal human length. Hair disappeared from his body to reveal pale skin and... no clothes.

"Whoa!" Tor put a hand before Mel's eyes, but she tugged it away. Because that was a sight. "Bloke, would you mind the lady?"

"Sorry." The wolf, now completely in human form, covered his erect penis with both hands. "That happens when I come back to were shape. Clothing never shifts with us. It's just the way things work."

Tor slid off his vest and handed it over to the man. Hart took it. It would not wrap completely about his waist, but he was able to hold it before him and clasp it at his hips.

"What are you doing out here?" Tor asked. "Hunting grounds?"

"You know it. If I'd known you were headed this way, I might have gone the opposite direction. What's going on here?"

"You didn't see the zombies?" Mel asked. The moonlight had a certain way of highlighting the man's incredible muscles, and she pulled in a sigh at the flex of his biceps. Did they glisten? Ahem. "They almost killed Tor."

Tor cleared his throat. "I had things under control."

"I thought you were going to stop the dead things from wandering about?" Hart asked.

"We did!" Mel hugged Tor with glee. "It's all over now. Hecate's heart has served its purpose."

"Yes, but we still have to secure that thing under lock and chain," Tor said, then asked the werewolf, "Did you ever track down the vampire from the yard?"

"Crying over a box of watermelon. Ha! That was a sight. He's been dealt with. But… I can still feel it." Hart pointed to the heart Mel hugged to her chest. "And other things do, too." He looked over a shoulder, scanning the darkness. "You two should probably get the hell out of here while the getting is good. Might be more zombies…" The werewolf sniffed the air. "That is the rankest scent. Maybe just one though."

"Then you can handle that. You've experience." Tor clasped Mel's hand. "Let's give CJ a call and tell him we're on our way with the heart."

"He won't appreciate being woken up so early."

"It's either that or the zombie apocalypse."

"A phone call it is!" Mel started toward the van, yet managed a look back at the werewolf. Yep. Nice ass. "We'll have to meet when there aren't zombies or revenants, Hart!" she called as she crossed in front of the van to the passenger side.

"I agree! Good luck to the both of you. Uh, Tor, you want your vest back?"

"Nope. You keep it."

"Doesn't fit." The wolf rubbed it back and forth across his groin.

"Really not interested in wearing it again," Tor said. With a wave, he sent off the werewolf, who dropped the vest and, as he ran toward the darkness, shifted to a four-legged wolf.

Tor slid inside and started up the van.

"I could wash the vest for you," Mel offered.

"I have others. And did I notice you were drooling over a certain wolf?"

"Well, come on. He was naked!"

Tor chuckled. "The guy does have some muscle on him." He wrinkled a brow as he thought about that statement. "So! On to the Archives. You call your uncle. And I'll prepare to face the dark witch's wrath yet again. Good times tonight. Good times."

Forty-five minutes later, Certainly Jones met them at the Council headquarters, which housed the Archives down a long, narrow alleyway that no one would ever suspect led to anything so fantastical as an organization that collected magical objects and was dedicated to policing paranormals of all breeds and species. And that was exactly the way they preferred it.

CJ strode down the alleyway, stopping Tor and Mel before they got close to the entrance. Mel figured her uncle wasn't about to let her get inside the building again. Fair enough.

She handed over the plastic container, and CJ whistled as he shook his head. "I can't believe you slipped this out without me noticing."

"Yes, well, I do have my talents."

"Thievery?"

"It did serve a purpose. Mom is now safe. Our family can finally begin to mend."

CJ glanced to Tor, who was looking the worse for wear. Blood was caked on his brow. A slash in his trousers revealed thigh, and his frayed shirt would have to be trashed, but he was smiling. Mel squeezed his hand.

"What repercussions should we expect?" CJ asked as he tucked the container under an arm. "Where did you perform the spell? What, exactly, was the result?"

Tor reeled off the latitude and longitude of the crossroads. "Just east of Versailles."

CJ nodded. "Our family land."

"I was able to talk to Amaranthe and get her to forgive Mom," Mel provided. "Then I gave her peace. And then Tor saved the heart from getting crushed by his dead girlfriend."

"Friend, not girlfriend."

"Crushed?" CJ rubbed his throat. "That explains a lot. A few hours ago, I thought I was suffocating. Was trying to figure who was working a spell on me. I warded myself quickly, but it lingered."

"That was the heart. It was almost destroyed. But it's all good now." Mel rapped the plastic box with her knuckles. "Put this in a steel box and throw away the key."

"Your visiting privileges have been revoked," CJ admonished.

"Oh, come on! I love researching spells in the stacks. That's how I learn. I promise I won't ever steal from you again."

CJ's look did not indicate trust. "I will consider it. But at the very least, you'll be grounded from the Archives for a good six months."

Mel pouted. "Fair enough."

"You call your dad?" CJ asked.

"Texted him. Didn't want to wake him. I would have texted you, but Hecate's heart really does need to be put away. Now."

Tor glanced behind them down the alleyway. "Yes, now."

"Got it." CJ shook a finger at Mel. "I don't approve of your methods, Lissa, but I am glad you got the job done. Your poor mom and dad needed this. You stepped up. You've done the family proud."

"Thank you. But I, uh…"

CJ tucked the plastic container under an arm and gave her his full attention.

"I'm not so sure I'm cut out to be a dark witch," Mel

offered. "It's not me. At all. But Dad would be so disappointed—"

"No, he won't." Her uncle clapped a hand onto her shoulder and bent to meet her gaze. "TJ loves you, Lissa. No matter what kind of magic you practice. And hell, maybe the family needs a light witch to balance out the dark, eh? Vika once practiced only light. I say you should honor the witch you are and don't try to be something you are not. You want me to talk to your dad about it?"

"Thanks, CJ." She hugged him, then tapped the container. "We should leave you to tuck that away. I've seen more than enough zombies in the past few days for a lifetime, thank you very much."

CJ extended a hand to Tor, who shook it. "Thank you. You've kept my niece alive. The Joneses owe you for that."

"You'll get my bill," Tor said.

CJ disappeared into the building, and the twosome strolled toward the van, hand in hand. Tor checked his watch. "Ah, hell."

"What?"

"It's already seven thirty?"

"Your interview is at eight."

"I don't have time to run home and change." They stopped at the van, and he opened the door for Mel and helped her up inside.

"Does that mean you're going to skip it?" she asked.

"I would never miss an appointment."

"Oh." Her shoulders dropped. She wasn't going to mention the memory potion. She'd seen him tuck the vial back in his shirt pocket. She'd lost him after all.

Her heart fell in her chest. But she lifted her head and did her best to keep back the tears.

"Besides..." Tor reached up to adjust the tiara on her

head. "I know exactly how this is going down, and I wouldn't miss it for the world."

But she wouldn't mind missing it. Mel nodded and forced a smile. "Onward?"

"Buckle up. We have to make the city limits through the crazy morning rush-hour traffic."

The office building was situated in the center of La Défense district, nestled amidst the tallest structures in Paris. It gave off the closest atmosphere to New York, Tor had once decided of the busy metropolitan area.

Having easily passed by the snoozing security guard in the building lobby, he now strolled down an aisle between cubicles that led toward the conference room, where the receptionist had directed him and where the meeting was to take place. As he passed the desks, workers turned to stare, openmouthed, hands to chests. A few gasps were audible.

When he neared the room, which was open, he straightened his tie and slid his hand down the length of it—which stopped midchest thanks to the zombie who had managed to slash a claw through the imported silk.

Shit happened.

"Monsieur Demengoet?" He entered the conference room and spied the bald man sitting at the end of a long table with a few file folders spread out before him. "Torsten Rindle. At your service."

Tor pulled out a chair. He set the machete he'd had tilted over a shoulder onto the glossy wood table, placed the gas mask he'd hooked at his belt next to it, then sat, put up his shoes on the table and offered a smile to the stunned interviewer.

"Monsieur Rindle, what is this?"

"Uh, the machete? It's standard gear for beheading vampires and zombies. It's sweet." He patted the weapon, then glanced out the doorway. Down the hallway, a bunch of heads observed, like gophers popping up from their holes. "It's a tool of my trade."

"This is highly uncalled-for. How did you get past security?"

"I strolled in. Don't worry. I'm not going to use it here. I just got off a job. As you can see. A bit untidy, but you know, that's what the job requires. And I am a man who goes all-in, full-out, whenever he's called to do the task. Would you like a list of my skills? Not only am I an expert with the blade, but my marksman skills are exemplary. I'm also keen on the chemical compositions required for proper crime-scene cleanup. I can twist any story to make your head spin. And…" He tugged a vial out from his shirt pocket and set it on the table before him. "I'm not afraid to use magic when necessary."

The man sputtered and slammed the file folder shut. "I don't know what sort of charade you are trying, *monsieur*, but I have had enough. Vampires and werewolves? You are a lunatic!"

"Far from it. I am a necessary asset to society. I make sure people like you don't believe in all the bad things that could happen to them, especially the bad paranormal things. If I didn't do my job? There would be chaos."

"Then why are you seeking a new job?"

Tor leaned forward onto his elbows. "You know, I thought I needed a change. To walk away from that which I have embraced all my life. Call it a ghost story. A silly fear. And toss in a bit of love story, as well. But I've overcome that, thanks to a helpful, weird and breathtakingly gorgeous witch."

"A witch—"

"She made me understand that I do what I do because I can, and because I enjoy it. Which I do. Can't lie. Taking out a clutch of zombies is incredibly satisfying. You've never seen something until you've watched a dead thing dechunk."

"I am going to call security."

"No need." Tor stood and propped the machete over his shoulder. "I just had to come here and put myself in this atmosphere. To know that it wasn't right. And it's not. I could never function enclosed in one of those confining beige cubicles. I need to remain freelance and ready for action."

He picked up the gas mask.

"Now, I know what you're thinking. If this guy is so good with spin, how's he going to spin an entire office building into believing he was never here? That he didn't march in with a big-ass machete and make a spectacle of himself?"

The interviewer merely huffed.

Tor clasped the vial. "Sometimes a guy has to rely on witchcraft. Thanks for your time, Monsieur Demengeot. Just hope you never see me in the future. Because the only way that'll happen is if the big bads have come for you. And if they do? I'll know. Have a nice day."

With that, Tor pulled the gas mask over his head and face. Next, he flicked the cork out of the vial and then waved it around in the room. As he strolled back down the hallway, he waved the vial before and behind him. Everyone dodged this weird action. One man fainted.

"Stay safe!" he called as he grabbed the door handle. Tossing the vial into the garbage can broke the thin glass. The spell would suffuse the room and overtake everyone in the vicinity with a memory relaxer that should erase what they believed to be paranormal. And since he was toeing the line of all things strange and paranormal, it should obliterate memory of his visit, as well. "Fight the good fight!"

He pumped a fist in the air and wandered out to the curb where the van was parked. Mel had moved into the driver's seat, so Tor hopped in the passenger side.

"You get the job?" she asked as she pulled away and onto the main road.

"Absolutely not." Her double take made him smile.

"Oh. Are you, uh…you bummed?"

"Nope. You got any more silly questions?"

"One more. Did you use the memory spell?"

"I did." Tor set the machete behind him on the van floor. When he looked up, Mel gaped at him. "When I was wearing this." He waggled the gas mask and then tossed it in the back. "The whole office will forget any strange talk of zombies and other creatures. But I will not."

"So that means you…don't want normal?"

"Absolutely, without question, no. That would be the most boring, obnoxious, unexciting existence I could imagine."

"And…" Her words were barely a whisper. "…us?"

"You still up for dating?"

She nodded eagerly. "You want to come home with me and crawl into bed and have wild sex until we both fall asleep from exhaustion?"

"Absolutely."

Epilogue

A week later...

Sinatra sang "Witchcraft" through the radio speakers while Tor held Mel in a close dance hold. The twosome swayed on the patio, their heartbeats synced, breaths tinged with the excitement of holding a lover. The sun had set and the night flowers had opened to release their heady perfume.

Bruce levitated near a red candle that flickered in the middle of a rose-petal circle. Duck waddled over the grass, plucking at unfortunate snails.

Off in another Parisian arrondissement, Thoroughly and Star Jones were packing their things in preparation to move out to the countryside and build a retirement cottage. They intended to enjoy every moment of Star's last life. In the safest way possible.

And somewhere in the neighborhood, a werewolf and

his vampire lover were cooing over their newborn daughter, who would grow into a half vampire/half werewolf, who would someday fall in love with a man who was her complete opposite in every frustratingly impossible way, and with whom, after much trial and romance, she would live happily ever after.

"Do you believe in happily-ever-after?" Mel asked Tor as she snuggled closer to his warm, hard, muscled chest smelling of sweet cherry tobacco.

"I want to."

"I'm not sure it's so easy to have."

"Wouldn't be worth having if it was easy."

"I don't know. I kind of like pushing the easy button every now and then."

He tilted her into a sudden, heart-pounding dip and bowed to kiss her. "I can give you *easy* every now and then." He waggled his brows and pulled her up and into his embrace.

"I like you easy. I also like you hard. Really hard." She hugged her hip against his groin, and Tor moaned as his erection tightened. "I like you any way I can get you, as long as I get you."

"You have me, witch. Two weirdos who will always be chasing normal—"

"But who never want to catch it."

"Exactly. I think Bruce is getting too close to the flame. Bruce!"

The frog ribbited and adjusted his angle to barely avoid the candle flame. Bruce then hovered away, but not without casting Tor a look of disdain.

"That is the most judgmental frog I've met," Tor said.

"He likes you."

"He tolerates me."

"I'll have a talk with him. You'll be spending a lot more time here?"

"You won't be able to get rid of me. Though I did get a text right before we came out to the patio. Something about a missing book on werewolves. The text was sent from the Agency CEO, Dez Merovich, in the States. Smells like trouble."

"Sounds intriguing."

"Sounds not normal. Just the way life should be."

"The normal stories are never very interesting."

"I prefer my stories weird."

"Here's to our weird story," Mel said. "May it be filled with adventure, romance, hot sex and that elusive happy ending."

Her lover bowed to kiss her and a flutter of sprites sparkled up from the grass to circle their heads, while off in the yard, Bruce levitated near Duck. If a man knew how to speak amphibian, he may have guessed the familiar's croak to have been, for once, approving.

* * * * *

Author Note

I hope you enjoyed this, the final story for Harlequin's Nocturne line. It's been such a joy to write paranormal stories for this line, and it is with great sadness I say goodbye to it. I wrote one of the first Nocturnes, *From The Dark*, and over the years have created a world I call Beautiful Creatures. All my Nocturnes (save a few) are set in that world, and while you don't have to read them in any particular order, they do all mix and match characters and families that are related. I've tried to list at the end of each book which secondary characters also have stories. For a complete downloadable pdf book list, visit my website at: MicheleHauf.com.

This is not my final paranormal romance by any means. I will continue to write in my world. As well, I will be writing for Harlequin's Intrigue line and get to exercise my love for romance, suspense and action-adventure (I'll try to keep vampires off the pages of those stories). For updates on my new releases, do follow me on social media:

Facebook.com/MicheleHaufAuthor
Twitter.com/MicheleHauf
Instagram.com/MicheleHauf
Pinterest.com/toastfaery
HaufsBeautifulCreatures.tumblr.com

Here's to a weird happily-ever-after!

Michele

Southern born and bred, **Kristal Hollis** holds a psychology degree and has spent her adulthood helping people and animals. When a family medical situation resulted in a work sabbatical, she began penning deliciously dark paranormal romances as an escape from the real-life drama. But when the crisis passed, her passion for writing love stories continued. A 2015 Golden Heart® Award finalist, Kristal lives with her husband and two rescued dogs at the edge of the enchanted forest that inspires her stories.

Books by Kristal Hollis

Harlequin Nocturne

Awakened by the Wolf
Rescued by the Wolf
Charmed by the Wolf
Captivated by the She-Wolf
Tamed by the She-Wolf

Visit the Author Profile page at Harlequin.com.

TAMED BY THE SHE-WOLF

Kristal Hollis

To everyone on the Nocturne team. Thank you for not only making my dreams come true, but also making them shine.

Chapter 1

"*Dayax!*"

Having shifted into his wolf form under cover of night, Lincoln Adams eased farther into the dilapidated two-story building, shot-up and abandoned long before he and his team had arrived in Taifa, a war-torn village in southern Somalia and home to the Yeeyi pack.

Wahyas, an ancient species of wolf shifters who were caught in the middle of escalating human conflicts, faced a greater likelihood of unintentional exposure. To minimize the risk, the Woelfesenat, the secretive international wolf council, developed elite Special Forces teams called Dogmen. Their primary function: safeguarding Wahyas in harm's way while aiding human allies in their worldwide peacekeeping endeavors.

Since their arrival in Taifa six months ago, Lincoln's Dogman team had been providing support to UN forces defending the area against militant insurgents and administering humanitarian aid.

Dayax, an orphaned wolfling who'd made himself somewhat of a daily pest at their base of operation, had disappeared from his village during the guerillas' morning raid.

Tonight, Lincoln's mission, though not officially sanctioned, nonetheless fell within the scope of his sworn duties. Still, he'd chosen to conduct the search and rescue alone.

Sensing movement behind him, Lincoln spun around, baring his teeth, and issued a low, threatening growl. Five dark, stealthy figures covertly closed in on the building.

Damn ass-wipes.

Affection flooded his wolfan body while he watched his team, in their human forms, fall into position as they had done on countless missions. Handgun drawn, Lila Raycen quietly and quickly entered the building, snapped a quick look around and then gave a hand signal to her teammates. Her gaze sweeping the street, she whispered, "Sorry, Cap'n. All for one and all that jazz."

Lincoln couldn't speak the words floating through his mind. Wahyas could only telepathically communicate with other Wahyas if both were in their wolfan forms. Unless, of course, they were mated, which he and Lila were not. Nor would they ever be.

Although grateful at the show of Lila's support, he growled to officially express displeasure at her disregard of his direct order for the team to remain on-base.

"You can thank me later—" she smirked "—with a fat, juicy steak."

She had a long wait. On deployment, Dogmen's diets consisted of water and rations—canned and freeze-dried. Lincoln couldn't remember the last time he'd eaten a real meal. But once this assignment ended and they returned to HQ, his first home-cooked meal would be fried, shredded beef empanadas. His weren't as good as the ones his mom made but she had the actual family recipe handed down from her *bisabuela*, while he had to make them from memory, since Dogmen weren't allowed contact with family or friends while in the Program.

One more team member entered the building; the remaining three set up watch outside.

"Are you sure this is the right place?" Damien Marquez asked. A member of Lincoln's team for less than a year and a royal pain in the ass, but the fresh-faced Dogman made a damn good soldier.

Lincoln nodded. Dayax had lived in the abandoned building ever since his parents died. On his first patrol of the village, Lincoln had discovered the wolfling scavenging in the streets. And Lincoln had been feeding him ever since.

He'd also notified his superiors of Dayax's plight, requesting an extraction and transport to a new pack. Their negative response didn't stop him from keeping an eye on Dayax or from planning to take the boy with him once the deployment ended. Screw HQ.

"All right," Lila said quietly. "Let's find the wolfling and get the hell out of here."

Using his snout, Lincoln motioned for Damien to stand watch at the entrance. Since he'd already searched the bottom floor, Lincoln signaled Lila to follow him upstairs. Remaining in his wolf form, he hoped the wolfling would either hear his telepathic calls or see his wolf and come out of hiding.

Lincoln bounded up the mostly intact stairwell. The bulletproof vest he wore, specially fitted for his wolf, chaffed despite a thick coat of fur.

Following close on his heels, Lila, his second-in-command, obeyed orders as well as she gave them. Except for tonight's excursion, she'd never disobeyed a direct command. But he wouldn't fault her for this one. Loyalty sometimes outweighed a crappy order.

Together for the last five years, he would miss her support and friendship when she got her own team. He knew she would because he had been the one to recommend her for promotion.

Lincoln continued reaching out telepathically to Dayax. Silence answered, time and time again.

The worry gnawing Lincoln's gut spread into his chest. As they carefully cleared the second floor, the probability that the wolfling had been injured in the earlier firefight or had been taken by the rebels became a clear and present concern.

"Más rápido!" Standing at the bottom of the stairs, Damien waved for them to hurry. "There's movement down the street and it isn't the Red Cross handing out lollipops and blankets."

Room by room they searched. The gnawing in Lincoln's stomach would eat through his chest before long. After seeing the cruel and evil side of man and wolf for so long, Lincoln had nearly lost hope in everything. Then Dayax came along. With his inquisitive mind, generous smile and trusting eyes, despite all he'd suffered, Dayax had renewed Lincoln's faith. If he lost the boy now, the last threads of his humanity would snap.

"Se acabó el tiempo!" Damien yelled.

"Almost done," Lila replied.

Lincoln exited the last room to the left of the stairs and returned to the corridor, shaking his head. He gazed out the large window into the empty alley below.

"Dayax, wherever you are, I will find you!" He sent the question telepathically in English and Somali, hoping the wolfling would receive the message and understand that Lincoln would not give up on him.

"Last one, Linc. Then we gotta scram." Lila stopped in front of the last door to the right of the stairs.

"All right, kid. Come out, come out, wherever you are," she said, turning the doorknob. "Hmm. Must be stuck."

Lincoln's stomach knotted and a horrible foreboding drove an icy knife into his gut. *"Lila, wait!"*

Unable to hear Lincoln's telepathic warning in her human form, she shoved her shoulder against the door. It swung innocently open and she darted into the room.

The breath stalled in Lincoln's chest continued on its path, though his heart still thundered.

"Vámonos!" Damien shouted, stomping up the stairs two at a time. *"Vámonos!"*

A flash of light accompanied a resounding boom. The percussive force slammed Lincoln against the window. Deafened from the explosion, he never heard the glass break. But the air swooshed around him and his stomach looped as he plunged downward.

He would be okay; his team would be okay. Dayax would be okay. The beautiful angel inside the thin silver case tucked in the pocket of his protective vest would make sure they were. She always did.

Nine weeks later

"I'm gonna wring his freaking neck!"

Angeline O'Brien glared at the man passed out on her brand-new leather couch, thrashing and yelling in his sleep.

She slammed the apartment door, envisioning her long fingers curling around Tristan Durrance's throat for giving his subletter the wrong key.

Friends since they were tweens, neighbors for nearly all of their adult lives, and both relationshipphobes, Tristan and Angeline had traded apartment keys with the understanding that they would look out for each other. Angeline had expected the arrangement to continue into their elder years.

Unfortunately for her, last summer Tristan had accidentally claimed a mate and subsequently fallen in love, breaking up their platonic cohesiveness. Angeline didn't begrudge Tristan's happiness, but she had felt a little lonely since he'd moved out of his apartment.

But not lonely enough to play nice with a *Dogman* who had found his way into the wrong apartment. Everyone in the Walker's Run pack had been anticipating the wolfan paramilitary man's arrival for weeks. Everyone except Angeline.

Turbulent emotions rose inside her. When her first and only love, Tanner Phillips, had chosen life as a Dogman over a mateship with her, Angeline had never wanted to hear the word *Dogman* again. Neither did she ever want to come face-to-face with one.

So instead of welcoming *this* Dogman like a hero, she had a mind to toss his ass outside into the cold and slam the door in his face. Next to the two empty beer bottles on the kitchen counter, she dropped her purse and the carry-out bag from Taylor's Roadhouse, her uncle's restaurant where she worked part-time.

"Hey!" she snapped. After being on her feet all night, Angeline wanted a hot shower to wash away the food odors from her body and to relax in the utter quiet and comfort of her home. Alone. The sooner she got the Dogman into the right apartment, the better. "Wake up!"

Curled on his side, face pressed against the duffel bag he used as a pillow, the man gave no indication that he'd heard her. Every muscle in his body remained tightly coiled. A muscle spasmed along his clenched jaw and the deep furrows creased his brow.

Angeline's irritation level dropped a few notches. "Are you all right?" She touched him. An unexpected electric current caused her fingers to tighten on his bare shoulder when she should've let go.

His large hand cuffed her wrist as he sat up. "Who are you?" he snarled. His glaring silvery-green gaze appeared to be clouded and unfocused.

"The person who owns the couch you're sleeping on." Angeline yanked her captive arm against his hold. Instead of freeing herself, she became more entangled with him as he rolled off the couch and stood, leaning heavily on her.

"Where's my team?" A shag of black hair curtained his forehead, dark brows slashed angrily over his eyes and his naturally brown skin lightly glistened with sweat. "Where's Dayax?"

"Wherever you think you are, you aren't!" She grappled against his effort to restrain her. "This is my apartment, not Tristan's, and I want you to leave."

Angeline's heart pounded with a healthy dose of adrenaline, but not outright fear. She'd had to contend with two older brothers growing up. Wrestling over one thing or another had been a daily sport and they hadn't given her any slack just because of her gender.

She wiggled one arm free, sharpened her elbow and jammed it into his solar plexus. An audible gasp filled her ear. His hold loosened. Falling away, he snatched the tails of her sweater.

With a resounding oomph, he hit the carpeted floor, flat on his back with Angeline sprawling on top of him. Immediately, his meaty arms caged her, then rolling her beneath him, he pinned her with his weight.

"I can't breathe!" At least not all that well.

Hands flat against his muscled chest, damp from sweat, Angeline shoved hard but nothing happened. Pushing over a concrete wall might've been easier than getting the wolfan male to budge.

"Who are you?" Though he allowed her some wiggle room, the timbre of his growl gave grave warning.

"The woman who will unman you if you don't get the hell off me!" Angeline scraped her nails down his taut abdomen to the waistband of his boxers. Odd, considering wolfan males didn't care to wear men's underwear. But it was winter and she was grateful that his bare ass hadn't christened her new couch.

The undergarment, however, didn't prevent her from gripping his heavy sack in a manner any man would recognize as anything but playful.

A painful snarl parted his lips. Each time she squeezed, his lids shuttered and his gaze became more focused and alert. She knew the moment his brain recognized that he was crouched intimately above a female whose body was perfectly aligned with his.

"Think carefully about your next move, Dogman."

"Oh, I'm not moving, Angel," he said calmly. Clearly. Seductively. "Not until you let go of my balls."

"Good," she said, ignoring the flutter in her stomach that his deep, quiet Texas drawl had started to stir. "Now that you're awake, do you know where you are?"

A whisper of a smile curved his mouth. "In heaven." Eyes drifting closed, he lowered his face to hers and rubbed his check against her jaw, snuffling her hair. "God, you smell divine."

Despite the awkward circumstance, Angeline didn't sense any threat in his manner. The reverent way he breathed in her scent seemed almost like an act of worship.

His clean male musk invaded her senses, sparking a primal interest better left dormant.

"All right. The sniff feast is over." She squeezed his sack.

Once she had his full attention again, Angeline let go.

He eased off her and she sat up, watching him hoist himself onto the couch. Only then did she realize that most of his left leg was missing. She also noticed the scattered scars on his arms and torso. Some new, others quite old.

Her heart pinched but she wouldn't allow sympathy to fester. She had no business feeling anything for a Dogman.

Leaning down, he picked up the blanket that had slid to the floor during their struggle and folded it. "Apologies for the intrusion, Angel."

"My name isn't Angel. It's Angeline." She sank into the oversize chair. "That was some nightmare you were having when I came home. Have those often?"

"Every time I fall asleep."

No wonder his eyes looked weary, and wary and sad.

"And why are you sleeping on my couch, *Dogman*?"

"I prefer Lincoln," he said quietly. "Tristan left the wrong key beneath the doormat. When I called, he said you wouldn't mind if I crashed here. Clearly, he made a mistake." He removed a nude-colored stocking from the oversize duffel bag. Grimacing, he began stretching it over his naturally bronze stump.

Angeline folded her arms over her chest, hoping he didn't notice her weakness, a traitorous heart that tweaked because of the traumatic loss he had suffered. "Tristan should've warned me."

If he had, she might've refused.

Watching Lincoln pull the state-of-the-art prosthetic leg from his duffel, guilt stabbed at her conscience. He would only be in town a few weeks. She could grit her teeth and be neighborly for that long, couldn't she?

Chapter 2

Half naked and legless wasn't how Lincoln had imagined meeting his guardian angel in the flesh. Angeline's long auburn hair framed a face Lincoln would have recognized even if he were a blind man with only his hands to feel the shape of her feminine brow, her high, angular cheeks and soft, full lips. God only knew how often he had traced every angle and plane of the woman in the worn photograph he'd carried with him for the better part of the last fifteen years. Now that he'd encountered the she-wolf in the flesh, his heart wouldn't stop fluttering and the tingly sensation in his stomach would make him sick if it didn't stop soon.

Attaching the prosthetic to his stump, Lincoln didn't dare take his gaze off Angeline, fearing she would disappear like she had so often in his dreams.

The old picture entrusted to him by the dying Dogman on Lincoln's first mission hadn't done Angeline justice because it had failed to capture her fire and strength of will. Unlike the fragile, ethereal female he'd envisioned, the real woman—strong, sassy, sexy—took him utterly by surprise.

"When is the last time you ate?" Despite the gentleness in her voice, Angeline's hard, no-nonsense gaze didn't soften.

"On the plane, somewhere over the ocean," he said over the loud rumblings of his stomach. Grabbing his camo pants, he stuffed his good leg into the pant leg and then slid the other pant leg over his prosthetic without embarrassment over his nearly nude state. For Wahyas, nudity was as natural as eating and breathing.

"I'm coming off a ten-hour flight from Munich. I got stuck in customs for over two hours in the Atlanta airport because the TSA agents had never seen the bionics used in my leg. Then I had a nearly three-hour drive to get here and all of the drive-throughs in town were closed."

He wouldn't starve, though. Inside his duffel were the rations he'd consumed for so long that he no longer remembered the taste of real food.

Wordlessly, Angeline stood and strolled into the kitchen. Lincoln quickly wiggled the pants over his boxers. He didn't particularly like the undergarments but had learned to tolerate them during his recovery when the friction from long pants made his stump feel as if it were on fire.

"Bon appetite," Angeline said, returning with a large foam box in her hands.

She opened the lid. The spicy scent of a mountain of buffalo chicken wings made his mouth water. His eyes might've, too, because she had offered him food. Actual everyday, take-for-granted, comfort food. Not canned or freeze-dried rations. Not bland, pasty mess hall slop or the airline's processed micro meals. Real, honest-to-goodness food, only mere inches from his face.

But, remembering the near-empty refrigerator and pantry, he waved away her offering. "Thanks. But no."

Times were tough and he didn't want to take advantage of her kindness.

Her nostrils flared slightly and her full, luscious lips flattened.

"I meant no offense," he said, pulling on a black sweatshirt. Wolfans took food seriously. Refusing food insulted the one offering it. "But I don't need your supper."

His stomach protested. Loudly.

"I'm not the one whose stomach is about to eat itself." She jabbed the box toward him. "Take them, they're yours."

"I saw the fridge." He gently pushed back the tempting container. "You need to eat those more than I do. I have rations that will hold me over. And I'll pay you for the beer." He dug a wallet from the duffel and held out a fifty-dollar bill.

Mouth open and shock rippling through her gaze, she stared at his hand. Suddenly, full-bellied feminine laughter shook her body.

Before the explosion, Lincoln had found a woman's laugh sexy. In his current circumstance, scarred and crippled, he felt belittled and hurt. He'd built up a fantasy about this woman. One where her kindness and gentleness had soothed and safe-guarded him. In reality, Angeline mocked him the same way the Program's bureaucrats had when Lincoln had insisted that he could still perform his sworn duties.

The money slipped through his fingers and drifted to the floor. Whether she used it or not, Lincoln didn't care.

He stood, steady and effortlessly. After a month of endless practice, he could stand, walk, run, jump and climb stairs with ease. Kneeling could be a bit tricky, but he managed. Shifting into his wolf form had proven to be the most challenging. No longer could he simply strip down and crouch before turning into his wolf. Now he had to carefully remove the artificial leg, otherwise it would turn to ash during the transformation.

As life changing as the loss had been, he was grateful to be alive. If he'd died instead of Lila, no one would go to the lengths Lincoln would to find his missing wolfling.

He slung the strap of the duffel bag over his shoulder then trudged toward the door.

"Where are you going?"

"To sleep in my truck until I can straighten this out with Tristan," he snapped, too exhausted to keep the frustration and anger from his voice.

"I wasn't laughing at you, Lincoln."

His hand froze on the doorknob.

"It's sweet of you to overpay for the beer to help me out with groceries, but I don't need it. The fridge is empty because I don't like to cook, not because I can't afford to buy food. That's why I laughed."

She eased behind him. "You see, I can take care of myself. And if I ever needed anything, my family and my pack would step up. That's how the Walker's Run Co-operative works."

A few years ago, while in Romania and assigned to a protective detail for the Woelfesenat's negotiator, Brice Walker, Lincoln had learned of the Walker's Run pack's co-operative. Consisting of wolfans and a handful of humans aware of the existence of Wahyas, the Co-op gave the Walker's Run pack a public, human face and a clever way to hide in plain sight among the unsuspecting townsfolk in Maico, a small Appalachian community in northeast Georgia where the pack resided.

Pivoting toward Angeline, Lincoln noticed the genuine concern etched on her face. Clearly, she hadn't meant to upset him and he felt like an idiot to have allowed a trivial misunderstanding to bruise his pride.

Nine weeks in the infirmary at Headquarters had turned him soft. Lincoln had hoped time away from HQ might help him regain his bearings. Now, he might need to reassess that decision.

How could he stay focused on increasing his stamina and sharpening his combat skills so he could return to Somalia and find Dayax when his guardian angel had escaped his dreams and lived only a few door down from where he would be staying?

"You can have this back." Slowly, her long, tapered fingers slid into his hip pocket to deposit the fifty. The ensuing jolt to his system rendered his entire body flaccid, except for his shaft, which instantly hardened.

"As I said before, bon appétit!" Moving her other hand from behind her back, Angeline presented him with the box of chicken wings. "And no there's no need to sleep in your truck. I have a key to Tristan's apartment."

"Why?" Lincoln wondered about the relationship between the two and why Tristan had failed to mention that tidbit during their brief call earlier.

"Neighbors look out for each other." She picked up a keyring from the kitchen counter, worked off a key and handed it to Lincoln. "Welcome to the neighborhood, Lincoln."

A key in one hand and food in the other, he should be happy to finally be getting into his temporary apartment. "I wouldn't mind some company for a while."

Her gaze slid down his torso to the erection his pants couldn't hide. Food and sex. A wolfan male's priorities.

"I gave you food. Now you need to take care of the rest

on your own." She reached past him and opened the door. The biting February air gusted into the apartment and nipped his skin beneath the sweatshirt.

"Good night, Lincoln." Angeline patted his chest, urging him to leave.

He'd barely stepped outside when the door closed behind him and locked.

"Whew! That was close." Angeline's voice reached his ears despite the barrier.

Turning, he strolled down the open corridor to the corner apartment, a smile budding on his face even as a weight settled in his heart. He had a mission to complete. Until he found Dayax, Lincoln would do well to resist the devilish diversion of his angelic neighbor.

Heart thumping and holding her breath, Angeline leaned against the door. The jumble of feelings knotting inside her were a fluke. Lincoln was a Dogman. Period. She could be neighborly but absolutely nothing else.

She squinched her eyes to banish the vision of him watching her beneath long, dark lashes as his silvery-green gaze caressed her face with reverence and awe. The effort merely branded the image into her brain.

Inheriting her mother's model looks, Angeline had grown numb to people's ogles, waggles and even jealousy-filled glares.

But the way Lincoln looked at her when she'd laughed and he'd misunderstood had felt like an iron fist slamming into her stomach, hard and painful.

Pushing away from the door, she trudged to the couch, slouched against the leather cushions and pulled off her boots. Next she peeled out of the thick sweater she wore over the long-sleeved T-shirt and tossed it in the chair. Picking up the afghan Lincoln had carefully folded, she inhaled his earthy male musk. Instead of trotting outside to hang the afghan on the balcony in the cold night air to remove his scent, she shook it out and laid it across her lap. After all, she couldn't leave her favorite blanket out in the elements.

Too keyed up to sleep, Angeline visually searched for the television remote and didn't see it on either end table or the entertainment center. Slipping her hand between the cushions, she not only found the remote but also Lincoln's wallet.

At the thought of returning it to him, her heart picked up speed. The sudden acceleration caused her body to tingle and anticipation coiled low in her belly.

Perhaps a brisk walk would cool things down.

Tossing aside the blanket, she didn't bother with a sweater or shoes. It would only take a minute to return the wallet. She walked outside and scurried down the corridor overlooking the parking lot to the corner apartment.

"Lincoln, it's Angeline." Knocking on the door, her fingers were as cold as ice cubes.

Tristan had disconnected the doorbell years ago. Too many people pulling him in too many directions. Once he turned off his phone to sleep, he didn't want to be disturbed by someone showing up at his door and pressing the bell until he got up.

Sure would've been nice for him to have reconnected the bell before subletting his place.

Still holding Lincoln's wallet, she tucked her hands beneath her arms to warm them. "Hurry up! I'm freezing."

"What are you doing out here, Angel?"

Angeline spun around, doing a little jig that could either be described as a startled jump or a stealthy self-defense move.

She preferred the latter.

"Whoa!" Lincoln's hands lifted in surrender. "I didn't mean to scare you."

"You didn't." Angeline stood tall.

"Uh-huh." Lincoln's disbelieving grin raised her ire and suddenly she no longer felt cold.

"Why didn't I hear you coming up behind me?" Wahyas had excellent hearing.

"You're not supposed to."

"Right. Because you're a Dogman."

Silent as a ninja, as deadly as one, too. Or so the rumors went. No one outside the Woelfesenat's militarized security force knew exactly what the Dogmen did, other than the generic job description of peacekeeping.

Considering the numerous scars on his body, whatever Lincoln had been doing, it wasn't so peaceable.

"You're right about one thing." Lincoln pivoted to block the gust of wind that caused her teeth to chatter and then reached around her to open the door. "You are freezing."

His broad hand heated the small of her back and he nudged her forward. Her mind mounted a protest but her feet didn't get the memo in time to keep her from crossing the threshold.

"What were you doing outside?"

"Cooling off." He tossed an odd-looking cell phone next to the take-out box on the asymmetrical coffee table. If he'd had the device in her apartment, she hadn't noticed it.

"Change your mind about sharing a snack?" Lincoln sat on the couch and opened the box of chicken wings.

"No." As a restaurant employee, she'd learned to eat only when truly hungry, otherwise she'd eat constantly and no amount of running in the woods would compensate for the extra calories. Ignoring the delicious scent taunting her stomach, Angeline held out Lincoln's wallet. "I found it between the couch cushions."

Mouth full of food, he gave a hand signal for her to leave it on the coffee table.

Angeline strolled around the living room. "This place is probably a culture shock for you. The furnishings are too modern for my taste. Tristan didn't like it much, either, but his mother is an interior designer and she loves this stuff."

Still eating, Lincoln watched her with the same quiet curiosity as he had in her apartment. And when she walked into the kitchen, his inquisitive gaze followed.

"You're in luck," she said, peeking into the refrigerator. "It's stocked with a few basics. At least you won't have to go grocery shopping on Sunday." Closing the refrigerator, she added, "Which technically is today, since it's after midnight, you know…in case your days are mixed up from traveling."

A chuckle accompanied Lincoln's slight head shake.

"You would think Sundays are good days to go to the grocery store." She sat on a stool at the bar rather than leaving. She and Tristan had their fair share of late-night chats. Being back in his apartment, it seemed natural to carry on tradition. Even though Lincoln was a Dogman, she could still be neighborly.

"Because everyone is either going to church or sleeping off Saturday night's good time. But actually, the early risers are buzzing around to get their shopping done to have the rest of the day free. Late-goers are trying to grab something on their way to wherever. And the rest are trying to find something to fix their hangovers."

"Good to know." Not one speck of sauce marred his mouth and very little dotted his fingers. An amazing feat considering most people who ate her uncle's wings required a plastic bib and a double stack of napkins.

And while looking at his mouth, Angeline couldn't help but notice the perfect shape of his masculine lips or how his straight nose balanced the angles of his cheeks. His black hair didn't conform to a human military's regulation cut but rather fell to his collar in soft waves. The muscles in his strong jaw, darkened by a shadow of stubble, worked in tandem as he chewed. When he swallowed, she watched the slow descent of his Adam's apple along his throat. The silver chain around the thick column of his neck held the dog tags hidden beneath his sweatshirt.

The thick dark slashes above his pale green eyes drew together as the curiosity in his gaze transitioned to something primal. "Angeline." He softly growled her name and it whispered across her skin, heightening her own awareness of him.

She shouldn't study him so intently. Wahyas' senses were acutely sharp and staring too long usually signaled a threat or sexual interest. Obviously, Lincoln wouldn't consider her a threat. He stood over six feet tall, while she only pushed upward of five-seven, and he out-massed her by at least seventy pounds.

However, underestimating her would be a mistake. Her brothers might not be quite as imposing as Lincoln, but they weren't pushovers. They'd never taken it easy on her and the skills she'd learned tangling with them had come in handy a few years ago when a hook-up had turned sour and she'd needed to escape the situation.

Like most wolfan males, Lincoln would misinterpret her interest as...well...*interest.* Which, of course, it wasn't. If she and a Dogman were the last Wahyas on Earth, she wouldn't be interested. Even if it meant the salvation of their race, it simply would not happen.

Too bad, thanks to a treacherous brain, her body had no troubling recalling the intimate heat of him crouched above her, while his fierce gaze mapped every inch of her soul. His light-colored eyes had presented a striking contrast to the rich brownness of his nearly naked body and thick black waves of hair. Unbidden desire curled inside her like wisps of steam rising from a cup of hot chocolate.

"Tuesdays," she said, throwing the brakes on primal instincts. Despite the close friendship with her former neighbor, Angeline had never experienced a sexual attraction toward Tristan. Considering her body's unexpected and wholly unappreciated reaction to Lincoln, she would not make a habit of being overly neighborly.

"Tuesdays?" Confusion clouded Lincoln's gaze.

"About midmorning." Angeline slid off the bar stool. "Trust me. It's the best time to go grocery shopping at Anne's Market."

"Appreciate the tip." From his neutral expression, Angeline couldn't discern if he truthfully did, or if he merely humored her.

"I should go."

Lincoln met her at the door. "Here." He tugged off his sweatshirt.

"Thanks." She kept focused on the faint scar below his eye rather than the short, dark hairs spread across the broad, chiseled expanse of his chest. "But I don't need it."

He slipped the sweatshirt over her head and onto her shoulders anyway. His clean, crisp, masculine scent immediately invaded her senses, and she obediently slid her arms into the sleeves.

The fabric still held his warmth, and she remained nice and toasty all the way to her apartment.

Standing watch from his doorway, bare-chested and unflinching against the icy wind winding through the corridor, Lincoln presented a striking image of a proud warrior. He reeked of confidence, but not the arrogance she had imagined to have infected all Dogmen.

Once inside, Angeline sighed against the locked door.

Hugging Lincoln's sweatshirt to her body, she held the collar over her nose, breathing his scent and absorbing his warmth like a she-wolf showing more than a casual interest in a male—

Like cold water to the face, the realization shocked her senses and she couldn't get out of his clothes fast enough.

This was all Tristan's fault!

Leaving the sweatshirt in a puddle on the floor, she stomped to the kitchen bar, snatched open her purse, whipped out her cell phone and began furiously typing.

Chapter 3

"Dammit!" Angeline swiped the pick down the guitar strings, abruptly halting the sappy tune she'd been composing for the last hour.

Sitting in the middle of her unmade bed, she stared into her open closet at the numerous prestigious awards her love songs had won. Hidden away from all eyes but hers because no strong, self-respecting she-wolf would ever pine over a man who didn't want her. Neither would she write songs about the devastating experience. Especially not a she-wolf raised by Patrick O'Brien. He'd be appalled to learn that his daughter had been reduced to inconsolable tears by the man who'd broken her young heart.

However, Angeline had turned the heartbreak from Tanner's rejection and the heartache from his death into writing love-lost songs that country and pop recording artists fought over to record.

Of course, she had long moved past the actual events.

But to write the music and lyrics people wanted, she had to tap into those old feelings, putting herself back into the maelstrom of all that pain. Lately, though, she had grown weary of the process.

Again, she blamed Tristan. His migration from her staunchest bachelor friend to happily mated had left her feeling off-kilter. A feeling magnified by her unusual reaction to Lincoln. Also, Tristan's fault. If he hadn't left Lincoln the wrong key, she wouldn't have his scent imprinted in her nose and lingering in the living room.

Obviously, she found the wolfan sexually appealing. Tall, broad-shouldered, with chiseled abs and sculpted pecs, and muscled limbs that proclaimed his strength without being ridiculously pretentious. The way he moved and carried himself proved he'd earned those muscles on the job rather than in the gym. But she was accustomed to physically fit wolfan males. Generally, they didn't stay on her mind.

But she couldn't stop thinking about Lincoln, whose commanding presence had not been diminished by the loss of his leg. The injury appeared to be fairly recent, considering the freshness of the scars on his stump and on the left side of his body.

However, it was the lost and lonely look in Lincoln's eyes that had haunted her all night and greatly interfered with her creativity today.

Sympathy infected her heart, causing it to ache for the Dogman. It shouldn't. Her heart should be cold and unfeeling toward them. They'd made their choices and should live with them. Why should anyone be sympathetic? Especially those they'd abandoned to pursue glory.

Growling, Angeline strummed the strings in frustration and set aside the guitar. She slipped off the bed, stretched and then padded out of the bedroom. The pounding at her front door halted her trip to the kitchen.

She opened the door to Tristan's famous grin.

"Hey there, Sassy."

"Hey there, Slick. Bite me."

Before she could close the door, Tristan thrust his arm through the opening, gripping a white paper bag. The scent of apples and cinnamon and sugar caused her nose to twitch. He nudged the door open a little wider and showed her the large coffee in his other hand. "I come bearing gifts," he said lightheartedly.

"Once upon a time that didn't work out so well for the Trojans." Regardless, Angeline lifted the coffee cup and bag of pastries from Tristan's hands. Ignoring him as he entered the apartment, she sat cross-legged on the couch and fished a bear claw with an apple filling from the bag.

Tristan closed the door and made himself at home in the overstuffed chair. "I'm not exactly sure what this means." He showed her the angry, emoji-filled text message she'd sent last night.

"Just delete it." Angeline wiped away the sugar sticking to her lips. "We're good now."

"I'm sorry that I didn't give you a heads-up about Lincoln." Tristan paused and suddenly the exhaustion he'd been hiding surfaced. "Nel and I were at the hospital most of the night."

"Is Nel all right? Did she have the baby?"

"False alarm. She's had Braxton Hicks pain on and off, but last night she got so uncomfortable, I took her in to be checked." Running his hand through his tousled blond hair, Tristan yawned.

Angeline did, too. Seemed they'd both had a long night.

"Lincoln called right as the nurse took Nel to an exam room. I meant to text you—"

"Forget it." She waved off Tristan's worry and he began to relax. "You're dealing with a lot. Seems to be your calling."

"I'm hoping to build a team to shoulder that burden." Everyone's problem solver, Tristan—a former sheriff deputy, had recently been named the Walker's Run Co-op's chief of security. A huge undertaking considering the pack now had its own police force.

"Don't look at me. I like my life the way it is." In defiance of Tristan's pointed, disbelieving look, she shoved another pastry into her mouth.

"I'm talking about Lincoln," Tristan said. "Brice wants him to remain in Walker's Run."

Not surprisingly, the Alpha's son had a habit of keeping his friends close. "Good luck to him. Lincoln doesn't seem the type to walk away from the Program, even if he could."

"Apparently, he's being forced into a medical retirement."

"Whoa." The only utterable word able to form on Angeline's lips. A Dogman losing his career, much like a wolfan losing a mate, hurt to the soul.

She would not sympathize with Lincoln, though. Not about that.

"I have a favor to ask," Tristan said quietly.

Over the rim of her coffee cup, Angeline watched him squirm in his seat. The hot liquid heated her mouth and the warmth traveled all the way to her starting-to-clench stomach. "I'm not going to like it, am I?"

"I need you to keep an eye on him."

"No." Angeline cut her eyes at her oldest, dearest friend. He should know better than to ask such a thing. "I'm not spying on a Dogman."

"Just be neighborly." Tristan leaned forward, his elbows planted on his knees with his fingers laced. "Brice trusts him, but I don't know this guy. Dogmen are just this side of feral. I need to know sooner than later if he's on the verge of crossing the line. The pack has been through enough violence."

"Why me and not Shane? He's only a few doors down." And a legitimate pack sentinel.

"Shane doesn't have your assets," Tristan said good-naturedly. "Lincoln isn't likely to let his guard down around a male. But you?" Tristan's expression turned serious. "You could make a wolf lie down at your feet, roll over and purr, if you wanted him to."

"You know why I can't do this." Angeline swallowed another mouthful of coffee but the kinks in her stomach tightened rather than relaxed.

"Lincoln isn't Tanner. Don't judge him for Tanner's mistake." Tristan stood. "If Lincoln is the man Brice believes, when the realty of his medical retirement sets in, he's going to need help coping. It can be you or someone else, but I strongly feel you're the best person he could have in his corner because you know how it feels to lose the life you thought you were meant to have."

Quietly, Tristan closed the door as he left.

"Dammit!" Angeline slung a throw pillow after him. Harmlessly, it glanced off the door. She snatched it up and punched it. "Damn you, too, Tanner." She smacked the pillow again, then hugged it to her chest and schlepped to the couch, knowing she'd do just what Tristan had asked. Because she did know exactly how it felt to watch the future crumble. No one, not even a Dogman, deserved to face it alone.

Bracing against the cold, Lincoln knocked on the door to Brice Walker's residence, two miles up the mountain from the family-owned Walker's Run Resort. Used to the heat in Somalia, the lower temperatures in Northeast Georgia would be a welcomed change if his stump didn't ache.

The heavy wooden door opened to reveal a petite, human redhead. A smile warmed the porcelain tone of her skin and her cinnamon eyes shimmered.

"Hello, Cassie." Though they had never met, he knew her from the late-night chats he'd had with her mate during a mission in Romania several years ago.

"Lincoln! Please come in." She stepped aside, welcoming him into her home.

Gratefully, he shook off the cold.

"Thank you for keeping Brice safe so he could come back to me," she said, closing the door. "If you need anything, let me know. I'll make sure you get it."

"I appreciate your kindness." But what he wanted she couldn't give. Her husband, however, could be the Ace that Lincoln needed. After all, he had saved Brice's life. "I was just doing my job."

"You went beyond your job. You were a friend when Brice needed one the most."

Uh-oh.

Reading her body language and seeing the intent on her face, Lincoln leaned down so that her arms reached his neck in the full-on hug rather than banding around his middle, which would've appeared quite odd and a bit too personal to her mate. Lincoln didn't have a visual on Brice Walker yet, but his ears honed in on the slight thump of the man's limping gait inside the house.

A tawny-headed wolfan, not quite midtwenties, stepped into the hallway. On his shoulders sat a toddler.

"Shane—" Cassie grinned at the young man "—this is Lincoln Adams, Brice's friend from his time in Romania."

Lincoln hid his smile. Humans often identified a personal connection when introducing people. Wolfans pointed out their rank or benefit to the pack.

"Lincoln, this is Shane MacQuarrie. He's a close friend of ours."

Neither he nor Shane made an effort to observe the human custom of shaking hands. Instead, they greeted each other with a curt nod.

"I hear we're neighbors at the Chatuge View Apartments." Shane's wintry gaze didn't warm. Close to the age Lincoln had been when recruited for the Dogman program, the young wolf reeked of confidence, piss and vinegar. Lincoln liked him immediately.

"Good to know."

"And this is my daughter, Brenna," Cassie said.

The little girl's bright blue eyes targeted him with the same intensity Lincoln had seen in her father's gaze years ago. And although her hair wasn't red like her mother's curls, the blond ringlets held a tinge of fire.

Cassie held up her hands and Brenna practically launched into her mother's arms. "More monkey than wolf, I think."

Although the little girl's mother was human, her father was Wahya and wolfan genes were dominant. All Wahyan offspring were born with wolf-shifting abilities.

"Just brave and confident." Lincoln extended his hand in a nonthreatening greeting. "Nice to meet you, Brenna."

"Mmm…five!" Grinning, she smacked her palm against his open hand.

"That's not how we greet guests." Despite Cassie's frown, no true reprimand sharpened her voice. She turned to Lincoln. "Come. The others are in the family room."

Others?

Brice hadn't mentioned others when he'd invited Lincoln to Sunday supper.

Shane took a step back, allowing Lincoln to follow Cassie, but remained close enough to respond to any threat, should Lincoln become one.

"Lincoln!" Brice stepped forward as they entered the family room. "Good to see you, man."

Fairly equal in height, Lincoln didn't need to crouch for Brice's brotherly embrace and friendly pat on the back.

"Thanks for the invite."

"My parents." Brice waved his hand toward the more than middle-aged couple sitting in the love seat near the fireplace. "Gavin and Abby Walker."

The Alpha and Alphena of Walker's Run. Lincoln had expected to meet them eventually. Just not on his first venture out.

After a handshake from Gavin and a hug from Abby, Cassie hustled them into the dining room. Brenna insisted Lincoln sit next to her and he complied, despite Shane's obvious annoyance.

Throughout the delicious meal, Lincoln politely answered questions and listened to their security concerns. Although what they'd experienced over the last few years alarmed the quiet Appalachian pack, it couldn't compare to the violence Lincoln dealt with daily on deployment.

When finished with supper, everyone returned to the family room. Lincoln sat in an overstuffed rocking chair, leaving the couch and love seat to the mated pairs while Shane claimed the recliner. Conversation shifted to planning a spring gathering for the pack. For fifteen years, Lincoln had been isolated from first-world normalcy and he found the sudden reentrance jarring.

Brenna climbed into his lap with a book. Glad for the distraction, he read and reread the story until she fell asleep. Only then did he notice all the adults in the room silently watching him.

Thank you, Cassie mouthed, easing the child from his arms.

"I wouldn't have expected a Dogman to know how to handle children." In spite of Gavin's stony expression, his sharp blue eyes twinkled.

"Wherever I'm deployed, I see children impacted by the conflict around them. I do what I can to help them retain their childhood, in spite of the circumstance." The ache in Lincoln's heart grew stronger. Dayax had no one but him, and Lincoln was thousands of miles away. Safe, warm and well-fed. The lost little wolfling likely was none of those things.

"Sounds like you will be a great father one day," Abby said.

"Dogmen can't take mates," Lincoln replied gently. "We aren't meant to be fathers." Or mothers, or sons, daughters, brothers or sisters. The Program required absolute devotion. All ties with family and friends were severed upon joining.

"Aren't you ready to retire?" Shane's gaze dropped to Lincoln's left leg.

"Not anytime soon." Lincoln shifted his attention to Brice, who stood.

"I've got something to show you." Brice motioned for Lincoln to follow.

After closing the French doors to the home office, Brice sat behind a messy wooden desk, pulled a photo from the drawer and handed it to Lincoln.

He fingered the snapshot of them sitting by a campfire, laughing.

"Remember that night?" With one blue eye and one green, Brice's direct gaze could intimidate lesser men.

"Hard to forget." Especially since Lincoln still bore the

scar from the bullet he'd caught protecting Brice less than an hour after the picture had been taken.

"When I talked to you a couple of weeks ago, I thought you were on board with the medical retirement."

"I only said that so the doctors would stop harping about adjustment issues. Yeah, I lost a leg, but I have more important things to worry about, which is why I need your help with something."

"Name it." Brice planted his elbows on the desk and steepled his fingers.

"I want to go back to Somalia."

To his credit, Brice didn't balk, blink or bat an eyelash.

"I was looking for a wolfling in an abandoned building when an explosion blasted me out of a two-story window." Lincoln fished out his wallet, removed a photo of him and Dayax and tossed it on the desk in front of Brice. "Insurgents took him. I want him back."

"I'm not a soldier, Lincoln. How do you think I can help?"

"Ask your friends at the Woelfesenat to grant me clearance to go back in." As the secretive international wolf council, the Woelfesenat not only had ruling authority over the packs but had executive power over the Dogman Program.

"I'm Dayax's only hope, Brice. I have to find him or die trying." Invisible fingers fisted around Lincoln's heart. His mission to rescue Dayax would be over before it began if Brice declined to help.

Brice glanced at the framed picture of his daughter on his desk. "I'll do what I can."

Lincoln managed to breathe again. "Thank you." Though grateful, he didn't allow himself even the smallest celebration. More than two months had passed since Dayax's disappearance. Finding him would take a miracle.

Chapter 4

Have you met him yet?" Madelyn O'Brien, sister-in-law number one, nudged Angeline.

"Who?" She shoveled another spoonful of creamed corn into her mouth. The once-a-month family supper at her father's house provided Angeline with her only full-course home-cooked meal. Her brothers supplied the meat, their mates provided the sides, and Angeline always showed up with a healthy appetite and plastic containers to take home leftovers.

"The Dogman." Isobel O'Brien, sister-in-law number two and affectionately known as Izzie, flashed a conspiratorial grin. "Haven't you been listening?"

No. She'd tuned out at the first mention of "Dogman." Her brain needed the break.

"He was supposed to arrive yesterday," Garret, Angeline's oldest brother, said. "Did he meet up with anyone for dinner and drinks at Taylor's Roadhouse last night?"

"Nope," Angeline answered between bites.

"I bet he's handsome." Izzie grinned. "But not as good-looking as you." She kissed Connor—her mate and Angeline's other brother—on the cheek and his soft, disgruntled growl ceased.

So cute. Mated thirteen years and the father of two kids, Connor still got a little jealous when Izzie mentioned other men. He had nothing to worry about. Izzie loved him to the moon and back. Stinky feet and all.

"Angeline, what have you heard about this Dogman?" Patrick O'Brien clasped his hands over the dinner plate. Angeline's father might not like the idea of his daughter waiting tables for a living, but he certainly liked pumping her for the tidbits of gossip she frequently overheard.

"His name is Lincoln," she said. "He got in late last night, he's friends with Brice, and that's all I know." Not really, but it covered the basics.

"Have you actually met him?" Connor asked.

"He's subletting Tristan's apartment." Angeline speared the green bean bundle wrapped in bacon on her plate and chomped down so she wouldn't have to answer the barrage of her family's questions.

"Dogmen don't just come for a visit." Patrick O'Brien's statement quieted the table. "Why is he really here?"

All eyes turned on Angeline.

"How should I know?"

"You're tight with Tristan," Garret said.

"So?" She never disclosed the things Tristan revealed in confidence.

"Are you going to talk to him again?" Her father's narrowed gaze forced Angeline to swallow the food she'd just stuck in her mouth.

"Tristan? I talk to him a couple of times a week." Texts mostly, that way he could reply when he had the time.

"The Dogman," her dad growled. "Why are you being so evasive? Do you know more than you're telling us?"

"Actually, Dad, I don't." Angeline put down the food-laden fork in her hand. "Why is everyone so concerned about his business? He's just a guy that traveled a long way to get here. He arrived exhausted and hungry. I gave him the food I'd brought home from the restaurant and the key to Tristan's apartment, and then I sent him on his merry way."

"Are you going to see him again?" Connor asked.

"He's staying a few doors down from me. And I work at Taylor's." Most wolfans couldn't resist her uncle's fire-grilled steaks. "What do you think?"

Connor squinted, and she knew he wanted to stick his tongue out at her, like when they were kids, but they'd grown past that childish expression—in the presence of others.

"You only work part-time," her father said, always ready to seize an opportunity to hassle Angeline about her employment choice. "When are you going to get a real job?"

"You may not like than I'm a server, but it is a real job. And in three nights, what I make in tips is more than some people earn in a week."

"Your mother and I wanted you to be more than a waitress."

"Mom would've wanted me to pursue music. But when she died, you sold the piano and wouldn't allow me to bring any instruments home."

Her father's jaw tightened. "Someone had to teach you to be realistic about your future."

"Shouldn't *my* wants determine the reality of *my* future?" Angeline's chest tightened and with every beat of her heart she felt a sharp pain stab her eye.

"Not if your head is in the clouds," was what her father

said. However, every time they had this argument, all Angeline heard was that her dad didn't want *her*—he merely wanted a version of her that she could never be.

"Dad, let it go," Garret said.

Angeline inhaled a few calming breaths, hoping to prevent a migraine.

Grumbling, their father stabbed his mashed potatoes and jabbed the fork into his mouth. Everyone else resumed eating in awkward silence, so everything had returned to normal.

After supper, Angeline collected the dishes and began loading the dishwasher.

Izzie leaned against the counter. "Your dad is worried about you."

"Worried that I might have a stroke from the spike in my blood pressure? Because that's what worries me."

"He's worried about what will happen to you—" Izzie lowered her voice "—after he's gone. You don't have a mate. Or a career. He thinks he failed you."

"No, not failed me," Angeline corrected. "Failed in raising me. I didn't turn out to be the daughter he wanted."

"Your dad loves you." Madelyn quietly joined them.

"I know." Angeline dropped the silverware into the utensils tray and closed the dishwasher. "But he doesn't understand me. All he wants is for me to fall in line with what he wants."

"Couldn't you give in, just a little?" Madelyn gave her a little shrug. "Maybe put your business degree to good use and help out your dad on one of your days off."

"No. He didn't teach me how to give in." Nor did she have a business degree, having chosen to secretly study music instead. Angeline dried her hands on the dish towel. "If you'll excuse me, I need to say good-night to the kids."

"Don't forget they're out of school for a teacher's workday on Thursday," Madelyn said.

"I have everything planned." Breakfast, sledding, watching a superhero movie on DVD while overloading on popcorn and hot chocolate.

"You haven't changed your mind about Sierra's birthday party, have you?" Mischief twinkled in Izzie's eyes.

"I'll be the one loaded with all the surprises." And Angeline couldn't wait to see the disapproving look on Patrick O'Brien's face when forced to wear one of the fringed pastel foil party hats she'd bought specially for the occasion.

Headlights briefly lit the dark stairwell. When they blinked off, Lincoln glanced toward the parking lot and stopped to watch Angeline slide out of her car.

Seeing him paused on the stairs, she waved but only a faint smile touched her lips.

He waited, his heartbeat falling into an unusual rhythm, pushing his blood more quickly through his veins.

"Hey," she said, climbing the steps behind him. "How was your day?"

The question caused a little flutter in his chest. Other than the nurses at the infirmary, Lincoln couldn't remember the last time someone had asked that question of him.

"Awkward," Lincoln said.

"Why?"

He remained one step behind Angeline as they continued up the stairs.

"Brice invited me to his home for supper. Didn't know his parents would be there."

"Guess that would be awkward, especially not knowing them."

"What about you?" He'd seen the rigidness of her stride

valking to the stairs and could feel the tension radiating rom her now.

"Monthly family dinner. My dad uses the opportunity ɔ chide me about my life's choices. He's gravely disapointed that, at my age, I'm unmated and have no viable caeer." Her entire body seemed to sigh. "If he only knew…"

"Knew what?"

They reached the third-floor landing.

"Doesn't matter." An artificial smile curved her tanlizing mouth.

Nearing his apartment, Lincoln bid Angeline goodight. He fiddled with his keys, listening to the rhythmic ump of her boots retreating down the corridor.

"Lincoln?"

"Yeah?" He turned.

"Wanna come in for a drink?"

"Sure." Shoving the keys into his pocket, he walked own to her apartment.

She'd left the door partially open, so he entered and shut ut the cold night air. Angeline had dropped her coat on the ack of the couch and had headed straight for the kitchen.

"Beer, wine or Jack?"

"Your choice." He sat on the couch rather than the chair, iving room for Angeline to join him, if she chose.

After living in tents and barracks, sleeping on the round, in cots, hammocks or in trees, Lincoln appreci-ed the upgrade to Tristan's modern-style apartment. But lacked the cozy warmth of Angeline's place. Walking side felt like coming home.

Or rather, what he imagined coming home would feel ke, if he had one.

Calm, comfortable and filled with the enticing scent of sexy, spirited she-wolf.

A fantasy. Nothing more than a fleeting dream the mind

called forth in times of extreme stress just so he could ge
through the ordeal.

Each Dogman had just such a dream. They'd go fera
without one.

Handing him a bottle, she plopped next to him on th
couch and kerplunked one furry-booted foot onto the cof
fee table, then the other.

"Cheers." Her bottle clinked against his, then she tippe
back her head, exposing the slender column of her smooth
creamy neck, and took a long swig. His mouth parche
with want of the taste of her skin despite the cold liqui
sloshing down his own throat.

In all the years he'd carried Angeline's picture in hi
pocket, Lincoln never imagined he'd actually share a drin
with his angel.

Oh, he'd tried to unravel the mystery of the woma
in the photograph in the months following the death o
the Dogman who'd entrusted him with the prized posses
sion. But Lincoln had very little to go on. Only the nam
"Angel" had been written on the back of the picture an
Tanner Phillip's next of kin had not known her identity.

In the beginning, Lincoln had reached for the phot
when hurt, indecisive or just plain lonely. Later he'd spo
ken to her upon waking and just before going to slee
Probably not the healthiest of habits, but his second-in
command, Lila, had said the rosary. By nature, Wahya
weren't religious. However, she had found comfort in th
tradition and repetitiveness. And so had he.

They all needed something larger than themselves fro
which to seek guidance, absolution and everything els
in between.

"What makes your family dinners stressful?" Linco
asked, restarting the conversation they began on the stair

"Irreconcilable differences." Angeline took anoth

drink. "It's insanity. My dad keeps picking the same fight, month after month, expecting that suddenly I'll conform to his expectations of a daughter." She snorted. "Not that he ever wanted one. After my mom died, he cut off my hair and dressed me in my brothers' hand-me-downs."

"You must've looked like your mother."

"I did." Angeline swirled her bottle. "Still do."

Lincoln took another swig of beer, unable to imagine the long auburn strands that fell below her shoulders stunted in a short bob. He much preferred the vision of her in masculine clothes...in particular, his sweatshirt enveloping her much smaller frame.

His thoughts drifted to the way the softness of her body had cushioned his when he'd rolled her beneath him while disoriented from a nightmare.

The mere memory of how perfectly their bodied aligned electrified his nerves, tingling and tantalizing his already sensitized skin.

"Everybody's curious about you," she said. "We've never had a Dogman in town." Her jaw tightened and her mouth pulled tight.

"Brice and I go back a few years. When he heard about my injury, he invited me here."

"Then why aren't you staying at his family's resort?"

"Not my style." Or in his comfort zone. He didn't need to be pampered or coddled. Besides, a couples retreat had been scheduled for Valentine's Day weekend and he definitely didn't want to be in the midst of a lovefest, especially during a full moon.

Wahyas were wired for sex. It regulated their wolfan hormones, keeping the primitive monster that lived inside them dormant. A full moon was the most critical time for Wahyas to have sex, but Dogmen had little time and opportunity to find willing partners every month.

So, Program scientists developed the hormone suppressor implanted into every Dogman before deployment. Only those involved in the Program knew of the implant's existence because of the known side effect of increased hostility.

Dogmen were highly trained to manage their aggressive impulses, whether naturally occurring or chemically induced. Unleashing the implant on the general Wahyan population could give rise to the very beasts that the drug had been created to suppress.

Removal of the implant proved just as challenging. After a wolfan's sexual instinct had been stifled for so long, some Dogmen found the deluge of natural hormones overwhelming.

Lincoln's implant had been removed after the last full moon. With less than a week until the next one, he needed to find a consenting sex partner. Soon.

He glanced sidelong at Angeline and his heart thudded all the way down to his groin. His wolf had declared his choice. Undeniably, Lincoln wanted to agree. But things could get oh, so complicated.

He liked simple.

And he knew one thing for sure. There was absolutely nothing simple about Angeline.

Chapter 5

"What is that god-awful noise?" It pounded in Angeline's head like a woodpecker drilling a tree for food.

Slowly and painfully, she opened her eyes. The shirt Lincoln had worn last night obscured her field of vision. Suddenly, the pillow her head rested upon moved.

"*Buenos días*, Angel." Lincoln's deep Texas drawl sounded thunderously close but at least the beep grating her nerves stopped.

The sluggish thoughts in her brain, however, kept going. Unfurling her legs, she sat up and rubbed her eyes. "Were you speaking Spanish?"

"Yeah. I grew up in a bilingual household. My maternal grandparents emigrated from Mexico to Texas when my mom was a child. But I also speak German, Tagalog and some Somali."

"Strange combo of languages."

"I learn whatever the Program tells me to." Lincoln began the process of putting on his prosthetic.

She remembered Lincoln asking if she was okay with him taking off his artificial leg because his stump hurt, but not much after he did.

"Um." She glanced at the coffee table littered with a Jack Daniel's decanter and likely every beer bottle she had in the fridge. All empty. "What happened last night?"

"You passed out and latched onto me in your sleep." He wiggled into his pants.

"I did not!" The screech in her voice made Angeline cringe.

"Oh, so it was a ploy to keep me here?" He cracked a smile. "Aw, Angel, all you had to do was ask."

She felt the weight of a frown on her jaw. "Tread lightly, I'm not a morning person."

Despite her warning, he laughed. "You certainly aren't. But you are quite adorable with your messy hair and grumpy face."

"You're not earning any brownie points, Dogman."

"That's not what you said last night." He had the nerve to wink.

"They only count if I remembering doling them out. Which I don't, so..." She massaged her temples.

"I'm not surprised." Lincoln stood, and Angeline felt woozy looking up at him. He began gathering the discarded bottles. "Most of these are yours."

"That can't be right," she said, trying to focus her fuzzy and somewhat incoherent memories. "I don't normally drink that much."

"Good to know," Lincoln said. "But I think your family dinners are more upsetting than you allow yourself to believe."

"Why? What did I say?" Angeline's heartbeat sped up,

lespite the sludge a night of drinking had deposited in ıer veins.

"Nothing that bears repeating." Lincoln dropped the ›ottles into the recycling bin underneath the sink.

"No, really. I need to know what I talked about."

"Tell me where the coffee is." Lincoln gave her an as-essing look. "Then I'll give you a play-by-play of all the ›eans you spilled."

Angeline's stomach churned and it wasn't from the ıangover. If her drunken self had told Lincoln about her nusic career…

"Check the pantry, third shelf. Coffee filters should be here, too."

While Lincoln busied himself in the kitchen, seemingly naking as much noise as possible, Angeline dragged her-elf into the bathroom, soaked a washcloth in cold water nd buried her face in it. This—the morning-after hang-ver—is why she didn't usually indulge in more than two rinks in one night.

Dampening the cloth, she glanced into the mirror and ımped back. Her bloodshot eyes were a little puffy, but er hair…yikes! What a tangled mess.

And Lincoln thought she looked adorable? Definitely, ıe man needed glasses.

At least nausea didn't accompany the hangover, but if he didn't take a painkiller for the pounding in her head, might split open.

She fumbled through the medicine cabinet for ibupro-en and downed two caplets with a glass of water. After crubbing her face and rinsing the funk from her mouth, ıe tackled combing her hair. Seriously, how did she get › many knots?

Emerging from the bathroom, Angeline looked much ıore presentable than when she'd gone in. Her nose twitched at the rich, robust aroma of fresh-brewed cof fee, and she followed the scent all the way to the kitchen

Lincoln handed her a big cup filled nearly to the rim.

"Thanks." Holding the ceramic mug between both hands, she took her first sip. The heat sloshed down he throat ahead of the flavor. The more she drank, the mor the tightness in her body began to ease.

"I would've made breakfast, but your fridge is nearl empty and so is mine."

"I'm not usually up this early. On the occasion that am, I grab a pastry from the bakery."

"Sweets for the sweet," Lincoln said. "I'll remembe that."

"I'm not really sweet." She tried to glare at him over th rim of her coffee cup, but his sleepy eyes and soft smil were just so cute.

"Difference of opinion then." He poured a cup of coffe for himself and sat on the bar stool next to her.

"Okay," she said, swiveling toward him. "*You* spill th beans. I want to know every word I said to you."

"I don't have that much time. You became quite chatt after that third beer."

"Why did you let me keep drinking?"

"You have pretty, white teeth, Angel. And they looke very sharp when you snarled at me for trying to pry th bottle of Jack from your hand."

She-wolves didn't blush from embarrassment, but An geline certainly felt mortified at her lack of self-contro "Why didn't you leave?"

"Clearly, you were upset. And drinking the way yo did, I wasn't going to leave you alone. Something could'v happened to you."

"Did anything happen?" They were both fully dresse

when she woke up, but she really didn't remember much about last night.

"No," Lincoln said without hesitation and holding her gaze. "You drank, said a lot of nonsensical things, and then you fell asleep. I stayed in case you got sick." He lifted the coffee cup to his mouth to drink.

"You're a good guy, Lincoln. Thanks." Angeline swallowed another mouthful of coffee, too. "So what sort of stuff did I talk about?"

"Your mom. You miss her a lot."

True, Angeline did miss her mother. And she missed how differently her life would've been if her mother hadn't been murdered during a mugging.

"You also kept saying if I were Tristan, you would tell me a lot more." Curiosity edged around the uncertainty glimmering in his eyes. "Sounds like you and Tristan have been more than just friendly neighbors."

A subtle tension crept into Lincoln's body and his gaze left her face.

"No." Angeline shook her head. "It's not what you're thinking."

"It's okay," Lincoln said. "I don't need an explanation."

He might not, but Angeline's instinct pushed her to clarify. "Tristan is like a brother, but closer than my own. He knows things about me that my family and other friends don't."

"Maybe you should've called him last night instead of inviting me in." Lincoln carried his cup to the sink.

"Tristan has a mate now."

"So I've heard."

"I don't expect him to be my confidant anymore. It wouldn't be right."

Lincoln finished rinsing out his coffee cup. "I guess you're in search of a new one and I didn't cut the mustard."

"I barely know you." How could she trust him the way she trusted Tristan, who'd been there for her for most of their lives? "Is it true that you're retiring from the Program?"

"That's what people keep telling me."

Not exactly the answer she wanted to hear.

"Well, who knows?" She shrugged. "If you stick around long enough—" They might eventually become friends... good friends...really good friends with full moon benefits.

"I'm not planning on it," he said abruptly. "Neither should you."

Well, if that wasn't a door being slammed in her face...

"Thanks for playing watchdog last night." She walked to her front door and opened it. "But I'm in control of all my faculties now. Time for you to leave."

He dried his hands on the dish towel, walked to the door and stepped outside into the breaking dawn.

"Angeline." He turned around. Of the myriad of emotions flickering across his face, confusion, regret, loneliness—those were the ones that tugged her heart strings.

Damn, she was too soft.

"I have a really busy day," Angeline lied. She didn't have to be at the restaurant until the afternoon. "See you around."

Locking the door, she hoped her heart took notice. Lincoln was no different than Tanner. Dogmen lived for the Program. Nothing and no one else mattered. And she would never put herself through that turmoil ever again.

Lincoln stepped into the Walker's Run Resort and shook off the cold. A large fireplace in the rustic seating area crackled with flames, and red roses and hearts decorated the main lobby. A Happy Valentine's Day banner hung behind the guest services counter. Coming from a part of the world where conflict and violence had become commonplace, he found the commercialization of love off-putting.

Intentionally early for his meeting, Lincoln walked to a seating area near the fireplace and sat in a high-backed leather chair to watch everyone coming and going. Brice had invited him to meet the security team leaders and unofficially consult on the upgrade process of the pack's well-being. He'd also given Lincoln access to the resort's state-of-the-art gym, which he planned to use to continue his fitness training.

Two sentinels dressed as resort employees casually patrolled the lobby. Outside, Lincoln had noted at least three sentinels working valet and four handling bell service. Lincoln expected those numbers would increase, depending on the number of non-pack wolfans registered for rooms.

He turned his attention to the three offices with interior glass windows that faced the lobby. Two offices were dark, but the middle one had the blinds up and the light on. Cassie sat at a desk, her back straight and her fingers tapping on a computer keyboard.

Hands paused and she turned, looking directly at him. He gave a slight nod as she waved.

A few minutes later, limping, Brice walked slowly out of the corridor. Cassie's attention turned to him.

Brice gave her a wink, which broadened her smile. Nearly an entity in and of itself, the palpable love bouncing between them was a phenomenon Lincoln had never witnessed.

His parents loved each other and loved him, in their own way. But their mateship, and their family life, had been centered on being the best of the best. Life was a competition to win and affection merely distracted one from the ultimate end goal.

If Lincoln had remembered what his family had taught,

he wouldn't have allowed his emotions to lead him and his team into a trap. While in Walker's Run, he needed to stay focused on his mission and not be led astray by indulging in errant emotions and human customs, or he would screw up his chance to get back on active duty and lose the only opportunity he had to find Dayax.

"Tristan's office is on the third floor," Brice said, approaching.

Lincoln matched Brice's stride but remained a half step behind him. As progressive as some wolfan packs were, a natural pecking order remained. Brice, the Alpha-in-waiting and a direct descendant of the first Alpha of Walker's Run, deserved his respect.

The Wahyas of Walker's Run had done well in choosing an Alpha family who, through the generations, had remained committed to serving the pack rather than accumulating wealth and power.

Not that the Alpha family didn't have both. The difference being that they shared the wealth and utilized the power for the benefit of the pack.

All able-bodied adult pack members were expected to work and contribute to the pack's finances—a tithe of sorts to the Walker's Run Co-operative that funded their health care, education, business start-ups and things for the pack's overall enjoyment. The Co-op's Family Park, for instance, included a baseball field, picnic pavilions and an entertainment stage. Unfortunately, the stage itself had been destroyed a few months back by a diversionary explosion in a domestic power struggle between a pack member and an outsider.

It might be easy for wolfan rogues to mistake the peace-loving Walker's Run pack as being ripe for a takeover. However, Lincoln had seen enough of the world to recognize that wolfans and humans who fought to defend their families and their ideals could become the deadliest forces on the planet.

They stopped at the brass elevators rather than continuing to the wide, curved hardwood stairs.

"I can make it up the steps," Lincoln said, trying to keep the strain from his voice. If he couldn't convince Brice of his fitness, he'd have no chance swaying the medical review board.

"Be my guest," Brice replied without censure. "But I can't. Cold weather wreaks havoc on my bad leg. It's a struggle to stand and walk today. Climbing the stairs will likely do me in."

Ding! The doors slid open and Brice stepped inside the elevator. Lincoln joined him.

"I meant what I said last night before you left." Brice held Lincoln's gaze as the elevator began to climb. "Regardless of when you retire, I hope you'll consider settling down in the Walker's Run territory."

"I appreciate the invitation," Lincoln said. "It's hard to look that far ahead when all I can think about is that scared wolfling waiting for me to keep my promise." A new pack, a new home, a new family to keep him safe: That was what Lincoln had vowed to find for Dayax. Until Lincoln fulfilled that oath, he couldn't begin to think of his own future.

The elevator doors opened. Instead of guest rooms, the third floor housed offices and conference rooms.

He followed Brice to an office with a large interior glass window looking into the corridor. No matter how civilized they became, wolfans didn't like being boxed in.

The wolfan sitting behind the desk and the one leaning next to him with his palm flat on the desk blotter studying the computer screen looked up as he and Brice entered.

"Lincoln, this is Tristan Durrance, our chief sentinel."

Brice waved his hand toward the blond man behind the desk beginning to stand.

"Finally, a face to go with the voice." Grinning, Tristan extended his hand in the customary greeting that Wahyas who worked closely with humans had adopted. "Sorry about the mix-up with the key."

"No worries. Angeline got me oriented and I've settled in." Lincoln pocketed the key Tristan handed to him.

"Great." Tristan hiked his thumb toward the man beside him. "This is Reed Sumner, one of our lieutenants."

Like Shane, Reed greeted him with an obligatory nod of acknowledgment rather than a handshake. After pleasantries were exchanged, they discussed the recent run-ins with illegal game poachers inside the pack's protected forest and a series of unrelated attacks by revenge-seeking wolfans. In Lincoln's experience, their concerns were generally consistent with what most first-world packs deal with from time to time.

"It would be a great help if you ran through our security protocols and advised where and how to tighten our current measures," Tristan said.

Reed cut his eyes at Lincoln.

He needed to be careful to avoid stepping on the lieutenant's paws.

"Sounds like Reed has a good handle on things," Lincoln told Tristan, then turned his attention back to Reed. "But I'd love to stretch my legs if you don't mind a tag along."

"I'd appreciate the company," Reed said, beginning to relax. "Is now too soon?"

"Not for me." Lincoln admired how their recent adversities had brought the Walker's Run pack closer together, making them stronger rather than tearing them apart. They were a united force working toward a common goal.

A team.

Something Lincoln no longer had.

His ribs seemed to fold in on his lungs. The immense sorrow he buried after realizing his team members had died because of their loyalty to him threatened to surface. If he gave in to the grief, it would simply consume him and their deaths would be in vain. He needed to keep a clear mind and a singular focus on finding Dayax.

Chapter 6

Five o'clock, and a few early birds were seated inside Taylor's Roadhouse. According to Reed, by eight the place would be packed and Lincoln wanted to be out before the crowd arrived.

Funny how masses of people had not bothered him while on active duty. However, a few days ago in the Munich airport surrounded by hundreds of people, he'd experienced the first panic attack in his life. Accelerated heart rate, shortness of breath, ringing in his ears, cold, clammy hands despite sweating profusely, had forced him to seek solace in the men's room. What an unwelcomed start to his first venture back into the civilian world. A splash of cold water on his face and a harsh internal dialogue had gotten him through the episode. And he'd sincerely hoped it would be the last.

However when Reed had invited him to meet up with some of the security team tonight, the same odd creepy-crawly sensation had tightened Lincoln's chest and he'd begged off with a rain check. Of course, that didn't mean he would deprive himself of "the best steaks in three counties." Nor did he want to miss a chance to talk to Angeline.

Last night, he'd made the right call not telling her about his connection to Tanner Phillips. But after the strained way they'd parted, she might not answer the door if he knocked. Clearly, he'd upset her, but the conversation was leading to a road he wasn't allowed to explore, no matter how much he might want to do so.

Visually, he searched the restaurant for her, but only spotted one server. A blonde a few inches shorter than Angeline, and human. Wahyas had an eerie sense that allowed them to recognize their own kind. And she did not let off any signals, wolfan or otherwise.

An older woman approached the hostess station. Silver threads glinted in her hair, the rich, robust color of chestnuts but her eyes matched the exact shade of Angeline's sapphire blues.

"Welcome to Taylor's." Her wide, genuine smile appeared all too human. "You must be Lincoln."

A prickle scaled his spine. "Yes, ma'am. And you are?"

"Miriam Taylor, Angeline's aunt," she said. "She's told me all about you."

Lincoln hoped otherwise.

"I'm surprised to see you this early. Angeline mentioned you were getting acquainted with the sentinels today. They don't usually come in until later."

"Jet lag." Lincoln used the same lie he'd given Reed. "I need to eat then crash for a while."

"We'll get your belly filled and then you'll sleep like a lazy pup until morning."

"Sounds nice, but I never sleep more than a few snatches at a time."

"I imagine out of necessity, considering your line of work. But you're in Walker's Run, not a war zone. It's okay to relax and enjoy yourself."

"Yes, ma'am." Lincoln smiled, although he doubted there would ever come a time when he could drop his guard. "Is anyone joining you for supper?"

Only in spirit. "No, ma'am."

Miriam picked up one hard-bound menu. "Table or booth?"

Lincoln glanced around the cozy interior of the restaurant. The bar area had stools at the bar itself, booths along the wall and bistro tables of two and four. In the other section, booths were also along the wall with tables of four and six in the center. Larger parties probably used the huge round table in middle of the restaurant. A small stage sat in front of the dance floor and the kitchen had a long glass window in front of the grill so that patrons could watch their steaks being cooked. His mouth watered even though nothing had been placed on the grill.

"A small table in the bar is fine." He hoped the steaks tasted as good as his new friends had insisted they would. The ones he'd eaten in the Program's hospital in Germany had tasted like cardboard.

"It will be about twenty minutes before Jimmy starts putting steaks on the grill, so make sure to start with an appetizer, on the house." Miriam seated Lincoln at a bistro table and handed him a menu. "Would you like something to drink while looking over the menu?"

"Water, for now," he said, flipping through the three pages of alcoholic beverages listed at the back of the menu. It had been so long since he'd eaten in a restaurant like this Lincoln had forgotten the variety of items to choose from.

"I'll send over Tessa when she's finished with them."

Tessa, Lincoln assumed, was the blonde server delivering drinks to a table of elderly wolfans.

"Is Angeline here?" he asked Miriam, internally volleying between the desire to see her again and the dread of needing to fulfill a promise to a dead Dogman, which would likely draw her censure.

"She's in the storeroom taking inventory." Locked on Lincoln, Miriam's gaze narrowed ever so slightly beneath the delicate arch of her brow. "I could ask her to come out."

"No." He pretended hunger caused the unpleasant tug in his gut. "I'll talk to her later."

"Angeline mentioned that you're staying in Tristan's apartment."

"For the next few weeks."

"Well, we're glad to have you here."

Once he told Angeline about Tanner Phillip's last words and the photograph he'd entrusted to Lincoln, he doubted she would share her aunt's sentiment.

At her departure, Lincoln closed the menu and pushed it aside. He didn't much care about what he drank and the plethora of options made him antsy.

Unease coiled inside his chest and his body tingled from the hairs rising on his skin, despite not being on any covert mission about to face untold danger. In fact, since joining the Dogman program, Lincoln had never touched a paw in a more peaceful place than Maico, the quaint little town at the center of the Walker's Run pack's territory.

Definitely, nothing like Taifa.

Lincoln dug into his pocket for the Program-issued satphone, a mobile device that connected to private satellites rather than cell towers on the ground, and dialed into a secure message line.

Nothing.

During his recovery at the hospital, Lincoln had been in contact with Colonel Llewellyn, the commander of the human forces in Somalia. Of course the colonel had promised to do all he could to find Dayax.

But sixty-three days had passed and the boy had not been found. In his gut, Lincoln knew Dayax was alive and waiting. Waiting for Lincoln to bring him home.

"I'm Tessa." The bubbly blonde appeared table side, holding a round tray with a glass of ice water balanced in the center. "You must be new in town. I haven't seen you before, and everyone eventually makes their way into Taylor's." Her broad grin and sparkling green eyes didn't stir his senses the way Angeline's unamused frown and blue eyes darkened with irritation had.

"I rolled in Saturday night."

"Staying or passing through?" Tessa placed the glass of water on the table.

From the dilation of her pupils and the subtle way she inched closer to him, Lincoln got the feeling her questions were more for personal interest rather than the friendly banter the owners would typically ask their servers to provide to customers.

"A little of both. I'm doing some consulting for the Co-op for a couple of weeks." Unless Brice's contact in the Woelfesenat managed to get Lincoln's active duty status reinstated sooner.

"Well." Tessa laughed lightly. "They have a sneaky habit of keeping those they hire, so I expect to see you in here for a good, long time."

Lincoln didn't share Tessa's expectation.

"Ready to order?"

"A steak, rare."

"The Co-op steak?" She pulled a pad from her apron and slapped it on the tray hooked in her arm. "It's an eighteen-ounce porterhouse."

Suddenly, Lincoln remembered Lila, smirking at him and saying that he could thank her one day with a big, juicy steak.

"Make it two orders."

"You get two sides per platter."

Lincoln look at her and shrugged.

"Baked potato, sweet potato, steak fries, potato salad, Caesar salad, mac-and-cheese, green bean amandine, grilled asparagus—" Her words rolled into an incessant buzz.

"Surprise me," he said, swallowing the uncomfortable feeling scaling his throat.

Tessa jotted on her pad. "We have an extensive selection of domestic and imported beers."

Lincoln rubbed his hand along his jaw, stubbled with a day's worth of beard. "I'll have whatever Reed usually orders and make it two."

She stopped scribbling and slowly lifted her gaze. Her smile flat.

"You know him, right? He said he's in here a lot."

"Yeah, I know him," Tessa huffed. "It's a small town."

Her reaction suggested more, but Lincoln didn't care to ask.

"He drinks Little Red Cap."

"Never heard of it."

"It's domestic with limited distribution. We order it and a few other ales from Grimm Brothers Brewhouse in Colorado." She tapped her pen against the pad on the tray. "Is Reed joining you later?"

"Not tonight."

"You ordered two meals."

"I did." But Lincoln only planned to eat and drink one. The other he owed to Lila.

"As much as I appreciate you doing this," Jimmy Taylor said, accepting the weekly inventory sheets Angeline handed him, "I could get one of the full-timers to handle counting the supplies."

"I've been doing inventory since I was sixteen," Angeline replied. "It would be weird to hand over the job to someone else."

Her uncle smiled, but his eyes were filled with worry. "I don't want you to feel obligated."

"I don't," Angeline assured him. "I like working for you and Aunt Miriam." Mostly she liked having a routine that got her out of the apartment and gave her a chance to interact with people. Since she didn't work with a partner, songwriting was a solitary endeavor.

As pack-oriented creatures, Wahyas thrived on socialization and there was no better place for it than Taylor's Roadhouse. At least in their human forms.

The protected forest of the Co-op's wolf sanctuary allowed pack members to fraternize as wolves, especially during full moons. Although, when temperatures dropped below forty degrees at night, she preferred to run in the woods behind the apartment building. Afterward, she could walk straight into her toasty apartment, rather than waiting for the heater to warm her car on the drive back from the sanctuary.

"Do you like it well enough to take over the business one day?" Jimmy's gaze fell just shy of hers.

"What about Zach and Lucy?" Angeline's much younger cousins were Jimmy's true heirs.

"Zach has been talking to a Dogman recruiter again."

Icy fingers twisted Angeline's stomach. She certainly didn't want her cousin to end up like Tanner or Lincoln. She and Zach would have a frank discussion about the very real possibility of death and dismemberment.

"Lucy is considering transferring to a bigger college out of state." Jimmy sighed. "The more their mama and I try to keep them close, the more they can't want to scramble away."

"They need time to see that the world outside Walker's Run isn't all they think it is." Angeline hugged her uncle. "They'll come home, just like I did."

"Still." He squeezed her tight before letting go. "You're the one who's put time into this place. Miriam and I would like for you to take over the restaurant when we retire."

"I'll consider it," Angeline said more to alleviate her uncle's concern than to suggest actual intent. "But I expect you to keep running this place for a long, long time."

Relief washed over Jimmy's face and his smile turned genuine. "Deal."

The daily grind of actually running the restaurant took more time than Angeline cared to invest, but she didn't mind giving Jimmy and Miriam some peace of mind while their children sowed their oats.

They walked out of the storage room into the kitchen. While one cook tended the large gas stove, the other dropped a basket of steak fries in to the fryer. Another cook and one more server would arrive shortly and stay through closing.

"Aunt Miriam," Angeline called to the woman entering the kitchen.

As a child, Angeline didn't think her aunt favored her mother very much. But as Miriam aged, not only had she grown to look more like her sister, she had developed some of the same mannerisms and quirks.

With Miriam, Angeline could almost imagine what it would've been like to have grown up with her mother. Her aunt had even encouraged Angeline's love of music and paid for her lessons when her own father refused to do so.

"I gave Uncle Jimmy the inventory list, but despite the numbers now, you might want to increase the meat order for more steaks and ground beef. The full moon and Valentine's Day is Friday."

"Thanks for the reminder." Miriam wiped her hand on the apron tied around her waist as she walked toward Angeline. "Did Jimmy talk to you?" she asked quietly, touching Angeline's arm.

"Of course I did." He brushed past them and headed to their office to thumbtack the inventory list to the bulletin board. More than once Angeline had suggested they modernize the books, but her aunt and uncle were old school and feared entrusting their tried-and-true manual accounting system to a computer program.

"Well?" Her mouth drawn in a pensive grimace, Miriam peered at Angeline with the same dark shade of blue she remembered seeing in her mother's eyes.

"I told Jimmy that I would consider his offer, but he had to promise not to retire anytime soon."

Miriam's eyes twinkled with tears, and she hugged Angeline. "Thank you for putting his mind at ease."

"It's the least I could do for all that you and Jimmy have done for me over the years." She stepped back from Miriam, willing her tears to stay deep in the wells. An O'Brien never showed weakness, a mantra her father had drilled into Angeline and her brothers after their mother's tragic and untimely death.

"I should get out there and help Tessa."

"Yes, you should. There's at least one customer anxiously waiting to see you." Miriam shooed her from the kitchen.

Angeline ducked into the employee room to put on her half apron and grab an order pad before walking into the dining room. Tessa finished taking an order at a table in Angeline's section then beelined for her.

"You have two orders in, plus this one." Tessa handed

her an order ticket. "Table twenty should have their food coming out in a couple of minutes. Seventeen just went in. And have you met Lincoln, the new guy in town?"

Angeline followed Tessa's gaze to the bistro table for two in the bar where Lincoln nursed his beer. An untouched bottle sat on the placemat across from him. Curious, but definitely not jealous, despite the little kick in her gut, she couldn't help wondering who would be joining him.

"He's really hot, even if he does keep company with Reed—the rat bastard." Although Tessa had mumbled the last part beneath her breath, Angeline's wolfan ears had heard every word her recently dumped friend had uttered.

"Lincoln is my new neighbor," Angeline said, watching a kitchen helper deliver two steak platters to Lincoln's table.

"Lucky you." Tessa sighed dreamily.

"No. Not me," Angeline said, but Tessa had already walked away.

Over the next hour Angeline had a steady flow of customers and only managed to say "Hey" to Lincoln on her way to and from the bar with drink orders. The beer and food at the second place setting remained untouched throughout his entire meal.

Periodically, she'd felt him watching her. Perhaps he wanted an explanation for her behavior this morning. She wasn't quite sure herself. His warning that she should not expect him to become her new confidant shouldn't have bothered her. She knew better than to expect anything from a Dogman. Though Angeline felt no obligation to provide an explanation for her reaction, she did want to let him know that she wasn't angry at him.

Waiting for the bartender to fill a drink order, Angeline casually strolled to Lincoln's table. The beer for his guest remained untouched. "How was your day?"

"Informative." His eyes still looked tired and barely a fleeting smile dusted his lips. "I spent most of the time running the woods with Reed."

"He's a good guy. Smart. Loyal."

"Cynical," Lincoln added.

"He got shot by a poacher a few months ago."

Lincoln swung his left foot out. The hiking boot concealed the prosthetic within. "A bomb blasted me out of a two-story window."

"You still have nightmares."

"I imagine he does, too," Lincoln said easily. "Our failures haunt us far longer than our victories stay with us."

"He took a bullet for Shane. I wouldn't call that a failure."

"The failure is in believing we are invincible." Lincoln guzzled the last few swallows of his beer and slammed down the mug on the table. "And learning we aren't."

"You sound a bit cynical yourself."

Lincoln shook his head, avoiding her gaze. "Cynicism colors one's judgment and clouds the vision. What happened, happened. All I can do is adapt and keep going."

"Are you waiting for Reed?"

"No." Lincoln fiddled with the edge of his linen napkin. "I owe an old friend a steak dinner."

"You've been a while. Did he take a wrong turn somewhere?"

The muscle in Lincoln's jaw twitched. He lifted his sorrow filled gaze. "Died in the line of duty."

Angeline's stomach dropped, a sick feeling rose in her chest and her heart hurt as if it had broken all over again. Not for her loss but for all those who'd lost loved ones, living and dead, to the Program.

Dogmen turned their backs on everything and everyone they'd ever known. All communication with family and friends ceased. No one ever knew what became of their loved one unless they received a death notification or an injury forced the soldier into retirement, like Lincoln soon would be.

Long simmering anger ignited Angeline's tongue. "Instead of eating and drinking with the dead, maybe your sympathies should lie with those he abandoned when he became a Dogman. And, for what? To feed his ego and die who knows where without regard to those he left behind?"

"Angeline—" Lincoln began.

"Have you called your family? Do they know what happened to you? Do they know you're even alive?"

His guilty look answered for him.

"Unbelievable!" Angeline barely managed to keep the shriek out of her voice.

"They're better off not knowing."

"That's a lie Dogman tell themselves to keep their consciences clear. Speaking from experience, it's not better. It's far worse than any nightmare you've ever had."

Though angry and hurt by Tanner's rejection, Angeline didn't immediately stop loving him. Not knowing his whereabouts or his situation had been an unrelenting torture. Until one day when a sharp pain sliced all the way to her soul. In that moment, she knew Tanner was dead. He would never come home to her. He would never come home to anyone, except in a box.

Despite Lincoln's request for her not to leave, Angeline walked away and collected the drinks from the bar. Delivering the beverages to appropriate patrons, she caught a glimpse of Lincoln making his way to the exit.

Good riddance, she thought without truly meaning it. Neither Tanner's choices nor his fate were Lincoln's fault.

A deep part of herself compelled Angeline to apologize for her behavior. Another part of her refused.

As a Dogman, Lincoln represented the very ideal she hated. She'd lost her first love—her only love—to the Program, and it destroyed the life they should've had.

Lincoln slipped out of the restaurant and Angeline's heart clenched, a phantom ache that his ridiculous homage had resurrected. It had absolutely nothing to do with the devastated look on his face when she'd left his table.

And if she told herself that enough times, by the time she got off work she might actually believe it.

Chapter 7

"Lila!"

Lincoln wrenched himself awake before hitting the ground in his nightmare. In reality, he couldn't remember anything past those first moments of falling out the window. His mind remained blank until the moment he woke up, alone in the hospital at the Program's headquarters in Germany a week later, missing a leg.

Whenever he asked about his team, the medical staff would merely pat his shoulder and say that he needed to focus on his own recovery. The tight smiles and averted eyes that followed told him all he needed to know.

His team was dead. And he was to blame.

Lincoln threw aside the sheets and sat up. His breaths continued to come hard and fast and would likely continue until his heart stopped forcibly pounding from the dream-induced adrenaline rush.

Swinging his good leg over the side of the bed, he stared

at his scarred stump. Life would never be the same but he refused to simply accept retirement and quietly fade into the background. Not until he finished what he started. For Dayax. And for his team, whose loyalty had been rewarded with death.

Heavy-handedly, Lincoln rubbed his stump, stinging with phantom sensations. The physical therapist had chided him for being too aggressive with the desensitizing massage. The doctors had said the same about his push for recovery. They didn't understand that the pain distracted him from the quagmire of self-pity and gave him a definitive obstacle to conquer.

He squirmed into his knee shorts and snatched the sleeve off the nightstand. Pulling on the elastic-like fabric, he smoothed out the wrinkles until the material gloved his stump like his own skin, except for the glaring pale color that was nowhere near his naturally brown skin tone. He reached for the bionic limb that had fallen to the floor and fitted the cup onto the remaining part of his leg.

Carefully standing, Lincoln rocked on the prosthetic, allowing his weight to push out the air while his stump slid securely into place. The first steps were tentative. By the time he reached the open bedroom door, his gait became as fluid as it could be walking on an artificial leg.

The lights were on in the living room and kitchen. Even though his wolfan vision allowed him to see clearly in the dark, he didn't want to take a chance of tripping over something he'd overlooked.

Staring into the refrigerator at the lunch meat and four bottles out of a six-pack of beer, Lincoln knew he'd have to get more substantial food soon. A creepy-crawly feeling spread across his chest. He shivered, shaking off the sensation that gave rise to a childhood memory he'd rather not revisit.

Lincoln grabbed a beer and closed the refrigerator door. Eating civilian food rather than rations and mess hall grub, and civilian life in general, felt odd. Especially since he didn't have his team alongside him. They had done everything together. And he missed them, more than he could ever express.

The satphone on the counter chimed and an unknown number flashed across the screen. His heart suddenly beat double-time.

Lincoln picked up the phone. "Adams."

"¿Que pasa, capitán?" The masculine voice shocked Lincoln's ear.

His heart stilled and the blood in his veins cooled. Without heat, his muscles froze up and yet his knees felt weak and rubbery.

Phone in hand and plastered against his ear, Lincoln leaned heavily against the kitchen counter. *"¿Quién eres tú?"*

"It's Damien," the man said. "Did the fallout of that two-story building screw up your brain?"

"Damien Marquez died over two months ago," Lincoln answered as his "screwed-up" brain tried to reconcile the familiar voice he heard to the belief that his team had perished in the explosion.

"I'm not dead, Linc," the man on the other end of the line continued. "In case you're wondering, neither are the others. Well, except for Lila. There wasn't even enough of her—"

"Shut the hell up, Marquez." The guy really had no tact.

"Now you sound like the guy I remember." Damien snorted.

"I don't see what's so funny."

"You never did." A stark pause hung between them.

"How did you make it out of the building before it collapsed?" Lincoln asked, not wanting to give in to a mounting sense of relief.

"The blast knocked me off the stairs and I landed on

the ground floor. Brax and Nico pulled me out." The dark emotion in Damien's voice as he spoke suggested he clearly remembered every horrifying moment. "Sam—she took care of you until the medics arrived."

All but one member of his team had survived. One of the worry knots in Lincoln's chest loosened.

"Honestly, I didn't know you'd made it until Colonel Llewellyn mentioned that you were dogging him to find that orphan kid."

"Dayax," Lincoln said beneath his breath. "The boy's name is Dayax."

"I guess you haven't heard from the rest of the team since you thought we were dead."

Was the relief in Damien's sigh real or imagined?

"If they weren't injured, protocol would be to reassign them after a debriefing." But why didn't his CO or someone at HQ simply tell him that his team was alive?

Lincoln strolled into the living room and stretched out on the couch. "I take it you're not on active duty, or we wouldn't be having this conversation. Are you all right?"

"I had a dislocated shoulder, a torn meniscus in my knee, some shrapnel lacerations. Smacked my noggin pretty good but it didn't crack."

"Good thing you're hardheaded."

Damien laughed.

"Where are you, man?"

"Miami. Using up the last of my medical leave. I've been reassigned to a new team and we're scheduled to deploy to the Amazon. Does HQ not understand how much I hate the fucking humidity?"

"Command knows. They just don't give a shit."

In the eight months Damien had been on Lincoln's team, he'd never quite jelled with them. Of course, Lincoln and the others had been together for considerably longer and e had fully expected that Damien would eventually find is groove.

Now he would have to start the process over with a ew team.

"How about you, Linc? Were the HQ doctors able to ix your leg?"

"I got a new one."

"Damn." Damien's sigh crackled in Lincoln's phone. How's that gonna work for you?"

"I'm still on medical leave. No new orders yet." A trange awareness prowled Lincoln's senses. "For now, m in Maico, Georgia, doing some security consulting or the Walker's Run pack."

Glancing at the clock—half past midnight—Lincoln ood, ambled to the door and looked through the peep-ole into the dimly lit, empty corridor.

"I may have some business in Atlanta," Damien said. If you're close by, we should meet up."

"Tell me when and where, I'll be there."

A shadow moved up the wall. The click of boots echoed om the stairwell.

"I'll text you details as soon as my plans firm up," amien said.

"Roger that." The line went silent.

Lincoln watched Angeline move lithely down the cor-dor. Then, she stopped and looked over her shoulder, asting a troubled gaze at his door.

Lincoln's heart thumped an unusual beat. His instinct aid he'd be a fool to let her go to bed without clearing the r between them. Then again, the last time he'd trusted is instinct a dear friend had died.

Behind the condensation on the bathroom mirror, the flection of a pissy she-wolf stared back at Angeline. A ot shower had not improved her disposition.

She knew what it felt like for a man to watch her ever move. And she'd felt Lincoln's gaze on her the momer she'd stepped onto the third-floor landing.

Had he waited up for her? Why hadn't he opened th door when he'd seen her staring back, instead of lettin her stand in the cold like a freaking idiot?

She finished towel-drying, dressed in her comfy clothe and wished her jumbled thoughts about the Dogman wer as easily flushed away as the tissue she tossed in the toile

In the bedroom, she picked up her guitar and sat cros legged on the unmade bed. After strumming a few chord she tuned the strings and began again. Unfortunately, wit her mind and fingers out of sync, everything she playe sounded crummy.

The doorbell rang.

Pick between her fingers, her hand stilled over th strings. When Tristan lived down the hall, he would oc casionally stop by for a chat when he got off work, knov ing she would be up.

Maybe Lincoln wanted company, too.

Well, she had a mind to tell him a few things.

She laid the guitar on the bed and scrambled out of th bedroom, then nonchalantly walked through the livin room. The doorbell rang again.

"I'm coming!" Agitation caused her to twist the dea bolt harder than normal and Angeline swung open th door with her chin tilted upward so she could glare in Lincoln's eyes.

Only, nothing but air looked back at her.

She dropped her gaze to the pizza delivery boy wh barely looked old enough to shave.

"Fourteen ninety-nine." His gaze slid up and down h body and back up to her chest, which, in her braless sta with cold air passing through the thin material of her long-sleeved T-shirt, clearly outlined her hardened nipples.

"Grow up!" She stepped back to shut the door.

"Hey!" He shoved the pizza box into the doorway, preventing the door from closing. "Pay up or I'm calling my supervisor."

"Call away. I didn't order anything. You have the wrong apartment."

"The ticket says Chatuge View Apartments, number twenty-one." He looked at her door proudly displaying the golden numerals two and one.

"Let me see." She snatched the ticket off the top of the box. Sure enough, the caller had given her address but the wrong name.

"This goes to Lincoln Adams," she said, waving the paper in front of the young man's face and pointing down the hallway. "He's in the corner apartment, number twenty-five."

"The delivery is for apartment twenty-one. Are you gonna pay up or what?"

Angeline matched the kid's exasperated huff. "Wait here."

Despite his protest, she shut the door. He retaliated by keeping his finger pressed against the doorbell until she returned with the cash and sent him on his way.

Glaring down the corridor, she thought about keeping the pizza. But wolfans took food seriously. Better to deal with Lincoln now rather than later, when he came looking for his food.

After closing the door behind her, Angeline beelined for apartment twenty-five. Taking a cue from the delivery boy, she pounded the door until Lincoln answered wearing only his boxers. With his dark hair in disarray and sleepy eyes narrowed at her, he loomed in the doorway.

"Here." She jabbed the pizza box into his chiseled abdomen. "Next time, give them the right apartment number."

He made no effort to claim the box. "It's not mine."

"Your name is on the ticket." Her teeth chattered as a cold wind blew through her.

"They delivered it to you."

"Because you gave them the wrong apartment number." Her nipples, definitely pointy after the last breeze, did not escape Lincoln's notice.

His entire body tensed and his Adam's apple prominently traveled down his throat. But when his gaze flickered back to her face, his eyes were clear. "It's not mine," he said again, then turned and walked away, leaving her standing in the doorway.

Since he hadn't shut her out, Angeline stepped inside to get out of the cold and closed the door.

"Sheesh! It's freezing in here."

Lincoln glanced at her from the kitchen. "Didn't notice." Opening the refrigerator, he pulled out two beers. "Grab a glass from the cabinet if you don't want to drink from the bottle," he said, strolling past her and into the living room.

First setting the beer on the coffee table, he eased onto the couch, grabbed the remote and muted the television. When she made no effort to join him, Lincoln's head slowly rotated in her direction. "I can resist a lot of things," he said as his gaze lifted from the box in Angeline's hands to her face. "Food isn't one of them. If you don't want to stay, leave the pizza on the counter. Otherwise…" He patted the seat cushion beside him.

A test, perhaps? To gauge her willingness to move past the kerfuffle at Taylor's.

"It's a little too frosty in here for me. I can almost see my breath." Angeline placed the pizza box on the kitchen counter.

Hand gripped on the couch arm, Lincoln hoisted himself up and went over to the thermostat.

"How about the fireplace?" Angeline opened the pantry and snagged a handful of napkins. "The controller should be on the mantel."

For the first time, she noticed the quiet thump of Lincoln's artificial foot as he walked.

Lincoln picked up the small device and the gas fireplace came to life. "You know a lot about this place."

Napkins and pizza box in hand, Angeline strolled into the living room and placed the items on the coffee table. "Tristan and I have been close since we were kids. We've always looked after each other."

"Sounds like me and Lila," Lincoln said, joining Angeline on the couch. "For the last five years, she was my best friend."

"What happened?"

"She died on our last mission."

Angeline's stomach dropped. "Is she the soldier you bought the beer and steak for?"

"Yes." Lincoln's head bowed slightly and his eyes squinted shut before his hand swiped down his face. "One of the last things she said to me was that I owed her a nice, thick, juicy steak."

"I'm sorry for your loss," Angeline said quietly. "I understand what it feels like to lose someone close to you."

Wordlessly, he turned his head, glancing sidelong at her.

"I should not have been rude to you at Taylor's. It's not your fault that someone I loved chose to be a Dogman rather than have a mateship with me."

"No apology necessary, Angel." Lincoln flipped open the pizza box. Inside was a large heart-shaped pizza loaded with meats and cheese. Slowly, he turned to Angeline. One dark eyebrow rose in a question while an irritating smile spread across his masculine mouth.

"It's probably a special promotion. Valentine's Day is next week."

Still grinning, he placed a slice on a napkin and handed it to Angeline.

"I didn't order this pizza."

"And yet you paid for it and brought it to me," he teased. "How sweet."

"It would've been sweeter if you had paid for the pizza before the guy delivered it to me."

"But then you wouldn't have had a reason to come over." After grabbing a slice for himself, Lincoln leaned back on the couch, closed his eyes and took a giant bite. A sexy growl of satisfaction rumbled in his throat as he chewed. "I haven't had pizza since college."

"Really? Why?" Angeline wiped away the cheese that dribbled on her chin.

"No one delivers to the jungle, or the desert or the swamp. Or Antarctica."

"You went to the South Pole?"

"If I confirm or deny that question, I'll have to terminate you." He made the statement with lethal seriousness but his mouth quirked into a smile before he took the next bite of pizza.

She playfully bumped his shoulder and was rewarded with a soft, playful growl that flooded her senses with an awareness of his undeniable masculinity. Common sense dictated that she should leave immediately. But his apartment was warm and toasty now. Neither her body nor her stomach wanted to brave the crisp, cold night to scurry down to her home and an empty refrigerator.

Chapter 8

Stone-cold determination.

Lincoln faced each and every mission with stone-cold determination. This one would be no different.

Get in, get the objective, get out. That was the plan.

He'd followed the same plan when trying to locate Dayax. That mission hadn't turned out so well.

Midmorning on Tuesday, only a few cars were in the parking lot behind Anne's Market. Just as Angeline had predicted.

Lincoln shut off the truck engine and opened the door. Slinging his good leg out, he pivoted in the seat and grabbed the door handle for support. He climbed out and adjusted his balance until he felt steady on the artificial limb.

Slowly, Lincoln followed the sidewalk to the front of the long building, housing several businesses facing the one-way street framing Maico's quaint town square. Keeping

focused on his agenda, he stared straight forward until h
reached Anne's Market.

Inside, he glanced around to get his bearings. It wa
a small store with a decent produce section to the left,
small deli and refrigerated section to the right, canned an
dry goods in the center and, according to the sign hangin
from the ceiling, a meat section in the back.

First, he needed a cart. Unfortunately, the one h
grabbed was jammed into another and wouldn't shak
loose. He looked around to make sure no one was watch
ing, then gripped the handle, lifted the wheels off the floc
and slammed it down. It made a terrible noise but the forc
knocked the buggy loose and, heart pounding, he went o
his less than merry way.

Though small, especially in comparison to the mega
size chain stores, the market seemed to have more tha
anyone could ever need. Aisles of canned goods lined th
center of the store with so many selections that Lincol
simply did not know what to choose.

He headed to the outer sections filled with produc
How hard could it be to buy a tomato? Apparently a degre
in agricultural science would've been beneficial. Ther
were heirlooms, grape-size, Romas, organic, home-grow
and imported. All he wanted was one to slice, salt and e
with a platter of scrambled eggs.

Closing his eyes, he picked one tomato then headed t
the refrigerated section. Eggs were eggs, right? Apparentl
they came in half dozen, dozen, a dozen and a half, tw
dozen, three dozen and four dozen containers. He reache
for the closest carton, noticing the slight tremor in his han

Seriously, he'd faced down terrorists and mercena
ies. How could grocery shopping alone rattle his nerves

He took a deep breath and slowly exhaled, which di

nothing to ease the sound of his heart thumping in his ears or the crackle of electricity that raised the hair on his arms.

"Better check those eggs." Unexpectedly, Angeline's Southern twang drifted over his shoulder. "You don't want to get home and find one cracked."

At the rate he was going, Lincoln would be lucky to get home with them at all.

She slid the carton from his death grip and opened it. "See?"

Two eggshells were broken, more than likely from the frustrated way he'd latched onto the carton.

Angeline set them aside.

"These are my favorites." Selecting a green foam container, she inspected the eighteen eggs inside, then set them in his cart.

Her handbasket crooked in her arm, Angeline continued on her way. Instinctively, Lincoln followed.

"I could use some good recommendations." He strolled beside her, the tightness in his chest easing. "It's been a long time since I've had so many things to choose from." He wasn't sure why anyone needed so many choices, especially when others in some parts of the world had none.

"You're going to need the basics, so let's start with the nonperishables."

"Lead the way." He waved his hand in an after-you gesture.

Wearing jeans tucked into her black, pointy-heeled boots and a long cardigan sweater, Angeline took the lead. If Lincoln wasn't careful, the mesmerizing sway of her hips might lead him to the edge of a cliff.

They stopped in the paper goods section.

"Do you like washing dishes?"

Lincoln shook his head.

"Neither do I." Angeline dropped a stack of paper plates

into his cart. Followed by a roll of paper towels and a box of garbage bags.

The next stop, the personal hygiene aisle, displayed at least a dozen brands of soap—and that was just the bars that came in boxes. The body gels and foams took up nearly as much room on the shelves as did the shampoos.

He simply stared at all of them. The flutter in his heart started again and his stomach tightened.

Just pick one!

He reached for a small, rectangular box and envisioned the slippery bar sliding from his hand and dropping to the shower floor. Since he didn't want to spend half of his shower time hopping on one leg, trying to retrieve the soap, Lincoln grabbed the first bottle of body wash within reach.

"You should smell it," Angeline said.

Lincoln carefully unscrewed the cap and sniffed. It smelled like soap and flowers.

He lifted it toward Angeline for her to get a whiff. Instantly, her nose wrinkled.

Okay, not this one.

It really shouldn't matter which ones she liked, but he couldn't stop himself from seeking her opinion on every damn one of them. When her eyes closed and she took a second sniff of the woodsy-scented body wash with a hint of citrus and amber, a soft, sexy smile curved her mouth. Lincoln nabbed two bottles. The full moon was only a few days away and if she was looking for a partner for the evening, or any other evening, he definitely wanted her to have that same response if she scented him. And he hoped she did.

His libido had reawakened the night they'd met. At first he'd wondered if his reaction had simply been a response to his hormones righting the chemical balance in his body after years of suppression. But none of the other women he'd encountered over the last few days had sparked the same feeling.

The air seemed to charge whenever Angeline was near and she pulled from him a need to protect and pleasure. A need that would intensify as the full moon drew near.

The way she turned and smiled made Lincoln feel as if she'd read his thoughts.

Silently, he laughed at the notion. In their wolf forms, Wahyas were telepathic with others also in their wolf form. The ability to mentally communicate did not transfer to their human forms, unless a mate-bond had formed. Not all wolfans in a mateship developed the ethereal connection, but those who did were synced mind and body, heart and soul.

Lincoln's heart and soul belonged to the Dogman program. His mind and body would do well to remember the commitment he'd made and not get used to Angeline's company. Despite pressure from his CO, Lincoln had no immediate plans to retire and settle down. But he was a long way from proving his readiness for active duty if he couldn't accomplish the simple task of grocery shopping on his own.

Humming the new tune that she was composing, Angeline drove into the parking lot of the Chatuge View Apartments. Admittedly, even if one climbed on top of the roof with a pair of binoculars, Lake Chatuge would be a distant blur. There was, however, a nearby retention pond the residents had jokingly named after the big lake.

She parked next to Lincoln's empty truck. Instead of following him to their apartment complex, Angeline had stopped by the gas station to top off her tank before coming home.

With one lightweight shopping bag in hand, she climbed

out of the car. Rarely did she purchase more than she coul
eat in a week. Lincoln, however, had loaded up his cart
From the stress the activity seemed to cause him, Angelin
figured he didn't want to return to the store anytime soon

At first Lincoln had relaxed when she'd begun help
ing him find the things he wanted. But before they'd bee
ready to check out, a dark mood had settled over him. Hi
side of the conversation had whittled down to grunts b
the time they'd parted. Except for the harsh words he'
snarled when she'd asked if he wanted her assistance get
ting his groceries to the truck.

Angeline peered at the two bags left in the truck bed
wondering if she should risk a repeat. When Lincoln didn'
appear after a full minute, she gathered his groceries wit
her own and headed upstairs.

His door had been left open and he stood in the kitche
guzzling a bottle of water. He turned as she walked int
the apartment. The storm in his eyes had yet to subside
His gaze dropped to the bags in her hands. "What are yo
doing?"

"I saw these in the back of the truck. Since I was com
ing upstairs, I thought I'd save you a trip back down."

"Did you not understand what I said earlier?" An angr
treble crisped his words. "I don't need anyone's help!"

"I'm just being neighborly." Angeline placed his bag
on the kitchen counter. "I would've done it for anyone."

"I'm not *just* anyone." The underlying snarl was quiet
menacing, and absolutely pissed off Angeline.

"Because you're a big, bad Dogman," she snapped, step
ping toward him. "Big freakin' deal!"

"It *is* a big deal." A tremor ran along his clenched ja
and his fingers tightened around the empty water bottl
crackling and collapsing it in his fist.

"Being a Dogman or accepting help?" Angeline stoo

lose enough to feel warm puffs of air on her face as Lin-
oln's chest heaved. "You're in the real world now, Lincoln.
nd while you're here, you are part of the community.
art of the pack."

Giving him the *get-your-shit-together* look she reserved
or the babysitting times when her nieces and nephews got
n her last nerve, Angeline raised on her toes. "Get used
people being neighborly and offering a helpful hand.
's who we are. It's what we do. And we aren't going to
hange for you—*Dogman*."

The corded muscles in his neck flexed as he swallowed.

After a glaring match that she refused to forfeit, pri-
al interest flickered in his eyes, defusing the anger but
hipping up emotions just as turbulent. His gaze drew
ack, as if taking in all of her face, which warmed with
e visual caress. When he focused on her mouth, her lips
ngled. Angeline could list a dozen or more reasons why
he should walk away. Only one to stay.

Her instinct ruled in favor of the one.

Pressing her lips against his mouth, she gave him a
haste kiss. Eyes open and intently watching her, Lin-
oln laid his hands on her waist and urged her closer. As
he snuggled against him, his arms wrapped around her,
olding but not restraining. His eyelids slid closed and
is lips parted.

Her eyes drifting closed, Angeline deepened the kiss.
ently, she probed his mouth, eliciting a soft, deep mascu-
ne growl. A shiver of satisfaction swept across her skin,
arming her despite the cold breeze drifting in from the
pen door.

He took charge of the kiss, branding her mouth, claim-
g her breath and heating her to the very core. Usually
he kept her head when kissing a man. Never allowing too
uch emotion or real feeling to emerge.

She'd lost her heart once to a Dogman. To do so agai would be foolish. Dogmen were committed to the pro gram every bit as much as true mates were to each othe

But that didn't mean she couldn't enjoy Lincoln's kisse or caresses, among other things.

The feel of his hands palming her curves and gliding u her back to cradle her neck sent an electric tingle down he spine. He tilted back her head, comfortably resettling he from her tiptoes to the flats of her feet. She sighed agains his mouth. Without breaking their kiss, he softly chuckled

Whatever worries that had darkened Lincoln's mood, h seemed to have forgotten. Angeline sensed no more ange and frustration, only curiosity and desire.

"Am I interrupting?" Tristan's voice carried above th knock on the open door.

Angeline stepped back from the kiss. Despite the les than friendly look she aimed at Tristan, he responded wit an irritating grin.

"We were, um..." Eyes still slightly hooded and a sma smile upon his mouth, Lincoln cleared his throat. "She wa helping me with the groceries."

"Never heard it called that, but okay." Tristan's gri broadened and a tease glinted in his dark eyes.

"Were we meeting up today?" Lincoln asked.

"Nah." Tristan waved his hand. "I was on my way t see Angeline and noticed your door was open."

Although Lincoln's expression and loose-limbed pos ture didn't change, Angeline sensed the tension creep ing into his body. Could feel it, actually, tightening he muscles.

If she didn't know better, she would think Lincoln wa a little jealous. More than likely, his heightened tensio was due to Tristan's sudden appearance.

"Nel's baby shower is today," Angeline said. "I asked Tristan to pick up the gift."

"Not going to the party?" Lincoln asked.

"Not my thing." Nothing against Nel. Angeline didn't quite fit in with Nel's circle of human friends. And because Angeline and Tristan had been intimately close friends, she felt a little awkward around his pregnant mate.

"Well, thanks for being neighborly." Lincoln lifted a couple of cans from the bag on the counter and stepped toward the small pantry.

Eyes narrowing ever so slightly, Tristan's gaze flickered to Lincoln and back to Angeline.

"Anytime." She snagged Tristan's elbow, tugging him along as she left.

"I'll catch up with you tomorrow," Tristan said to Lincoln, stopping to close the door.

Angeline hurried down the corridor to her apartment. Tristan followed at a leisurely stroll.

"So." He stepped inside and shut out the cold. "You and Lincoln seemed cozy."

"I don't do cozy." Angeline walked into the kitchen and put away her few groceries before gathering the gift basket in the bedroom. "Give Nel my best."

"I didn't do cozy, either, until I met Nel."

"Lincoln is a Dogman. No matter how strong of an attraction we might have, his heart will always belong to the Program." And Angeline wouldn't set herself up for another broken heart.

Chapter 9

The icy fingers of the crisp, Wednesday morning air pinched Lincoln's face. Standing near the edge of the ledge at Walker's Pointe, he gazed over the Walker's Run territory and down at the sleepy little town of Maico below. Calm, serene. Peaceful.

After all of the violence he'd seen and been required to do, Lincoln never expected to experience those feelings again. Yet, here he was, in the most idyllic place he would ever set his paw upon, daydreaming about accepting Brice's invitation to make Maico, the gentle town in the heart of the Walker's Run territory, his home.

But what would Lincoln do if he stayed?

A career soldier accustomed to watching tanks rolling past instead of ordinary trucks and cars and motorcycles, he lacked any useful civilian skills.

"This is my favorite place." Brice stepped beside Lincoln.

"I can see why." Lincoln deeply inhaled fresh, crisp mountain air. "It feels…"

"Like home?"

"Surreal. I'm not used to all this tranquility."

"It's not hard to adapt to Walker's Run. This place settles in your blood and roots in your soul. Makes it difficult for some wolfans to leave."

"I'm not here to settle down." Lincoln stuffed his hands into the pockets of the thick jacket he'd received in the shipment of clothes from headquarters.

"When we met in Romania, I saw the same restlessness and longing in your eyes that I had felt before returning home. Even then, you were growing tired of the Program. There's nothing wrong with wanting out."

"I don't want out." *Not yet.*

The news today from Colonel Llewellyn did not deviate from the script he'd given Lincoln every time he'd called. No one had seen or heard from Dayax, and his body had not been found.

This time, though, the Colonel had spoken the grim truth that the boy might never be found, alive or dead. Lincoln still had to try. "I can't help Dayax if I'm not a Dogman."

"My friends in the Woelfesenat agree."

Lincoln's entire body switched to running on silent mode. The breath stilled in his lungs. The steady thump of his heart quieted to a whisper. Even his thoughts paused as he watched and waited for Brice to continue.

"A new Dogman team will soon join the human forces in Taifa. When they deploy, so will you. Your only mission will be to find Dayax and the other missing children."

The tiny hairs at the base of Lincoln's neck began to rise. "I sense a *but* coming."

"You have to pass the readiness evaluation."

"Damn!" The test was a three-week assault of a recruit's senses, strength and willingness to die for the Program.

"Since you're already a Dogman, I convinced them to simply put you through the final physical obstacle course."

"Fair enough." As a weight lifted from Lincoln's shoulders, cold determination settled in his gut. Weeks of rehab had kept him physically fit, but he needed more practice shifting. No longer could he simply shuck off his clothes and go wolf. Now he had to carefully remove his leg or risk disintegrating the state-of-the-art prosthetic prototype the Program had entrusted to him.

"I bargained with the Woelfesenat to grant you one last mission, Linc. But I couldn't stop your mandatory medical retirement. Whether or not you come home with Dayax, your career as a Dogman will be over."

"I appreciate everything you've done." He was more than humbled by it, actually. Lincoln had seen the impact of Brice's hard-hitting negotiating skills in Romania. Brokering peace in the midst of pure, unadulterated hatred required more than talent. One needed divine favor.

Something Brice seemed to have in spades and wasn't stingy in dispensing.

"After you find him, what then?"

"Hadn't really thought much further than that."

"You need to, for yourself and Dayax."

Lincoln returned his gaze to the tranquil community below.

Home. The word pulsed through his mind.

Perhaps his pain medication had skewed his senses. Southwest Texas had been his home. And the Big Bend pack had always buzzed with activity and competition to be the best.

There was nothing inherently wrong with that mindset. It had propelled his mother forward in her career a a Texas Ranger and had kept his father alive as an undercover DEA agent. It had also formed the foundation of Lincoln's career. Unfortunately, no one could stay at the top forever. And his topple had caused his best friend her life.

"If the Woelfesenat allows me to bring Dayax to the States, would someone in Walker's Run be interested in fostering him?" Lincoln would be able to keep tabs on the boy if he was adopted into Brice's pack.

"What about yourself?"

"I'm not father material," Lincoln said. Dayax deserved so much more than a washed-up Dogman for a father.

"Are you sure about that?"

It was the one thing Lincoln had utter confidence in.

Angeline paused beside the babbling river, careful not to get her paws wet. A slight breeze ruffled her fur. The thick coat locked in her body heat against the cold night. A near full moon shimmered in the dark, velvety expanse of the sky.

There was a time when she'd eagerly anticipated the coming of a full moon. She never had to worry about finding a sex partner, full moon or otherwise. Usually she hooked up with a customer from the restaurant for a bit of fun.

A few years ago she'd picked the wrong man and narrowly avoided an unimaginable predicament. Still, the near miss caused her stomach to turn whenever she remembered the incident. Since then she'd toned down her flirtations and vowed never to have casual sex with a man she didn't know and trust.

That had become a complication in and of itself. Wolfan males could become possessive, especially of a female sex partner. However, some had managed to forge successful full moon partnerships. The caveat was that the male and female did not engage socially nor did they have human style sex. Their full moon rendezvous and romps were always in wolf form, thereby eliminating the development of emotional attachments.

Angeline had yet to find such a partner.

It would probably help if she actually started looking for one. Her throat grew tight. Lowering her head, Angeline stretched her neck to lap the water. The icy wetness dislodged the lump of regret and sloshed it all the way down into the pit of her stomach.

She had a good life. Maybe not the one she once wanted, but good nevertheless.

Backing away from the stream, she padded along the path worn by many sleepless nights. Though they had experienced trouble in the recent past, the Walker's Run territory was generally safe. Sentinels were never more than a howl away, especially inside the wolf sanctuary. But Angeline preferred to stick to the woods behind her home. Easy access to a quiet place to shift and run at a moment's notice was one reason some unmated Wahyas resided at the Chatuge View Apartments.

Without any thought to time, Angeline meandered along the winding trail, trying to sort out the mixed feelings Lincoln's arrival had caused.

For the period they had dated, not once had Tanner mentioned his interest in the Program. When he'd broken the news, Tanner had even admitted that, deep in his soul, he believed Angeline to be his true mate. But he wanted to be a Dogman more than he wanted her love.

Lincoln had also left behind everything he'd known and loved to live the life Tanner had coveted. Facing mandatory retirement, Lincoln was forced to watch his dreams slip through his fingers. Sometimes in his eyes Angeline caught a glimpse of the horrified sadness of seeing all he'd sacrificed for being so easily dismissed.

He seemed more disappointed than angry, which surprised her. She'd always imagined Dogmen to be selfish, arrogant adrenaline junkies.

Lincoln displayed none of those traits. It would be better for her if he had. Maybe she wouldn't have been so drawn to him if he'd acted like a pigheaded jerk.

Making the turn toward the apartments, Angeline lifted her nose. Lincoln's scent drifted on the currents. Sensing no advancement in her general direction, she presumed that he must be sitting on his balcony. He would see her coming home, and might even consider that it would be a good idea for them to run the woods together. It wouldn't be. Other than being neighborly, she should have no interest in the Dogman.

Her body disagreed. A solid mountain of muscles, Lincoln was as sexy as a wolfan male could be. With a full moon coming, she was tempted to give in to its aphrodisiac effects with him.

Even in her wolf form, Angeline's lips warmed and tingled. She'd had her fair share of kisses, but none had stayed with her the way Lincoln's kiss had.

The leisurely stroll quickly turned into a fast trot. Despite her mind's stern attempt to slow the pace, her paws maintained a steady rhythm. Only when she caught a flicker of movement through the bushes ahead did her canter ease to a stop.

Lincoln removed the long, slender tote slung across his shoulder, peeled off the cover and opened the folding chair. Slipping off his untied boots, he yanked the sweatshirt over his head and dropped it on the ground. The silvery shimmer of moonlight glanced off his sculpted chest. He shook off the cold and unzipped his pants, sliding them from his hips and allowing them to puddle at his bare feet. Or rather, actual bare foot and one artificial.

Protruding from a nest of dark hair, his long cock bounced free and easy. Angeline's mouth watered for the salty, masculine taste of him. She could blame the lustful desire on the nearing full moon, but the accusation would be a lie.

Despite his career choice, she wanted him, even though she wished otherwise.

Careful to stay downwind, she watched him ease into the chair and begin the laborious process of removing his leg. His movements were slow and methodical, and it hurt her heart to understand that he would never be able to simply shuck his clothes and run free. Not if he wanted a leg to stand on when he returned.

With one hand, he lifted his thigh and carefully worked off the prosthetic cup. Each time he grimaced, Angeline did, too.

He laid the artificial limb on top of his clothes. Lincoln's naturally bronzed skin appeared several shades darker that the flesh-colored stocking covering his stump. Carefully, he began the tedious process of removing the protective sleeve.

A new ache rose in her heart at the independence he'd lost and sacrificed.

She wanted to go to him, to help so the task wouldn't be so difficult. Instead, she remained perfectly still. He'd resented her assistance with the groceries. How much more upset would he be if she tried to help him now?

The leg and sleeve wrapped in his clothes and stowed beneath the chair, Lincoln eased out of the chair and onto the ground. Balancing his weight on one knee and both hands, he shifted.

His wolf, black with glints of gold dust on the tips of

his fur, looked as magnificent as the man. He took a few wobbly steps, but then his stride grew more confident. He lifted his snout and scented the air. Since she stayed downwind, he didn't pinpoint her current location but he quickly picked up her scent trail when she'd started her run. He stared in the direction she'd gone, then darted down the same path.

There could've been any number of reasons as to why he'd chosen to track Angeline. But that he did made her happier than it ever should have.

Chapter 10

Lincoln jarred awake, the deafening explosion still ringing in his ears. His heart pounded unmercifully and he struggled to breathe normally. The sweat coating his body seemed to burn his skin rather than cool it down.

Even with the glow of the television lighting the room, it still took a few seconds for him to realize that he was safe inside the apartment and not falling out of a two-story building. Shoving aside a lightweight blanket, Lincoln wiped the troubled sleep from his eyes and rubbed his hands along his jaw covered in several days' worth of stubble.

He'd dozed off on the couch again. The bed seemed too much a luxury to get used to sleeping on.

Muting the television didn't silence the noise. The rumble outside grew louder, chased by the tinkling sounds of laughter and giggles.

After putting on his leg and sweatpants, he stood slowly

shook off the sludge the nightmare had cast and limped to the door. The peephole gave him a perfect view down the corridor but not of the ruckus coming from the stairs.

He cracked open the door and leaned out for a quick peek. The flurry of activity storming the stairwell moved en masse to swarm him, firing questions and exclamations at him faster than a semiautomatic AK-47.

Angeline stepped up behind the crowd of children, their ages anywhere from six to sixteen. Despite the chaos ratcheting up his raw nerves, she appeared unflustered and unconcerned by the swirl of activity.

For a fleeting moment, Lincoln wished he would've caught up with her in the woods last night. He still needed to tell her about Tanner. After all, he had made a promise. But what if fulfilling that oath did more harm than good?

"Whoa! Whoa!" Angeline held up her hands. "Settle down, please."

The kids quieted, except for one. Obviously the youngest, she stepped forward. Her wide, rounded eyes were just as blue as Angeline's but her hair was a deep chestnut.

"Are you the... *Dogman*?" She whispered the last word. So adorable and brave.

"I am." He crouched to her level and flattened his palm over his heart. "Lincoln Adams, at your service."

A dazzling smile cracked the serious mask on the little girl's face, but it wasn't her brilliance that heated his skin. He slid his gaze to Angeline. The natural feminine curve of her mouth didn't waver. The heat he felt radiated from her eyes. All sparkly and bright, they warmed him to the depth of his soul.

The little girl's hand darted toward Lincoln.

"Sierra! No!" The oldest boy clamped a hand on her shoulder and pulled her back into the safety of their huddle.

Fear now filled the little girl's eyes.

Like a splash of ice water to the face, Lincoln regained his senses. Dogmen, though generally held in great esteem among Wahyas, were also feared for the awful things they had to do.

Peace came at a price. Dogmen were the ones who paid it.

Lincoln stretched to his full height and met each of the children's uncertain gazes. How brave Dayax must have been, alone and starving, to face a Dogman for the first time and ask for food.

"I hope we didn't wake you," Angeline said.

Lincoln checked his watch. Quarter past eight. "I needed to get up, anyway."

"Aunt Ange." The youngest boy spoke out of the side of his mouth. "Is he going to kill us?"

"Not if you study hard, finish your homework and don't talk back to your elders," Angeline said seriously.

"You said the same thing about getting presents from Santa Claus," the middle boy said.

"Who do you think Santa gives the naughty list to?" Lincoln stuffed his hands into his pockets.

The oldest girl, a teenager, rolled her eyes. "I'm hungry. What's for breakfast?"

"Well, that depends." Angeline stepped around the pack of children and stood in front of Lincoln. "Can we borrow some eggs?"

"And bacon!"

"No, sausage!"

"Bread! I want French toast."

Everyone shouted over each other, and Lincoln had difficulty determining who wanted what.

Angeline whistled, shrill and effective. The kids fell silent.

"Help yourself." Lincoln pushed open the door.

"We're going to need the kitchen, too," she whispered, ushering the kids inside.

"All right, then." He closed the door, watching them file into the kitchen, each diverging into a specific area and setting up like a team of breakfast sprites.

"It's a teacher's workday at their schools." Angeline peeled off her coat and collected the ones the children had discarded on their way in. She laid them in a chair by the entertainment center. "And they always spend them with me. This—" she waved her hand toward the kitchen "—is tradition. We start the morning with a hearty breakfast."

"You don't cook."

"No, but Tristan does, so I always brought them here. Even after he moved in with Nel, we still came here because he has a larger kitchen." Angeline gave him a sidelong look. "We can gather everything and go to my place if we're disturbing you."

"What's in it for me if I let you stay?"

"Breakfast, and the kids clean up the dishes." Angeline's blue eyes sparkled and her mouth formed a pretty-please smile.

"Hard to say no to that."

"Hey! Mr. Dogman!" Sierra waved at him. "We're going sledding after we eat."

"You are?" Lincoln noticed an ebbing warmth deep inside. Had he made a different choice, he could've shared his life with a mate and a brood of kids.

"Yep. It's fun and then we drink hot chocolate." The little one gathered the silverware.

"Want to come?" Angeline asked.

"I probably shouldn't."

"Your loss. We always have a great time." The tempting smile curving her mouth wreaked all sorts of havoc on Lincoln's mind and body.

"I bet you do." Lincoln started toward the bathroom. "Don't let them burn down the place while I'm in the shower."

"I'll keep Aunt Ange out of the kitchen," the teenaged girl said. "She's more apt to start a fire than we are."

"Roslyn!" Angeline pointed a long, slender finger at her oldest niece. "Keep talking like that and no more driving lessons."

The carefree giggles and unrestrained laughter that filled the apartment were sounds like nothing Lincoln had every experienced. He dwelled in a world of strife and fear and desperation. He couldn't imagine adapting to civilian life, yet longing broke inside him.

After lumbering into the bathroom, Lincoln stripped off his clothes. Sitting on the shower chair, he removed the prosthetic leg and turned on the water, allowing the icy-cold stream to numb his skin. Too bad it couldn't do the same with his wayward thoughts.

Brice had asked what Lincoln planned to do after he found Dayax. "Bring him home" had been the only response Lincoln's heart would provide. But Lincoln had no home. No future, really. His entire life had been devoted to the Program. Watching Angeline with her nieces and nephews, he began to truly understand the tragedy of Tanner's choice. And now, possibly his own.

"We killed the Dogman!" Sierra shrieked.

Angeline's heart had not yet restarted after watching Lincoln's sled go airborne, flip twice and slam to the snow-covered ground with Lincoln tumbling behind. A thunderous howl had chased him down the hill.

"Everyone stay here!" She gave a look to Roslyn and Caleb, her teenaged niece and nephew. Immediately, they gathered Logan, Brent and Sierra closer and assured the younger kids that Dogmen were Wahyan superheroes, so they couldn't die from falling off a sled.

Angeline darted to the spot where Lincoln had landed. The snow boots provided her feet with some traction, but she would have made faster progress in her wolf form. Seeing her shift on the fly would likely panic the children, who were already frightened and worried.

The muscles in her legs burned and tightened as she trudged through the snowdrift. The sunlight glinting off the stark white landscape caused her eyes to water, not the sight of the man, flat on his back, still as death.

"Lincoln!" Her breath steamed the air.

Don't be dead! Don't be dead!

Dropping to her knees, Angeline yanked off her mittens and brushed away the snow flurries dotting Lincoln's face. She didn't see any signs of blood, his body didn't appear twisted, and his neck wasn't crooked at an odd angle. "Hey, are you all right?"

His closed eyelids didn't flutter open, no sound escaped his slightly parted lips, and not one muscle twitched in response. Lightly, she pressed her hand to his nose and mouth. Not one puff of warm breath heated her palm.

"Oh, no." She yanked open his jacket and laid her ear against his chest. The layers of clothes could've obscured the sound, but she didn't hear the beat of his heart.

Maybe she should've taken the CPR class Tristan had suggested.

Angeline leaned over Lincoln's all too still body and lowered her face to his. Just before she touched his jaw to pry open his mouth, Lincoln's eyelashes lifted. Mischief sparkled in his pale green eyes.

"Hello, Angel." His hand rose to cup the back of her neck while the other slid around her waist, pulling her on top of him.

His mouth, cold from the wind, captured her lips, muffling her surprise. A rush of desire followed on the heels of utter relief. Without meaning to do so, she relaxed in the warmth spreading through her.

Lincoln deepened the kiss, the taste of coffee and syrup still on his tongue. Probing gently, he explored her mouth, unleashing peals of excitement low in her belly.

Encouraging Lincoln's attention was reckless. He stirred up feelings no other man had since Tanner had left her. A feeling she wouldn't mind exploring with someone other than a Dogman.

So why didn't she want to resist his kiss?

His hand slipped beneath her jacket. His hand branding her skin despite the layers of clothes.

"He *is* dead," Sierra yelled from the hilltop. "Aunt Ange is giving him air!"

"No, silly." Caleb's voice carried down the snow-covered slope. "They're kissing."

"Ewww!" a choir of voices chimed.

"Obviously, they have no idea what it's like to kiss an angel," Lincoln murmured against Angeline's lips.

She drew back and gave him her scrunched up I'm-not-impressed face. "Not funny, Dogman. Not funny at all."

"And yet I'm smiling."

Indeed he was. Mouth. Eyes. His entire face beamed.

"Are you all right?" Angeline kept her serious mask in place.

"Never better. But, I—um." Lincoln frowned. "I'm numb from the snow. Is my leg still on?"

"I think so." She patted the fleshy part of his left thigh

Lincoln's head fell back and his chest rumbled with a deep groan that definitely had not come from a place of pain.

The sound sent a shock down her spine that spread

through her body until it settled like a swirl of heat in her abdomen. Gritting her teeth, she danced her fingers lower until her fingertips felt the hard ridge of the prosthetic cup. "Yep. Leg in place."

The chatter of children drew closer.

"Can you take them back up the hill?" Lincoln sat up, his gaze falling to the artificial leg. "It might take me a while to get up."

"Nope," Angeline said. "It's tradition. After the first person falls, we all make snow angels."

She watched the kids' rosy faces as they made their way down the hill to her and Lincoln.

Sierra trudged up to Lincoln. Her small, mittened hands clutched his face. "I thought you were a goner."

"We all did. The way you flew through the air." Brent flopped onto the ground a few feet away. "It was spectacular."

"No," Angeline said. "It was a dangerous stunt and no one is going to repeat it."

"It wasn't dangerous." Lincoln pulled a wide-eyed Sierra into his lap. "No one was shooting at me." Mercilessly, he tickled her.

Her giggles of delight echoed around them.

Logan lobbed the first snowball and after tucking Sierra behind him, Lincoln returned the volley. Soon, all the kids had joined the fight.

Angeline no longer felt the cold in her fingers as unbidden affection warmed her inside and out. Lincoln truly knew how to connect with kids and that was the very reason why Angeline should not have invited him to come. The fastest way to her heart was the path carved by her nieces and nephews. And if he left them brokenhearted when he left, she just might kill him.

"How about those snow angels I heard about?" Lincoln said.

"It's easy." Sierra sat on the ground, lay on her back and spread her arms.

The others, including Angeline, joined her, plopping around Lincoln as if they'd known him their whole lives. And he gave each of them the attention and praise they craved.

Angeline's brothers loved their children, but like their father, had difficulty showering them with affection. And why she made a conscious effort to do so.

She hadn't expected that a Dogman would understand how much kids needed encouragement and acceptance. But there he lay, sprawled in the snow, giving time and attention to children he'd just met.

Snow angels made, they began getting up. Tension crept into Lincoln's body.

"All right, guys," Angeline said. "Lincoln is almost frozen solid, so let's get him up."

"Uh, no." Lincoln sat up, his face deadly serious.

Too late. The munchkins swarmed him and, despite the ferocious look Lincoln flashed her, he didn't speak one cross word to the kids.

Roslyn and Caleb each grabbed an arm. Brent and Logan pushed from behind and Sierra hugged his good leg. In no time, they had Lincoln up and standing.

Angeline sent the kids ahead, then grabbed Lincoln's arm. "Pull another stunt like that, don't bother playing dead. Because you will be, after I strangle you."

"Now why would you do that, Angel?"

"Because I don't want them trying to imitate you." She pointed at the kids.

"They won't." Lincoln draped his arm over Angeline's shoulders. "I'll talk to them."

"Thank you."

"And thank you." He squeezed her shoulder.

"For what?"

"Worrying about me." He smiled. "That was nice."

"Know what's nicer? Not doing something to make omeone worry."

"Duly noted." He laughed softly and a feeling of con-entment settled into Angeline's bones. And she started inking that being neighborly to a retiring Dogman wasn't uch a terrible thing after all.

Chapter 11

Ice-cold beer sloshed against the back of Lincoln's throa
His second, in what looked to be a very long evening. A
full moon on Friday night and Taylor's Roadhouse wa
standing room only in the bar area and not a single empt
table in the restaurant section.

The swollen crowd might've been overwhelming i
he had time to focus on them. But he stayed occupie
with keeping track of Angeline. As suspected, more tha
a few customers had gotten overly handsy with her. She
of course, had expertly handled the overzealous wolfans
Didn't make him want to break their thick necks any les

He never should've gone sledding with her and the kid
yesterday. A switch had clicked in his brain, moving he
from the sexy next-door neighbor with whom he wante
to have a good time to a home-grown family woman wh
deserved so much more than a fast and furious tumble be
tween the sheets.

Adored by her nieces and nephews, Angeline was as kind and loving and encouraging as she was beautiful. And she deserved to be at home being loved by a mate instead of pawed and drooled over by horny males merely looking for a full-moon hookup. Lincoln included.

He'd wanted Angeline from the moment he'd met her in the flesh. And had hoped she would be the one he bedded on the full moon. But he had trouble reconciling the growing feelings complicating what should be nothing more than pure, unadulterated sex.

"Earth to Lincoln." Reed snapped his fingers in front of Lincoln's face.

He cut his eyes toward the younger man. "Do that again and I'll bite them off."

Reed smiled good-naturedly. "Coming from you, I'd believe it." He turned to the other sentinels gathered at the table. "On our first run together, I saw him catch a rattlesnake midstrike and chomp off its head."

Though there had been snow on the ground, the sun had been out, bright and warm. Likely the snake had surfaced from its den to bask in the sunshine and they had accidentally disturbed him. Normally, Lincoln left forest critters alone. But they'd been in the woods behind the Co-op's housing community and he hadn't wanted to risk a child getting bit.

"Good reflexes, huh?" one of the younger sentinels asked.

"Yeah," Lincoln said rather than going into detail about the extensive training he'd received to be able to dispatch a deadly threat with nothing more than his teeth.

The table buzzed with comparison stories, each trying to top the last.

"Are you all right? For a full moon night, you're awfully tense." Reed leaned across the table and lowered his voice. "There are a lot of single she-wolves here tonight. I can introduce you."

"Thanks, I'm good for now."

Angeline squeezed through the crowd and made her way to their table. "Hey, fellas. I'll be taking care of you tonight. Everyone want the usual?"

"Isn't this Tessa's section?" Reed asked.

"Trust me." She gave him a pointed look. "You don't want her near your food. She's still mad at you."

Conflicting emotions flashed across his face. He nodded but said nothing.

Everyone agreed to have the usual and Angeline jotted down their drink orders.

Reaching Lincoln, she looked up from her pad and smiled. "How about you? The usual or something else?"

"I haven't been around enough to know what the usual is."

"For these guys, it's a plate of ribs." Angeline leaned down and whispered in Lincoln's ear, "So messy, so not sexy."

"I'll have a burger, medium rare."

"Excellent choice." Her laugh zipped through him like a jolt of electricity. She leaned even closer. "See those ladies at the bar?"

Lincoln glanced at the trio of she-wolves wearing short skirts, spiked heels and low-cut tops. They were beautiful, maybe even sexy, but they didn't charge his senses the way Angeline did.

"They're dying for you to buy them drinks."

"I don't mind paying, but tell them they're from someone else."

"Not interested?"

"Not in them." He held Angeline's gaze and the wall holding back the blatant desire he had for her crumbled.

Satisfaction flickered in her eyes. "Good to know, Dogman."

She walked off, and Lincoln swore she put an extra dose of sass in the swing of her hips.

"You've got a thing for Angeline, don't you?" Reed's eyes narrowed on Lincoln.

"What's it to you?"

"Nothing." Using his thumb, Reed wiped the condensation beaded on the side of his beer bottle. "But she gets a lot of attention. Especially on a full moon."

"I've noticed."

"And I've noticed that you noticed." Reed shook his head. "Look, man. She doesn't do relationships."

"I'm not looking for one."

"You sure about that? Because you gotta look in your eyes and it's not the kind a wolfan gets when all he's after is a good time."

"Yeah?" Lincoln stared straight into Reed's eyes. "What's that look telling you now?"

Reed held up his hands. "Just offering a friendly piece of advice."

"I'll keep that in mind."

Reed rejoined the table conversation, and Lincoln kept up with it, as well. But he remained cognizant of Angeline's whereabouts. And it seemed whenever she sensed him watching, she'd lift her gaze and smile.

Never coy about sex or selecting partners, he could only guess that the hesitant gnaw in his gut had to do with Tanner. The man had entrusted him with his final words, yet Lincoln had not offered them to Angeline.

He needed to come clean about the man linked to both their pasts, but Lincoln didn't want to risk a chasm opening between them.

"Damn you, Tanner." Lincoln chugged his beer.

"Who's Tanner?" Reed asked.

"The first man to die in my arms."

The table fell silent.

"On my first deployment." Lincoln slammed the empty bottle on the table. "You never forget your first, boys." Or any of the ones who came after, and there were quite a few. Including Lila.

Lincoln left the table and headed into the men's room. After relieving himself, he bumped aside a few males preening at the sinks to wash his hands. One took issue, but one look from Lincoln and a clearly threatening growl, and the man backed away. Drying his hands, he suddenly had a sense of Angeline. Startled. Hurt. Angry.

Darting out of the restroom, he visually searched for her but the crowd obscured his view. He did, however, see Reed and two more sentinels making their way toward the bar.

"Excuse me," Lincoln said once, shouldering his way through the crowd to see Angeline bring her knee up sharply between a man's legs then smash her fist into his face.

Atta girl!

Another man stepped up. "You bitch!"

"Touch her and I'll rip off your arm and shoved it up your ass," Lincoln said, walking up behind the man.

"You and whose army?" The human male turned. His bloodshot eyes were filled with deadly anger and he reeked of liquor.

"Mister, I am an army."

"That bitch needs to pay for what she did to my brother."

"Looks like he needed to be taught some manners. Be thankful she served up the lesson and not me." Grabbing the man's shirt instead of his throat, Lincoln shoved him at Reed. Then he reached for the other guy, still doubled over.

"I'm going to make this simple for you." Lincoln macked his palm against the man's forehead and tilted back his head to look him in the eyes. "She's off-limits. This establishment is off-limits. If you don't stay away, I'll natch your balls off and feed them to the birds."

Fear flooded the man's eyes. Sometimes a healthy dose of it cured future problems.

Lincoln handed the man off to the sentinels.

"The show is over, folks. Go back to minding your own business." He turned to Angeline. "Are you hurt?"

"You can't go around threatening a man because he got a little handsy." The anger in her voice didn't quite each her eyes.

"That's not an answer to my question. And for the re-ord, I don't threaten. I explained the principle of action nd reaction in terms he'd understand."

Angeline rolled her eyes. "I can handle myself. I don't eed you to interfere."

She bumped past him and headed into the kitchen.

Lincoln rubbed his jaw. If she thought that was the end f it, she was oh, so wrong.

"Angeline?"

Coming through the kitchen doors, she narrowly voided colliding with her uncle.

"What's wrong?" Jimmy's large hand gently cupped er shoulder.

"A couple of customers got rowdy when I refused to erve them liquor." Obviously intoxicated, they'd probably een cut off at the last stop on their bar hop and decided come to Taylor's. "They're gone now." After giving is wrist a gentle squeeze, she headed to the ice machine.

"Are you all right?" Jimmy asked.

"I'm still waiting for an answer to that question, too.
The double doors closed behind Lincoln.

"I'm fine." Angeline pushed up her long sleeve. Mark
from the man's tight grip reddened her skin. She scoope
a small amount of ice into a clean bar rag and pressed
against her arm. More to cool the notions running ram
pant inside her than to soothe her skin.

Lincoln's essence wrapped around Angeline second
before his actual touch. "I should've kept a closer watch.

No, he shouldn't have. His searing gaze following he
every move had kept Angeline distracted. Otherwise sh
would've been more alert and better able to defuse or de
flect the drunk men's actions.

"I don't need a bodyguard. I've been handling drunk
long before you came to town."

"You shouldn't have to," Jimmy said. "That's why w
have sentinels here every night."

"Is it usually like this?" Lincoln coaxed the makeshi
icepack from her fingers and gently inspected the bruise

"No." Angeline closed her eyes, trying to ignoring th
wild fluttering in her belly that his touch had sparked. "B
it's Friday night and a full moon."

"It's also Valentine's Day," Jimmy added. "A trip
whammy."

Lincoln's gaze caressed her face and raw passion heate
his eyes. "She needs a break," he said to Jimmy.

"No, I don't." Angeline pulled down her sleeve.

"Got a place I can take her?" Lincoln continued. "Som
where private?"

"The office. Miriam is in there, but she won't mind.'

"I don't have time for a break. We're packed." Angeli
looked hard at her uncle. "I'm fine, really."

Lincoln's low, soft growl grated her nerves as much
it stimulated.

"He's the one you need to convince," Jimmy said. "Besides, you haven't taken a break all shift and the others have had two each."

"Fine," she said, because Lincoln blocking the doorway would slow service and then they really would have a problem on their hands.

Angeline sensed rather than heard his steps behind her. Awareness tingled her skin. Gritting her teeth, she knocked on the door of the office before opening it.

"Hi, Aunt Miriam. Mind if we use the office for a few minutes?"

"Everything all right, dear?" Miriam pulled off her glasses, her gaze shuttering between Angeline and Lincoln.

"Yes. Uncle Jimmy insisted that I take a break and Lincoln is making sure that I do."

The way Miriam looked at them made Angeline wonder if her aunt could see the energy bouncing between them. The full moon wasn't to blame. The current connecting them had begun well in advance of the lunar phase.

"Take all the time you need." Miriam turned the computer monitor off and pushed away from the desk. "I'll help with the hostess station for a while."

Lincoln closed the door behind Miriam as she left.

"How long do I have to—" she used air quotes "—*rest?*" Angeline perched on the edge of the desk. "I'm losing tips, you know."

Lincoln eased closer and she didn't stop him from entering her personal space.

"I know you are okay," he said quietly. "But I'm not sure that I am."

A storm raged in his eyes and a nearly imperceptible tremble shook his hands. "When I saw that guy's hands on you…" Lincoln's nostrils flared and his nose twitched. "I really did want to kill him."

"He was just drunk." A mean one, apparently.

"That's no excuse. For him or me." Lincoln cradled her cheek. The warmth of his palm sent a wave of heat through her body. "May I?"

Instinctively, Angeline knew he wanted to scent her. Warily, she nodded consent against her brain's instruction to the contrary.

Leaning in, Lincoln carefully planted his hands on top of the desk, caging her between his strong arms. His eyelids closed and he lightly grazed his stubbled cheek along her jaw. Goose bumps scattered across her skin, and she shivered.

He moved closer, drawing his hands up her hips.

Working her fingers up his chest to his shoulder, Angeline cozied into Lincoln as he nuzzled her neck on the way to the sweet spot behind her ear.

"God, you smell good." His hot breath puffed against her skin.

"So do you." She breathed in the heady scent of wolfan male musk. Desire threaded through her body like wisps of steam rising from a cup of hot chocolate.

If he was anything other than a Dogman, she wouldn't resist the pull between them. But tonight's full moon weakened her resolve and with his scent invading her being, she couldn't think of anything except coupling with him.

"Lincoln," she whispered against his ear.

He shifted ever so slightly to look at her. His masculine lips parted with a soft breath.

She kissed him and found his soft, firm mouth welcoming, drawing her in for a long, deep kiss. The taste of beer on his tongue wasn't overwhelming and she relaxed, knowing that he had full command of his senses. And so did she.

Her hands fell to Lincoln's waist and fumbled with his belt.

He broke the kiss. His eyes brilliant and branding her with their intensity, he cupped her face. "Are you sure I'm the one you want tonight?" he asked hoarsely.

"I wouldn't be unzipping your pants if I had any doubts." She wrapped her hand around his shaft. The hot, velvety hardness had her clenching with need.

Biology overrode any warning her brain may have signaled. She pulled off her shirt and slid off her bra.

Lincoln's soft growl of appreciation gave her a rush of feminine power. He yanked off his sweatshirt and pulled her tightly against him.

He dotted kisses down her throat, and she arched, allowing him more access. Gently, he kneaded her breasts. When he strummed his thumbs over her nipples, tiny bites of electricity sparked.

She grabbed his face, kissed him hard and insistently.

His hands palmed her back and slipped inside the waistband of her jeans. He slid them off her hips as she did the same to him.

Wet and wanting, she turned around. Lincoln wrapped her in his strength and warmth.

Closing her eyes, she luxuriated in the feel of his fingers sliding through her feminine folds.

He kissed her temple, gently bent her over the desk and nudged her legs apart. He entered her in a swift, deep thrust. The delicious shock caused a throaty rumble to erupt from within. His hands tightened on her hips, holding her steady as he rocked against her, harder and faster.

She loved the feel of him inside her and had no worries of pregnancy or disease. She-wolves could not get pregnant unless a male claimed her with his bite during intercourse.

And her sharpened sense of smell would have warned her of sickness the moment she'd scented him.

Maddening tension balled in her lower belly, priming her entire body for climactic release, and Lincoln drove her right over the edge. Waves of pleasure buoyed her.

Behind her, Lincoln groaned in release and then stilled

"You okay, Angel?" He eased out of her.

"Better than all right." She turned in his arms and he kissed her sweetly.

Normally she didn't engage in postcoital affection with her full-moon partners. But the way Lincoln held her tight and rested his chin on her head felt nice.

A knock fell at the door.

"Angeline?" Jimmy called. "Everything all right, hon?"

"Couldn't be better." Angeline and Lincoln scrambled for their clothes and began dressing.

"If you need the rest of the night off—" Jimmy laughed

"No. We'll, um, be out in a minute."

"Your shirt is on wrong," Lincoln whispered.

Groaning, Angeline readjusted her top. "How's this?" She held out her arms.

"I liked it better on the floor."

"You would." Angeline headed out of the office, her body humming. She glanced over her shoulder at Lincoln one step behind her. He winked and the hope that now the itch had been scratched, the attraction between them would wane went up in flames.

Chapter 12

Lincoln stared at the shadows beneath his eyes and the
ines feathering out from the corners. His brown skin had
veathered from years of exposure, responsibility and the
veight of the things he'd done. And he could use a good
have and haircut.

He didn't look quite like a vagabond, but neither would
is face grace the cover of *GQ* magazine. Not that he cared.

Before joining the Program, he'd been popular with
he ladies. They'd said he had a devilish smile and was
asy on the eyes.

In recent years he hadn't had a lot to smile about and
is once charming manner had become more than a little
ough around the edges. After all he'd seen and done, who
ould blame him?

Well, Angeline did. Or had when they'd first met.

He wondered how she now saw him. As a man or
ogman?

Foregoing the shave, he reached for the crutches an
turned from the bathroom mirror to make his way into th
bedroom. He'd left the prosthetic on the bed, his stum
slightly sore from the friction caused by the sexcapad
with Angeline a few hours ago.

Given the chance, he'd do it again.

And again…

Despite a good, long run in the woods behind the apartments and a cold shower, he couldn't shake the desire fo
more.

Vivacious and independent, for Angeline their encoun
ter had been all in good fun. However, it would've bee
damn impossible for him to have stayed at Taylor's with
out his fist connecting with a face whenever someone go
too friendly with her. He felt far too protective and pos
sessive of her for their own good.

A full moon encounter shouldn't generate feelings o
any kind. Jealousy was a dangerous emotion for Dogme
and Lincoln wasn't proud to be infected with it. Ange
line was simply his first full moon partner in a very lon
time. There could be nothing between them and yet whe
they coupled, Lincoln had been filled with a comfortin
sense of home.

Strange, because his real home had been less than coz
His parents were strict, career-focused and had the high
est expectations. They were disappointed with anythin
less than perfection.

He picked up the photo Tanner had entrusted to hin
Thankfully, the picture had been tucked safely inside a thi
silver case when he fell from the second-story windo
The moment Lincoln had lost consciousness, he'd shifte
back into his human form. The shift energy would've de
stroyed the photo without the protection of the silver cas

He stared at the worn, familiar image of Angeline that had been his lifeline too many times to count.

Mine!

"No," he sighed, tracing the angelic face of the woman in the picture. "She's not."

Lincoln's jumbled emotions were simply a confusion of instinct. For years he'd studied Angeline's picture, memorizing every detail, imbuing it with the belief she was his guardian angel, and treating it as if it were a living, breathing entity. As a result, his instinct had forged a bond with the figment of his imagination. Now his wolf didn't understand the difference between fantasy and reality.

Yes, he'd had sex with Angeline. But full moon sex was nothing more than the quenching of a biological necessity.

He needed to keep his distance until his body, his brain and his wolfan instinct understood that Angeline was not the fantasy he'd concocted to get him through some really bad times.

A flesh-and-blood woman, she had feelings and a heart that had already been broken by a Dogman. Considering Lincoln had one last do-or-die mission to complete, he couldn't encourage anything to develop between them. To do so wouldn't be fair to either of them or to Dayax, who was depending on Lincoln to find him.

From the dresser drawer he pulled out a clean pair of boxers and a T-shirt then sat on the bed to get dressed. Barely 10:00 p.m. and too keyed up to sleep, he used the crutches to hobble out of the bedroom.

The satphone he'd left on the kitchen counter had not received any messages while he was in the shower, which meant no news on Dayax's whereabouts. He scrolled to the only picture stored in the phone's memory: Dayax hugging him. Lincoln had just given the wolfling some beef jerky. The sheer pleasure on the kid's face always made Lincoln smile.

He tossed the phone onto the kitchen counter and made his way into the living room. Laying the crutches on the floor, he stretched out on the couch. Nothing caught his interest on the television but he left it on, hoping the light and sound would keep the nightmares away. At the very least, it would mask Angeline's footfalls as she came up the stairs. She didn't have heavy steps, but somehow he always heard her coming home.

Barely had his eyes closed before his stomach started gurgling. He'd skipped supper, ducking out of Taylor's before being served. Deli meats and condiments were in the fridge, but preparing a sandwich would be cumbersome on crutches and he simply lacked the motivation to get up.

Knowing how to ignore hunger, he grabbed the blanket off the back of the couch and settled into a comfortable position beneath it. The crawly feeling spread into his chest and a pricking sensation ran up his spine.

Someone pounded on the door.

"Lincoln."

He sat up, his heart beginning to rev.

"Lincoln, are you home?" There was a slight pause. "Sheesh! It's freezing out here!"

He reached for the crutches despite his brain's warning to not answer.

Maybe if Angeline saw him this way, she would start avoiding him, saving him the trouble.

Halfway to the door, he saw it swing open.

"Oh!" The downward curl of her mouth slid into a vivacious smile. "You're home."

"What are you doing here?" The gruffness in his voice didn't deter her from coming inside and toeing the door closed behind her.

"You left without eating." She waggled the carryout ags in her hands.

"Since when does Taylor's deliver?" His fingers tightned around the hand grips on the crutches.

"It's a perk of being my neighbor." She waltzed past im, dropped the food on the coffee table and stared at e pillow and rumpled blanket on the couch. "Still sleepg on couches?"

"Aren't you supposed to be working?"

"I got off early. It's a tradition." She went into the itchen and opened the refrigerator. "Before Tristan met el, he and I always hung out on Valentine's Day. Strictly atonic. We'd eat and watch a movie." Holding a couple bottles of water, she returned to the living room and sat the couch. "Since you're here, I thought..." Her voice ailed off.

If Lincoln intended to turn her away, he needed to do now.

Taking a deep breath, he joined her. She didn't flinch grimace watching him come toward her, legless and utch dependent.

"What do you usually watch?" He eased down beside r.

"Anything non-romantic." When she opened the bags, e delicious scent of saucy chicken wings made his mouth ater. "Tristan likes all the comic book movies. Great speal effects, over-the-top action."

"All right." He tried not to tense, thinking of the epic ttles and explosions.

Looking over her shoulder, she gave him a pensive look. prefer something with less drama tonight."

"Be my guest." He handed her the television remote.

Her fingers grazed his hand and warmth ebbed beneath r touch. She pulled up a pay-per-view channel then fin-

ished unpacking the food and handed him a container fille
with chicken wings.

“Thanks.” He loved the soft smile she gave him.

“So.” Settling next to him, she stole one of his wing
“Does your prosthetic always make your leg red?”

“No,” he said. “It’s a friction burn.”

“Is it because we…you know.” She bit into the wing.

“Probably.” Not sensing pity, he began to relax. “M
stump is still a little tender from everything that hap
pened.”

“I didn’t realize that it bothered you.”

“I do exercises to help desensitize the nerves, but I’
still getting used to my new…” He couldn’t bring himse
to say “limits.”

“Way of life?” Genuine understanding shimmered i
Angeline’s eyes.

“Yeah.” One that he began to think could be better tha
he’d ever imagined.

Angeline inhaled Lincoln’s clean masculine scent. Th
warmth spreading through her had little to do with th
blanket she snuggled beneath. She smiled, despite hersel

“Hey, Dogman.” She elbowed the lump next to he
“What time did the movie end?”

When he didn’t answer, she sat up, opening her eyes,
little disoriented with the darkened living room.

“Lincoln?” Even as she called out for him, Angeli
knew he wouldn’t answer. The apartment felt too emp
for him to be there.

Uncurling her legs, she tossed aside the blanket. No
mally, she’d leave it where it landed. But she noticed Li
coln had removed the take-out containers filled wi
chicken bones and dirty napkins from the coffee tab
folded her jacket across the chair and placed her boots ne

the door. He seemed to like things neat, so she smoothed the blanket over the back of the couch.

"All righty." She clasped her hands between her knees. "Guess I should go."

Normally, she didn't do sleepovers. Watching a comedy with Lincoln last night had been fun and relaxing. She hadn't meant to fall asleep and apparently her staying all night had freaked out Lincoln so much that he'd left. Pulling her phone from her purse, she checked the time.

Nearly ten in the morning, she might as well get to work on that song niggling her brain. Maybe she could figure out the bothersome last refrain and come up with some lyrics that didn't churn her stomach with their sappiness.

Slinging her purse over her shoulder, Angeline collected her coat and boots and padded to the door. She felt sad leaving this way, but clearly understood Lincoln's hesitation about facing her the morning after.

Their full-moon coupling wasn't meant to be anything more. But coming over last night didn't have anything to do with it. She and Tristan really did have a V-day tradition and she didn't want to spend it alone. It had been a mistake to assume Lincoln had felt the same.

So much for being neighborly.

Turning to leave, she heard footfalls nearing Lincoln's apartment. Her heartbeat picked up speed.

After quickly finger-combing her hair, she opened the door. "Hey, I was— Oh!"

"I'll be damned." A man a few inches shorter than Lincoln, with a short crop of dark brown hair and a jagged scar slicing across his handsome face, slowly removed his mirrored sunglasses. The accompanying smile lacked real warmth. "What's your name, sweetheart?"

"Not *sweetheart*."

His laughter rang hollow.

"Are you lost?" She knew every resident in the small apartment complex and this wolfan was not one of them.

"Definitely not." He adjusted the shoulder strap of his duffel bag that looked an awful lot like the one Lincoln had.

"You're a Dogman, aren't you," Angeline said, flatly. She'd gotten used to Lincoln because he didn't resemble what she'd imagined a Dogman to be.

"I am." Now the stranger's broad smile turned genuine and arrogant and expectant. "Is Adams up? Or sleeping off a long full moon night?"

"I didn't catch your name," she said instead of slamming the door in his leering face.

"Marquez." Lincoln's voice drifted up the stairwell.

Angeline's heart began that fast-paced *tha-dump* again.

Reaching the landing, carrying two large coffees and a small white bag, he smiled at Angeline. "I picked up breakfast." His gaze shifted to the man. "Should've told me you were coming."

"My business in Atlanta ended sooner than expected. Didn't think you would mind if I dropped in."

Lincoln's stoic look gave no hint as to whether or not he was glad to see Marquez. However, his eyes twinkled when he handed her the paper bag.

Angeline wasted no time checking the contents. "Oo-oh, raspberry éclairs. I haven't tried these yet."

Instead of grabbing one and dashing home in the cold, she dumped her things in the chair and made herself comfortable on the couch. Lincoln set the drinks on the coffee table.

Marquez closed the door and dropped the duffel bag on the floor next to the entertainment center. "Are you going to introduce me?"

Sitting next to Angeline as she took her first bite of the

delicious pastry, Lincoln tipped his head toward her. "Angeline O'Brien, Damien Marquez."

A mouth full of food saved her from expressing the sentiment that it was a pleasure to meet him. It wasn't. She could manage dealing with one Dogman, but two?

"Nice place you have," Damien said, glancing around the apartment.

"It isn't mine." Lincoln sipped his coffee.

Damien's gaze darted to Angeline. Instead of answering the man's silent question, she turned to Lincoln. "These are really good."

"Glad you like them." He wiped away a dot of raspberry-cream filing from her mouth and sucked the confection off his thumb.

"So." Damien looked at the chair filled with Angeline's coat, purse and boots. "You two are—?"

"Neighbors," she and Lincoln said in unison.

"Right." Damien grabbed a chair from the round table in the dining area off the kitchen, turned it around and straddled the seat.

"You two worked together?" Angeline asked Lincoln.

"He's my captain." Damien shrugged. "Was, anyway. I'm going to a new unit. I guess Linc will be going into retirement."

A subtle tension crept into Lincoln's body, and Angeline noticed a gleam of satisfaction in Damien's eyes. Instinctively, she'd disliked the man upon opening the door. His standing hadn't improved in the last few minutes.

Angeline finished off the éclair and picked up her coffee as she stood. "I should get home."

Disappointment flashed in his eyes as Lincoln pushed to his feet. "Thanks for stopping by last night," he said softly.

"It was fun, wasn't it?"

"Especially when you started snoring," Lincoln said, walking her to the door.

"I do not snore."

"Yeah, you did." He smiled. "Until I let you hog the blanket and you curled up in my lap."

"No, I didn't."

The truth in his pale, wistful eyes convinced her otherwise.

She gathered her things and he walked her to the door.

"See ya later." She meant to give him a quick peck on the cheek but he responded with a soft nuzzle that had her curling into his warmth.

"Stop by anytime."

She nodded then hurried down the corridor to her apartment. Tucked safely inside, she headed into the bedroom to get her guitar. She needed to write down the notes of the new tune running through her mind.

Chapter 13

You lying bastard." Damien's short laugh raised Lincoln's ackles. "I never understood your obsession with a stranger a photo, but you've known who she is all along. And ow you're up close and personal with her."

"I didn't lie." Lincoln closed the door after Angeline isappeared inside her apartment. "I accepted an invitation finish out my medical leave here rather than in the in-rmary at Headquarters. Finding Angeline, nothing more ian a coincidence."

"No such thing. Isn't that what you always said?" amien migrated from the dining table chair to the leather ne in the living room.

"Apparently, I was wrong." Lincoln returned to the ouch, popped the lid of his coffee cup and swallowed e hot drink. All the while his mind spun with ideas.

Ideas of the quickening that brought together true mates.

Dangerous ideas with a promise of a future he wasn't en titled to have.

"What did she say when you told her how long you'v been carrying around her picture?"

"I haven't mentioned it." Lincoln didn't want to risk he rejection, even if they were nothing more than friendl neighbors. He fished out the éclair Angeline had left fo him and bit into it. "I would offer you breakfast, but I didn know you were coming."

"I grabbed a sandwich on the way up from Atlant this morning. Good thing I hooked up with a flight a tendant last night. If I hadn't, I might've interrupted you sleepover."

Lincoln's skin prickled, but he dismissed the erran warning because the peculiar smile on Damien's face wa likely caused by the deep scar running down the side o his face.

"That picture of her must be pretty damn lucky Damien continued. "No one would know that you wer knocked out of a two-story window. Not one damn scratc as far as I can see."

"I lost my leg." Lincoln hiked his pant leg, revealing th prosthetic. "I'd say that's more than a scratch."

"At least the Program gave you a new leg." Damie traced the long, deep, jagged scar down his cheek. "The wouldn't give me a new face. Apparently cosmetic recon struction isn't worth their time."

Young and more than a little cocky about his looks, o course Damien considered the Program's refusal to eras the scar to be a deeply personal affront.

"Sorry, man," Lincoln said regretfully. If Lila hadn convinced the team to follow him, she would be alive an Damien would still have his perfect face.

He waved off Lincoln's concern. "The ladies still lo

me. I've been told I look dangerous and sexy." Damien grinned. "Damn right I am."

Lincoln laughed, glad that Damien had taken what had happened in stride, but it tweaked his heart that he'd never get the chance to talk it out with Lila.

"It's good to see you, but what are you doing here?"

"I have some time to kill before my next deployment." Due to the Program's restrictions, a Dogman's social circles consisted entirely of other Dogmen. "Is there a hotel in this flea-sized town?"

"A resort, but they're hosting a couples retreat."

"Just my luck." Damien frowned.

"You can bunk here. You can even take the bed. I'm partial to the couch."

"What about your neighbor?"

"She's off-limits," Lincoln said a bit too abruptly.

"How about passing along her picture? I could use a good-luck charm."

"It's not mine to give away." Before he left Walker's Run, Lincoln would return the photo to Angeline and give her the message he had sworn to deliver.

Damien shrugged. "It was worth a try."

"If you're going to stay awhile, you'll need a key." Lincoln stood and went to the door. "Help yourself to the fridge, the shower, whatever you need. I'll be back with a key in a few minutes."

"She has the key, doesn't she?"

"Her name is Angeline and, yeah, she has the spare." Lincoln stepped into the corridor. The cold air nipped his face and hands. Memories of Angeline snuggling against him in her sleep heated his blood. He could've woken her up after the movie ended, but he was comfortable, she was comfortable and he simply didn't see the need to disturb either of them. And for the first time since waking up in the Program's hospital, he'd had a peaceful night's sleep.

The faint sound of music touched his ears just before he rapped on Angeline's door. "Hey, Angel, it's me."

The music stopped. A funny feeling tickled his stomach right before she opened the door.

"Tired of your company already?" She stepped back to allow him to enter.

"Well, he's not you."

That earned him a stellar smile and put an extra sparkle in her deep blue eyes.

Lincoln saw the guitar on the couch and sheets of music spread over the coffee table.

"Planning on joining the band at Taylor's?"

"Keeping up my skills. In college, I majored in music, but don't mention it to my family. They think I have a business degree."

"Why would it matter to them?"

"The family business is handcrafted cabinets and furniture. My dad and brothers are carpenters. They expected me to handle the administrative and financial tasks." The shimmer in her eyes faded. "It never mattered to them what I wanted."

"What do you want?"

"Neighbors who aren't so nosy."

"I guess asking you to play a tune for me is overstepping my welcome." Lincoln shoved his hands into his hip pockets.

Instead of answering, Angeline moved the guitar off the couch and sat, tucking her bare feet beneath her legs. "Is there something I can help you with, Lincoln?"

Apparently he'd unintentionally exposed a nerve.

"Damien is staying for a few days and since I don't want to be stuck with him 24/7, I need the spare key."

"Oh!" Shock then disappointment registered on her ace. "Sure. No problem."

She reached for the large purse lying on its side on the loor. After digging through the contents, she worked a ey off a key ring and held it up. "All yours."

Electricity sparked in his fingertips as he grazed her ingers retrieving the key. "As soon as Damien leaves, it vill be yours again."

"Why?"

"Are you kidding? You bring me food, make me watch novies that put you to sleep, but mostly because I enjoy 'our company."

Her smile reappeared.

Lincoln turned to leave.

"Hey, Dogman," Angeline called after him. "I like being 'our neighbor, too."

Walking back to his apartment, Lincoln barely regis-ered the cold because of the warm, fuzzy feeling bub-ling in his chest.

"Have a hot Valentine's date?" Tessa stowed her purse nd jacket in the locker. "You ducked out pretty early last ight."

"No." Angeline tucked an order pad in her half apron. Just keeping to tradition."

"With Tristan?"

"Of course not. He and I were always just friends. Be-ides, he's madly in love with Nel and their baby is due ny day."

"So what did you do?"

"Stuffed my face and watched a movie." Snuggling with incoln on the couch. "Pretty boring."

"Then why are you smiling?"

"No reason." No, really. She had no reason to be smil-

ing. Her new neighbor might possibly evolve into a frien
But that was the extent of things.

While Brice might want Lincoln to make Walker's Ru
his permanent home, Lincoln had not once mentioned re
tirement. He often seemed preoccupied and checked hi
service-issued phone frequently. Regardless of his injur
he belonged to the Dogman program and as long as he di
Angeline couldn't develop feelings for him and be mad
the fool twice in a lifetime.

"I think Reed wanted to talk to you last night." Angelin
glanced at Tessa, sympathizing with her human friend
heartache. After all, Angeline had been the one to intro
duce Tessa to Reed.

"I thought I'd have a lot to say when I saw him again, b
I realized I don't want to be with someone who doesn't lig
up when I walk into a room, the way Lincoln does with you

"Um, Lincoln isn't interested in me."

"You really should get your eyes checked." Tessa smile
"It's so cute the way he watches you. And last night, th
way he handled those drunks messing with you..."

"I handled the drunks."

"He's so protective." Tessa didn't seem to be listenin

"I didn't need protecting."

"And he's so sexy."

On that matter, Angeline would be hard-pressed to argu
Incredibly attractive, tall, muscular and, even missin
a leg, he had an air of strength and grace that she foun
irresistible.

"Is he coming in tonight?"

"No. One of his buddies dropped by unexpected
and they're off doing guy things." Actually, Lincoln too
Damien to meet Brice and Tristan. Afterward the two Do
men would likely run the woods, swim in the icy riv

nd race to the top of Walker's Pointe to see who would ›ap off first.

Wolfan males, in general, were competitive. Dogmen ›ok the competition to a whole new level.

"Angeline?" Miriam walked into the employee room. Will you be at Sierra's party tomorrow?"

"Have I ever missed one of my nieces' or nephews' irthdays?"

"What about Lincoln?"

"He told Sierra that he would come, but one of his bud- ies just arrived and I'm not sure what his plans are now."

"Could you give him a call? I'd like a final head count › I know how much food to prepare."

Angeline reached into her locker for her cell and auto- ialed Lincoln's number.

"Hello, Angel," he said soft and low before the third ring.

"Hey." Even Angeline heard the breathiness in her oice. Cringing, she glanced at Tessa, her brow arched nd her hand cocked on her hip. "Um, Aunt Miriam needs final head count for Sierra's party tomorrow." Angeline ırned her back on Tessa and dropped her voice. "It's okay you can't go."

"A promise is a promise."

"What about Damien?"

"I don't think a little girl's birthday party is up his alley."

"But you're okay with going?"

"I never go back on my word."

"Okay, then. I'll see you tomorrow."

"Not tonight?"

Despite her initial reservations, she didn't mind spend- ıg time with Lincoln. But Damien put her on edge.

"I'm working until closing and I have some things to nish up."

"If you change your mind, I'll be up."

"I won't be home until after two." Her heart skipped a beat. "Are you planning to wait up for me?"

"Being a good neighbor doesn't stop at five p.m."

A feeling of warmth wrapped around her like a big generous hug.

"I guess it doesn't." She felt the smile stretching her mouth.

"'Bye, Angel."

"'Bye." The breathiness returned, accompanied by a certain giddiness.

"I've never seen you googly over a guy," Tessa said. "There really is something between you and Lincoln, isn't there?"

"We're neighbors like Tristan and I used to do."

"You never got dreamy-eyed over Tristan."

"I'm not dreamy-eyed. Tristan knew I could take care of myself. I think it's sweet that Lincoln thinks he's looking out for me."

"See…protective." Tessa unfolded her crossed arms. "This might be a game changer for you."

"What do you mean?"

"You can kick ass with the best of them."

"Thanks to my dad and brothers."

"Yes, but you didn't seem to mind him stepping in with those two drunks. I heard Lincoln threatened bodily harm before tossing them out, then he went to check on you."

"He didn't toss them out. Reed did."

"You were off the floor for quite a while. When you and Lincoln came back out, you both looked quite rosy."

"Jimmy forced me to take a break and Lincoln made sure that I didn't sneak back before my time was up."

"Uh-huh." Tessa touched Angeline's arm. "There's nothing wrong with *liking* him."

Oh, but there was. Lincoln's heart belonged to the Program. As long as it did, Angeline would not risk hers.

Chapter 14

Lincoln!"

Nothing rivaled the delighted squeal of a little girl on her birthday.

"You came!" The pure joy on Sierra's face nearly caused Angeline's heart to burst.

Lincoln picked up the newly turned six-year-old. "A Dogman always keeps his promise."

In the living room sat Izzie and Connor and Angeline's dad. Their mouths fell open when Lincoln strolled in like an ordinary man, carrying the birthday girl on his shoulders. Obviously, he wasn't what they'd been expecting, and she liked that about him.

"I told you he would come," Sierra announced triumphantly, then promptly stuck her tongue out at her brother, Logan.

Angeline introduced Lincoln to Sierra's parents, Connor and Izzie.

"Thanks for coming." Connor nodded at Lincoln in greeting.

"We're so happy you're here." Izzie hugged Lincoln's neck. "Sierra's been talking about you coming to her party for days."

Sierra looked around the room devoid of birthday decorations. "It doesn't look like a party because Pawpa doesn't like froufrou."

"Pawpa would be my father, Patrick." Angeline casually flicked her hand in his direction.

The two men silently regarded one another for a moment. Angeline's father pursed his lips the way he always did before a lecture.

"No froufrou, huh?" Lincoln lifted Sierra from his shoulders and gently set her feet on the floor. He leaned down to her eye level. "A close friend once told me that a little froufrou was absolutely necessary in the right circumstances."

"Sounds like something Angeline would say," Patrick scoffed.

"Actually, her name was Lila." Lincoln's attention remained focused on the little girl. "She died on our last mission."

"She was a Dogman?" Sierra's eyes and mouth rounded.

"Yes, and she loved parties. Froufrou and all."

Despite the harsh look from her father, Angeline couldn't tone down the ridiculously big smile staked on her face.

"Sierra, why don't you and Logan play upstairs?" Angeline's father said. "I'm sure Lincoln would rather talk with the adults."

"Actually, I wouldn't." Lincoln's smile didn't quite mask the subtle, not-so-friendly undertone in his voice. "I'm here for Sierra."

"Let's have a tea party." Sierra's small hand clasped Lincoln's large one.

"Lead the way, princess."

Angeline could almost hear her father's teeth grinding.

Midway up the stairs, Sierra turned. "Coming, Aunt Ange?"

"I need to help your mom, first."

When Lincoln, Sierra and Logan disappeared upstairs, Angeline faced her family. "So." She held up a bag. "I brought some decorations."

"Of course you did." Angeline's father frowned.

"This is a fabulous idea, Ange. A surprise party at the party. Sierra doesn't suspect a thing." The happiness in Izzie's eyes matched her radiant grin and it was easy to see which parent Sierra took after the most.

"Good! Lincoln is in on the surprise. He will keep her occupied until I get them."

"He's a Dogman, not a babysitter." Patrick O'Brien's disapproving look might've worked when Angeline was a child, but now she simply ignored it.

"Lincoln is a man who knows how to make a little girl happy on her birthday." Angeline placed a shiny, pointy hat on her father's head. "And so do I."

"Keep your father occupied while Angeline and I get the decorations up." Izzie gave Connor a sparkly party hat. "I expect both of you to wear them during the party."

Angeline caught a glimpse of her father's stunned face before her brother whisked him into the home office.

"We'd better get started." Angeline pulled the ladder from the laundry room and began hanging streamers in the family room.

Shortly after, Garret and Madelyn arrived with their three kids—Rosalyn, Caleb and Brent—to help. By the time Angeline tied the last balloon, Jimmy and Miriam, along with their daughter, Lucy, and their son, Zach, came in with platters of food.

Angeline followed them to the kitchen and once Zach's

hands were free of the large platter, she pulled him into a corner.

"Is he here?" The golden flecks in Zach's brown eyes glittered. "Mom said the Dogman was coming."

"Let's get a few things straight," Angeline said. "One, this is Sierra's party and Lincoln is her guest. You will not talk to him about the Program. Got it?"

Some of the enthusiasm faded from Zach's expression.

"Two, you're not going into the Program."

"Ange, I'm almost twenty-three. I can make my own decision."

"This isn't up for debate, Zach." She rested her hand on his shoulder. "I can't explain tonight, but there are things I want you to know about being a Dogman that you don't fully understand."

"Wouldn't it be better for me to talk to Lincoln? An actual Dogman?"

"I'll ask him to meet with you, but first you need to hear what I have to say. Deal?"

"Do I have a choice?"

"No. We'll do lunch tomorrow."

"I have classes at the college tomorrow, but I could swing by your place around seven." His eyes narrowed. "In the morning."

Ack! A morning person she wasn't.

But if she could get up early to take her nieces and nephews sledding, Angeline could get up early to talk her younger cousin out of signing his life over to an organization that would rip him away from everyone who loved him. "I'll need sugar and caffeine."

"Spot me a twenty and I'll pick up an assortment of pastries and a couple of large coffees to-go from Morning Glories."

"Deal." Angeline squeezed Zach tightly, rememberi

when he had reached the age when he thought himself too cool for affectionate expression. Thankfully, he'd outgrown the phase and freely returned the hug.

"It's time to get the birthday girl!" Izzie said when Angeline and Zach walked into the living room.

"On it!" Angeline's steps quickened on the stairs and she tiptoed to the playroom.

Lincoln, Sierra, Logan and their cousin Brent were sitting in a circle on the floor. The Dogman tossed a card onto the stack in the middle of their circle.

"No, silly." Sierra giggled. "That's the wrong one."

"Are you sure?" He gave her a dubious look. "I think someone is changing the rules."

"It's called cheating," Logan said.

"Nuh-uh!" Sierra's bottom lip protruded.

"Did you know that on a little girl's sixth birthday, she gets to make up the rules on all the games she plays?" Lincoln said to the trio.

"No way," Logan and Brent exclaimed in unison.

"Really?" Sierra squealed.

Lincoln held up two fingers. "Dogman's honor."

"He's a natural." Miriam's soft whisper startled Angeline. She had been so focused on the scene in the bedroom, she hadn't heard her aunt coming up the stairs.

"Yeah, he is." A bubbly feeling filled Angeline and she wasn't as resistant to it as she should be to her growing fondness for Lincoln.

"In case you haven't noticed, he's good with you, too."

Oh, she'd noticed.

Miriam squeezed Angeline's shoulder then slipped away quietly.

Sierra tossed down a card and threw her hands in the air. "I won!"

"The game isn't even over." Brent pouted.

"The birthday girl always wins on her birthday." Lincoln gathered the cards.

"Well, everything is going back to normal tomorrow." Logan huffed.

"Hey, you guys." Angeline stepped into the room. "Everyone is here and the food is ready."

Sierra stood and held out her hand. "Come on, Lincoln."

"Give me a sec." He straightened his prosthetic leg. Flattening his palms on the floor slightly behind his hips, he drew up his good leg and pushed from a squat to stand. The flawless motion made Angeline wonder how long he'd practiced those moves for it to look so effortless.

She admired his tenacity and persistence. He also had a calm, steady manner that she more than appreciated, especially in the company of her family.

Sierra stopped her brother from getting ahead of her exiting the room. "Birthday girl first."

"I can't wait until this day is over." Logan rolled his eyes.

The birthday girl snuggled up to Lincoln when they reached the stairs. "Why is it dark down there?"

"Maybe the power breaker blew," Angeline said. "I think they're coming back on, right now."

Right on cue, light flooded the house to the chorus of "Happy Birthday!" Balloons and streamers decorated the living room filled with family.

"It's a party!" Sierra squealed. "For me!"

She darted down the stairs, her brother and cousin following behind.

"Everything looks great," Lincoln said. "Well done."

"Kudos to you, too." Angeline took his hand as they slowly descended the stairs. "We couldn't have pulled this off if you hadn't kept Sierra busy. She adores you."

At the bottom of the landing, Lincoln drew Angeline

whisper-close. She loved his scent. Clean, masculine and woodsy, the smell made her feel grounded.

"I wish her aunt could be as easily enchanted." His understated smile wrapped around Angeline's heart.

"Maybe I am." She kissed his warm cheek, and the contact caused her lips to tingle.

"Only in my dreams."

"Lincoln!" Sierra waved madly across the room.

"See? You have a new best friend."

"I hope so." Lincoln's hand trailed down Angeline's arm and brushed her fingers. Reluctance filled his eyes. Still, he obeyed the birthday girl's summons, treating her like the princess he'd professed her to be.

An undeniable fondness welled inside Angeline.

"He really knows how to handle kids." Madelyn walked over to Angeline. "Not what I expected from a Dogman."

Nor what Angeline had presumed, either. A Dogman's likelihood of stealing her heart rivaled a snowball's chance of surviving the gas fireplace in Lincoln's apartment that she coveted. But if she wasn't careful, a man who played games with children, made them laugh and gave them his undivided attention just might beat the odds.

Angeline's scent filled the truck. Each breath, her essence, invaded Lincoln's senses, drawing him deeper into a life he coveted but could not yet claim.

"You're really good with kids," she said, gazing out the window.

"I've had a lot of experience. During my down time on deployment, I gave out treats and played games with any kids I found."

"That's so sweet." Angeline laid her hand on his thigh. Suddenly, he didn't need the heat blowing out of the air vents.

"It's actually pretty sad." The gravity of what many of the kids faced had a profound effect on Lincoln. "Their world was falling apart. I just wanted to give them something that resembled a normal childhood. At least, what I thought might be normal."

"What do you mean?"

"I'm an only child and my parents never gave me treats or played games with me. For them, life is a competition. They placed a lot of pressure on me to be the best."

"So you never got to be a kid." Angeline's tone mirrored the heaviness he felt when remembering his childhood.

"I guess not."

"My mom died when I was six." She stared straight ahead. Her hands clenched in her lap. "My dad chopped off my hair, threw out my dolls and dresses, and I had to wear my brothers' hand-me-downs. He also sold our piano even though I begged him to keep it. Mom had been teaching me to play. She loved music. I do, too."

"He didn't want any reminders of her?"

"He didn't want me to be weak." Angeline anchored her arms over her chest, her fingers digging into the sleeves of her green sweater. "A mugger killed my mother. She was human and my Dad thought if she'd been Wahya, she would've scented the danger and would've had a better chance of defending herself. So he became a drill sergeant instead of simply being our father."

"He didn't want to lose you, too." Lincoln couldn't imagine the depths of a father's fear. Dayax wasn't his son, yet sometimes the uncertainty of the wolfling's safety and well-being nearly ate him up inside.

"I worry that my brothers will become like him."

Angeline looked at Lincoln. "So I make sure their kids get plenty of fun time with me."

Slowing to stop at the red light, Lincoln squeezed her

and. "Your nieces and nephews are lucky to have you in
ıeir lives."

"You were great with them. Tonight and when we went
edding." She offered him a small smile. "I'm lucky to
ave you as a neighbor."

"Really?" He snickered. "When I arrived, you weren't
xactly thrilled."

"I only saw you as a Dogman, then." She hesitated. "In
ollege, I had a bad experience with one."

"Did he hurt you?" If he did, Lincoln would go to his
rave without revealing Tanner Phillip's last words.

"No, no. We were really good together." Angeline's
oice cracked.

The sadness that suddenly enveloped her hurt Lincoln's
eart.

"He simply chose to be a Dogman," she continued,
ather than become my mate."

"Angeline—"

"Don't." She waved off further discussion. "Ancient
istory."

The light turned green and Lincoln continued driving.
micable silence filled the space between them. Though
e sensed no real tension from Angeline, she appeared
st in her thoughts.

Lincoln teetered with the decision to tell Angeline the
uth about her Dogman. But what would the man's final
ords of longing and regret do to her? Rip out her heart
l over again?

Lincoln wouldn't do that to her.

She'd called the relationship ancient history. Maybe
incoln shouldn't resurrect ghosts while dealing with his
vn present demons.

Dayax remained unaccounted for and it could be an-
her week or more before Lincoln returned to Munich

to take the readiness test for active duty. He missed th
wolfling terribly. Lila had warned him about becomin
emotionally attached to the young orphan, but Dayax ha
burrowed into Lincoln's heart and he simply couldn't re
until the wolfling was safe.

Once he'd located and retrieved Dayax, Lincoln ha
no idea what would happen next. Brice had suggeste
that Lincoln adopt the orphan wolfling. After all, on
the mission was completed, Lincoln would no longer
a Dogman.

Having been a soldier for the last fifteen years, he wou
have a hard enough time learning to cope long-term in t
civilized world. Unmated and with no place to call hom
how could he even think of raising a young boy?

Still, the time spent with Angeline and her family h
brought his longing for family sharply into focus. Angeli
had a natural ability in handling the kids. She listened. S
supported him. And she responsibly indulged their nee
to simply be kids. She would be great with Dayax, too.

But Lincoln had no business making that leap. Not ev
in his dreams.

"It's still early," Angeline said as he parked. "Do y
have plans with Damien?"

"No." Although Lincoln had been the team leader,
and Damien weren't exactly friends. They had differe
ideas of fun and had very little in common. "Why?"

"I need to burn off the calories from those cupcake
Angeline opened the passenger door, climbed out a
waited for him at the front of the truck.

"What do you have in mind?"

"It's a beautiful night." The sinking sun tinged t
cloudless sky with streaks of red and orange. Althou
the temperatures had warmed to the midsixties, it wo
come down a few degrees after nightfall.

"There is a nice trail in the woods behind the apartments," she continued. "Care to join me?"

She-wolves didn't run with just any male. The moments of nudity and the vulnerability of the smaller female wolf in the presence of a larger, more dominant male required a lot of respect and a great deal of trust.

"I'd love to," Lincoln said.

Their fur would keep them warm once they shifted, but their human forms would be subjected to the chill while they stripped down. The thought of seeing Angeline naked again caused his breathing to go wonky.

Following her into the woods behind the apartment building might not be the smartest decision, but Lincoln did it all the same.

She led him to a thick patch of evergreen bushes that provided some privacy in case someone looked out of an apartment window. Turning his back to her, Lincoln tried to concentrate on something other than the zipper sliding down her boots and the rustle of her jeans.

Leaning against a tree, Lincoln removed the boot and sock from his good leg. Despite the lack of new snow, the ground felt ice-cold against his bared foot. His sweatshirt and T-shirt came off together. He shoved his jeans down his legs to his ankles and stepped out of them.

No breeze wafted through the trees. Still, the crisp, chilled air nipped his bare skin. He sat on the ground, his buttocks clenching in protest at the cold, hard earth. Carefully, he removed the prosthetic and wrapped his clothes around the artificial limb to protect it. Then he peeled off the protective sleeve covering his stump.

Completely naked, he maneuvered into an on-all-fours position. Well, except for him, it was on-all-three since he no longer had his left knee.

He looked over at Angeline. Crouched in a ready position, she gave him a soft smile.

"Ready?"

"I'll give you a head start."

"What?"

"You wanted a run, so run!" He growled the last word as he shifted.

Angeline didn't shift quite as quickly, so Lincoln watched her transform. Though the process took only a second, he glimpsed the soft, silvery glow engulfing her body before she turned into a beautiful wolf. Her fur remained the same rich auburn as her hair, and her eyes were just as strikingly blue. She had a tuft of white beneath her chin and down her slender neck, and white cuffs around her paws that looked like socks.

Without hesitation, she launched from her perch and disappeared into the woods.

Mine!

The declaration drummed in his mind.

It wasn't the first time he'd heard it in Angeline's presence. Nor did he expect it would be the last.

He'd connected with the real woman as easily as he had fallen for her photograph. But until he came clean about the past that linked them together, they couldn't be anything more than friends.

Lincoln also decided not to tell Angeline about his reinstatement to active duty. She'd said not knowing Tanner's whereabouts or whether he was safe had been the worst kind of torture. Lincoln wouldn't put her through the turmoil again.

Once he returned from Somalia, then and only then would he tell her everything.

Chapter 15

Heart pounding, Angeline bounded down the mile-long ail. Her paws barely touched the cold, hard ground be- re propelling her forward again.

Dogmen were competitive by nature and conditioning. Vinning was held in the highest regard. If racing against a ılly able-bodied Dogman, she would lose without a sub- antial head start. Lincoln, with only three legs, had still iven her the lead. Any other she-wolf might've foolishly elieved the race would be easily won.

Angeline doubled her efforts. Though she couldn't hear incoln coming, she sensed him closing the distance.

Her instinct had become highly attuned to Lincoln's pres- ıce. And her thoughts often either dwelled on moments they ıd shared or obsessed about when she would see him again.

There were a lot of reasons as to why they often sought ut each other's company. Only one frightened her—the ssibility that they were true mates.

She had loved Tanner with all of her being and his rejection had nearly broken her. Never had she imagined the possibility of wanting to bond so intimately with another again.

With Tristan, Angeline had felt a kinship to him closer than the one she had with her brothers. He had actually understood her and encouraged her to nurture the things important to her.

Lincoln also seemed to sense the layers no one else saw in her. She hadn't told him about her secret career as a songwriter yet, but she wanted him to know.

Ever since Tristan had claimed a mate, Angeline had scaled back the more personal aspects of their friendship. That had left a big, gaping hole in her life. One that in a very short time, Lincoln had filled.

Except with him, her feelings had quickly spread beyond the plateau of platonic friendship to become more emotionally intimate than she had anticipated.

Now she had to figure out what to do about it.

Following the well-worn path, she cut sharply to the left. The chilly air ruffled through her fur, invigoratin her senses. Lincoln's scent grew stronger. Anticipatio tightened her stomach as she wondered when and wher he'd finally catch her.

Angeline glimpsed movement between the thickets o trees ahead, but Lincoln's scent remained behind her. O dinarily someone else running the woods at the same tin wouldn't have bothered Angeline. Tonight, however, sh wanted an exclusive run with Lincoln and an interlop would spoil the moment.

"Angeline, stop!" Lincoln's calm command echo through her mind.

Immediately, she halted. Although she didn't detect a

arm in his telepathic communication, Angeline doubted
: would use a ploy to win a race.

"Don't move."

Standing absolutely still, she felt the sudden rush of Lin-
oln's essence pour into her. Strong, masculine, protective.
second later his sleek, powerful, sable-color wolf form
ared over her. He landed about five feet in front of her,
s front legs absorbing the impact of the landing before
: touched down his hind right foot.

Magnificent, she mused silently. Even missing a leg,
incoln's wolf form commanded respect.

His soft chuckle tickled her mind. *"Thanks, Angel."*

Uh-oh. She needed to keep a better handle on her
oughts. *"What's going on?"*

"We've got company."

About fifty feet ahead, a large brindle-colored wolf
nerged from the shadows and blocked their path. Ange-
ie didn't immediately recognize the male wolfan, which
eant he didn't belong to the Walker's Run pack.

The unknown wolf trotted toward them, and she sensed
subtle tension creeping into Lincoln's body.

"What are you doing here, Damien?"

"Same as you. Getting fresh air and exercise."

Damien stopped in front of Lincoln. The moonlight cast
otesque shadows on Damien's face, distorting and exag-
rating the appearance of the jagged scar down his cheek.

"Angeline?" The look he gave her made the skin be-
ath her fur crawl. *"You are absolutely stunning."*

Angeline didn't reply with the customary "thank you"
nce his compliment gave her an icky feeling that she
anted to wash off.

Lincoln sidestepped, blocking Damien's view of her.

"Why don't we go out and get a drink?" Damien con-
ued to stare.

"I'll pass." Working three nights a week at Taylor's Roadhouse, Angeline didn't want to spend her time off hanging out in a bar.

"Rain check," Lincoln confirmed.

"Any suggestions on what I can do tonight? I've had a royally boring day." There might've been an undertone of resentment in Damien's response, but since Angeline didn't know the man, she dismissed the thought.

"Maico is pretty tame on Sundays." And every other day, mostly.

"I should've stayed in Miami." Damien shook his head. *"I'm gonna die of boredom here."*

"I told you that I had plans with Angeline today." Lincoln's matter-of-fact tone held no sympathy for Damien's little pity party. *"Tomorrow, I'll introduce you to some o the sentinels. I'm sure they can plug you into all the excit ing things Maico has to offer."*

"Tomorrow it is, then." Damien bumped past Lincoln

Not wanting Damien to do the same with her and sprea his scent along her fur, Angeline stepped aside to let hin pass. He continued on his way at a leisurely trot.

"I feel a little bad for him." Angeline stepped next t Lincoln. *"He came to see you and I've been hogging you attention."*

"Do not feel bad. I prefer your company to his." Lin coln's gaze remained fixed on the path behind them. *"I' not sure why Damien came to see me."*

"Obviously, to spend time with you." A brisk win sifted through Angeline's fur.

"We weren't close."

"Maybe the explosion changed things."

Both Lincoln and Damien had been injured and lo a colleague, although Lincoln likely felt the loss mo sharply.

He turned his muzzle toward Angeline, and the hard look in his eyes softened. *"It certainly did."*

Her heart fluttered and a flood of awareness caused her to shiver.

"Cold?" Cautiously, he stepped closer and lowered his snout.

"Maybe." Angeline leaned in, encouraging Lincoln to nuzzle her.

His heat wrapped around her, sheltering her from the chill, and the gentle way he scented her made Angeline feel cherished. Burying her snout in the thick fur of his neck, she slowly and deeply inhaled his clean, woodsy scent, drawing part of him inside her with each breath. She missed this closeness, the ethereal connectedness of two souls merging.

Before Lincoln, Angeline considered herself a smart woman. The inability to race back to her apartment and lock Lincoln out for good suggested a significant problem with her common sense.

"We should head back." Lincoln's thoughts nudged her mind.

He was right, of course, which made a little piece of her heart inexplicably sad.

"I'll race you," she told him and then darted down the path toward the apartment building.

No longer sensing him behind her, Angeline looked back to see Lincoln headed in the opposite direction.

Boy, had she misread his signals.

Setting her sights ahead, Angeline bolted home.

"You look awful." Standing in the kitchen, squinty-eyed and sporting dark shadows beneath his lashes, Damien lifted one of the two large coffees from the cardboard drink holder in Lincoln's hand.

"Seen a mirror lately?" Lincoln dropped the bag filled with breakfast sandwiches and pastries onto the counter, popped the lid off his foam cup and swallowed a large gulp of dark, rich coffee.

After the night he'd had, one cup would not be enough. Too bad he'd canceled the order for Angeline's coffee. A late riser, she probably wouldn't have been happy if he woke her, especially after he'd intentionally ditched her.

Plucking an egg, cheese and bacon croissant from the bag, Damien straddled the kitchen bar stool. "I take it things didn't go well with your *angel* after I left."

Damien was not wrong.

Instead of accompanying Angeline home, Lincoln had chosen to finish his run alone. And he'd sensed the awful moment when Angeline had slammed the door on their growing closeness.

Even though he'd never been in love, Lincoln suspected the reason his instinct kept drawing him to Angeline was that the ethereal ties of the mate-bond were at work. However, now was not a good time to delve into the possibility of a mateship with Angeline.

Dayax remained his priority. Once he and the wolfling were safely reunited and Lincoln officially retired from the Program, then he would be free to indulge in his feelings for Angeline.

Until then he expected a lot more sleepless nights.

"It's complicated." Lincoln popped the lid off the drink container and swallowed a mouthful of coffee.

"You don't do complicated." Damien's inquisitive gaze tracked Lincoln's every move.

"That's why I look like this," he said, pointing his index fingers at himself. "What's your excuse?"

Damien shrugged, taking his time chewing his food.

Lincoln hazarded a guess as to the young Dogman's eplessness. "Nightmares?"

"How did you know?"

"I have them, too." Post-traumatic stress syndrome, the ych doctor at Headquarters had called it. Then he'd pre-ribed Lincoln medication and assigned him to a ther-y group.

But the pills fogged his brain and listening to stories out someone else's traumatic experience didn't help Lin-ln deal with his own. It merely made him angry.

"Does it get better?" Damien stared at Lincoln over the n of his coffee cup.

"God, I hope so." Lincoln held the young man's gaze. m sorry, Damien. I never intended to involve the team my search for Dayax."

Damien's eyes glazed and he seemed to be watching a emory play out in his mind. Methodically working his ht jaw, he slowly shook his head. "*No es tu culpa*, Cap'n. u ordered us to stay put." A dark look briefly drew his ck brows together. A moment later his expression light-ed. "We all liked that little scamp."

In the long weeks of separation, Lincoln was beginning realize that he didn't simply like Dayax. He loved that mali wolfling as his own.

Nudging aside the cherry turnover in the bag, Lincoln ted a bear claw and bit into the sticky-sweet delicious-ss. If he wanted to pass the physical readiness test, he eded less junk food and more exercise.

"I haven't been the greatest host since you arrived." He ve Damien a half shoulder shrug apology.

"Word of advice," Damien replied lightheartedly. "Don't nsider B and B operator as your next career. You have solutely no hospitality skills."

"You have a comfortable bed and running water. Plus, I

brought you food that's actually edible." Lincoln lifted his cup in a mock salute. "What else do you need?"

"A mint on the pillow would be a nice touch."

"I'm not a PEZ dispenser."

"Good one, *Capitán*." Smirking, Damien returned the coffee cup salute.

Fresh out of training when assigned to Lincoln's unit, Damien had been a royal pain in the ass to command. Cocky, self-centered and a self-important know-it-all who really didn't know anything about an actual deployment, he had not been any different than any other Program graduate who believed himself to be invincible.

Damien had found out sooner than most that he wasn't.

"When are you headed to the Amazon?" Lincoln finished devouring the pastry and licked the sugar from his fingers, making a mental note to put in an extra hour at the resort gym later.

"What?" Damien squinted at Lincoln.

"How long before you meet up with your new team?"

"Oh." Damien shook his head. "HQ put the brakes on that deployment. I'm awaiting new orders. Why?"

"I'm being stepped up to active duty—"

"How the fuck did you manage that?" Damien leaned toward Lincoln, curiosity glinting in his eyes.

"I called in a favor from a friend in tight with the Woelesenat," Lincoln said.

"Of course you did."

"They're allowing me to go back to Somalia. And I'm going to track down Dayax."

"How do you know the kid is still alive?"

"He's scrappy, smart, resourceful and managed to stay alive six months on his own before we arrived. He's doing whatever it takes to survive. I made a promise and I will find him." Failure was not an option.

Damien absently scratched his stubbled jaw. "Does your sexy guardian angel know what you're planning?"

Lowering his gaze, Lincoln shook his head. How could he tell Angeline that he planned to go on a suicide mission to save a child no one really believed was still alive?

But Lincoln knew. He could feel the truth gnawing at his gut. Dayax was waiting, and watching and wondering if Lincoln would come for him.

"Yeah, well, you better tell her," Damien huffed. "You're going to need all the divine intervention you can get, or else you might lose more than a leg." Damien pushed aside his coffee cup and half-eaten sandwich, then shoved off the bar stool and headed for the bedroom.

"Wait," Lincoln called after him. "You're here for some R & R, so no more Program talk. Come with me to the resort. I'll introduce you to the pack's security team. Maybe you can tag along with the sentinels on their patrols."

"Beats doing nothing." Damien's demeanor lightened. "I could give them pointers on perimeter surveillance and bringing down interlopers."

"I suppose you could," Lincoln told him. Although young and brash, Damien had elite military training. If they listened, the sentinels probably would learn a thing or two from him.

"Are you going to run with the sentinels, too?"

"Not today. The resort has a gym and I need to buckle down for some serious workouts. Before I'm certified for active duty, I have to take the readiness test."

"Oh, man." Damien scrunched his face. "There is nothing that would make me go through those three days of hell ever again."

If—no, *when* Lincoln got Dayax back, everything he endured would all be worth it.

Chapter 16

Having a rough…" Lincoln checked his utility watch. "I would say night, but it's not yet six o'clock."

Angeline slammed the office door shut. "This is all your fault." She snatched the bag from his hand and dumped the contents onto Miriam's desk.

"I was nowhere around when that happened." Flashing an insufferable grin, he zigzagged his index finger in her general direction.

So far, a pitcher of beer had spilled down her leg, someone's kid had slung mac-and-cheese at her ass, and her favorite sweater got splattered with barbecue sauce from the platter of ribs in her hands when she'd collided with Tessa.

"Turn around," she said, clenching her teeth.

"I've already seen you naked."

Angeline shook her finger. "Full moons don't count."

Still smiling, Lincoln turned his back to her and stuck

his hands into his hip pockets. "What's got you agitated, Angel?"

"You!" Angeline toed off her shoes, then peeled off her jeans.

Last night, things had been going so well until Damien had showed up and Lincoln had suddenly decided he needed to get far, far away from Angeline. Despite her resolve to write him off, she'd barely slept. Her mind had kept trying to figure out how she'd misread the signals while her instincts argued that she hadn't.

Then, after a sleepless night, she'd had to get up early to talk to Zach. She'd told him about Tanner but it was hard to gauge if anything she said got through to him. But he had promised to speak with Lincoln, as well, and she had already texted him Zach's number.

"Is this about last night?" Lincoln glanced over his shoulder.

"Eyes facing the door or this stapler is going to land right between them."

Lincoln complied, and Angeline was grateful he didn't call her bluff.

"I needed to clear my head. For both our sakes."

"You could've said something to me." Angeline stuffed her legs in the clean jeans and then yanked off her top to put on the soft blue sweater Lincoln had brought her. "When I looked back and saw you hightailing it in the opposite direction—"

She balled up the dirty clothes and dropped them into the bag. "I would have understood. I can see how you might've been weirded out by spending the afternoon with my family and then me asking you to go running."

Having Lincoln at Sierra's party had felt natural and the get-together had turned out better than most of the family events she'd attended. "I wanted to run with you because I sensed a connection that I haven't felt in long time. If I'm wrong, I would rather know up front."

Lincoln's posture stiffened. Of course his body language affirmed that she had made a grave mistake.

"Just forget it." She slipped on her shoes and combed her fingers through her hair. "Being around my family puts me a little off-kilter."

"I can't forget it." Slowly, Lincoln turned around. "I feel it, too, Angel. From the moment I first saw you."

"Oh?" Angeline's heart thumped faster, then seemed to drop straight into her stomach. She leaned against the edge of the desk. "Is it a mate-bond I'm sensing between us?"

Although Lincoln nodded, he didn't look happy.

Having been in this situation before, Angeline's own concerns doubled. "We have to stop interacting. You don't come to my place, I won't go to yours. And definitely no more invites to family functions."

A mate-bond could be circumvented if one or both parties resisted the ethereal connection.

"It's not okay." Closing the distance between them, Lincoln opened his hand for her to take.

She did and static electricity snapped at the contact. Before she could pull away, Lincoln's fingers closed around her hand. Immediately, she sensed his essence infiltrate her being.

Pulling her close, Lincoln nuzzled her neck. "Only a fool wouldn't want this with you."

The sincerity in his voice and touch couldn't mask the conflict she sensed deep within him.

"I'm being forced out of the Program," he said softly. "Mandatory medical retirement."

Understanding how difficult the circumstance must be for Lincoln, Angeline pressed her cheek against his chest. Although unable to hear his heart thumping beneath the ick pullover, she sensed the strong, steady beat pulsing ongside her own.

"But I have final orders to complete before my papers e processed."

"Final orders? That doesn't sound good." Angeline's omach tightened.

"A formality, mostly. Just a few loose ends that I need tie up. Nothing to worry about, I promise."

"How long will your final orders take?" Angeline arched Lincoln's face, wondering if he could or would de the truth from her as Tanner had done.

"Not long, I hope."

"When will you leave?"

"Whenever they call me up."

Angeline's entire body tensed. She'd have no time to epare. One minute Lincoln would be here, the next he ouldn't. Just like Tanner.

"Hey." Lincoln hands slid up and down her back. "I on't be gone any longer than absolutely necessary."

Angeline wanted to believe him, but she refused to set erself up for another heartbreak. A lot could happen bere Lincoln came home. *If* he came home.

"I'll be fine."

"You're already reading my thoughts?" When concted by a mate-bond, a couple could communicate telethically in their human forms.

"Body language." With both hands, Lincoln cradled her ce. Then, using his thumbs, he pushed up the corners of r mouth. "Much better."

He brushed her lips with a feather-soft kiss.

Suddenly, everything did seem better.

Wrapping her arms around his shoulders, she pressed gainst his body. Lincoln slipped one hand behind her ck, tilting her head to the perfect angle for a long, deep kiss. All the while, his other hand trailed down her arm then migrated to the small of her back.

He was holding on rather than pushing her away.

Hope sparked in her heart despite the reservation that Dogmen seldom, if ever, went quietly into retirement.

Lincoln broke the kiss and pressed his forehead to hers "I must not be doing this right if I can't get you to stop thinking about all the things that could go wrong."

"I wasn't..." Angeline stopped talking because Lincoln's gaze became so intense that she knew he could see straight into her soul.

"I never make a promise that I can't keep," Lincoln said. "I will come back." He sealed the oath with a kiss The softness of the previous one dissipated. This possessive and all-consuming kiss stole her breath and branded every inch of her mouth. His essence flooded her senses claiming the very core of her being.

She would be frightened of the developing bond if she hadn't watched Lincoln playing with her nieces and nephews. Every time he'd made Sierra giggle, every word encouragement he'd given to Brent and Logan and the wa he'd listened to Roslyn and Caleb revealed Lincoln's longing for family. From what she sensed, Lincoln Adams wa ready to make a *home*.

"Angeline? Tessa said you had an accident." Miriam entered the office. "Oh, oh! I didn't mean to intrude."

"Busted." Lincoln smiled against Angeline's mouth before taking a step back.

"I'm fine, Aunt Miriam." Angeline brushed her lip with the back of her hand. "I asked Lincoln to bring m a change of clothes. I couldn't work feeling like I we swimming in the garbage can."

"Thank you, Lincoln. For helping my niece—" Miria gave an exaggerated wink "—clean up."

"My pleasure." Smiling good-naturedly, Lincoln touched Angeline's hand. Her nerves lit up. "I should go."

"Stay for supper," Miriam said. "It's on the house."

"I'd love to, but I made plans with Damien to shoot pool with Reed and some of the sentinels." Lincoln edged toward the door. "Call me if you need…anything, Angel."

Angeline finger-waved as he left.

"I've never seen such a huge smile on your face." Miriam said. "I think Lincoln coming to town has been good for you."

"Yeah, I think so, too." But Angeline couldn't help wondering what would happen when he left.

"Something's changed." Damien tipped another beer bottle to his lips and took a long swallow. "You scored with Angeline, didn't you?"

All the chatter around the pool table ceased. The young blond man about to break the balls in an opening shot froze midstrike.

Slowly, Shane straightened, the cue stick sliding through his fingers until the rubber bumper touched the floor and his hand tightened around the tapered shaft. "What did you say?" His steely gaze cut from Damien to Lincoln.

"His neighbor is really hot," Damien said to Shane, then turned to Lincoln. "Caught up with her for an afternooner, didn't you? Must've been really good to have loosened that stick up your ass."

"Angeline is my neighbor, too," Shane said with lethal softness. "A packmate and a friend."

The air charged with the energy of pack mentality. The other sentinels quietly and effortlessly moved to close ranks. If Shane pounced, the rest would follow.

Except for Reed. Holding his position across the pool table, he slowly laid his cue stick on the felt top. A lead sentinel, he merely observed and assessed the situation without falling victim to an emotional reaction. When he acted, it would be swift and calculated.

Lincoln didn't consider any of them a viable threat. He wouldn't have lasted long as a Dogman if a few pissed-off wolfans could bring him down.

Not nearly as drunk as he appeared, Damien seemed to enjoy the heightened tension. Lincoln suspected the younger Dogman wanted to intentionally provoke the hometown sentinels.

"What Angeline does or doesn't do with me or anyone else is not your business," Lincoln said to Damien, then swung his gaze to Shane. "Or yours."

"It is when someone disrespects her." Shane made no effort to back down, and Lincoln admired his grit.

"Damien, apologize."

"For what?" He dropped the empty beer bottle onto the table.

Lincoln slowly turned his head and gave Damien a look that meant he expected the order to be followed. It didn't matter if they were both on medical leave. Lincoln was a superior officer and it would be an outright act of insubordination if Damien failed to comply.

Defiance flashed in Damien's eyes. Hot-tempered and reactionary, he needed a lot of seasoning that only time and experience would provide. At least some of his training had taken root because he shook off the attitude and presented a sincere face. "I meant no offense to Angeline."

"Shane, are you going to break or should I?" Reed picked up his cue stick.

The young sentinel studied Damien for a few seconds longer then gave a nearly imperceptible nod to Damien. "I won the toss." Shane turned back to the pool table. "I'm not giving up my advantage."

As if a switch had been flipped, the tension around em dissipated. Apparently, among these wolfans, once n understanding was reached, everyone simply moved ast whatever hurdle had tripped them.

Kara, their server, stopped by the table and collected amien's empty bottle.

"Keep 'em coming, *bomboncita*."

"You got it, sugar." Kara placed her hand on Damien's oulder and glanced at Lincoln. "Anything for you?"

"Nix his beer for now. We'll both have water."

"Gotcha." As she left, Kara flashed a bright smile and terest glittered in her hazel eyes.

"You're the one nursing a single beer," Damien said. "I now how to hold my liquor."

"Apparently not tonight," Lincoln said. "What's going n?"

"There's not much to do in this town. I'm getting antsy oing nothing.

"Didn't you join the sentinels on patrol today?"

"Yep." Damien rolled his eyes and slumped back in his air. "Buh-orr-ing."

After a lifetime of being on guard against bullets, incen- iary devices, poisons and knifings, the threat of torture pon capture, Lincoln appreciated the calm, slow pace he'd iscovered in Walker's Run. But he understood Damien's stlessness.

The Program's training taught recruits to thrive on ex- eme levels of adrenaline for extended periods. It kept em sharp, quick and deadly.

"How are you not crawling out of your skin?" His face young and earnest, Damien looked at Lincoln.

"Who says I'm not?" Lincoln watched the surprise flicker Damien's eyes. "I need to get back in the field. It's eating e up to be here, knowing Dayax is still missing."

"Huh." Damien scratched his ear. "You don't look bothered."

"It's all about focus. I'm still on a mission. The first part is to prove readiness for deployment. If I'm melting down over a little R & R, HQ will pull the plug on the second part." Lincoln paused. "If you can't handle the downtime, they will do the same to you."

"I'm not having a meltdown," Damien shot back.

"Inside, you feel jittery. Your mind is racing. The tightness in your chest makes it hard to breathe. Everything is closing in, you feel trapped. Desperate. Angry," he said watching Damien's hands curl into fists. "You're in withdrawal."

Dangerous and habit-forming, high levels of adrenaline enhanced the Dogmen's natural abilities and often kept them alive in extreme circumstances. The downside was that when the levels returned to normal, a Dogman's body protested significantly.

The best way to mitigate the side effects was to creat an adrenaline rush.

"I'm not in withdrawal," Damien snapped. "But I ar angry."

"Do tell." Lincoln opened his hands. "I'm all ears."

Damien glanced toward the pool table. Absorbed in th game, the sentinels appeared relaxed and unconcerne with the two Dogmen in their company. Except for Ree who kept a friendly watch as any good leader would.

"I don't want to be here." Hands balled, Damien reste his arms on the table and leaned toward Lincoln, beginni to bare his teeth. "I didn't become a Dogman to trot th expanse of some lame territory. I should be out there— he pointed in no particular direction "—making a diffe ence. Not stuck here with you."

"You came to me. And you can leave at any time," Lin-
oln said.

"Where should I go? I can't go home. You know the
ules."

All too well. It was one reason Lincoln hadn't called
s parents. The other being that they would consider what
ad happened to be a failure. See him as one, too. After
l, his leadership had cost him a leg, a friend's life, a re-
uit's face and the young wolfling he meant to find was
ill missing.

"I thought you'd want to get out of here," Damien said.
We could go anywhere. Do anything."

"I want to get to know Angeline better."

"You are so twisted, you know that?" Damien shook
s head. "Obsessed with a photo and now finding the ac-
al woman... It's creepy."

"I think it's fate."

"Unbelievable." Damien's short laugh sounded harsh
ad hollow. "You really are sick."

"Never felt better."

"Well, yippee ki-yay for you." Damien stood. "I feel
ke shit."

"And it's my fault."

"Damn straight, it is." Damien's knuckles thudded
gainst the table. His elbows and shoulders locked as he
aned forward. "We wouldn't be here if—"

"If I hadn't gone looking for Dayax."

Damien's glare focused on Lincoln.

"Then Lila wouldn't have convinced everyone to fol-
w and none of us would've been caught in that explo-
on. Is that it?"

"You should've been looking out for *us*." Frustration
d bitterness laced Damien's soft-spoken words.

Lincoln had. That was why he'd ordered Lila not to come after him.

"Are you a Dogman or a toddler?" Lincoln stood.

Damien's face darkened, turning his scar a purplish-black. "You know damn well what I am."

"Prove it." Lincoln intentionally kept his body loose. "Outside. I'm not paying for damages inside the bar."

"Are you serious?" Some of the anger in Damien's expression faded. Extremely competitive, a Dogman could no more turn down a challenge than a steak when starving.

"We need some fresh air," Lincoln said to Reed. "We'll be back in ten."

"Ten?" Damien scoffed, following him to the door. "I can take you in five."

Lincoln hid his smile. Ten was merely a generous time allotment to spike Damien's adrenaline and ease his withdrawal. Otherwise, he'd take down the kid in less than one

Chapter 17

Nothing below the waist. And no leg kicks or sweeps." In an empty area of the bar's back parking lot, Lincoln raised his arms, held his fists in front of his face and stood with his feet shoulder-width apart. "Upper body only. Break my prosthetic and you'll get the bill for a replacement."

"Are you sure you want to do this, *old man*?" From the unnecessary display of twinkle-toed footwork, to the pre-emptive air jabs and all the way up to his single-minded gaze, Damien reeked of arrogance.

Lincoln preferred the young Dogman figure out how to handle the downside of adrenaline withdrawal without turning himself into a punching bag. But he'd been in Damien's shoes before and had had a mentor do the same for him.

"Have at it, *pup*." Lincoln punctuated the intentional slur with a broad grin and achieved the exact response he wanted.

Damien jabbed a right hook that Lincoln could've blocked with his eyes closed. Instead, he let the punch connect. It rattled his teeth, but he didn't taste blood, so he shook it off.

"Is that all you got?" He watched Damien, fists close to his face and rocking from one foot to the other. "Don't see how you ever made it out of Basic with those weak-ass hands."

"I'm just warming up." Damien shuffled back and forth in a half-circle perimeter, periodically quick-punching the air to see if Lincoln would take the bait.

"Is this a fight or a dance?" Lincoln taunted. "Because if it's a dance, I'm going to find a prettier partner."

"Hey!" Shane called out. Most of the sentinels seemed to have come along with him. "What's going on?"

Damien took advantage of the momentary distraction and threw a punch that would've landed dead center of the solar plexus if Lincoln hadn't turned in time. The blow glanced his ribs. He drew a sharp breath, but was otherwise okay.

"This is what we do for fun." Lincoln shoved Damien away and eyeballed Reed, who stood to the side of the small posse with his arms crossed high on his chest. "Stay out of this or someone will get hurt and it won't be us."

"You heard the Dogman," Reed said. "Look but don't touch. Anyone who intervenes forfeits their spot on the security team." Despite the grumbles, all took a healthy step back.

Emboldened by the audience, Damien launched a full attack. Lincoln absorbed each punch with only a few forcing him to take a step back. Sentinels shouted, some cheering for Damien, whom they viewed as the underdog. Others yelled warnings to Lincoln in misguided attempts to be helpful. By the time Damien's fist slammed

to his body, Lincoln had already calculated where the
xt would land.

Damien's punches grew more aggressive and his
endly banter turned surly. An uppercut to the jaw caused
ncoln to bite down on his cheek. He spit out the blood,
d a feral gleam lit Damien's eyes.

"You've had enough adrenaline tonight."

"Are you conceding? 'Cuz I'm just getting started."
mien threw a right jab, followed by a right cross and
n a left hook. But he left himself open, and Lincoln
ponded with a power-packed, one-two counterpunch
d finished the combination with a right hook to the jaw.

Damien sprawled to the ground.

The sentinels fell silent.

Lincoln crouched over his opponent. The young man's
s were glassy and an odd smile distorted his face. "Are
ı all right?"

When he didn't answer, Lincoln snapped his fingers.
asked you a question, Dogman."

Damien blinked rapidly and the glaze cleared from his
cant gaze. "Yes, sir. I'm fine, sir."

"Feel better?"

Damien sat up and spit, then wiped his mouth on his
eve and grimaced. "I would, except I think you broke
jaw."

"It's not broken." Lincoln offered him a hand up. "Put
ne ice on it to help with the swelling."

The sentinels swarmed the younger Dogman with acco-
es of his putting up a good fight and advice on how to
e a better fight next time. Escorting him back into the
, the group promised he wouldn't have to buy another
ık tonight because each of them would buy him a round.

"You could've ended this before he took his first swing."

Reed hadn't moved from his position. "Why did you let him get in all those hits?"

"He needed the rush." Lincoln rubbed his jaw, tende and swollen from Damien's last punch. "Better for him to unload on someone who could handle it."

"You don't think me and my guys could?"

"This isn't personal, Reed." Lincoln liked the guy and didn't want to make an enemy unnecessarily. "Damie is a Dogman, plain and simple. Pit him against someon who lacks that level of training and Damien will likely kil them, albeit unintentionally. He's still green and nearl died on his first deployment. There's a lot of chaos whirl ing inside him right now. I know how to help him dea with it in a constructive way."

"Getting your ass kicked is constructive?" Ever-so-se rious Reed cracked a smile.

"My ass is fine." His jaw, chest and ribs, however, hu like hell. He needed to get home and soak in ice if h wanted to be able to get out of bed tomorrow. "Come o I'll buy you a drink."

"I'll take a raincheck and let Damien bask in his ne found fame with your sentinels."

"Are you and Damien good?" Reed asked. "The seemed to be a lot of anger in those punches."

Lincoln had noticed that, too. But after what had ha pened in Somalia, he couldn't blame Damien for harb ing some resentment.

"We're good. He just needed to get it out of his systen

"I hope he got it all out," Reed said. "I don't like t idea of him going off like that on someone else."

"He won't." Lincoln would make sure of it.

"You let him hit you?" Angeline stared at Lincoln. I neath his darkened eye and bruised cheek, an arrog grin split his face. Thankfully, he didn't seem to be missing any teeth. "On purpose?"

"Last night, it seemed like a good thing." Lincoln picked up the plastic-covered breakfast menu the waitress had left on the table.

At Mabel's Diner—a staple in Maico's town square for more than thirty years—the fare was always the same. Good, ol' fashioned, Southern-style cooking. Anything that couldn't be loaded down in butter was deep-fried in lard. Just a whiff of the delicious scents wafting from the kitchen could harden the patrons' arteries.

But people kept coming. For the food and for the company.

Enjoyed by unsuspecting humans and wolfans alike, Mabel's Diner was the heart of Maico. Mostly because of Mabel, a lively senior who sported a red beehive hairdo and resuscitated bright sky-blue eyeshadow that should've been left to rot in the eighties. Treating everyone like family, she nosed into everyone's business, doling out advice and scolds as readily as she served good eats.

"He needed to release some pent-up energy," Lincoln said.

"So you volunteered to be his punching bag?" Angeline waved away the menu he offered after reading it. She'd known exactly what to get the moment he'd mentioned brunch.

"Better me than someone else." Fingers laced, he rested his hands on the table. "It was a friendly brawl. We're both fine."

"I'll hold off agreeing with you until after I've seen Damien." Though, she had to admit, Lincoln certainly seemed more relaxed and some of the weariness in his eyes had faded. "He's not in the hospital, is he?"

"I said he's fine."

"You always say you're fine and you're missing a leg," Angeline said. "Are Dogmen trained in the Black Knight mentality? ''Tis but a scratch… It's just a flesh wound…'" she said, imitating the movie character. "'I'm invincible.'"

Lincoln's laugh, deep, rich and masculine, wreaked mayhem on every feminine molecule in her body. She crossed her arms over her chest to rein in the hormonal circus.

"I wouldn't peg you as a Monty Python fan."

"I'm not. Tanner was."

"Oh." Lincoln's smile tightened at the corners of his mouth.

"Well, well." Mabel Whitcomb's heavy Southern twang pinged them from three tables away. "Angeline O'Brien, here for breakfast no less."

"Brunch," Angeline clarified. "It's almost noon."

"Doesn't matter." Mabel leaned over and gave Angeline a friendly hug. "Always good to see you, hon."

"Same here, Mabel."

"Who's this fella you got with ya?" Mable winked at Angeline, then turned to Lincoln. "Haven't seen you before."

"First time visiting Maico." Lincoln held out his hand to the vivacious, human restaurateur.

Accepting his handshake, Mabel whispered loudly to Angeline, "Make sure he stays."

Gracefully, Lincoln hid his smile.

"I bet you're military," Mabel continued in her nosy way. "You've got an air about you. One that says *Special Forces*," she said, flashing jazz hands.

"Thanks, but…" He lifted his pant leg to reveal his prosthetic leg.

"Oh, I'm sorry, hon." Sympathy dampened the tease in her eyes. "How did that happen?"

"I fell out of a two-story window. Shattered the knee and twisted the leg so bad nothing could've saved it." Lincoln spoke without attachment or emotion, as if the injury hadn't cost his career.

"I'm glad you came through it all right," Mabel said. "And happy you came with Angeline. It's always nice when her pretty face brightens up the place."

"She brightens a lot more than she realizes." Lincoln's gaze caressed Angeline's skin.

"Could I get a refill on the coffee?" Angeline asked, not wanting to add more fodder to the diner's gossip circle.

"Sure thing," Mabel said. "Do you want the Co-op's special to go with it?"

"Two, please." Lincoln handed Mabel the menu.

"Um, I'll have the stuffed French toast, a ham and cheese omelet, and an order of bacon." Angeline smiled sweetly at Lincoln.

"One Co-op special and one special order coming up," Mabel said.

"No," Lincoln said before Mabel walked away. "I'll have two orders of the Co-op special."

"Hon, that's a lot of food." Mabel looked him up and down. "Even for you."

Lincoln glanced at Angeline. "I've been in the resort's gym since six this morning and have another workout planned for this afternoon."

"All right. Two it is." Mabel waved to a nearby server before moseying into the kitchen. The young woman hurried over and refilled their mugs nearly to the rim before rushing off to the next table.

"So, Tanner..." Head slightly bowed over his coffee cup, Lincoln's troubled gaze lifted to Angeline. "The Dogman you called ancient history?"

"Yes."

"I'd like to know about him."

"We met in college." Angeline looked out the large glass window at the Wyatt's Automotive Services building across the street. "I thought he was so handsome, smart, and funny." Arrogant at times, and proud. "He believed in me, in my talent."

Or maybe he simply wanted her to have something to pursue when he left.

"The night we met, I had gone to a secluded spot on campus to play my guitar. Since no one was nearby I also sang my heart out. Tanner said the voice of an angel had led him to me." The chemistry between them had been instantaneous and undeniable.

And yet he still walked away, abandoning the life they could've had together. For what? To die before he'd really had a chance to live?

A masculine essence gently ebbed inside her, pulling her back from the edge of the dark hole on which she teetered. Lincoln's hands were molded around hers, keeping her anchored in the present. And although his beautiful silver-green eyes were brimming with tenderness and worry over her past, in them she saw a hope for the future.

"Maybe your history with him isn't so ancient," he said softly.

"It is." Angeline withdrew from his touch. "He made his choice and then he died. End of story."

"I think you skipped a lot of parts." Lincoln's gaze didn't waver. "It's okay to talk about the good times and the bad ones. I'll listen to whatever you want to say, whenever you need to say it. Always."

She believed he would, too.

"Music is an important part of my life. It helped me heal after the ordeal with Tanner. You've seen my guitar, but I also play the piano, a clarinet and a little on the fiddle."

"I'd love for you to play and sing a song for me." A dev-
sh grin spread across Lincoln's face.

"Oh, no, you wouldn't." Surprisingly, Angeline's laugh
lt like it sounded. Lighthearted and genuine. "Tanner
as tone deaf. I sound like a banshee being strangled by
roll."

"Didn't know they existed." Lincoln laughed.

"According to Connor, they do. He once suggested that
y vocal cords be removed to avoid attracting the murder-
s creatures to our treehouse."

Deep peals of laughter caused Lincoln's shoulders to
ake.

"It's not that funny." Angeline rested her arms on the
ble.

"Easy, Angel." Eyes twinkling and mouth broadened
th a generous smile, Lincoln reached over and patted her
m. "No one is perfect, but you are close enough for me."

All the irritation building inside her immediately turned
rm and gooey, and a dopey smile took control of her
outh.

"What's your imperfection? And don't say your miss-
g leg, because that is definitely not one."

Lincoln's expression blanked, and he sat back in the
at.

"Come on. Confession is good for the soul."

"I don't like spiders," he finally said.

"That's not a deep, dark secret. You can do better."

"No," he said, growing visibly uncomfortable. "It re-
y is spiders." Eyes wide and rounded, Lincoln stared at
r without blinking, and his mouth folded down into a
t curve so tight that the edges of his lips turned white.

She lowered her voice. "You're really afraid of spiders?"

He shook off a hard shiver and wiped his palm over his
e. "Can't stand them."

The thought of a big bad Dogman afraid of a little bi arachnid was comical, but Angeline didn't dare laugh. L coln had shared a deeply personal tidbit and she would make him regret it.

"What happened?" Most phobias, she figured, w rooted in bad experiences.

"I had just learned to shift and my parents took me the woods for my first run. They were so proud of pouncing and tracking by pure instinct until a Texas bro tarantula dropped on me. I felt it scurrying through fur." Lincoln rolled his shoulders. "I thought it would me. I howled and cried and my parents thought I wa coward for panicking over a spider.

Angeline's heart tweaked for him. Wahyas were fai young when they developed the ability to shift.

"So, to teach me to be a brave wolf, they locked me my room at night with a tarantula. Oh, and they took the light bulb so I wouldn't sleep with the light on. stead, I used my wolfan vision to watch it. I didn't sl for three nights, sitting in the middle of the bed, worr the spider would bite me."

"What happened on the fourth night?"

"I spent it in the hospital. I had stopped eating drinking because I couldn't stop worrying about that da spider getting on me. I became dehydrated and deliri from sleep deprivation. To make matters worse, I refu to go home until our pack Alpha swore he'd person check my room and tell my parents not to bring any m spiders into the house."

"Lincoln." Angeline rubbed her chest bone to loo the tightness. "What your parents did was wrong on many levels."

He let out a long breath. "They actually thought it wc help."

Bobbie Sue stopped at the table and unloaded a tray of food. "Let me know if you need anything," she said, then hurried back to the kitchen.

"After that story, are you sure all that food will settle well in your stomach?" Angeline pointed at the double serving of eggs, pancakes, grits, biscuits with sausage gravy, ham and bacon.

Lincoln glanced around the restaurant. "No spiders, so I'm good."

Head down, face set in firm determination, he dug into his meal with gusto.

Angeline smiled, cutting into her French toast stuffed with strawberry cream cheese. Lincoln had trusted her with a deeply personal secret simply because she had asked. At the very least, she needed to reciprocate.

"The National Music Awards are on tomorrow night." She paused. "Interested in watching them with me?"

If he comes, I'll tell him. If he doesn't, I won't.

Lincoln's unreadable gaze lifted to hers and he took his time chewing the food in his mouth.

A sudden, large dose of anxiety caused her stomach to plunge. "Um, I just remembered that I have something else to do. I'll set the DVR and watch it later."

"I'll be home if you change your mind."

She wouldn't. If her family couldn't see the value in her musical talent, how could a hot-bloodied, near feral Dogman?

Chapter 18

What's up with the flowers, Slick?" Angeline stepped back, welcoming Tristan inside the apartment. "You usually show up with sweets."

She closed the door before the cold air leeched the heat from the living room.

"The National Music Awards are tomorrow night." Tristan handed her the lovely rainbow carnation arrangement. "Congratulations on your nominations."

"Thanks, but you usually don't give me flowers for the occasion." Since he had, Angeline appreciated that they came in a vase because she didn't own one.

She placed them on the kitchen counter. The sweet, floral scent filled the apartment and the bright colors balanced the muted shades of the decor.

"Because I'm usually celebrating with you on the night of the ceremony, but I can't this time." Tristan's apologetic expression tugged at Angeline's heart.

"I completely understand. You have a mate, and she's
ɔing to pop out your baby any day now." Angeline gave
ım a tight, friendly hug. "Me and you, we're good."

Looking like some of the weight on his shoulders had
fted, Tristan sat in the sofa chair. "Writing a new song?" He
pped his head at the scatter of papers on the coffee table.

"Yeah." Moving aside the guitar, she sat on the couch.
t's different from what I normally write."

"Meaning, it's about finding love instead of losing it?"

Angeline nodded. "Definitely not my bread-and-butter
arket, but it's exhausting to keep revisiting the emotions
the breakup with Tanner and his death."

"You've found new inspiration. Is it Lincoln?" Tristan's
ow dipped over his woried dark brown eyes.

She could always depend on him to have her back.

Angeline drew her socked feet beneath her legs. "I started
cperimenting with a new style before Lincoln came to
wn. But my muse has been more cooperative lately."

"He hasn't mentioned extending the sublet beyond the
ıd of the month," Tristan said. "Do you think he'll stay?"

"He has some things to take care of at the Dogman
adquarters but said he'll come back when his retirement
ıperwork is processed." She paused, mentally and physi-
lly taking a steadying breath. "Lincoln and I sense the
ate-bond." There, she'd said it. With much more convic-
ɔn than she'd practiced.

Fingers laced, Tristan leaned forward, resting his fore-
ms on his knees. "I don't want you to get hurt again."

"Neither do I." Angeline's heart smiled at her friend.
Ve aren't jumping into a mateship. I need time to really
ust him and Lincoln needs time to process how dramati-
lly his life is changing."

"That's smart." Tristan relaxed in the chair. "With the

accidental claiming, Nel and I didn't have the getting-to-know-each-other period before beginning a mateship."

"She loves you, Tristan. And I know you love her."

"I do." His eyelids pressed closed and his jaw tightened. "Once the baby comes, we'll have very little time for just us."

"Make the time," Angeline said. "When you and Nel need a few hours, a night or a weekend alone, call me. Aunt Ange will always be happy to babysit her." She studied Tristan's neutral expression. "Or him." Still nothing.

"Oh, come on." She tossed a pillow at Tristan. "Are you actually going to make me wait until Nel delivers to find out?"

"We don't know, either." Tristan grinned. "Nel and didn't have a chance to explore the mysteries of each othe before she became pregnant. So we wanted to share this one It's been so much fun, guessing and planning for a baby not a gender. We don't regret one moment of not knowing.

"That's really sweet." Tears stung Angeline's eyes "You're going to be a great dad."

"I hope so." Worry dimmed the joy in Tristan's expression. "I didn't have the best role model."

"Lead with your heart, like you always have, and you'll b getting those World's Greatest Dad gifts before you know it

"Thanks." A charming grin erased the tension Tristan's face. "In case I've never mentioned it, I'm gla we're friends. You helped me through some rough times

"That river runs both ways." Angeline offered a smi "I know things have changed between us and will contin to change. We'll adapt. We always do."

Tristan's eyes narrowed at her. "You're not going to tu this into a song, are you?"

She answered by slinging another pillow at him, whi he easily caught.

"I'm proud of you," Tristan said, turning serious. " your talent, your success. And I really hope your son

in tomorrow night." He gave her the "but" face. "I wish
ou wouldn't hide it from your father. Give him a chance
be as proud of you as I am."

Angeline shook her head. "Someday, maybe. Tomor-
w is way too soon."

"So you're gonna hole up in here and watch the cer-
nony all alone?"

"I invited Lincoln."

"Have you told him your top-secret identity?"

"I'm not a spy," she laughed. "I'm a songwriter."

"With how many awards?"

A closet full.

And a bank account that didn't need padding from a
aitressing job at her uncle's restaurant.

Tristan shook his head. "I get why you don't want to tell
ur dad, but you shouldn't keep who you really are a se-
et from Lincoln, especially if a mate-bond is involved."

"I'll tell him when I'm ready."

"You said the same about your dad. How long has it
en?"

Nearly fifteen years. And the way things were going,
could be fifteen more before she felt ready to endure
s censure.

"It'll be different with Lincoln." She wanted to share her
isic with him. And when the time felt right, she would.

"Hey, Angel." The sudden rush of excitement that filled
ncoln upon opening the door tanked. "What's wrong?"

Tight-lipped and clenching her teeth, Angeline stood
id in the doorway. Her laser-intense gaze bore straight
ough him.

"Damien!" Anger and fear strained her voice.

Lincoln glanced over his shoulder at the young man

seated at the kitchen bar, a homemade beef empanada paused halfway between his plate and mouth.

"You bastard!" Balling her hands, Angeline stormed past Lincoln.

"Marquez? What did you do?"

"I need a little context." Slowly lowering his hand, Damien laid the empanada on his plate. His spine stiff-ened and his demeanor slipped from relaxed to ready.

"Zach is just a kid!" Shaking, Angeline stood in fron of Damien.

"Ah." A cocky smile slid mockingly into place. Damie looked Angeline up and down. "I guess he signed the con tract."

"What's going on?" Edging close behind Angeline, Lin coln slipped his hands around her waist, hoping his nea ness would calm her distress.

She pointed her index finger an inch from Damien nose. "He bullied Zach into signing his life away to th Program."

Damn!

When Lincoln had talked to Angeline's cousin last nig after leaving the bar, Zach had already made up his mir to join the Program but he was worried about his famil Lincoln briefly spoke about the personal sacrifices the Pr gram required and asked him to wait until after his colle graduation before completing the paperwork. His fami needed the time to prepare for the inevitable.

Angeline pushed away from Lincoln. The anger twis ing her lovely face immediately morphed into a look betrayal.

"You knew he planned to do this?" Angeline's furio frightened voice shrieked in Lincoln's mind.

Suddenly the situation had turned from bad to worse.

she could sense his thoughts and he could hear hers, then a mate-bond was forming faster than expected.

He'd be more excited about the ethereal connection syncing them, body and mind, heart and soul, if he wasn't going back on active duty soon. But the distraction of sensing her turbulent emotions while trying to extract Dayax could get them killed.

"Sweetheart, wait!" He reached for her hand to stop her from storming off.

"I'm not your sweetheart," she hissed, jerking free.

The slamming door as she left rattled Lincoln to the very core of his soul.

"I'm beginning to sense that your *angel* really doesn't care for Dogmen." Damien snorted. "She does know that you are one, or did you keep that a secret, too?"

Lincoln ignored the question. "What, exactly, did you say to Zach?"

"Dogmen are born knowing their path. There is no hem-hawing." Damien resumed eating. "I'm surprised, actually. I didn't think he had the balls to commit."

Swallowing a mouthful of curses, Lincoln dug the cell phone from his pocket.

"Lincoln!" Zach cheerfully answered the call. "Have you heard the news?"

"Please tell me that you haven't emailed the docs to the recruiter."

"Not yet. I promised my folks that I would have Brice read over the contract."

"Smart idea." Lincoln breathed easier. "If you don't mind, I would like to be there, too."

"You're still on my side, right? I have enough people against me right now."

"Yeah, Zach. I'm on your side," Lincoln said. "When are you meeting with Brice?"

"Tomorrow afternoon. Hey, I'm celebrating with some friends tonight. Wanna come?"

"Not this time." Lincoln needed to do some damage control with Angeline. "I'll see you tomorrow."

Disconnecting the call, he turned to Damien, who had resumed eating. "You should've stayed out of this mess."

Damien gave a halfhearted shrugged. "Bunch of hillbillies. I don't know why everyone is upset. Becoming a Dogman is an honor and privilege."

"For *us*," Lincoln snarled. "Not for Zach's family, who he will have to turn his back on once he earns his tags."

"Either they support him or they don't. Either way, his life. His choice."

"It's not that simple." Not for close-knit families or their packs. They needed time to process, even time to grieve, because when the time came for Zach to say goodbye, in all likelihood, it would be the last time they'd see him.

Lincoln packed the food he'd made in plastic containers and headed to the door. "Whatever you do tonight, don't make this situation worse."

Damien raised his drink. *"No problema."*

Reaching Angeline's apartment Lincoln didn't hesitate. He walked in without knocking. "I brought supper. Made it myself."

"I'm not hungry." She stood, staring through the balcony sliders, her arms wrapped around her middle. "I don't want you here."

If that were true, she would've locked the door.

He left the food on the kitchen counter and walked to her. Standing close, but not quite touching, he leaned over her shoulder and waited.

It wasn't a long one.

"I've known Zach his entire life. I changed his poopy diapers, taught him to throw a snowball and helped him with

iework. I even let him borrow my car for prom." Her
:e broke. "I don't want him to be scarred or maimed.
d I don't want him to die, Lincoln."

Cupping Angeline's arms, Lincoln turned her around
wrapped her in a giant hug. She trembled against him,
he felt the hot sting of her tears splash against his heart
n though his shirt absorbed the actual moisture.

'Aunt Miriam and Uncle Jimmy are devastated, and
y haven't told Lucy. Roslyn, Sierra and the boys will be
rtbroken. Zach is like a brother to them, too."

"Zach is lucky to have so many people who love him."
coln swallowed, trying to dislodge the stubborn lump
iis throat. "I can't imagine how difficult this is for you
your family, but it's hard on Zach, too. Can you imag-
how scared and lonely it is for him to make this deci-
1, knowing everyone he loves is against it?"

'I can, actually."

'What?" Lincoln hooked his finger beneath Angeline's
1 and tipped up her face.

'We aren't talking about my decisions right now. This
bout Zach." Emotion contorted her face. "How could
be a party to convincing him when…?"

'When what?"

'Tanner died." Turbulent emotions darkened Angeline's
s. "I don't want anything to happen to Zach."

Lincoln cradled Angeline's face, gently brushing away
ggling tears from her cheeks. "Zach's decision isn't
ut you, Angel. It's about him."

'No one should have to go through what I did."

'If anything happens to Zach, your family will be there
each other. Just like they were when you lost Tanner."

Angeline slowly shook her head. "They never knew
ut him."

'Why?"

"His rejection nearly broke me. My father raised us be strong, to not be vulnerable. How could I tell him h weak I was?"

"You aren't weak, Angel." Lincoln saw in her an in strength that had called to him, comforted him and sav him from the brink too many times to count.

"You didn't see me when I felt Tanner die. I thoug would die, too. If not for Tristan, I might have."

"I thought you and Tristan…"

"We were never more than really good friends."

"I'm glad," Lincoln said, holding her tightly. "Glad was here for you back then. But I want to be the man you now. I will never intentionally hurt you."

"But?"

"I've talked to Zach. His heart is set on the Progra He needs everyone's support now because the next f months will be what he carries with him. Don't let it full of arguments, because that's what he'll dwell on d ing those long, lonely deployments."

"Tanner and I argued the last time I saw him."

"I'm sure he knew how much you must've loved hi

"I did love him," Angeline said. "And I had put all t behind me, but you came into my life and now this sit tion with Zach has stirred it up again. I don't want to l him, and I don't want to lose you."

"Me?" Lincoln rubbed his hand down her back, inf ing his strength into her spirit.

"Until your retirement papers are finalized, you still a Dogman. What if I lose you, just like I lost Tanne

"You won't lose me." Now that he'd found her, not e the devil himself would keep Lincoln from Angeline long. "I'm like a boomerang. I will always find my w back to you. I promise."

And Lincoln never made a promise he couldn't kee

Chapter 19

The situation with Zach escalated quickly," Brice said, watching Lincoln come into the Alpha-in-waiting's official office inside the Walker's Run Resort. "The whole damn pack thinks you and Damien are recruiting for the Program."

"We're not recruiters. And Zach told me that he's been planning to do this for quite some time. His parents really shouldn't be surprised."

"They're scared and upset. Walker's Run is family-centric. Conflict is not a conscious reality for the people here."

"And yet you're upgrading the security system, employing surveillance tactics and expanding the pack's sentinel program," Lincoln said, taking a seat.

Brice tipped his head.

"I didn't come to help you talk Zach out of his decision. However, I do want to give him a truer picture of how one becomes a Dogman, the sacrifices and the realities of living with the consequences 24/7."

"I expect no less." Brice pushed back from the desk. "It takes a special kind of wolfan to do what you do, Lincoln. When bullets started flying in Romania, you didn't hesitate. Even after catching one in the shoulder meant for me, you continued to mobilize your team and eliminated the threat. It was damn amazing."

"It's what we're trained to do. Being a Dogman isn't about us, it's about being a shield. We're expendable. Those we protect are not."

"Do you think Zach has what it takes to succeed in the Program?"

"He has the heart and motivation," Lincoln said. "But he'll have to endure grueling physical training, learn to take orders and follow without question and pass an intensive psychological evaluation. Realistically, less than a quarter of the recruits make it past the first six months of drills."

"Seventy-five-percent failure rate. That's steep."

"That's only the first round. Half of those who begin the second six months will successfully complete the endurance training program. After that, another third are eliminated with the final psych profile." Lincoln shrugged. "In the end, the Program is about service, not egos."

"Are you ready to take the final readiness test for active duty?"

Lincoln nodded.

"And if you don't make it?"

"That's not an option. Dayax is depending on me." Lincoln folded his hands over his stomach. "I will find him, and then we're coming here because I plan to claim Angeline as my mate."

"Is she in agreement?"

"Yeah." Lincoln felt his smile broaden. "Well, at the moment, she isn't too happy with me because of the situation with Zach. But we're starting to bond." And Lincoln damn sure wouldn't make the same mistake as Tanner Phillips.

The rich, buttery scent of fresh popcorn filled the air. In the comfort of her home, Angeline stooped in front of the microwave, watching the expanding bag and listening to the rapid eruption of the kernels. Usually, her nerves weren't jittery until the category and song titles were announced.

However, two hours ago her stomach had started doing low-impact flip-flops. More so because tonight, she had no moral support.

If she'd gone to LA to participate in the awards show, at least her agent, Sandra Lively, would've accompanied her. Win or lose, there would've been someone to share the moment with her.

After last night's meltdown, Angeline wasn't sure if Lincoln would show up. He'd remained levelheaded when fear had caused her emotions to overload. Like a pro, he'd helped her see that Zach's choices were his to make, and family supported each other, no matter what.

Helping Miriam and Jimmy accept Zach's decision? Lincoln proved to be good at that, too.

In the end, everyone realized how much becoming a Dogman meant to Zach. Including Angeline.

He had chosen to follow his heart. How could she not support him? Especially knowing how it felt to not have her family's support.

And she didn't want Zach to disappear into the Program believing his family had turned against him.

Angeline didn't like his choice, but it was his to make.

The microwave dinged. From the cupboard over the sink, she pulled down a large plastic bowl and filled it with the popcorn. Tucking a handful of napkins beneath her arm, she carted a cup of hot chocolate and the snack bowl into the living room, placed the items on the coffee table then settled comfortably on the couch with her drink.

Lincoln opened the front door and walked in. "Hey, Angel."

"What are you doing here?" Happily surprised, she didn't mind that he hadn't knocked.

"You invited me, remember?"

"I didn't realize you accepted the invitation, but I'm glad you did."

"Did I miss anything?"

"Nope. It should start after the next few commercials. Oh, there's beer in the fridge or hot chocolate in the electric kettle."

Lincoln detoured to the kitchen and poured a cup of hot chocolate before joining her in the living room. He sat close to her. He smelled of winter, clean and crisp.

"Has it started snowing again?" she asked.

"A few flurries. Nothing to worry about." He picked up the popcorn bowl and propped his foot on the coffee table.

"Oh, the show is starting." She took the sound off mute and got up to turn down the lights.

Returning to the couch, she snuggled against Lincoln. He tilted his head toward her so they touched. Cozy and comfortable, in that moment, she was the most content she'd been in a long time.

He watched the opening number raptly and laughed at the emcee's joke. She filled him in on tidbits about the nominees and added a little trivia.

"How did you learn so much about country music?" he asked during a commercial.

"Well," she said, "I do play a little guitar."

"And sing." Lincoln grinned.

"Not according to Connor."

"I'm a man who can make up his own mind." Lincoln

ghed. "Even if your brother is right, any song you sing me will be beautiful."

"Careful, Dogman." Angeline playfully bumped his oulder. "You're starting to turn sappy."

He flicked a piece of popcorn at her. It glanced off her nose d tumbled down her chest, landing between her breasts.

"If I didn't know better, I'd think you did that on purse." She plucked the popcorn from her cleavage and pped it into her mouth.

Lincoln winked. "Skill is making something look like accident."

"Oh, really?" She grabbed a handful of popcorn and a ht ensued, quickly turning into a tickling fest with Anline succumbing to giggles. And then they were kissing. Long, deep, soul-bending kisses that nearly made her get why the television was on.

"Wait!" She pushed against Lincoln's chest. "They're out to announce best song of the year."

Lincoln eased back into his seat with only a muffled oan in protest. Angeline sat up, increased the volume d perched on the edge of the couch. Her folded hands essed against her mouth.

"And the winner is..." The camera panned from the anuncer's face to her hand opening the envelope.

The air in Angeline's lungs stilled. No matter the dozen so awards stashed in her closet, she always awaited the nouncement with bated breath.

"'Heartache Lane.'"

"Yes!" A joyous howl erupted as Angeline jumped up dance her happy jig. Each win felt like the first and she ok none for granted. Every musical note and lyric she had bued with pure emotion. Recognition of her talent and owing how loved her songs were nearly burst her heart.

Typically, Tristan joined the celebratory dance. However, Lincoln remained on the couch. A warm smile tc the chill off his piercing silvery-green gaze tracing l every move.

The air whooshed out of her inflated excitement.

"I, uh…" She sat on the couch. Hands pressed toget between her knees, she fixed her attention on the tele sion. Jolene McKenzie, the woman who'd lent her vo to the words and lyrics Angeline had written, finisl the acceptance speech. She would take home the aw. for the vocals, Angeline's gold-color statue would co in the mail.

"I really like that song," Angeline said, feeling the h from Lincoln's gaze sizzle her skin.

"It's a memorable tune," Lincoln said. "I've heard few times on the radio. That Jolene girl who sings it doe look old enough to have endured that kind of heartbre

"Really?" Angeline had been a few years younger tl Jolene's current age when Tanner had left her. "I did think there was an age restriction on when a woman co have her heart broken."

"Maybe it's her eyes. They don't reflect the deep p. that the song is about." Lincoln tapped Angeline's l drawing her gaze. "But yours do."

Awkward silence strained the space between them.

"The announcer said the songwriter was A. R. O'Bri Any relation?"

Angeline's stomach clenched. Lincoln was opening proverbial bag and her secret was the infamous cat. S could either allow the truth to escape or leave it muff inside the bag.

"What gave me away? The dance?"

"The song." Lincoln squinted at her. "When I hear on the radio after you mentioned the ancient history w a Dogman, all I could picture was you. I didn't think yo wrote it, though. Until that little dance of yours. Come on." He laughed. "What was that?"

The tension broke as Angeline laughed with him.

"That was my happy dance."

"Kinda looked like an octopus on ice skates," he said playfully. "Arms and legs flailing in all different directions."

"Hey, that's my signature move."

"Anyone else seen it?"

"Just Tristan, and he's sworn to secrecy. He'll never admit to it."

"Is the secret just about the dance?"

"No." Angeline took a breath, for courage. "Come with me."

Without looking back, she led Lincoln into the bedroom and opened her closet. A waist-high cabinet provided a divider between her winter clothes and all the rest. The cabinet shelves displayed the trophies awarded for her music. She stepped back so that Lincoln could see.

"No one except Tristan knows that I'm a professional songwriter."

Lincoln's silence weighted the room. He knelt on one leg and seemed to read the inscription on each statuette.

"You've got amazing talent, Angel. Why don't you want anyone to know?" Concern laced his curious gaze.

"You've met my dad. How well do you think this would go over with him?"

"He should be damn proud of you."

"He would be ashamed that I allowed my heart to be so easily broken."

"Then he doesn't understand the nature of love," Lincoln said quietly. "It's a gamble. Sometimes it pays off, sometimes it doesn't. But I believe it's worth the risk."

On the other side of a once broken heart, Angeline wasn't sure she quite agreed.

Chapter 20

Lincoln eased over to the bed where Angeline had sat. "Are you still hurting over the past?"

"No," she said without hesitation. "When I wrote those songs, I had to put myself back into the heartbroken woman I used to be. It's exhausting."

"Why do you keep doing it?"

She gave him a quizzical look. "Have you seen what's in my closet?"

"Is the payoff worth the torture?"

"Not so much anymore." Angeline sighed. "I've been talking with Jolene—"

"Jolene McKenzie?" During his last deployment, Lincoln had seen the popular country-pop recording artist performing at a USO holiday function. "The woman who gave the acceptance speech, you know her?"

"Yes." Angeline gave him a funny look. "I know quite a few recording artists. It's my job to write songs for them."

"I didn't realize… Never mind. So, you were talking th Jolene?"

"She's young and doesn't want to get typecast as only ging one type of song. She wants to expand her reper- re and so do I. We've been brainstorming ideas and I've ven her a few sample pieces."

"And?"

"She likes them." Angeline smiled. "And I like writ- g them. It was hard at first. My brain kept defaulting to the hurt and turmoil I've lived. After a while, though, iting more upbeat music and lyrics became easier."

Lincoln grazed his knuckles over the skin of her cheek. ch a delicate appearance she had. Fine-boned and slen- r, she looked almost fragile. All the years he'd carried r photo, he'd thought of her as an ethereal beauty. One at might shatter at the touch.

But Angeline wasn't like that at all. Sass fired her soul d though she might look breakable, she had a will of eel.

Lincoln leaned in, brushing his lips against her mouth. e opened for him to deepen the kiss. She tasted of pop- rn, chocolate and hope.

Her fingers slid past his ear to cup the back of his head d he felt her essence ebb inside him. His inner wolf wled in tandem with his heart's declaration. *Mine, mine, ne.*

Both admitting to the mate-bond growing between them ade courtship easier. But Lincoln wanted to be careful. ate-bonds didn't guarantee a conflict-free relationship. nd he didn't want to rush getting to know Angeline. eally knowing her. The preconceived notions that he'd d needed to be unscripted so that he could see the real oman, not the fantasy.

Most important, he never wanted to cause her the pain

that she drew upon to write those haunting, achingly beau tiful songs.

Without breaking their long, deep, sweet kiss, she drev him down to the bed with her.

Desire had been coursing through his veins prior to th kiss and his body was already hot and ready for coupling Settling over her body would be a bit tricky. Though h could never be totally unaware of his prosthetic, most c the time he could ignore the feeling of the artificial lim cupped to his stump.

However, in the current situation, he found the pros thetic distracting him from a pleasurable experience.

"What's wrong?" Angeline whispered against his lip as her eyes fluttered open.

She had been straightforward and honest with him, h could do no less.

"I should probably take off my leg," he said.

"Okay." Her hands fell away, allowing him to chang positions.

"This will be the first time…since losing my leg."

"Um, are you forgetting the full moon?" She playful poked his arm.

"I was standing. This is different." Rubbing his han against his jean-clad thighs, he felt the upper edge of th prosthetic cup snuggled high on his stump. "Things mig get awkward."

"No, it won't. We'll figure this out, together."

Lincoln bent down to untie the laces, then pulled o his shoes.

"That's so cute," she said, looking at his feet. "You ha a sock on your prosthetic."

"I feel weird wearing only one sock."

Obediently, he lifted his arms for her to pull off h shirt. Next, she straddled his lap and kissed him, posse

his mouth as her fingers laid claim to his shoulders
l glided down his chest to his jeans. Deftly, she undid
button and inched down the zipper, then she slid her
ıd inside his boxers to stroke his shaft. His body ached
much as it hummed from her touch.

She urged him to lie back on the bed. Though his vision
uded with lust-laden lashes, he couldn't take his gaze
the sparkle in her eyes or the soft, genuine smile curv-
her luscious mouth. She was his. Not because some
tinct demanded her to be but because she'd made the
ive choice to follow where the instinct led.

As she eased off his lap, her fingers curled around the
istband of his pants. Adjusting his weight, Lincoln lifted
hips, allowing her to slide down his jeans and boxers
in one swoop.

"My God, Lincoln. How many times have you been
rt?" Her gaze seemed to bounce from one scar to an-
er. Not counting the ones on his stump, he had twenty-
en.

"That's really not what a man wants to hear when he's
ked in front of the woman he wants to have sex with."

"It's startling." An apology shimmered in her eyes. "I
an, I got a glimpse before, but I really didn't compre-
ıd…"

"I've been a Dogman a long time." Lincoln pushed up
his elbows. "Battle wounds are par for the course."

Her bright blue eyes blinked back tears. She hurt for
n—he could see the pain twisting her features.

"These scars aren't worth your sorrow, Angel. They
aled and I'm still living." He sat up. "I don't regret any
it." Especially because the path he'd chosen had led
n to her.

He clasped the cup of his prosthetic. "Should I take this
? Or get dressed?"

Angeline took his face in her hands. "I'm not put by your scars. And I want you. Very much." She kis him hard and passionately, breaking away to remove sweater and yoga pants. The black lace bra and pant against her pale skin made his mouth water even as throat dried.

"Your turn." She pointed a slender finger at his leg

Carefully, he worked off the prosthetic.

"Can I hold it?" Angeline held out her open hands.

Gently, he entrusted her with the state-of-the-art lir

"Wow! It's—"

"Expensive," he interrupted.

"I was going to say heavy." She carried the prosthe to the dresser and propped it against the drawers.

"It shouldn't weigh more than my natural leg woul

"Have you seen your leg?" She sashayed toward hi "Tree trunk size and solid muscle."

He scooted farther onto the bed as she stalked up body, then straddled him. Her sizzling kiss short-circui the higher functions in his brain, reducing his ability talk to a series of grunts and groans and growls.

Her lips trailed down his throat. The floral scent of hair was as feminine and intoxicating as her touch. S kissed each and every scar on his chest and arms, m ing them more than worth the pain he'd suffered obta ing the wound.

Following the dark line of hair below his belly butt she licked, nibbled and kissed his skin all the way do to his groin. Never in all the nights he'd been alone had dared to hope for a moment like this with her.

Maybe he had died in that explosion and been fou worthy of a little piece of heaven.

The tip of her tongue traced the seam of his sack to top of his cock. The anticipatory tension inside his gr coiled tighter, making it difficult to breathe normally. His pants sounded as ragged as a man dying from thirst yet inching his way toward a lush, beautiful oasis.

That was what she was to him. Hope. Soft and wonderful and incredibly beautiful.

Taking him into her mouth, she laved her tongue over his slit and down his shaft. His mind turned into a quagmire of images and instinct, all driving him toward claiming his mate.

"Mine," Lincoln said in a harsh, hoarse whisper.

Angeline ignored the declaration in favor of savoring the salty, masculine taste of him. Beneath her hand, the taut skin of his stomach trembled.

He was close, so close, and she took pleasure knowing she had brought him to the pinnacle of agony and ecstasy. She wanted him to teeter there a little longer, to share the experience of aching and clenching with need.

Men, always in a rush to the finish line, often missed the softer nuances of coupling that a woman wanted.

Slowly, she eased his shaft from her mouth and kissed a trail from his belly button to the hollow spot at the base of his throat. A sigh drifted on his long, drawn-out breath.

Though his lashes fluttered, his eyes did not open. Large, calloused hands gripped her hips and the contact unleashed a flood of hormones in her body already raging with feminine desire.

She looked down Lincoln's body, his bronzed skin marred with scars but no less beautiful. His loss of a leg didn't diminish his vitality or lessen her want of him.

His long, thick shaft pressed intimately against her lacy panties. She rocked back and forth, teasing him.

"Angeline." It sounded like a croak.

She did it again and again until his eyelids lifted and he seared her with his molten gaze.

"Now that you're awake..."

He growled, menacing, with a slight undertone of desperation.

Reaching behind her, Angeline unhooked her bra then took her time drawing her arms out of the straps before lowering the cups to expose her breasts. Lincoln seemed to stop breathing. His chest stilled completely and not one muscle in his body flickered.

Slowly, she leaned over him and softly touched her lips to his mouth. As they kissed, Lincoln slid her panties down her hips. Easily, she maneuvered out of the undergarment one leg at a time. Completely naked and straddling him, she watched his gaze follow his hands over every curve.

He brought her forward to take her breast into his mouth. Her growl competed with his as he fast-flicked his tongue over her nipple. With his arms wrapped securely around her middle, she couldn't escape the unbearable pleasure.

Though his hold did not lessen, she felt his hand move down the curve of her ass and his fingers caressed her inner thigh before teasing and sliding against her folds.

"So wet," he panted against the valley between her breasts as his mouth moved from one to the other.

The response on her tongue became a deep feminine groan as his finger traced her opening before pushing inside. Dropping her head, she rested her forehead against his shoulder as every muscle in her body went slack except for those in her lower belly. Those grew tighter and tighter, coiled and primed for release.

Lincoln grinned, damn him. Though he had every right. Turnabout was fair play and she had teased him to the point of ecstasy. Only she'd stopped at the pinnacle, hoping to rolong the moment. From the rhythm and pressure of his istoning fingers, he had a different agenda.

Each time she tried to call his name, a passionate groan scaped. With her muscles refusing to cooperate, she simly indulged in the pleasure each stroke provided.

"Oh, God." The words were a chant in her mind.

"Want me to stop, Angel?"

"Do and die." She barely managed the thought before iattering in sheer ecstasy. Buoyed on the feeling, she arely noticed Lincoln rolling her onto the mattress.

He crouched over her; a wildness in his eyes she'd never en made him all the sexier.

"Grab a pillow and put it under my leg," he said hoarsely.

It took a moment for her brain to process the words bere her arm reached over to do as he'd asked. As soon as e did, some of the strain eased in Lincoln's shoulders.

Angeline molded her hand around his shaft and guided m inside her. Though it took a few positional adjustments him to comfortably thrust, the trials and errors were rth the effort. They sighed in unison as he filled her.

His essence entangled with hers, heightening the sention of completeness. She'd never expected to expérice that feeling again, especially with another Dogman.

Lincoln had expressed his intent to retire from the Proim and she found herself less afraid to open her heart to n. They had a long way to go, though, before they comtted to a mateship but the getting to know each other t was rather fun.

"Mmm." His lips whispered along the curve of her neck, ning her insides giddy.

'No biting," she gasped.

A wolfan bite during sexual intercourse established a e-claim and was binding until death. A mate-claim did guarantee that a mate-bond would form. And some

couples, like Tristan's parents, never became a cohesiv
pair after the claiming.

Lincoln licked a spot that instantly became her nev
favorite, causing her hips to arch and her fingers to di
into his back.

"Same goes for you, Angel." Lincoln's voice floate
through her mind.

Peeking open her eyes, she realized how close her teet
were to his shoulder. Moving away from the danger zon
she captured his lips in a breath-stealing kiss that brok
only when her head tipped back from the force of the o
gasm pulsing through her body.

Wave after wave battered her senses, drowning her i
an ocean of pleasure. Only Lincoln's strong, steady pre
ence kept her from slipping into oblivion.

He shuddered against her and stilled, except for the ri
and fall of his chest with each panted breath.

Her breaths easing, she brushed her fingers through h
dark, wavy hair and tried to imagine how different the te
ture would feel if shorn in a military buzz cut.

Slowly, his eyelids fluttered open. "Hello, Angel,"
softly growled. The gleam in his gaze was possessive a
smugly satisfied.

Mine, mine, mine. Her heart thumped the declarati
with every beat. Though neither had physically claim
the other, she sensed the power of the mate-bond stitchi
them together mind and body, heart and soul.

"That was fun." She kissed him lightly on the mout

"Fun?" His brow scrunched though humor lit his ey
"Admit it, that was pretty amazing."

"I admit nothing." She made a turning-the-lock g
ture over her lips.

"My training included techniques used to make peo
talk." Settling on his right side, he drew his left hand fr

her hip across her ribs and traced the curve of her breast, causing her to suck in a breath. “Shall I continue?”

“Please do.”

He chuckled and Angeline reminded herself that unless she wanted Lincoln reading every thought that crossed her mind, she needed to remember to shield them from him.

Using the pad of his thumb, Lincoln strummed her nipple until it tightened into a sensitive bud. “Still not talking?” he teased and then lowered his head to suck her peak into his hot, moist mouth.

The comfortable ebb of satisfaction that had lulled her into a relaxed state suddenly churned with want and need and the knowledge that Lincoln could quench both.

Teasing and tormenting, his tongue flicked against her nipple a dozen times before he sucked it long and hard, driving her to near madness, and releasing it only to start the cycle again. On the fourth round, his hand slipped down her abdomen and between her legs, parted in welcome.

Gingerly, he fingered her folds. She wanted to stroke his shaft in tandem, but the way he was positioned prevented her from reaching his groin. Since his face was practically planted in her chest as he continued to lick and suck her breasts, she gripped the back of his neck, massaging the thick, corded muscles beneath her palm. A slight shiver rolled across his shoulders but didn’t impede the attention he showered on two particular parts of her body.

Once more on the cusp of ecstasy, she arched her hips. A few more strokes would send her plunging over the edge. Only he stopped.

“Lincoln?” His name tore raggedly from her throat.

Silently, he cocked his head at the open bedroom door.

“Okay,” she nearly panted, “I admit it. Sex with you is downright amazing. So, can we get back to it?”

"I need to answer my phone!" The urgency in his voice made her heart race.

They both sat up. He swung his leg over the edge of the bed and looked toward the dresser where his prosthetic rested.

"I'll get it." She scrambled off the bed and dashed into the living room, following the sound of the ring to the satellite phone on the coffee table. Someone from the Program was calling.

Her heart sinking into the pit of her stomach, she grabbed the device, rushed into the bedroom and handed it to Lincoln.

"Adams," he answered, his voice tight and his body rigid.

Angeline placed the prosthetic leg next to Lincoln on the bed. Then she quickly gathered her clothes and went to dress in the bathroom. Playtime had ended. And more than likely, her days with Lincoln were numbered. He'd warned her that he'd have to return to the Program for a while. She couldn't help but wonder if the Program would really let him go.

Chapter 21

Dayax is alive!

Lincoln's heart nearly cracked his chest with its furious beating. The adrenaline-laced blood rushing in his ears made it difficult for him to comprehend much of what had been said afterward.

All this time not knowing but hoping and praying. Refusing to believe any other outcome. To learn that the boy he loved like a son had been found, Lincoln came as close to tears as he'd ever been in his entire life.

"Are you orders clear, Captain?" The CO's crisp voice snapped Lincoln to attention.

"Yes, sir."

"Then I'll see you soon, Adams. Safe journey."

"Thank you, sir." A deluge of relief and determination rocked his body. The allied forces had eyes on Dayax and a group of children rounded up by the insurgents. But the wolfling wasn't safe yet.

Lincoln dropped the phone on the bed. Pocketing his fist into his other palm, he pressed his hands against his mouth and clenched his eyes, sending a silent proclamation.

I'm coming, little wolf. Hold on for me a bit longer.

His senses returning to baseline after the adrenaline boost, Lincoln noticed the leg on the bed and Angeline's absence. A different set of emotions now churned inside his chest. Time with her had become extremely short and there were so many things he needed to explain.

He and Angeline might recognize the mate-bond drawing them together, but there was so much they didn't know about one another. Despite the warnings from the CO that the wolfling might not be cleared to leave the country, Lincoln had every intention of bringing Dayax home to Walker's Run.

But Angeline knew nothing about the wolfling and Lincoln had no idea if she wanted to be a mother. Or what he would do if she didn't.

"Angeline?" He sensed her in the apartment, but she neither answered nor returned to the bedroom.

Quickly and carefully, he secured his prosthetic and pulled on his boxers and pants, then put on his shoes. Strolling out of the bedroom, he stuffed his arms into his sweatshirt and yanked it down over his chest.

"Hey, we need to talk," he said, walking around the couch to stand in front of Angeline.

"Shh!" She flicked her open hand at him without looking up. "No, not you," she said into the phone. "Lincoln just walked in. Never mind about him. I'm on my way. I'll deal with your parents. Just get in there and help Nel deliver that baby!"

Angeline disconnected the call and looked at Lincoln, her face all aglow. "I'm going to be a godmother." Her happy shriek rolling into a squeal, she jumped up from

: couch, her arms askew, and hopped around in a dance niniscent of the one he'd seen earlier.

For someone with such musical talent, Angeline didn't ve any rhythm when it came to dance moves. Still, he ınd her jerky, uncoordinated movements quite endear- ;.

"My purse!" She dashed into the bedroom.

Lincoln snagged his keys from the coffee table. Wait- ; at the door, he took her coat off the stand and picked her boots.

"Here." She rushed to him, holding his Program-is- ed phone.

Now that he'd been notified about Dayax's whereabouts d received official orders, Lincoln doubted he'd receive y more calls from HQ tonight.

"Thanks, Angel." Dropping the device into his other cket, he kissed Angeline's temple then passed her the ots.

"Sorry, I'm rushing off," she said, holding on to him th one hand while using the other to pull on her boots. ut the baby's coming. And I—" She looked around. lave you seen my keys?"

"Are they in your purse?"

"Maybe." She glanced around the room. "Do you see ınywhere?"

"On your shoulder." He lightly tugged the strap.

"Duh," she said. "I don't know why I'm so scattered. 'e been around babies. Five, in fact."

"Is this your first time being a godparent?"

"Yeah." Her face lit up with a huge grin and some of ; worry faded.

He'd watched Angeline with her nieces and nephews. e was an absolute natural in handling them and they 'ed every minute spent in her company. Dayax would be lucky to have her as a mother—if she could accept a package deal.

Lincoln helped her into her coat then flipped up th hoodie on his sweatshirt as they stepped out while sh locked the door.

"This was…fun." She offered a half shrug and a smil "See you around?"

He didn't like the way that sounded. Was she brush ing him off?

"You'll see me for the rest of the night," Lincoln sai walking her to the stairwell. "I'm taking you to the hos pital."

Instead of arguing, she looked relieved. "Thanks. didn't expect to be this nervous."

They started down the three flights of stairs.

"I wasn't asked to be involved with the births of m neice and nephews." Though Angeline's voice remain cheerful, Lincoln sensed the deep hurt the slight ha caused. "Tristan and Nel have no siblings and Nel's pa ents were killed in a car accident when she was youn Tristan's parents—" she peeked at Lincoln "—well, you see for yourself."

"In case no one has ever told you," Lincoln said, "you great with kids."

"You've mentioned it." She smiled. "After Sierr party—which, by the way, she hasn't stopped talki about. I think she's your biggest fan."

"I was hoping her aunt would be."

Angeline laughed softly.

"Have you ever wondered about becoming a mothe

Her steps faltered slightly. "When I was younger," s finally said. "But life happens and now I'm not sure t I want to do the whole pregnancy thing."

"There's always adoption," he said quietly.

She touched his arm as they reached the first-floor landing. "Do you want be a father?"

"I've started thinking about it," he said, dodging the question rather than providing a direct answer. If she was resistant to the idea of an instant family, then he didn't want to put pressure on her with the knowledge that he had realized how very much he wanted to be a dad.

"Gavin Walker is a big supporter of wolfan adoptions," Angeline said.

Good to know that about his future Alpha. Not all packs were keen to the idea.

"In fact," she continued, "his godson, Rafe, was adopted from another pack. I heard Gavin faced down the Woelfesenat when they challenged the transfer."

"They didn't want Rafe removed from his birth pack?" Lincoln had the same fear regarding Dayax.

"No, an illness wiped out his birth pack. The Woelfesenat objected because Rafe's adoptive father is human."

"I can see why they were concerned." The general human populace had no idea of the existence of Wahyas.

"They couldn't see past Doc being human. But Gavin knew him. Trusted him. And he fought to give a little wolfling a loving home and a son to a human who has dedicated his life to our pack."

"Brice once told me the backbone of the Walker's Run pack is family."

"It is. Even the dysfunctional ones, like mine."

With his hand gently pressed against her lower back, Lincoln led Angeline to his truck and helped her get settled in the seat.

"Thanks, again," she said as he slid behind the steering wheel.

"Anytime, Angel." He started the engine and adjusted the heater control so that she would be comfortable.

Even catching all of the red lights on the main road, they made it to the hospital parking lot in less than ten minutes.

Angeline took his hand as they entered the emergency department and led him through the waiting room, past the check-in station and down a long corridor with locked double doors. She swiped her Co-op ID through the card reader mounted on the wall.

"Where are we going?" Warily, Lincoln watched the doors slowly swing open.

"The west wing," she said. "When the Co-op built the hospital, as a precaution, it was set up to keep injured and sick wolfans separated from human patients."

She held his hand as they walked. He liked the warmth that the physical contact produced. It made him feel as if she didn't want to let him go.

Very soon, she would have to do that very thing. But for now he wanted to stay connected to her for as long as possible.

"Jayson Nathaniel Durrance. What a fine name for such a handsome wolfling." Angeline lightly tapped the baby's little button nose. Yawning, he balled his hands and pointed his toes in a rigid, full-body stretch for about five seconds, then returned to a snuggly position in her arms.

Her heart nearly burst with love. She kissed his forehead, and he peeked at her beneath half-opened eyelids. His little mouth formed a cute little grin that reminded her of his father's trademark smile.

"Oh, you're gonna be a little charmer, just like your daddy." She glanced at Tristan, sitting next to his mate and holding her hand as she slept. The labor had been difficult, and Angeline was glad mother and son were doing well.

"So how does it feel to be a dad, Slick?"

"Terrifying," Tristan said in all seriousness. "The only

time I've felt more afraid was when I thought I would lose Nel." His fear in that situation had been justified. Nel had been at the mercy of a deranged wolfan. In the end, Tristan had been forced to put down his own blood-kin to protect her.

Angeline had no doubt he would do the same for his son. "You are going to be great at this."

"I will try my damnedest." Using his cell, he grabbed a snapshot of her holding Jayson.

"Text that to me," she said. "I have virtual scrapbooks of my nieces and nephews, and I want to start one for ayson. I plan to make videos and make everyone watch hem at important events, like graduation parties, re-earsal dinners. Whenever they think they're too old for heir breeches, I'll be there to remind them they aren't."

"Done." Tristan laughed. "Where's your purse? I didn't ear your phone ding."

"I left it with Lincoln. He's in the waiting room."

"You brought Lincoln?" Tristan's demeanor changed ightly with the protective-brother gleam coming to light n his eyes.

"He brought me." The baby stretched his arm and his ny fingers tangled in her hair. Cradling him with one arm, he carefully worked opened his hand and swept the er-nt strands over her shoulder. "I was too excited to drive. nd he volunteered."

"Things are going good with you two?"

Angeline shrugged. "He got a call on that clunky phone. n pretty sure it was someone from the Program. Lincoln entioned that he had a few things to take care of before s retirement papers are processed." But what if the Pro-am decided he could continue? Would he make the same oice as Tanner?

Deep inside, she feared he would.

"Hey, Sassy." Tristan caught her attention. "If Lincoln told you that he's coming back, he will."

"Since when did you become a prognosticator?"

"I haven't been around him a lot. But when I have, and someone mentions you, he lights up like Mary Jane McAllister's house at Christmas."

Warmth rushed through her. "That much, huh?" Mary Jane, an elderly human woman whose homestead bordered the wolf sanctuary, put out so many lights and animated decorations that one needed sunglasses driving by her house, even at midnight.

"Lincoln's at a different place in his life than Tanner was, and so are you."

"It scares me sometimes, the mate-bond."

"Preaching to the choir, sister." Tristan's phone dinged and he checked the message. "I think this is for you."

"Why? What does it say?"

"'You're a natural, Angel.' Oh! And there are three hearts and a kissy-face smiley emoji." Mischief lit Tristan's eyes. "I am never gonna let the Dogman live this down."

"Play nice," Angeline said. "Remember, he's licensed to kill."

"That's James Bond, a fictional character. And there's no such thing as a license to kill."

"You sure about that?"

"I'm sure," Tristan said. "Fairly sure."

Scrunching his reddening face, Jayson squirmed in Angeline's arms and his mouth opened in an ear-piercing wail.

Tristan jumped up. "What's wrong with him?"

"He's either hungry or having his first poo. Neither of which I can help with." Angeline carefully stood with Jayson and walked to Tristan. "Time to go to daddy." She placed the crying infant in his father's arms.

"What am I supposed to do with him?"

"Bring him to me." Nel's soft voice sounded tired. "I nk he's hungry."

"Okay, little one." Tristan kissed Jayson's balled hand. Iama says it's time to eat."

The baby made loud sucking noises as Tristan laid him Nel's arms.

"That's my cue to leave," Angeline said. The new fam- needed bonding time. "I'll come back later with Su- nah and Ruby."

Tristan's mother and aunt were a handful to deal with, ich was why Angeline had promised to "handle" them.

"Thanks for everything," Tristan said.

"No thanks necessary." She slipped out of the room, her rt full and heavy at the same time. Her joy for the new nily was immeasurable but the bubbly excitement con- led a heavy ache of uncertainty regarding her future.

She quietly entered the west wing waiting room. Shortly er she'd arrived last night, Tristan's parents had de- rted. Mostly because she'd demanded they leave since y wouldn't stop arguing. Accidentally mated nearly ty years ago and still they had never learned to get ng.

Since she'd gone in to see Tristan and Nel's newborn n, dozens of pack members had arrived. Prominent ong them was the Alpha-and Alphena-in-waiting, Brice d Cassie Walker, and their close companions, Rafe and ace Wyatt, and Ronni and Bodie Gryffon. In their midst Lincoln. Her heart tweaked at how comfortable he med with them.

Although Tristan and Nel were part of the inner circle, geline had kept her distance.

"Well?" Brice's voice boomed across the open area.

Everyone fell silent. Expectantly, they looked at Angeline for the revelation of the pack's longest kept secret—the gender of Tristan and Nel's wolfling.

"I'm proud to announce the newest member of the Walker's Run pack is Jayson Nathaniel Durrance." She paused for the collective cheer, knowing it would've been the same enthusiastic cheer had Angeline announced a girl's name. "Mother and baby are fine. Dad is still a little green."

Everyone laughed and happy chatter followed.

She made her way to Lincoln, sitting comfortably among the cluster of Tristan's closest friends. Although Tristan was tight with the Alpha-in-waiting and his circle of companions, Angeline felt a little awkward in their midst. Mostly because they were a tight-knit group whose members trusted one another with their secrets, and she wasn't willing to do the same.

"Are they up for visitors?" Brice asked.

"Right now, Jayson is nursing. But as soon as he's done, I'm sure they'll be glad to see you." Angeline glanced around at the others in the room. "Maybe the rest should wait until later. Nel's pretty worn-out."

"You've been here all night," Cassie, Brice's mate, said with a friendly smile. "Why don't you go get some sleep?"

Good advice, especially since Angeline would need to come back later with Tristan's mother and aunt.

"Come on, Angel." Lincoln helped Angeline into her coat then whispered in her ear. "Let's get you home."

His presence made her feel all snugly. She did want to go home and go to sleep. The problem was she wanted Lincoln warming the spot next to her.

Chapter 22

Sweat glistening on his skin, Lincoln finished the last rep in his final set on the bench press and racked the bar. He performed a series of deep breathing exercises before sitting up and checking the time.

In the three hours he'd been working out at the Walker's Run Resort gym, he still had not figured out how to break the news to Angeline that he was returning to temporary active duty and that he would come back with custody of an eight-year-old boy.

She'd fallen asleep in the truck as they'd left the hospital. He'd hated having to wake her upon parking at the apartment building, but carrying her up three flights of stairs wasn't a smart idea. He hadn't practiced carrying more than seventy-five pounds going up and down steps and wouldn't risk stumbling with her in his arms.

Lincoln had walked Angeline to her door and made her promise to get some rest. Later, they'd have dinner and he would tell her everything and do his best to put her mind at ease.

"Quitting time already?" Zach Taylor racked his bar and sat up. Since announcing his recruitment, he'd joined Lincoln for daily training sessions in the hope of getting a jump start on his physical readiness.

It would take a while before Zach could handle the weight Lincoln did, but the new recruit would be able to hold his own during Basic.

"Yeah, we're good. You want to push your endurance, but not to the point of exhaustion or injury." Lincoln grabbed his hand towel and patted down his face, arms and bare chest.

Zach did the same. "Thanks for taking me seriously from the start. You're the only one who ever did."

"How are your mom and dad coping?" Angeline seemed to have come to terms with her cousin's decision, but most parents had a difficult time accepting that they were losing their child to the Program.

"They say they're proud of me," he said. "I know they're scared. But I told them that just because I got accepted into Basic doesn't mean I won't wash out before the end of the program."

True. A lot of recruits wanted to be Dogmen. Few had the tenacity and fortitude to endure the grueling training to the end.

"Washing out isn't a bad thing." Lincoln shoved his arms into the sleeves, then stuck his head through the neck of his sweatshirt. "It means your heart is somewhere else and you need to figure out where it is."

Zach pulled on his long-sleeved T-shirt. "I know exactly where mine is."

Lincoln knew where his heart was, too. With the ones he wanted to call family.

:ach's phone pinged and he dug the device out of his
'el bag. "Shane wants to grab an early dinner at Tay-
;. Want to join us?"

'Thanks, but no."

I'm in good with the owner." Zach grinned. "I can get
free meal."

I have plans. Another time?"

You got it." He stood, hooking the strap of his duffel
his shoulder.

.incoln swiveled on the bench, swinging his good leg
e same side as his artificial one. He dropped his hand
el into his duffel and slung the bag over his shoulder
e stood.

Come on, pup." Lincoln used a friendly tone. "I'll walk
out."

I'm not a pup." Zach gave him a cross look.

You're gonna get called that a lot. Get used to it."

'hey walked out of the resort gym and took the stairs
o the lobby.

It's amazing," Zach said. "If I didn't know you, I'd
:r suspect that you have an artificial leg. It's not no-
ible at all."

I notice it." The stump sleeve and cup felt nothing
his real leg and he was keenly aware of each pros-
ic step.

What's it like? To lose a limb?" Zach gave him an
:st, open look.

.wkward. Frustrating. Humbling.

Life-changing." And in more ways than the obvious
;ical and emotion ramifications of adapting to having
one leg. Because of the injury, he'd been invited to
ker's Run. Although he'd searched for Angeline after
ıer's death, Lincoln likely never would've met her oth-
se. "It helped me find a whole new world to explore."

They crossed the lobby and exited near the valet
tion. Lincoln greeted the car jockeys, recognizing tw
them as sentinels who were at the bar a few nights ag

"I have classes tomorrow," Zach said as they wal
between two of the waiting vehicles. "But I'm out at th
Want to meet me here around four?"

Waiting on the median separating the incoming tra
from the outgoing traffic, Lincoln watched a car leav
the self-park lot and drive past them.

"Sounds like a—"

Boom!

Suddenly, Lincoln was standing on the second floo
that abandoned building in Somalia. Bits of glass and p
ter and wood flew all around him in slow motion.

"Lila!" He yelled for his second-in-command, his v
loud, clear and panicked. But that was impossible beca
in his wolf form he couldn't speak.

His nostrils stung from the spontaneous fire and
could barely breathe because billows of black smoke g
bled up the oxygen. Sensing the percussive wave com
he scrambled to latch onto something that would keep
from being swept out the window.

Heart pounding, he struggled against the invisible f
grabbing and snatching at his chest. He had to get to L
Had to save her.

The more he fought to stay upright, the heavier his a
and legs became. He called desperately for Lila, pray
she would answer, even though his training had taught
that no one survived an explosion at the point of orig

Each gasp drew more of the thick black smoke into
lungs. He coughed, trying to get a clear breath. He
himself slipping.

No! He would not go through that damn window.
again.

* * *

"How is he?"

At the sound of Tristan's voice, Angeline turned from he hospital room window and smiled at him in the door-/ay.

"You should be with Nel."

"She wanted me to check on you and him. I wanted ɔ, too." Hands in his pockets, he stepped into the room. Brice and Cassie are with Nel and the baby. If she needs nything, they'll take care of her until I get back to the oom."

"They just left here." Still hugging herself, Angeline ank into the chair beside the hospital bed.

"Brice said Lincoln had some sort of episode at the esort."

"Doc called it a traumatic flashback." She glanced at incoln, sleeping peacefully now, but it had taken a high ose of sedatives to calm him down. "Zach was with him.)ne of the resort guests drove by them in a car with a herry-bomb exhaust and intentionally made it backfire. pparently, it sounded like an explosion."

Angeline rubbed her shoulders. "Zach said Lincoln sud-enly blanked out for second and then started yelling and ırning around. The sentinels tried to help, but ended up aving to take him down.

"Before they did, Lincoln had broken one man's nose nd cracked another's ribs." She took a deep breath. "He ould've killed them."

"But he didn't. And this isn't his fault."

"I know." She nodded.

"Why don't you grab a bite to eat in the cafeteria? I'll tay with him."

"I'm not hungry." If she tried to eat now, it would sit in

her stomach like a rock. “Besides, Lincoln gets restless if I move too far from him.”

“It’s good he knows you’re here.”

“Will this keep him from joining the pack?” Brice had assured Angeline that it wouldn’t, but she had a constant nagging in her gut that wouldn’t go away. “What if Gavin thinks he’s a danger to the pack?”

“No one thinks Lincoln is a threat,” Tristan said. “I’m sure Doc is doing everything he can to help Lincoln.”

“He is.” Still, she couldn’t help feeling that things were about to get worse. Like the universe had decided to play a sick joke on her because she’d fallen in love with another Dogman.

“I’m going to pick up some coffee from the cafeteria. Want some?”

“Sounds good.”

“I won’t be long,” he said, heading out of the room.

“I’m not going anywhere.” She reached between the bed rails and squeezed Lincoln’s hand. He was still too sedated to respond.

Someone knocked at the door.

“Forget something?” She turned. “Oh! Damien.”

“I came as soon as I heard. I was tagging along with some of the sentinels on patrol.” He walked into the room and stood at the foot of the bed. “How is he?”

“Physically fine.” His mental state had her worried. What if the episode had triggered some sort of psychosis and he couldn’t find his way back to the real world?

“I guess you really are his guardian angel.”

“What do you mean?”

“The picture of you he carries in his pocket. It goes everywhere he goes. He told us that you were his guardian angel and as long as you were with him, everything would be all right.”

"What picture?"

"It's an old faded photo. I think you were sitting in a café because you were holding a large foam coffee cup and there's a pastry on the plate in front of you."

"It couldn't be me. I didn't know Lincoln before he came to Walker's Run."

"Oh, it's you." Damien tucked his hands into his pockets. "If the team was here, they'd all agree."

"Your Dogman team?"

"Yep. In fact, a couple of times when we were pinned down by hostile fire, the lieutenant would ask Cap if his angel was still in his pocket." Damien laughed. "We did all kinds of crazy shit. Sometimes one of us caught a bullet or two, or some shrapnel, but nothing too serious. Until—" he shrugged "—the explosion."

It didn't make sense. "Where would Lincoln get an old picture of me?"

"Off a dead guy is what I heard."

Angeline's heart froze, but her stomach churned nauseous waves. The man couldn't have been Tanner. What were the odds?

Why hadn't Lincoln told her? About the picture? About the man?

"How long is he going to be out?" Damien tapped the bottom of Lincoln's foot.

Lincoln showed no sign of waking up.

"He'll probably sleep through the night." At least, that was what Doc had said.

"I'm going to meet up with some of the sentinels for dinner. I'll check on him later."

Damien nodded his goodbye and Angeline was glad for him to leave. She'd always felt a sense of unease around him and he hadn't earned any brownie points with his revelation.

Quietly, she closed the door and then searched throug
Lincoln's things. She found no photo in his pants' pocket
or duffel bag, so she opened his wallet. Three photos wer
stuffed in the card slots.

One was of an adorable little boy with a short cro
of Afro-textured hair. His face radiated with pure joy a
Lincoln, kneeling on one knee, gave him a tight hug. On
of the sweetest things Angeline had ever seen, the tende
moment tugged at her heart.

Dogmen did not claim mates while in the Program, s
the child obviously could not be Lincoln's biological so
But even in the photo, Angeline could see the two wer
bonded. It must've broken Lincoln's heart to have left hi
behind. It broke hers just thinking about it.

The second photo was a group picture of Lincoln an
five others standing in front of a tank. All were dresse
in camouflage pants and T-shirts, wearing mirrored sun
glasses, bulletproof vests and holding assault rifles. Hi
team. As in the photo with the boy, Angeline could se
the bond between the soldiers.

She didn't see Damien in the group, but Lincoln stoo
next to a woman with his arm casually draped across he
shoulder. *Lila?*

More petite and not at all how Angeline had picture
her, the woman had to be Lila. Lincoln had mentioned sh
had been his best friend. And according to Zach, she ha
been the one Lincoln had called out for several times du
ing his traumatic flashback.

Jealousy nipped at Angeline's heart but she ignored th
feeling in favor of the empathy she had for Lincoln losin
two important people in his life.

Removing the third photo, Angeline dropped the walle
Her hand flew to her mouth to silence the gasps.

Tanner had taken the snapshot on their first date at the é on campus.

Tears stung her eyes. She'd assumed when Tanner had her for the Program that he'd gotten rid of any remind- of her and the time they'd spent together. But if Damien s right and Lincoln had taken the photo from a dead n, then he must've been with Tanner when he died.

Heart hurting, she walked to Lincoln's bedside. "Why n't you tell me?"

Whatever his reason to hide the truth, when he woke Angeline expected answers.

Chapter 23

Suddenly awake, Lincoln tried to get a bearing on his
roundings. The smell of antiseptic lingered in the ai
droning beep behind him and to the right sounded at re
lar intervals. He lay in some sort of bed, covered in a w
sheet. Window blinds were closed but a soft light lit
room.

He tried to sit up, but something held him down. "W
the hell?"

"Glad to see you're awake." A voice drifted from
dark corner.

"Brice? What's going on?" Lincoln forcibly blinke
sharpen his vision.

Brice stepped forward. "How are you feeling?"

A bit panicked at the moment. "Why am I tied do
What's going on?"

"Easy. You were combative when they brought you

Brice placed a calming hand on Lincoln's shoulder. "Do you remember what happened yesterday?"

"Yesterday is relative." Lincoln tried to force the fog from his brain. "What day is today?"

"Friday." Brice worked his way around the bed, unfastening the restraints.

"I remember leaving the hospital with Angeline after Tristan's baby was born. Oh, God. Did we get into an accident?" Lincoln's stomach clenched and he struggled to sit up. "Where's Angeline?"

"She's fine. Cassie took her to the cafeteria."

"What happened? Why am I here?"

"Doc thinks you suffered a traumatic flashback. Do you remember being at the resort with Zach yesterday?"

Lincoln concentrated on mentally retracing his steps, but nothing came into focus. "I'm blank after Angeline and I left here. How did this happen?"

"A car with a modified muffler backfired as you and Zach were leaving the resort. Zach said you stopped talking in the middle of a sentence and had a faraway look. When he touched you, suddenly you began yelling for someone name Lila. The sentinels had to subdue you."

Lincoln's gut fisted. "Did I hurt anyone?"

"A broken nose and some cracked ribs, but the guys are not too sore about it. They can claim bragging rights with those injuries."

The sentinels might not be too upset, but the news thoroughly horrified Lincoln. "I must've been acting out my nightmare and didn't see them as a threat."

"Has this ever happened?"

"I have nightmares most nights, but never acted on one while awake." A flashback like that could screw up everything. "Yesterday, I got the call from my CO. They want me back at HQ and are putting me on a flight from Atlanta Saturday evening.

"They found Dayax in a rebel camp. He's being held with about a dozen other kids, and he isn't the only wolfling the insurgents grabbed. HQ wants me to go in with ground forces for hostage extraction. If they find out about this flashback, they could scrap me from the mission."

"Doc wants a psychologist to see you. If she says you're okay, then our lips are sealed. But if she thinks you're unstable, there's no way I'm letting you board a plane to HQ alone."

"I'm not unstable." Lincoln felt fine, except for his dislike of hospitals and the worry beading in his gut because he hadn't had time to tell Angeline that he had to leave. "If it makes you feel better, I'm sure Damien wouldn't mind flying back with me."

"About Damien." The grim line of Brice's mouth made an unhappy curl downward.

"Has the pup done something wrong?" Young Dogmen were often brash, egotistical and a little bullish at times.

"Did he mention to you that he suffered a traumatic brain injury in the explosion in Somalia?"

"He mentioned smacking his head but didn't say anything to me about a brain injury. How bad is it?"

"I don't know the specifics, but my understanding is that his neuropsychological evaluation revealed some significant concerns. He was suspended from active duty, pending further evaluation."

Damien had told Lincoln that after his med leave expired, he would be deployed with a new team. But he hadn't mentioned how long that leave would be. "When is his next eval?"

"There isn't one." Brice's gaze seemed to inspect every inch of Lincoln's face and Lincoln wondered if Brice was looking for signs of instability in him. "Damien suffered iolent breakdown when HQ advised him of the medical pension from active duty. Once he stabilized, he was charged from the Program."

Lincoln sucked in his breath as if he'd been punched in gut. Dogmen lived and breathed the Program. Getting sed out was a fate worse than death.

He'd gone through significant denial and anger upon rning of his own medical discharge. But Lincoln had nd Angeline. No longer resentful, he looked forward iis discharge and starting a new life.

"Damien hasn't mentioned any of this to me. How long e you known?"

"Councilman Bartolomew called this morning. He'd rd that two Dogmen were here and wanted to confirm t Damien had come here to see you.

"He also knew Dayax had been found. Before the elfesenat started the paperwork to get the wolfling out Somalia, he wanted to know if Walker's Run would ac-t a refugee into the pack, even if something happened you on the mission."

Lincoln's heartbeat paused and he didn't dare to breathe.

"Of course we will. We would never turn away a child." ce offered a small smile. "My best friend was an orphan m another pack and he's become an invaluable member Walker's Run. I'm sure Dayax will, too."

The air in Lincoln's lungs rushed out. "I plan to be on t return plane with him."

"I have no doubt about that." Brice's grim expression irned. "What concerns me is Damien."

"You thought I knew?"

Brice nodded. "It would almost be better if you did, iough I would've been disappointed that you kept the ormation from me."

"I only keep secrets that I'm required to by the Program.

That would not have been one of them." Except he ha
told Angeline of his plans.

Tonight, he would, although it would be a water
down version because he did not want to cause her
necessary worry.

"Good to know." Some of the strain in Brice's exp
sion eased. "Is Damien wanting to settle in Walker's Ru

"Honestly, I don't know. He showed up, said he
nowhere to go and wanted to stay with me until his
ployment."

"It's my understanding that Damien needs ongo
treatment. If he wants to remain in Walker's Run, he'l
required to be compliant with the Program's recomm
dations. Neither my father nor I will put the pack or
human neighbors at risk."

"I'll talk to him." Lincoln didn't want anyone to
hurt, either.

"I trust that you will." Brice's demeanor became
formal and his expression turned friendly.

Lincoln had seen the same transformation in Roma
when Brice had switched modes between a hard-hitt
negotiator dealing with hostile, warring Alphas anc
easygoing nightly campfire companion telling Linc
stories of Walker's Run. Stories that had made his h
ache for a home and family of his own.

"I noticed that you and Angeline have become q
close. Does she know of your plans to return to Somal

"I told her that I have some things to wrap up be
my retirement is finalized."

Bound by a mate-bond, he had faith she would un
stand. Once Lincoln returned with Dayax, he would cl
Angeline as his mate and they would become the fan
he'd always wanted.

A simple plan, really. What could go wrong?

* * *

ifting a cup of fresh coffee to her lips, Angeline in-
ed the robust aroma and forced herself to relax as the
, bold flavor laced with hazelnut slid down her throat.
glanced at the digital clock on the wall behind the reg-
ation desk in the waiting room.

en forty-five.

reat! She'd been waiting an entire fifteen minutes. The
chologist said she'd be with Lincoln for at least an hour.
etween having breakfast with Cassie in the cafeteria
the nurse kicking her out of the room for Lincoln's
ch consult, Angeline had barely had five minutes alone
h Lincoln since he'd woken up this morning. Maybe
as for the best. The hospital wasn't the place for the
versation they needed to have.

eaching for her purse, Angeline fumbled through the
tents for her phone then dialed Miriam's number.

Good morning, dear," her aunt answered on the first
. "How's Lincoln?"

Awake and alert." Angeline slouched in the chair. "He's
h a specialist now. If all goes well, Lincoln will come
ne today."

A specialist? That sounds serious."

Just a precaution." At least, that was how Doc had ex-
ned it.

And how are you?"

Better now that Lincoln is awake."

If you need tonight off, I'll call Ginger to come in."

That won't be necessary," Angeline said. "She cov-
d for me when I left early on Valentine's Day. I'm not
ng to ask her to give up another Friday night." If Lin-
came home, he'd need to rest. If he didn't, Angeline
ld need to keep herself busy.

Jimmy and I don't need to be at the restaurant for a

while. Do you want us to come to the hospital and v
with you?"

"No." She glared at the clock's red LED display,
nouncing the time as ten fifty. When had a morning e
passed more slowly? "How's Zach?"

"He's fine. A little shaken to have had a front-row v
of a Dogman's meltdown."

"Lincoln didn't have a meltdown," Angeline said
fensively. "He suffered a traumatic flashback and reli
the most horrific moment of his life. He didn't lose just
leg in the explosion, he also lost his best friend."

"I didn't mean to upset you, dear."

"I know. I'm just edgy."

"Everything will work out." Always positive, Mir
truly believed her mantra.

Life had taught Angeline that although everything ev
tually did work itself out, it wasn't always the way
expected.

"I'll see you at Taylor's later."

After her aunt said goodbye, Angeline pulled up S
taire on her phone. Though not particularly challengi
the card game allowed her mind to vegetate rather t
race.

When the nurse called her name, more than an h
had passed.

"Yes?" Angeline put away the phone.

"Lincoln is asking for you." Carmen smiled pleasar

"Thanks." Angeline tossed her empty coffee cup i
the nearest garbage can.

"I bet it's exciting," Carmen said, grinning. "Datir
Dogman."

"To me, he's just Lincoln." Angeline had once imagi
Dogmen as narcissistic, coldhearted bastards but be
with Lincoln had helped her see past her own prejudi

"Aww." Carmen laid her hand over her heart. "That is o sweet."

"I'm gonna go check on him." Angeline collected her acket and purse then walked down the corridor to Lin-oln's room.

The door was partially closed, so she knocked before asing into the room.

"Hey, Angel." Lincoln's smile warmed her inside and ut. "Come to break me out of this place?"

"That depends on whether or not you've been cleared or discharge," she said, watching him put on his pros-hetic leg.

"Where's your sense of adventure?" He winked. "Mind anding me my pants?"

Angeline doubted he would be in a playful mood if the octors had wanted to keep him longer for observation.

She retrieved his clothes from the small corner closet nd laid them on the bed. "Mind telling me what the psy-hologist said?"

Lincoln put on his jeans. "I'm okay, but she wants me get counseling to help me cope with what happened."

"Do you plan to follow through?"

Lincoln shoved his arms down the sleeves of a black weatshirt, poked his head through the neck and tugged down over his scarred, muscular chest. "I agreed to a ew sessions because I don't want to snap and hurt you or nyone else."

Angeline's heart melted. She hadn't expected him to dmit that counseling might be beneficial. Her father and rothers would've flat out refused.

Lincoln closed the distance between them, then drew er into his arms and held her snugly against his chest. Al-ough warm and safe in his embrace, she sensed a cold chasm emerging between them. One she hoped to close once she learned the meaning of the photo.

After the nurse brought by the discharge papers, Lincoln held Angeline's hand as they left the hospital.

He seemed his regular self, yet Angeline knew he was keeping secrets.

A Dogman and their missions were often top secret. Those secrets, she wouldn't demand to know. But the one concerning *her*...absolutely.

They made a quick stop to pick up sandwiches for lunch before returning to the apartment. Lincoln blocked the wind nipping at her back as she unlocked the door and hustled inside. Dropping the sandwich bag on the coffee table, she shucked off her coat and tossed it onto the sofa chair before plopping on the couch.

Lincoln took his time removing his coat and laid it carefully across the back of the couch. His movements were always deliberate, as if he had mentally calculated every possible move and chosen the most direct and efficient one to employ. She appreciated that he wasn't reactive or impulsive. Simply strong, steady. Solid.

Still, he kept secrets and, if they were going to be mates, Angeline needed to know that she could trust him and show that he could trust her.

"Lincoln, there's something I need to tell you."

He met her gaze and worry troubled his eyes. "Same here, Angel."

"Damien told me about the old photograph of me and I went through your wallet to find it."

Lincoln sat next to her, then curled his fingers around her hand.

"Tanner took that picture on our first date. How did you get it?"

'He gave it to me," Lincoln said quietly. "Right before died."

'You were with him?" Tears stung Angeline's eyes, and ıustic knot rose in her throat.

'Yes."

Suddenly, Angeline felt as if all the strength had drained n her body. Although sitting, she swayed from the dizng assault.

Lincoln pulled her close, tucking her beneath his arm, she rested her cheek on his shoulder.

'My first deployment," Lincoln began, "the team I was got sent overseas to replace Tanner's team. There was overlap so they could bring us up to speed on the prools and mission plans. We were doing a ride-along with human forces when Tanner's Humvee ran over an IED. convoy took heavy fire. By the time I reached him, e was nothing I could do."

'Was he in a lot of pain?" The words were barely a sper because her throat had tightened.

'No," Lincoln said after a pause. "He was clutching r picture and told me if he had a second chance, he'd ose you."

Angeline wanted to cry, but so many tears had already n shed that no more were left to fall. All this time she'd eved that Tanner had abandoned her without a sec- thought. Knowing he hadn't filled her with a genuine se of peace.

Lincoln took out his wallet and gave Angeline the pic-. "I asked HQ to find you, but no one from Tanner's k knew you."

He was in his senior year in college when we started ng. I never met his family or pack." Angeline turned photo over. On the back, Tanner had written her name, but over time the ink had worn off and only the first f letters—Angel—were readable.

"I couldn't bring myself to throw away an angel, so I' kept her with me ever since. Sometimes, knowing that c day I had to find this woman is what kept me going." L coln stared hard at the picture in her hands and she kr it was much more than a photo to him.

"I want you to keep it." She handed him the photo. "I good luck."

"She certainly is." Lincoln's finger lightly traced t woman in the picture. His gaze lifted to Angeline. "I you are so much more to me."

Cupping Angeline's face, Lincoln pressed his l against her mouth and kissed her so sweetly, her he ached because in that moment she absolutely knew t Lincoln was already planning to leave.

Chapter 24

Do you want to talk about what's bothering you?" Lincoln asked, watching Angeline shove her barely touched sandwich into the refrigerator. He couldn't pinpoint exactly when her mood shifted but it had definitely worsened during lunch.

"You're leaving. I can feel the inevitability of it coming much sooner than later." Uncertainty shimmering in her eyes, she flattened her hands on the kitchen counter. "How much time do we have?"

Lincoln's lunch suddenly felt like lead in his stomach. He'd wanted to break the news to her gently and with a lot of reassurances. Instead, he'd have to blurt it all out and hope for the best.

"I'm waiting for HQ to finalize the return flight to Munich. I expect it will be sometime Saturday evening."

"I see." She tensed, her muscles tightening to the point of rigidity.

"I don't think you do." He gathered the paper his sandwich had been wrapped in and his empty glass, then joined her in the kitchen. "I mentioned there are a few things I have to take care of before my retirement papers were processed."

"Is your retirement a lie?" She didn't meet his gaze.

"No." Lincoln placed his glass in the sink, disposed of the trash, then took the picture of Dayax out of his wallet and handed it Angeline. "I promised this little wolfling that when I left Somalia, I would take him with me. His parents were killed and his pack can't support him."

Tears filled Angeline's eyes as she traced the boy's outline in the photo, and a lump formed in Lincoln's throat.

"My final orders are to give him a home." His voice cracked. "Brice has been helping me with the adoption paperwork, but I have to be the one to go get him."

"What's his name?" Angeline's voice was barely a whisper.

"Dayax."

"Why didn't you tell me that you're going to be a dad?"

"I wasn't sure how you would feel about the situation." Lincoln's heart began to race. "Because if you accept me as your mate, then you become—"

"A mom!" Angeline slipped her arms around his neck and silently sighed against his body. Her essence touched his and he could feel the happiness bubbling inside her.

The tension balled in Lincoln's stomach eased. "Once HQ gets everything arranged, I'll pick up Dayax, sign a lot of paperwork and then we're flying home." An oversimplification of the truth, but he didn't want Angeline worrying. If her fears leaked into their strengthening mate-bond, he wouldn't be able to concentrate on the mission.

"So it's not dangerous?"

"No." Lincoln would swear to the lie as many times as it took for her to believe it.

He'd spent years holding on to her photo. Now that he'd found the real woman, nothing would keep him from returning to her.

"Can I call you?" she asked.

"No, it's against regulations. Everything will be fine, Angel. I promise." So much had happened in such a short time, Lincoln looked forward to things slowing down once he officially retired. "We should get some rest."

Angeline's brow arched in a beautifully delicate curve. "By rest, you mean—"

"Rest," he said, despite his body's instant response to her unspoken suggestion.

"I don't want to sleep away what little time we have."

"We have a lifetime ahead of us." He hoped.

"Fine!" She clutched his hand and led him to the couch. "Take off your pants."

"Angeline." He growled soft and low, but it didn't have quite the warning he'd intended and didn't stop her nimble fingers from unfastening his belt.

Playfully, she tugged his zipper. "If you want me to stop…" Her beautiful blue eyes slowly gazed up at him. "Just say so."

An impossible feat considering his mouth had gone dry and his tongue felt so thick that forming the word seemed an impossible task, even for a Dogman.

Holding his gaze, she inched down his zipper, taking nearly an eternity to open the fly. A sexy smile widened her luscious mouth a second before her hand cupped his sack and lightly squeezed.

Already hard, his shaft strained against his boxers and his inner wolf prowled anxiously, eager to claim his mate. Lincoln drew a deep, deliberate breath into his lungs.

There could be no claiming today. Otherwise he'd never be able to leave her and do what needed to be done to get Dayax back.

She stroked his shaft through his clothes. "Last chance to say no." As she dragged out the last word, a very clear picture of her soft-looking lips taking him into her mouth formed in his mind. His entire body primed to receive the laving attention the vision promised.

If she wasn't a she-wolf, he might've expected to hear her purr as she slid his pants and boxers over his hips and down his legs. Instead, a possessive, feminine growl rumbled softly in her throat.

Oh, boy!

Slowly, Lincoln sat on the couch and clasped the prosthetic.

"You don't have to take that off," she said softly.

"I want to be comfortable and this—" he tapped the stump cup "—will only get in the way."

Angeline perched on the coffee table, giving him seductive smiles and searing glances as he removed the prosthetic and took off his other shoe.

"Mmm." Her gaze warmed his groin before lifting to his face. "Lose the top, too. I want you completely naked."

She didn't need to ask twice. Yanking the sweatshirt over his head, he dropped it behind the couch.

"Now, you." Lincoln cradle his sack with one hand and slowly stroked his shaft with the other.

Employing the same torturous speed she used to bring down his zipper, she unzipped her boots and tossed them aside.

Lincoln groaned. He'd never make it through the striptease.

After the second boot came off, she took her time inching up her sweater before pulling it off to reveal the lacy ra hugging her creamy breasts. Lincoln squeezed the base of his shaft, stalling the orgasm clamoring for release.

"Angeline." The menace in his growl warned that his ontrol was waning.

She gave him a perfectly innocent look as she slowly ushed down her leggings. Not once did she break eye ontact. Stepping out of the leggings, she moved directly n front of Lincoln.

"I need a little help with the rest," she said, all breathy nd sexy. She turned around and wiggled her lace-clad ackside.

Lincoln grasped her waist and pulled her into his lap.

Startled, she let out a small gasp. Instead of pulling way, she relaxed against him.

His hands glided over her smooth abdomen and his fin- rs toyed with the waistband of her panties before delving neath the lace to find her wet and wanting.

"Mmm." She arched and rocked her hips to match the ythm of his strokes through her folds.

Lincoln smiled against her cheek then nosed her hair ide to pepper her jaw with wet kisses. The slightly salty ste of her skin made him hunger for so much more.

Dipping his finger into her opening caused her to iver. She was close, so close, to ecstasy because of his ich. He wouldn't disappoint her.

Teasingly, he slipped two fingers inside her, alternat- g the rhythm of each stroke. She writhed against him, aning incomprehensible words that grew louder and der until her inner walls began to spasm and her body mbled.

Closing his eyes, Lincoln breathed in her scent, allow- her essence to invade to the depths of his soul. Never d he hoped to find such deep and utter contentment.

Even becoming a Dogman hadn't filled him the wa
she did.

He belonged here with her, he knew that to the marro
of his being. Once he returned with Dayax, they woul
be a family and nothing would ever separate them agai

Limp as a wet noodle, Angeline forced her eyes to ope
Lincoln's soft, rhythmic breathing replaced the hum in h
ears. And his strong, muscled arms caged her in a way th
made her feel safe and treasured.

"Wow," she sighed. "I needed that."

"I know you did, Angel." Lincoln's words whisper
across her ear. Gently nuzzling her neck, he retraced t
kisses he'd placed earlier.

She tilted her head, granting more access to his war
lips. Every touch, caress, stroke and kiss, she committ
to memory. As much as she wanted to believe Linco
would come back to her, part of her feared he wouldn't

Blinking back unbidden tears, she pushed open his ar
and stood in front of him. His gaze freely roamed h
body, branding her skin along every inch where it linger
When he lifted his face to hers, she slowly removed h
bra and panties, then returned to straddle his lap.

Needing to be close to him for as long as possible, s
held his face between her hands and kissed him deep
drawing in his essence in the hope he would becom
very present part of her soul. She probed the depths of
mouth, wanting to brand his taste on her tongue.

His rough but gentle hands kneaded her buttocks as
took control of the kiss, laying claim to every inch of
mouth before abruptly breaking away. Pulling her clo
he lifted her so that her breasts were but a hairbrea
from his face.

He flashed a wicked grin then blew a breath across

skin. Anticipatory chills ran down her spine and her nipples tightened into rosy buds. In an erotic game, he sucked one peak into his warm, wet mouth, flicked his tongue against the nipple until she squirmed and slowly released it with a noisy pop, only to do the same to the other one.

Angeline drove her fingers through Lincoln's thick black hair, clutching him to her chest. All the while, his hands roamed her body, warming, teasing, possessing. Claiming her with his touch.

No one had ever turned her into a quivering ball of need and want the way he did. She could think of nothing else but joining with him. Merging completely.

His hands caressed her shoulders then slid down her back until they fastened around her waist to lower her until they were face-to-face again. When he looked into her eyes, she felt the masculine touch of his essence fill her soul.

Trailing her hand down his muscled chest, she felt the warmth of his skin, the beat of his heart and the tremble of desire the closer she came to his groin. Dark and angry-looking, his erect shaft strained toward her open legs.

Gently molding her hand around the base, she rubbed the tip through her folds before guiding him inside her, inch by glorious inch, until he filled her completely.

His groan rolled into a possessive growl. One hand pressed against her lower back while the other snaked up her spine and cupped her neck. She clung to him as his hips lifted with each thrust and hers rocked in tandem.

Earlier, his fingers had teased her to the brink of ecstasy and kept her hovering there until she'd thought she might go mad with need before finally succumbing to orgasmic release. Now, there was no playful torment. Only a hard, fast pace, driving her onward until she shattered.

Ribbons of color dazzled her mind. Lost in the overwhelming sensation of wave upon wave of pleasure pulsing through her body, she would've drifted into oblivion if not for Lincoln's essence tethering her to him.

Groaning with his release, Lincoln tightened his steely arms around her as his hips stilled. His pants synced with hers and gradually eased to soft, even breaths.

"Still with me, Angel?" he said in a hoarse whisper.

"Uh-huh," was all she could manage to return.

He smiled smugly and she could almost hear him congratulate himself on giving her a bone-melting orgasm.

"Two." His voice whispered through her mind, a manifestation of their deepening mate-bond. *"I gave you two bone-melting orgasms."*

"I was faking," she answered in kind.

Lincoln laughed out loud. Deep, rich, satisfyingly male. And she loved every arrogant note.

Closing her eyes, she squeezed him tightly, knowing that soon they would say goodbye. "I don't want this to end."

"It won't, Angel." His deep, masculine voice was a soothing whisper.

Knees beginning to ache, she eased off his lap.

He clasped her hand before she had a chance to stand. "Lie with me for a while."

In his eyes, she saw that he wanted her as close as possible for as long as possible. Despite the affirmations that his trip to pick up Dayax would not be a long one, she saw a flicker of doubt.

He stretched out on the couch, turned onto his right side and hooked his arm beneath the sofa pillow. Then he urged Angeline to lie on her right side and snuggle into him. Once she settled, he rested his stump against her thigh and pulled the sofa blanket over them.

"This is nice." She relaxed in the heat of their bodies and the ebb and flow of their mingling essences.

Lincoln didn't say anything but she could feel him smile

ainst her head. Angeline also sensed his thoughts turn vard, so she reached for the remote, turned on the tele- ion and lowered the volume. After flipping through the annels, she stopped on a home and family talk show.

A few minutes later, Angeline yawned. The lack of ep over the last couple of days had caught up to her. e closed her eyes, waiting for the commercials to end.

"Hey." Lincoln nudged her.

Angeline glanced at the clock. Nearly three thirty. "Oh, I have to get ready for work."

She sat up and Lincoln caught her hand.

"I saw a commercial for the Academy of Country Music vards. Is your song nominated?"

"Two are. Why?"

"You should tell your family and accept the award in rson."

"Um, no." Angeline reached down to pick up her clothes. here's no guarantee that my songs will win. Even if one l, my father and brothers would not be impressed."

"I am," Lincoln said quietly. "I'm proud of you and your ent. Your family deserves a chance to be proud, too."

Angeline kissed Lincoln lightly on the lips. "You're eet to think so, but my dad won't be impressed."

"What about Miriam and Jimmy?"

"They don't need to know, either." Not sharing the mu- al side of her life with them tweaked Angeline's heart, t she couldn't tell them because it would be too hard to ep the news from her father and brothers. She was better keeping that secret. Besides, her aunt and uncle would ist she quit working at Taylor's, and they needed her.

"I'm happy with the way things are."

No, not really. But the secret had gone on so long that let it out now might do more harm than good.

Chapter 25

"¿Dónde has estado?" Lincoln used the remote to turn
the television. He'd been texting Damien to call or co
home ever since Angeline had left for work.

"No estamos en servicio activo." Damien closed
front door. "I don't have to report to you."

"I'm an officer. And active duty or not, you would
port to me if you were still a Dogman."

Damien's face reddened and the jagged scar along
cheek turned a blackish-purple. "Don't get all high
mighty. You're on your way out of the Program, too."

"Not yet."

"Oh, Somalia." Damien waggled his hands. "Do
really think the Program is going to put you in a hot zo
They're jerking you around, man."

"I'm headed to Munich tomorrow night. My orders
I'm going back to Somalia."

"Who at HQ fucked up?" Damien dropped into the liv-ng room chair. "You're missing a goddamn leg!"

"This one works fine." Lincoln tapped his knuckles gainst the stump cup.

"You're going back for that kid, aren't you?"

"I won't leave him behind."

The muscles in Damien's jaw flexed. "How did you onvince HQ to actually put you back in?"

"Brice has connections to the Woelfesenat. And I asked im to put in a good word for me."

"He's got that much sway?"

"I guess someone on the Council owed him a favor." incoln knew Damien well enough to know the wheels ere already turning in his mind. "Brice won't help you t reinstated."

"You know that for a fact, do you?"

"He's the one who told me that you were discharged d why."

"There's nothing wrong with me," Damien snarled. 'hey had no right to kick me out."

"You suffered a head injury and refused treatment. If u can't prove mental and physical fitness for duty, you t booted."

"HQ is letting you back in and you're missing a leg."

"I have to take the physical readiness test." Lincoln ped the training he'd been doing would pay off. Oth-vise he'd be sidelined and it would be a crapshoot as whether or not Dayax trusted an unfamiliar extraction m enough to go with them rather than going wolf and nning away. "I'm flying out of Atlanta tomorrow after-on. I'd like you to come with me."

"For what?"

"HQ is better equipped to help you deal with your in-ies."

"Then why didn't they fix my face?"

"I don't know. Maybe they would have if you'd und gone the psych treatment."

"My brain works fine. I'm not going to become one their lab rats."

"So you'd rather leave the Program for good?"

"Yes." The flicker in Damien's eyes betrayed him.

"Why didn't you go home?"

"Yeah," he scoffed. "Going home a washout isn't h on my list of things to do this year."

"So you tracked me down for what? To reminisce ab the good ol' days?"

"I thought—" Damien snapped his mouth shut a stared hard at Lincoln. "Doesn't matter now."

"You were looking for a place to fit in and, since here, you thought Walker's Run might welcome you, to Lincoln knew he'd guessed right by the surprised look Damien's face. "They might, but if you want to stay, yo have to get the counseling recommended by the Progra

"You're the one who had the meltdown yesterda Damien shook his head. "Yet I'm the one who needs th apy."

"I met with a psychologist and I agreed to follow recommendations because I don't want anyone to get h because of me."

"A little late for that, don't you think?" Damien snort

"Not a day goes by that I don't think about what h pened. But I'm not entirely at fault. I gave a specific ord Lila, you and the rest of the team chose to ignore it. I ca undo my decision any more than you can undo yours."

Damien responded with silence.

"Once I return from Somalia, I'm retiring. I plan make Walker's Run my home."

"Because of *her*?"

"If you're referring to Angeline, then yes."

"What is it about the she-wolf that has you so wrapped up in homesteading?"

"She's my true mate." From the moment Tanner had given Lincoln the photograph, he unknowingly had been on a path leading him straight to her.

"And HQ thinks I'm the crazy one." Laughing harshly, Damien rolled his eyes. "You're a Dogman. How can you think of being anything but that?"

"Because after this mission, the Program doesn't want me and I've found someone who does." Not once in the last fifteen years did Lincoln have the courage to dream of a happy ending with the woman in the photo. To him, she had been as ethereal as an angel. And too good for the likes of him.

Then he'd met the real flesh-and-blood woman—strong, sassy and independent—and had fallen madly in love with her, not the photograph.

"What about me?" Damien's voice rose and bitterness laced his tone.

"Your whole life is ahead of you. You can go anywhere, do anything."

"The only thing I've ever wanted to be is a Dogman."

"Me, too." Lincoln's heart squeezed at the anguish in the young man's face.

"It isn't fair."

"No one ever said it was. But we're trained to adapt to any situation. This is no different, for either of us."

"So you're adapting by taking a mate and settling down?"

"Yeah."

"Lame, man. So lame. With your skills you could get contract work with any pack in the world."

"I'm settling in Walker's Run. It's time I learned a new set of skills." Such as how to be a good mate and father.

"Such a waste." Damien stood, his face twisted into a grotesque mask of disgust and despair. "I need some air."

"Hey," Lincoln called out before Damien reached the door, "I'm staying with Angeline tonight and leaving tomorrow afternoon. But Tristan doesn't mind if you squat here until you figure things out."

"Gee, thanks." Sarcasm weighted Damien's words.

"Walker's Run is a great place and you've made friends among the sentinels. Give some thought about staying. If you agree to follow a treatment plan, this could become your home, too. You could make a good life here."

Damien answered with a derisive snort and slight head shake. He left, closing the door with a quiet click, which unsettled Lincoln more than a resounding slam would have.

Lincoln started to go after Damien, but the kid had a lot to process and needed some space. If Lincoln had been sidelined so early in his career, he might not have reacted very well, either. Hopefully, Damien would see what lay before him as an opportunity rather than as a dead end. Because a Dogman with no options could quickly turn feral. And Lincoln didn't want to be forced into putting down one of his own.

I'm going to be a mother!

The roar of the Friday night crowd at Taylor's could not drown out that one singular thought in Angeline's mind.

Mixed emotions jumbled her nerves and caused her stomach to clench. She had no idea how to be a mother. Being a fantastic aunt was what she knew, and Angeline made a conscious effort to shower her nieces and nephews with as much love and attention as she could muster. But

ı her own experiences, she realized that an aunt was
he same as a mother. Miriam had been a strong and
ıg influence in Angeline's life and they had forged a
ː bond, but their relationship had never pinnacled that
parent and child.

he wondered how the relationship between her and
ax would evolve. Mother. Aunt. Or something else.
egardless, she would do her best to help Lincoln raise

Angeline!"

Hmm?" She glanced at Avery, the bartender.

Your drink order is ready." She pointed to the four tap
s and one specialty bottle on the bar.

Thanks." Angeline began placing the drinks on the
d tray in her hands.

Are you okay?" Avery dropped ice cubes into two
d glasses. "You haven't seemed yourself all night."

'm fine, just have a lot on my mind." With drink order
ınd, Angeline squirmed through the swell of people
nd the bar and headed toward the tables.

Here you go." She placed the glasses in front of the off-
sentinels and the bottle in front of Reed. "Is Damien
ing?"

ince his arrival, Damien seemed to have bonded with
ral of the sentinels who were close in age.

He might come later," Shane said. "He's training with
ı."

Why? Lincoln has been working with him." Angeline
't like the idea of her younger cousin joining the Dog-
program, but since he was dead-set on it, she trusted
Lincoln would help him prepare.

Lincoln spazzed out. Zach got freaked. Can't say that
me him," Shane said.

Give Lincoln some slack," Reed snapped. "You have

no idea what it's like to—" He sealed any further w
behind firmly pressed lips, picked up his ale bottle
left the table.

The color in Shane's face faded and he stared ha
his glass. An awkward silence blanketed the table. Li
they were all remembering that only a few months
Reed had faced his own mortality at the end of a poac
shotgun. And he hadn't quite gotten over it yet.

"Shake it off, guys," Angeline said. "Lincoln and I
need understanding, not pity. Besides, we all have th
that get to us from time to time."

Lance, a newly deputized sentinel, raised a toast an
young men's spirits seemed to lift. Except for Shane,
picked up his glass and joined Reed at the bar.

"I'll check on you guys later." Angeline left to at
her other tables.

The rest of the evening went by in a blur, with the
not slowing until closing.

Slumped in the booth she'd been cleaning, Ang
propped her feet on the opposite seat and closed her
feeling like she could sleep for a week. Of course,
couldn't. Once she got home, she wanted to spend e
waking second with Lincoln. Not that they had many
before he had to leave for Atlanta.

Though he promised not to be gone long, she h
nagging feeling things wouldn't go as smoothly as he
dicted.

"Hon, why don't you go on home?" Jimmy sque
her shoulder.

"I haven't finished cleaning my stations." She h
yawn.

"We'll take care of it." Her uncle held out his ha
help her stand. "You all right to drive home?"

"I'm tired, not drunk. I just need some coffee."

"There might be a pot on in the kitchen." Jimmy picked
p the cloth from the table and began wiping down the
eats.

"Thanks." Angeline headed to the kitchen, swallowing
e urge to ask for Saturday night off. She and Lincoln had
iscussed her accompanying him to the airport but he'd de-
ded it would be too difficult to say goodbye at the termi-
al and preferred to make the near three-hour drive alone.

After pouring the last of the coffee into a large to-go
ip, Angeline put on her coat, said good-night to the late-
ight staff, went out the back door and walked to her car.
he chilly night air wasn't as cold as it had been last week,
ut it was still frosty enough for her to appreciate the car
eater.

Sitting behind the steering wheel, she jabbed the key
ito the ignition and turned it, expecting the vehicle to
oar to life. Sadly, it didn't.

She tried again and got the same result. "Damn battery."

At least she wasn't stranded. Jimmy and the others were
ill inside the restaurant.

Leaning across the middle console, she reached for her
urse on the passenger side floorboard.

Rap, rap, rap!

A squeal accompanied Angeline's startled jump. Twist-
ig in the seat, she saw Damien outside the car, his face
eering in the window.

"Everything okay?"

Angeline took a calming breath. "The battery is dead."

"Want a lift?" Damien looked perfectly decent, but a
reepy-crawly sensation rose from her clenched stomach.
'I'm parked over there." He pointed to the car near the
ght.

"A jump would be better," she said. "I have cables in
e trunk."

"I'll bring the car around." Damien jogged across th
parking lot.

Guilt replaced the uneasy feeling she had. Damien ha
never actually done anything to warrant her distrust. Stil
she remained inside, instead of climbing out to get th
cables.

He parked in front of her vehicle and opened his hoo
"Pop the trunk," he said, walking past her window.

Obediently, she pressed the button to unlock the trun
then pulled the lever to open the hood. Damien worke
quietly and quickly. In only a few minutes he called o
for her to crank the engine.

The car roared to life. Shortly afterward, he closed bot
hoods and returned the jumper cable to her trunk.

"I'll follow you out," he said, walking past her windo
without stopping.

"You really are a nice guy, Damien Marquez." Dismis
ing the annoying nag in her mind, Angeline waited for hi
to get into his car before backing out of the parking spac
and driving home.

Chapter 26

The first time Lincoln had knocked on Brice Walker's ront door, his life had been in chaos. Now, only a few hort weeks later, he knocked at the door again with a lear hope for the future.

He squeezed Angeline's hand, and she looked up at him. The fragile smile on her lips tugged his heart as much as he reticence in her eyes at attending a Saturday-morning runch at the Alpha-in-waiting's home.

Brice opened the door. Almost immediately they were reeted with a high-pitched squeal and the fast patter of iny feet headed toward them.

"Link-ed!" Arms wide-open, Brenna headed straight or him.

Brice swiped her up and gave her a stern look. "Manners."

"Puh-leez, comes in." Brenna waved her arm, motioning them inside the house.

Lincoln's hand gravitated to Angeline's lower bac guiding her to enter ahead of him.

Brenna tapped him on the shoulder and held out h arms with a happy grin on her slightly slobbery mout Brice handed her off and Lincoln held her in a tight hu

"Good morning, Brenna."

Her chubby cheek pressed into his shoulder for barely second before her attention turned to Angeline. "Who dat

"You don't remember me?" Angeline gave the child playfully exaggerated frown and then pulled the knit ca off her head. "How about now, munchkin?"

"Ann-jeel!" Brenna clapped her hands and leaned t ward Angeline to give her a kiss on the cheek.

"All right." Brice gently took his daughter from Li coln and set her feet on the floor. "Go check on mama."

"Mmm, 'kay." The little girl darted down the hallwa to hunt for her mother.

"She's growing so fast," Angeline said.

"Some days it's hard to believe she's almost two." Bric took their jackets and hung them on the coatrack insid his home office.

They followed him into the open living area, and th delicious smells of cinnamon rolls, ham and eggs mad Lincoln's mouth water.

"Help yourself to some tea or coffee," Cassie said chee fully, putting Brenna in her high chair.

"Juice?" Brenna lifted her sippy cup toward Angelin

"Thanks, munchkin. But I'll stick with coffee." A geline poured a cup for Lincoln and then one for hersel

"You two—" Cassie looked at Brice and Lincoln "– out!" She shooed her hands at them. Although the kitche was large and open, with two wolfan males, two female and a child in a high chair, space was in short supply.

Lincoln hesitated long enough to see that Angeline ha

ed next to Brenna and the two of them were engaged in e imaginary game. A rush of pride caused his heart to ll. Not only would Angeline be a fine mate, she would terrific mother. Of that, he had no doubt.

urning from the heartwarming domestic scene, he fol- ed Brice into the living room. While Brice sat in the iner without the footrest engaged, Lincoln chose the rby love seat.

Are you ready to go back on active duty?" Brice rested right ankle on his left knee and massaged his calf.

Yes," Lincoln said without hesitation.

How about becoming a father?"

hat made Lincoln's heart skip a beat or two. "I never gined becoming a father, so I don't know if I'm ready. I'll never rest easy if he's not in my care."

Will you return to your birth pack to raise him?"

They are good people, but there's a lot of pressure to he absolute best. I want Dayax to have a more balanced ringing." Lincoln glanced toward the kitchen. Watching geline play with Brenna while talking to Cassie filled with a great sense of contentment.

I've decided to bring him to Walker's Run and make mily with Angeline. I just need to figure out how to port them." Though he'd have a sizable pension, Lin- wanted to be useful and productive.

The Co-op's revenues pay for housing, health care, cation and provides startup money for business ven- s. Once you join the pack, all those benefits will ex- l to you and Dayax."

I'm a Dogman. I don't know how to be anything else."

Talk to Tristan about joining the sentinels."

I'm not sure that would be a good idea. I think it could ome problematic within the ranks, and I don't want my ence to undermine the chain of command already es-

tablished." Neither did Lincoln want to start over i
omega position doing grunt work.

"Would you be interested in becoming a personal
tinel to the Alpha family?"

If Lincoln had been in his wolf form, his ears woul
perked.

"A bodyguard?"

Brice nodded.

"Is one necessary? Or are you tossing me a pity bo

"My father thinks one is necessary and Cassie w
feel better if someone we trusted traveled with me w
ever I'm away from home." Brice folded his hands ac
his waist and tented his index fingers. "Our pack is o
cusp of a vulnerable transition. My father will retire
few years. According to tradition, the Alpha's first
becomes the Alpha-in-waiting. Technically, I'm sec
born, but my brother was killed a few years ago, lea
me to inherit the Alphaship."

Brice glanced over at Cassie then back at Linc
"Brenna is my firstborn and it's her birthright to suc
me. Even though we're decades away from her step
into that role, some packs have already expressed conc
not only with her gender, but that her mother is huma
was her paternal great-grandmother."

Lincoln easily understood Brice's concerns. Less
gressive packs were likely already positioning themse
to overtake the Walker's Run pack if the opportunity a

"To make matters even more interesting, Cassie is p
nant. If we have a son, we could face pressure from
Woelfesenat to put him forth as the Alpha heir."

"But you have friends on the Council."

"Not enough. Yet." Brice's expression remained
tral, but Lincoln had no doubts of the weight his fr
carried on his shoulders. "We have no intention of us

ing Brenna's birthright. Nor will we allow anyone to pressure her into abdicating."

As the pieces of information began clicking into place, Lincoln understood why the Walker's Run Co-operative had taken measures to create a legitimate police force, along with its own emergency services and establishment as a municipality.

He had to give Brice credit. A lawyer, trained by his uncle, the renowned Adam Foster, Brice had figured out how to use the full extent of human laws to protect his family and his pack.

"So." Brice's gaze—one blue eye, one green, both of equal intensity—pinned him. "Are you interested?"

And just like that, Brice called in the favor of his help for getting Lincoln returned to active duty.

"Yeah, I am."

A fierce negotiator, Brice went to extreme lengths to resolve issues peacefully, but as those scars on his throat could attest, he was also damn lethal when he had to be. And if the Walkers were gearing up for a dogfight, Lincoln sure as hell wanted to be the one standing with them, not against them.

Saturday afternoon, after using nearly half a bottle of eye drops and a cool compress, Angeline's eyes were no longer red and puffy.

All day, she'd held in tears so Lincoln wouldn't see her weakness, but the moment he'd left, the floodgates opened and unleashed the despicable waterworks. She was lucky if there was any moisture left in her body.

"You big baby," she said, scowling at her reflection.

There was comfort knowing Lincoln had promised to return. When she'd said goodbye to Tanner all those years ago, there had been no hope of ever seeing him again.

This time it's different, she told herself. Tanner had been at the beginning of his career. Lincoln's career was coming to an end and he wanted to start a new life with her and Dayax.

In a matter of weeks, she would unofficially become a parent. Most mothers had nine months to prepare for their newborn. Angeline had far fewer days to prepare for an eight-year-old she'd never met.

What if he didn't like her? Or worse, what if he *hated* her?

"I think I'm going to be sick." She hung her head over the sink and pressed a cool cloth to the back of her neck.

Immediately, a comforting masculine presence chased away her panic. Hugging herself, she promised to keep better control of her emotions. There was no need to worry Lincoln with her insecurities.

Dropping the cloth and the towel she'd used after showering into the laundry hamper, she padded into the bedroom. Crisply folded, Lincoln's sweatshirt lay on top of her pillow. Her heart melted.

He'd left a token, rich with his scent, to keep her company in his absence. Rubbing the soft fabric against her cheek, Angeline smiled, thinking about the surprise she'd tucked inside his duffel bag.

She draped the sweatshirt over her pillow and dressed for work. Staying busy would keep her mind occupied so she'd have less time to worry.

After putting on her coat, she grabbed her phone and purse and headed outside.

The sun was bright and the sky was clear, giving the false impression of a nice warm day. Still, it was decent enough for folks to enjoy Maico's Art and Craft Show likely in full swing down at the town square. One day she would like to check out all the handmade crafts. Perhaps one in the fall would be a fun activity that she, Lincoln Dayax could go to as a family.

Angeline hurried carefully down the stairs and to her gritting her teeth against the cold nipping at her face hands.

"Come on, baby. I need some heat." She shoved the key the ignition. Something clicked. The engine made a ining noise then died. "I don't have time for this."

She counted to one hundred and tried again.

Nothing.

Spotting Damien's car in the near-empty parking lot, got out of her vehicle and hurried upstairs. Cold and f, her knuckles hurt when she knocked on the door to coln's apartment.

"Damien? It's Angeline."

A moment later she heard footsteps and the door ned. Dressed in camouflage pants and a dark sweat-t, Damien peered curiously at her.

"What's up?"

"My car won't start again. Would you mind helping out?"

"No problem." He put on a jacket, pulled a skullcap n his pocket and fit it snugly on his head, then followed down the stairs.

"I appreciate your help. Come by Taylor's tonight. Din-is on me."

"Thanks," Damien said. "But I have other plans."

"Some other time then."

"We'll see."

They crossed the parking lot to her car.

"Pop the hood." Damien turned up his collar, making look like he had no neck.

Angeline sat behind the steering wheel and pulled the er near the floorboard.

Damien propped up the hood. "How old is your batte
"A year." Same age as her car.
"Maybe you have a loose connection." From the sc
of his tinkering, Damien seemed to be checking more
the battery.
Angeline checked the clock on her phone. Miriam
Jimmy wouldn't care if she came in a few minutes
but Angeline hated to not be on time.
"How about another jump-start?" That would at
get her to work and she could ask Jimmy to give the
tery a jump after her shift ended. She wouldn't need
car on Sunday. And Monday she could ask Damier
another jump to get her to the service station.
"You should take a look at this," Damien said grin
Angeline didn't relish the idea of standing in the
while staring at engine parts that she knew nothing ab
but she climbed out of the driver's seat and joined hi
the front of the car.
"What are we looking at?"
"You've got a loose wire."
"Really? Where?"
"Right down there." Damien pointed behind the bat
She leaned farther over the open hood to get a be
view. "I don't see anything." Even though she'd sharpe
her wolf vision because of the low light.
Damien stepped out of her way to give her a better v
"Nope. Still don't—"
Damien's arm locked around her neck and his o
hand pressed against the back of her skull, pushing
head forward. Even as she dug her nails into the fle
part of his arm, her vision darkened until there was n
ing but blackness.

Chapter 27

nety miles north of Atlanta, Lincoln began to feel antsy. flow of traffic had been good and there hadn't been delays, so he didn't know why he suddenly felt like vas about to crawl out of his skin.

quick glance at the console showed the truck had just er a half tank of gas. After checking the rear and side rors, Lincoln eased the vehicle into the far right lane. 'aking the next exit, he drove to the nearest gas station. nbing out of the driver's seat, he did a few stretches, ed up the tank and then walked inside the store. Not icularly hungry or thirsty, he purchased a package of wing gum and a couple of magazines to read on the ht, then returned to the truck.

s he drove away from the pumps, his phone pinged 1 a text message, mostly likely from Angeline. He led because it felt really good to know someone actu- missed him and eagerly anticipated his return.

Having had no contact with his parents since joi
the Program, he had no idea if they remembered havi
son. Or if they would be interested in knowing that
would soon be grandparents.

Lincoln's parents were only children and he had no
lings. At least Dayax would grow up with cousins f
Angeline's side of the family.

Family.

The word resonated in his being.

For the longest time he'd believed having a family
well beyond his reach. Now one was within his grasp
because of a photograph and a little twist of fate.

Instead of pulling onto the road, he parked in a spot
the air pump and vacuum station and picked up his ph
The alert showed a text from Damien. Lincoln swiped
screen to open the message.

A picture of Angeline appeared on the screen and
coln's heart stopped. Lying on a dirty wooden floor,
appeared unconscious. A cloth had been stuffed into
mouth and silver-dipped zip ties bound her wrists and
kles. The silver collar fastened around her neck was
tached to a long silver-coated wire connected to a ne
explosive device. When frightened and trapped, a wolf
natural instinct was to shift. But if Angeline transfor
into her wolf, the silver would act as a conduit for the s
energy and ignite the bomb.

Lincoln called Damien's phone. "Hurt her and I'll
out your throat," he snarled.

"Whoa! Whoa!" Damien laughed. "Settle down, *C*
tán. If HQ knew you were threatening people, they m
revisit your active duty status."

"Where is she?"

"I'm going to hazard a guess that you're asking ab
Angeline. Isn't she working at Taylor's tonight?"

"I'm not playing games with you, Marquez."

"That's too bad." All the humor in Damien's voice was one. "Because right about now, you're approximately half-ay between Maico and Atlanta. Am I right?"

"Yes," Lincoln hissed between clenched teeth.

"So, you get to choose between two outcomes. If you oard that plane in Atlanta, you'll save the boy and lose the irl. If you turn around and come back to Maico, you *might* ave the girl, but will lose your chance to find the boy."

Lincoln's heart felt like it would split in two. How could e choose between Angeline and Dayax?

"Tick, tock. Tick, tock. You have two hours."

"When I find you, I will kill you," Lincoln shouted nto the phone.

"I didn't figure you would abandon your promise to the oy so quickly." Damien's heartless laugh made Lincoln ringe. "Then again, if your guardian angel dies, what appens to you?"

The line went dead.

Lincoln's heart pounded furiously as fear unleashed a eluge of adrenaline into his system. His hands trembled o badly that he nearly dropped the phone while searching he contacts for Brice's number. It took three tries before e managed to hit the call button.

"Damien has Angeline," Lincoln shouted before his riend finished saying hello. "He's tied her to a bomb and only have two hours to find her!"

"I'll mobilize the sentinels to track them," Brice said almly. "Where are you?"

"On I-75. I'm ninety minutes away." Lincoln heard the anic in his own voice and some part of him believed this vas all a dream. "He's making me choose between Ange-ne and Dayax. If I miss the plane, I won't make it to HQ n time to meet up with the team heading to Somalia. If I atch the plane, I'll lose Angeline."

Worse than the nightmare reliving the explosion inside

the abandoned building in Somalia, this situation woul
likely kill him or some part of him. Because losing eithe
Angeline or Dayax would leave a gaping wound in his soul

"Do you know where he's holding her?" Brice's clea
level voice helped modulate Lincoln's rising panic.

"No, but he sent a picture."

"Text it to me. We'll start looking as soon as the senti
nels are gathered."

"If they find her, tell them to not engage." Swallowin
the caustic lump lodged in his throat, he forwarded Bric
the picture. "I'm coming to get her."

He'd made the best decision in the midst of an awful cir
cumstance, and it was the one he knew Damien expecte
him to make. Dogmen prioritized rescues based on th
most eminent and immediate threat of danger. Angelin
was tied to a bomb. Dayax had a hostage extraction tean
working to free him and the other children.

"I just received the picture. I'll keep you updated."

"Brice, get word to HQ. I'm not going to make the fligh
so the team will have to go without me. As soon as the
make contact with Dayax, they need to tell him that they'r
bringing him to me. Or he'll run away at the first oppor
tunity." And Lincoln would likely never find him.

"Will do."

Disconnecting the call, Lincoln focused his mind o
the rote mantra he used to prepare for dangerous mis
sions. Once all emotion had drained from his conscience
he slammed the gearshift into Drive and spun out of th
parking lot with a singular thought.

Damien Marquez is a dead man.

Something hard and cold pressed against Angeline'
cheek. Opening her eyes, she saw a black snake coiled i
the wake of a parallel sunbeam about six feet away.

ler startled gasp never left her throat because of the
e wad of cottony material stuffed into her mouth and
l in place with a strip of cloth tied around her head.
ckly, she visually scanned the room, at least what she
d see from her angle, lying on the floor.

leither seeing nor hearing Damien, Angeline tried to
p. Since her wrists and ankles were bound behind her,
ok several attempts before she was successful.

rom the weight around her neck, she suspected Damien
collared her and the silver wire dangling down her
t and beneath her arm was some sort of leash.

eally?

he would've thought a Dogman would be more origi-
n kidnapping a she-wolf. Her gaze followed the wire
ss the dusty floor to a strange device sitting in front
everal gas cans.

un!

ler instinct flew into panic mode. With her hands and
tied, all Angeline could do was scoot away from what
ared to be a homemade bomb. The silver tether didn't
v her to get far.

ormally, shifting would be her first response. The en-
from the transformation disintegrated any material
hing her skin. Except silver.

hanging into her wolf form wouldn't free her but it
ainly might kill her.

he tried to maneuver her legs and discovered that not
were her hands and feet tied behind her, they were
trussed together. Somehow, she had to find a way to
ree.

hidden knife inside her boot was the perfect solution.
bad she'd scoffed at the idea when one of the human
ers at Taylor's suggested it. Why carry a knife when
could shift into a wolf and use her razor-sharp teeth?

At the time she'd never considered a scenario in whi
Dogman would kidnap her and chain her to an explo
device.

Think. Think. Think!

What would her father and brothers do?

Angeline huffed. They wouldn't have gotten themse
into this situation.

She'd broken the first rule: never let your guard do
People like Damien were the reason for the rule. H
gained her trust and, *wham*, used the Sleeper Move to
capacitate her.

Unable to do anything else, Angeline studied the ro
The dusty windows were boarded up with old plank
the outside. The walls and floor were wood, termite
fested and rotten, from the looks of the panels. The h
door appeared to be solid oak, with rusty iron hinge
doorknob and slider lock.

A hole in the baseboard at the far right corner of
room, might've been where the snake had entered. U
her knees to scoot around, she saw an old stone firepl
Black marks scored the bottom of the pit and up the f

From what she could tell, Damien had dumped her i
old abandoned antebellum but she had no idea where
particular house was located. There were several thro
out the area and Tristan knew each and every one. But
geline had no way of contacting him. Even if she co
she had no idea how long she'd been out. Damien coul
driven her anywhere, including right out of the Walk
Run territory.

Damn! All the years she'd resented her father's d
to make her tough, to make her capable, to make her
as hard-boiled as her brothers, now she understood w

She fought against the restraints. The thin silver
bit sharply into her skin but there was no give, no ma

ow hard she pulled. Exasperated, she roughly rubbed her heek against her shoulder until she worked the gag loose nd spit out the cloth.

Sharp pain shot through her jaw as she closed her outh, the muscles in her face and neck sore from being orced open for an unknown period of time. With no moisure in her mouth, dry-swallowing felt like sharp barbs iding down her throat.

Creaking boards distracted her from the pain. She atuned her ears to follow the sound of movement. Booted otfalls seemed to echo from different directions inside e house, as if someone was moving back and forth beveen rooms. Then silence.

Angeline tried to quiet her breathing in the eerie quiet. he sunbeam warming the snake faded. Slowly lifting s head, it stuck out a forked tongue to scent the air for anger.

The footfalls began again. This time in a linear path at seemed headed toward the door to Angeline's prison. er heart raced.

On her knees, with her hands and feet fastened together ehind her back, she had no means of self-defense. She ouldn't even count on the snake, a black racer without e tiniest bit of poisonous venom.

Booted steps stalled at the door. The iron lock wiggled en turned. Slowly, the door creaked open and Damien epped inside the room.

"Untie me, right now!" Angeline's voice cracked from e dryness of her throat.

"I'm not in the business of taking orders." His cold, ark gaze flickered over her.

"You're a Dogman! You take orders all the time!"

Madness churned in the arctic depths of his fathomless

eyes. "No and no. Not anymore." His precise enunciatio
sliced the chilly air.

"What does that mean? You're *not* a Dogman?" In he
current predicament, Angeline figured it was best to kee
him talking. Maybe she could find a way to reason wit
him and convince him to let her go.

"HQ's quack doctors think I'm…" Damien tapped
finger against his temple. "I'm not. But they cut me fro
the Program anyway. So the answers to your question
are no and no."

Oh, Angeline begged to differ. Damien might not b
a Dogman now, but he definitely needed professional in
tervention.

"I don't have any sway with the Program." She softene
her voice, hoping to lure him closer. "Why do this to me?

"I don't give a damn about the Program," he snarle
"Not anymore."

"Then what does this accomplish? Why have you rigge
me to a bomb, Damien?"

He paced a wide berth around her. "Lincoln always be
lieved in his guardian angel. The rest of us thought yo
were nothing more than one of those photo inserts foun
in new wallets. Turns out—" he shrugged "—you're rea
And you're his true mate."

Damien stopped in front of her, but far enough awa
that she couldn't lunge forward to topple him. "That i
why you're here, *Angel*. Dogmen don't have true mates.

"Lincoln isn't a Dogman anymore. He's retiring."

"Aww." Damien squatted so he was eye level with he
"Is that what he told you?" His toxic laughter made he
flinch. "Here's the truth. Captain Lincoln Adams is pa
of a team headed to Somalia and his mission is to extra
hostages from the rebels' camp."

"You're lying." Lincoln promised he wouldn't be in da

er, promised he was only signing paperwork and then ould bring Dayax home.

"I have no reason to lie," Damien said. "I already have ou here and my plan has been set in motion. Lying serves ne no purpose."

"Except to hurt me."

Damien's mouth twisted into a grotesque smile. "That's hat the bomb is for, *Angel*."

"Stop calling me that!"

"Never heard you object to Lincoln saying it."

"You're not Lincoln!"

Damien's creepy smile faded as he replaced her gag. And you're no angel. I checked." He waggled his hands. No wings."

What she was, was a pissed off she-wolf. And the mo- nent she got loose, Angeline would show him how much f an angel she wasn't, using nothing but her bared teeth.

Chapter 28

Dirty old snow flew past the windows. The truck jostle
from the deep potholes on the unpaved road but Linco
did not let up on the accelerator.

Within twenty minutes of his call to Brice, the Wal
er's Run sentinels had tracked Angeline's phone using
GPS tracker. Unfortunately the device and her jacket ha
been found down the embankment of the ravine where h
crumpled car rested at the bottom.

No one believed she'd hit an ice patch and missed th
curve at Wiggins Pass. The consensus was that the acc
dent had been staged. Recovery crews hadn't found a bod
but Lincoln knew they wouldn't because the mate-bond
shared with Angeline had not been severed.

Periodically, he could sense her during moments
strong emotional reactions. However, he intentional
blocked feeding his emotions back to her, because

nien knew they were communicating through the mate-
d, he might escalate his plan before Lincoln arrived.
Which would be within minutes, thanks to Tristan.
After arriving home from the hospital with his mate
newborn son and getting them settled, Tristan had an-
red Brice's text with the picture Lincoln had forwarded.
Tristan recognized the room where Angeline was being
l and had sent a handful of sentinel scouts to the aban-
ed MacGregor homestead.
As Lincoln barreled into town, his phone had pinged
a photo confirmation that Damien had been sighted at
location and a message that they were still trying to
a visual on Angeline.
He had responded with a request to pull the sentinels
k to at least a half-mile radius. If Damien got wind of
interference, he might simply level the house with
geline inside.
Sharply jerking the steering wheel, Lincoln swung the
k onto the overgrown driveway dusted with melting
w. Despite the initial fishtailing of the back tires, he
d toward the dilapidated house overrun with thick ivy
es and hardy weeds.
Nearing the porch, he slammed on the brakes and cut
wheels to the left while engaging the emergency brake.
truck swung in a complete circle before stopping.
Lincoln jumped out of the truck and bounded up the
h steps. Not fooling with the lock, he planted his shoul-
in the center of the large, double mahogany doors with
r rusted hinges and gave a good, hard shove. A sec-
shove with his full weight behind him brought the
rs down.
Angeline's essence suddenly rushed him. Relief, worry,
er, fear—all of it a tidal wave of emotion that nearly
cked him off balance.

"I'm here, Angel." He stood in what once might h
been an elegant entryway flanked on both sides b
curved marble staircase leading to the second-floor
cony, which looked like it might collapse at any mon
The row of doors vaguely reminded him of the buildi
Somalia where he'd been searching for Dayax. No sur
that Damien had picked this place for whatever twi
game he wanted to play.

"Lincoln! It's a trap."

"Don't worry, sweetheart. I know what I'm doing."
coln cautiously stepped around the jagged remains
glass chandelier. When this ordeal was over, if he n
stepped inside another abandoned building again, it w
be too soon.

"Are you hurt?" Lincoln focused internally, trus
his instinct to lead him to his mate.

"I'm tied up, but okay."

Lincoln began walking down a corridor toward a
on the left. Perhaps once a study or a cigar room of
main floor.

"I don't know where Damien is."

"I'll find him once I get you out." Lincoln rappe
knuckles against the door panel.

"Someone's knocking."

"It's me. Do you see any wires running along the
frame?"

"No!"

Holding his breath, Lincoln slowly and carefully tu
the knob and opened the door. His heart dropped a
sight of Angeline bound and gagged in the center o
room.

After a quick visual inspection to determine there
no trip wires, Lincoln darted to Angeline. Tears sh
mered in her big, blue eyes.

"I will get you out of here." He pulled the gag from her mouth and she spit out a wad of cloth. "Did he hurt you?"

She shook her head.

Lincoln lifted the silver-coated wire running from her neck collar to the explosive device. "Did he say anything about the collar? Can we take it off?"

"No," she said hoarsely. "He said the bomb would go off."

Lincoln carefully ran his finger along the inside of the collar. He didn't feel a second trigger but wouldn't tempt fate.

Pulling out a pocketknife, he sawed through the silver-coated zip ties fastening her hands to her feet. Angeline began to topple forward. Lincoln caught her shoulders and helped her maneuver into a position to maintain her balance.

"Hang tight." Lincoln slipped the blade beneath the ties at her ankles. "You'll be free in a minute."

Less than that with any luck.

"Lincoln! Look out!"

Damien's wolf slammed into Lincoln with enough force to knock him across the room and push Angeline to the floor.

Lincoln shook off the momentary surprise and saw the brindle-colored wolf crouch over Angeline with his teeth bared, growling a challenge.

"Damien," Lincoln said, knowing the wolf could understand him. "You're a Dogman. We don't hurt innocents."

The wolf's growl got louder.

"You're making it hard for me to believe that you don't want to hurt her." Lincoln slowly and carefully rose on his hands and knees. "Back away from her."

Mouth open, Damien swung his muzzle toward Angeline.

Lincoln sprang forward, shifting into his wolf at th
same time Angeline thrust her knees into Damien's ribs
As Damien fell back from her self-defense move, Lincol
knocked him clear.

Both wolves hit the floor and skidded into the wal
as a tangled heap. Uninterested in a parlay of bites an
scratches to gain dominance, Lincoln immediately lunge
for Damien's neck.

His mouth filled with fur, but before Lincoln clampe
down on the young Dogman's throat, Damien wrangle
free.

"What the hell is wrong with you, Marquez?" Lincol
positioned himself between Damien and Angeline.

"I'm finally seeing things clearly," he snarled. *"
would've followed you anywhere. Hell, I did follow yo
and lost half of my face."*

*"You're angry at me because you disobeyed my orde
and got disfigured in the process?"*

"I would've worn this scar like a badge." The wol
shook his twisted muzzle. *"You and me? We could'v
worked together. Lots of packs would've taken us on con
tract. Hell, the one in Miami already made an offer. D
you know how much money we could've made? The fu
we could've had?"*

*"You kidnapped the woman I want to claim as my mat
because you wanted us to be business partners?"* Prima
rage rustled in the deep, dark, dangerous recesses of Lin
coln's being. But he needed to rely on his training to re
solve the current conflict without unleashing the primitiv
beast within.

"I looked up to you," Damien snarled. *"Hell, I wa
happy that the Program put you back on active duty sta
tus. And then you said you were giving it all up for her."*
Damien glared at Lincoln. *"Traitor!"*

Lincoln anticipated Damien's launch toward Angeline l intercepted. Both wolves crashed to the ground in a nzy of gnashing teeth and slicing claws.

Never did Angeline imagine in all the times her broth- had tied her up when they were kids that the experi- e would one day come in handy.

Though her hands and feet were still bound, they were longer tied to each other. Which meant she could wig- around, working her hands below her feet and…voilà, hands were now in front of her.

She sat up, saw the pocketknife Lincoln had dropped l scooted close enough to pick it up.

Angeline's bound hands made it awkward to use the fe to saw through the silver zip ties. Lincoln had cut ough the first restraints effortlessly. Then again, his ds hadn't been tied together.

Lincoln's and Damien's growls were no longer warn- s. She glanced up as they collided in the air, their bodies gling as teeth gnashed and claws slashed with deadly ent.

Crashing to the floor, the wolves wasted no time scram- ng to their feet. Lincoln continued to block Damien's ances. The problem was that once Angeline freed her- , she'd have nowhere to go because Damien was clos- to the door.

She might've caught him unawares with a knee to the ly once, but doubted he'd give her a chance to do it in. Continuing to awkwardly saw at her restraints ped to keep her focused on not freaking out. Although had no idea what to do once her arms and legs were because the wire to the collar around her neck was nected to a freaking bomb.

Lincoln will figure it out, she told herself.

A blood-curdling howl of pain caused her to drop
knife. She jerked in the direction of the fight.

Missing part of an ear, Damien bled from a gap
shoulder wound and multiple bites and scratches. Lin
had several deep scratches and two really bad bites,
still had both of his ears.

Neither wolf moved. Perhaps a temporary truce?

Angeline fumbled for the pocketknife and continue
work the blade through her wrist bindings.

Someone barked. Startled, Angeline jerked and
knife sliced across the back of her hand. She clam
down on the cry of pain before it passed her lips, af
any noise from her would distract Lincoln, who was
tively engaged with Damien again.

She forced her attention from the wolves ripping
each other with their teeth to her own wound. The cut
freely, but when she wiped her hand against her shi
clean away the blood, the wound looked shallow and
already started clotting. Holding her hands in front of
face, Angeline studied the marks on the zip ties. He
tempts had barely scratched through the silver coatin

If she couldn't get the bindings off, it would do no g
to go wolf. Silver morphed in tandem with the shift
body, which meant she'd still be bound in her wolf fo

Clearly, she understood why some animals chewe
a limb when caught in a trap. Sometimes it was the
alternative. However, she had not reached that poi
desperation. Yet.

Picking up the knife, she wedged the handle betw
her teeth with the sharp edge of the blade safely prot
ing beyond her lips. Then she positioned her wrists o
ther side of the blade, pulling downward on the tie as
sawed backed and forth until the binding broke.

Yes!

he glanced at the wolves. Blood and spittle matted their :s, puddled on the floor and smeared along the walls.

)h, God!

'hey would both bleed to death unless they stopped iting soon.

lands now free, Angeline feverishly attacked the bind- around her ankles with the knife until they broke. She tched her legs and wiggled her toes, trying to rush the ing back into her feet.

n her peripheral vision, she saw a flicker of move- it and looked up to see Lincoln's hind paw slide into a dle of blood, causing him to lose his balance. Damien nced, biting and swiping at Lincoln until he went down.

Get the hell away from him!" she screamed.

)amien swung his muzzle around and his cold, dark, dly gaze targeted her. She sensed the threat of attack re one muscle flexed to propel him in her direction.

nstinctively, she flipped the knife so that the handle ited upward when she raised her hand, then threw it, like her father had taught her to do.

'he knife sailed toward Damien. The rotation could've ı better but the weapon struck the target and stuck. Un- unately, it didn't stop him. But it did make him angry.

ngeline's instinct screamed for her to shift.

incoln's wolf rose up behind Damien and slammed to the ground. The force of the landing caused them ide straight toward her.

'here was no time to get out of the way. Upon impact, flew in one direction, the two wolves in another.

haking off the daze from the hard landing, Angeline d her gaze. The silver wire dangling from the collar ind her neck was no longer tethered to the explosive ice.

"Run!" she screamed at Lincoln, who had Damie the throat in a kill strike.

She shifted. Darting out of the room, she raced dow corridor, leaped over the broken glass on the foyer f bounded across the broken doors at the entryway, ski across the porch, sailed over the steps and kept runn

Lincoln shadowed her, barking nonstop. Urging h run faster.

Dammit! She was trying.

At one time, the meandering, oak-lined drive might've been a delight, but covered in melting snow petrified acorns, it was a bitch to run.

The first glimpse of the dirt road beyond the prop gave her the adrenaline boost she needed. Her spee creased, and Lincoln kept pace.

They were going to make it. Surely they would.

Lincoln suddenly slammed into her. She landed in deep ditch alongside the road with him on top of her.

The tremble in the cold, wet ground beneath them g into a seismic force. Only then did she hear the per sive force of the house exploding along with the sh of glass, the whoosh of debris sailing past and the t when it dropped to the ground. It was over in seconds it felt like an eternity.

When all fell quiet, she felt the buzz of shift energ Lincoln returned to his human form, naked and wit his prosthetic. He eased his weight from her body.

"Baby, are you all right?" Uncertainty sharpened voice as he removed the silver collar around her neck

Angeline shifted. "I'm okay."

Bloody and dirty, Lincoln hauled her against him hands gliding over her nude body as if to make sure spoke the truth. Seemingly satisfied, he let out a breath.

“Do you think Damien made it out?” she whispered.

“No. He didn’t want to make it out.” Lincoln buried his ace in the curve of Angeline’s neck.

Even though the danger had passed, Angeline realized he was shaking. Lincoln, however, was rock-steady and miling against her bare shoulder.

His secret thoughts whispered through Angeline’s mind. n that moment she knew. Damien hadn’t lied to her.

But Lincoln had.

Chapter 29

Lincoln's plane to Munich was flying over the Atlanti
and, instead of seeing blue skies and even bluer wate
he stared up at the ceiling lights in the emergency bay
Maico General Hospital.

"Okay," Doc Habersham said. "That's the last stitch."

"Thanks." Lincoln sat up on the gurney and glance
at the new patchwork on his body. Then, he fingered th
gauze covering some nasty gashes on the side of his nec
that would definitely leave obvious scars when healed.

"You get used to them," Brice said. And he shoul
know, having a similar reminder of when someone ha
tried to rip his throat out, too. He pushed up from the cha
in the corner and handed Lincoln some clothes and shoe
"You look about my size, so I hope it all fits."

Lincoln was grateful for the hand-me-downs since hi
clothes were in the duffel bag in the passenger seat of th

:k that had been destroyed in the explosion. Along with rything else he owned—which was very little.

Shoving his right foot into the pant leg, he had to roll he left to pull the jeans over his hip, then roll to the it after putting his stump in the other pant leg. He ap- ciated that Brice didn't offer to help. Dressing wasn't easiest task but it was one Lincoln could do indepen- tly, even covered in stitches.

Once he put on the long-sleeved shirt, sock and shoe, coln felt somewhat normal again, except for the miss- prosthetic. HQ would not be happy that his bionic limb been destroyed.

Hell, they probably wouldn't even issue a wooden re- cement now. Crutches might be his only available ns of ambulation for a while.

"I'm going to need a new place to stay," he said qui- . "Without my prosthetic, three flights of stairs will problematic."

And that wasn't his only worry. Through the mate- d, he felt Angeline distancing herself from him and ensed the real possibility that she would reject a mate- with him.

Have you decided not to return to Somalia?"

I missed the last flight that would put me at HQ in time ake the physical readiness exam and join the team be- they leave."

After what you just went through to save Angeline, no at HQ will doubt your readiness."

I appreciate the vote of confidence, but I don't see how uld make it to Munich before the team leaves."

I happen to know that Councilman Bartolomew is ing Atlanta for Munich on a private jet tonight," Brice . "There's a seat reserved for you, as well."

"A member of the Woelfesenat just happens to be gc to Munich. Tonight?"

"I believe he said there was some paperwork at HQ garding the transfer of a minor wolfling that required personal attention."

Lincoln rubbed his temple. "Exactly how many fa does the Woelfesenat owe you?"

Brice smiled but said nothing.

A nurse came in with a pair of crutches for Lincoln. " said he put through your discharge papers. You're all set tc but he wants to see you in ten days to check your stitche

Though he politely nodded his agreement, Lincoln pected to be gone a lot longer than ten days if he cc wrangle HQ into giving him a new prosthetic in time to dezvous with the team going to Somalia. "How's Angeli

"A little dehydrated. Doc has her on IV fluids. should be ready to go home soon." The nurse handed some paperwork and left the room.

Using the crutches, Lincoln got up from the bed. "I v to see her before I leave."

"I'll wait for you in the lobby," Brice said.

Lincoln carefully maneuvered down the hallway, instinct leading him to Angeline's room. She looke fragile sleeping in the hospital bed that he couldn't lieve she was the same woman who'd stood up to a ranged Dogman, freed herself from captivity and esca a deadly bomb.

It was difficult to be quiet, easing into her roon clumsy crutches.

Opening her eyes, she smiled at him, but it was br and stiff.

"Hey, baby." He leaned down, giving her a soft k "The nurse said you can go home soon."

"What about you?"

"They've already kicked me out." He curled his hands around her fingers resting on the bed. "I don't have much time, Angel. Brice arranged for me to hitch a ride to Munich with Councilman Bartolomew."

Her body went rigid. "Damien said your medical retirement was rescinded and you're back on active duty. You're not just signing paperwork, you're going into a war zone. How could you lie to me?"

"You've been lying to your family for years because you're afraid of telling them the truth." As soon as the words finished spilling from his mouth, Lincoln regretted them.

"How dare you!" She jabbed her finger in the direction of the door. "Get out!"

"Angeline, I'm leaving and I don't know how long I'll be gone. The last words you say to me will be the ones written in my heart when I go into Somalia."

Tears glistened in her eyes. "Just go," she whispered.

Lincoln had hoped that Angeline would put her faith in him. But on the heels of everything that had happened, she simply didn't have the courage to do it.

Leaning over her, Lincoln kissed her sweetly on the mouth. "In case these are the last words you hear from me, I want you to know that I love you and I believe in you."

In silent agony, Angeline had watched Lincoln leave. After his profession of love, a vacuum had opened in her chest, crushing her heart and stealing her breath.

She'd gone through this with Tanner. He had loved her, too. But not enough to choose her over the Program.

What a fool she'd been to fantasize about a mateship with another Dogman and motherhood. Now her heart was doubly broken. And the only thing Angeline could tell herself was that she should've known better.

"Angeline?" Her father stood in the doorway, holding a

bag of her clothes and personal items to wear home afte discharge. "Are you all right?"

"I'm okay," she said, noticing the worry lines creasin his forehead. "Doc said I can go home once I've finishe the IV fluids."

The strain on her father's face didn't ease as he sat i the bedside chair and reached for her hand. His gaze swep her head to toe and back again before the stiffness in hi posture faded. "Coming in, I met Lincoln leaving. He sai a curious thing."

I bet he did.

Her emotions raw and ragged from allowing herself t end up in the same devastating position she knew she neede to avoid, Angeline didn't want to deal with the impendin inquiry. Especially because Lincoln was right. She had bee hiding the truth from her father for most of her adult life be cause she was afraid of his ridicule and rejection.

"What is this whole other side of you that he mentione I should get to know?"

Continuing to keep the truth from her father woul only prolong the inevitable. The time had come to fac the music.

Figuring the beginning was the best place to start, An geline told him all about pursuing music instead of a busi ness degree. About falling in love with Tanner and hov much his rejection had hurt when he'd chosen being a Dog man instead of her, and how she'd channeled those difficul emotions into writing award-winning songs.

When she finished unfolding the details of her secre life, Angeline waited for her father's response.

And waited. And waited.

"Are you going to say something?" she finally asked.

"Why did you wait so long to tell me?" Her father's dis appointed gaze searched her face.

Angeline folded her hands in her lap. "You never approved of my musical interest. Instead, I had to take karate classes to make me tough. How could I tell you that I'm earning a living writing songs about getting my heart broken?"

"Don't you think I understand heartache? Your mother was everything to me. Those first few months, even a year or two after she died, I was so lost that I didn't know what to do." Her father swiped his hand across his jaw. "I regret giving away her things, but at the time I couldn't tolerate the reminders."

"Is that why you cut off my hair? I've always thought it was because I looked like mom."

"I was a single father with three young kids and no time to primp and curl a little girl's hair."

"What about the music lessons? Aunt Miriam paid for them because you wouldn't."

"I thought you were going through a phase and I didn't want to waste money." His sigh sounded sad and tired. "Until now, you've never explained to me how much music meant to you."

"Would it have mattered?"

"I wouldn't have been happy to learn that you wanted to write songs for a living. A career like that is a risk. I would rather know that my children have a solid foundation for their future."

"Is that why you're always badgering me during Sunday dinners to join the family business?"

"I thought you were floundering. You don't have a mate and I'd hoped you would eventually have higher aspirations than being a part-time server at your aunt and uncle's restaurant."

"There's nothing wrong with waiting tables for a living."

"No, there isn't. But I was right. You did want more for

yourself. I just wished you hadn't kept your talent a secret. Songwriting isn't a job I would pick for you, but I'm proud of you, no matter what you do for a living."

"One of my songs is nominated for an Academy of Country Music Award. The event will be televised live from Las Vegas in April. Maybe we can get everyone together to watch."

"How about we go there instead?" her dad said in earnest.

The heaviness in Angeline's chest gave way to an effervescent joy. "I'd love it!"

Her father stood, then leaned over and kissed her forehead. "Lincoln should join us, too."

Some of Angeline's happiness dimmed. "He's a Dog man, Dad. He isn't coming back."

"That's not what Lincoln told me." Her father squeezed her hand. "What's this about a new grandson?"

Angeline's heart paused while her brain processed her father's words, then it kicked into overdrive as a jumble of emotions fought for dominance. "What did he say exactly?"

"He's going to get his boy and they're both coming home to Walker's Run, if you'll have them."

"I need your phone!"

Clasping the device her father handed to her, Angeline dialed Lincoln's number. Her heart, which seemed to have climbed into her throat, tumbled into her stomach when the recording announced incoming calls were no longer accepted.

All she could do was pour all of her love and support into the mate-bond and trust that her intentions were getting through because she did not want her last words to Lincoln to haunt him the way they did her.

Chapter 30

unfire echoed in every direction, though no one on
rescue team had fired a single shot. Still, they took
'antage of the confusion and advanced on the insur-
its' compound.

Waiting for the team leader's next signal, Lincoln
ised a gentle feminine essence graze his spirit. Always
intrusive, Angeline had reached out to him through
ir mate-bond on a daily basis for the three and a half
eks he'd been on active duty.

More than once he'd been tempted to respond, but en-
iraging the connection was a Program violation and
ild distract him at an inopportune time and devastate
if something terrible happened. Though touched by her
pressions of support, especially after the way they had
ted, Lincoln closed her out of his thoughts and senses.

Redirecting his focus to the rebels who kidnapped chil-
n and forced them to become soldiers in their militia,

he watched two adult males with rifles slung over t
shoulders walk within a few feet of his hiding spot.
urge to rip them to pieces for their parts in the atro
grew as they passed him on their rounds. But the tas
take out the foot patrols fell to someone else.

Lincoln was on point for first contact with the k
When the time came, he would have to maneuver thro
the enemy compound to the building the reconnaissa
scouts had identified as the children's barracks. Ne
midnight, all should be asleep in the common quar
making it easier for Lincoln to get them in one swoo

He glanced around the compound, his wolfan vision
hindered by the suffocating darkness. The cloak of o
nous clouds provided an additional layer of coverag
the team, already dressed head to toe in black clothing
wearing camouflage paint on their faces. Lincoln ho
his appearance didn't frighten the children. He nee
their trust to get them out alive.

The gunfire ceased one minute and twelve seconds a
it started, just like the last five times. Too patterned t
actual gunplay, he suspected the rebels were brainwash
the children into believing their captors were protec
them. Depending on how long the ploy had been in use,
children could be affected by Stockholm syndrome. W
ever their condition, Lincoln prayed that Dayax would
ognize that he was not the enemy.

"All clear." The CO's voice whispered through Linco
earpiece. "Go, go, go!"

Immediately, Lincoln sprang forward and ran. His t
porary prosthetic didn't have the versatility the previ
one had, but it fit comfortably and provided solid, ste
support.

With his heart practically in his throat, he reached
of the trucks the rebels used to gather and transport c

dren after a raid. Hunkered down, he glanced around to ensure he'd not been seen. Then, he slipped a tactical knife from the sheath fastened around his good leg and jabbed it into the back tire. Jerking the weapon free, he heard the hiss of escaping air.

Carefully, he eased along the driver's side, the body of the vehicle shielding him from the view of any foot patrols. After puncturing the front tire, Lincoln broke radio silence.

"The mongoose is in the pocket."

"The mongoose is in the first pocket. Hawks stay frosty." The CO's whispered instruction went out to the entire team.

One obstacle down, five more to go.

Random foot patrols slowed the team's progress and their standing orders were not to engage unless discovered. In that event, hand-to-hand combat was preferred. No one wanted to alert the rebels of their presence. The likelihood of successfully escaping with all twelve children unharmed dropped dramatically if all hell broke loose.

Still, every team member had been equipped with an M16A4, just in case.

Finally reaching the barracks, Lincoln dispatched the unsuspecting lone guard, then pressed his ear against the door. Not hearing any suspicious movement, he carefully entered the single-room building. Thirteen children were sleeping on small mats strewn on the floor.

Damn!

The recon team had only counted twelve.

Lincoln broke radio silence. "The mongoose is in the ring with a baker's dozen. Repeat, *baker's* dozen."

In the ensuing radio silence, he scanned the room, his gaze settling on Dayax's small form. Lincoln's heart nearly leaped from his chest. After nearly thirteen weeks of separation and worry, he'd found his wolfling.

Lincoln swallowed the gasps of joy and relief rising in his chest. Danger surrounded them, and he had a lot to do before allowing himself to celebrate.

The team had five escorts—three of whom were Lincoln's former teammates—assigned to whisk two children at a time to safety, with Lincoln providing cover as they retreated. Either someone would have a trio to wrangle through the woods and protect, or he would have to keep number thirteen with him.

The CO made the call for the latter.

Quietly, Lincoln woke up Dayax first.

The boy's dark eyes widened. "Lincoln!" He threw his thin arms around Lincoln's neck. "I knew you'd come."

Lincoln's throat closed around a sharp, ragged breath that he had to clear before he could speak. "Shh. We must be quiet." He held the boy tightly, his heart pounding so hard, he thought his ribs might break. Since the wolfling had gone missing, Lincoln had hoped and prayed for a moment just like this one.

But they weren't out of danger, not yet.

Lincoln gently pulled back, gritting his teeth against the painful resistance of every muscle. "I need you to help me explain to the others. We're taking them home." Although Lincoln could speak Somali, he knew the children were more likely to trust one of their own than a stranger.

With Dayax's help, they quickly and quietly woke up the remaining twelve. Lincoln paired up the six oldest children with the younger ones, leaving Dayax as the solitary spare.

Lincoln checked the perimeter and radioed the CO.

Once he received instruction to begin the evacuation, he sent them two by two to the first spotter stationed less than thirty feet from the building, who then sent them to the second spotter, and so on and so forth until each had two children they would escort through the woods to the endezvous point. Once the final pair made it safely to the ast spotter, Lincoln knelt in front of Dayax.

"Do exactly what I say when I say it. Don't think, just o it. Okay?"

Dayax nodded.

Lincoln shouldered his weapon and eased out of the arracks. Almost immediately, his senses tingled.

Drawing the tactical knife from its sheath, he spun to e left and threw the weapon at the guard racing toward em. The target dropped silently to his knees, clawing at e knife lodged in his throat.

Clutching Dayax's hand, Lincoln quickly followed the ath the other children had taken. Shouts went up behind em. From the sound of the chatter, someone had found e guard Lincoln had dispatched.

Lincoln and Dayax stayed their course. When gunshots ng out and bullets whizzed past Lincoln's head, he pulled ayax behind the nearest tree, readied his weapon and re- rned fire.

Above the commotion, he heard the rebels' shouts and eir advancing steps. Outgunned and outmanned, their pture was certain if they remained where they were.

He hadn't come this far to end up dead.

Lincoln grabbed Dayax's arm. "Run!"

The boy dropped to his hands and knees, shifted into s wolf and bolted through the woods. Lincoln did the me, only he was much faster. On the fly, he picked up e wolfling by the nape of the neck and ran like the devil d lit his paws on fire.

Chapter 31

Sitting in a large auditorium filled with famous face
Angeline twisted the note card in her hands.

"Don't be nervous." Sandra—Angeline's longtime agent
squeezed Angeline's hand. "You've got this."

I hope so!

However, Angeline's reasons for wanting to win t
Songwriter of the Year Award were likely entirely diff
ent from her agent's reasons.

Angeline had not heard a peep from Lincoln in ove
month, despite flooding the mate-bond with love and po
tive vibes at random times throughout the days and nigh

She firmly believed that he remained unharmed a
that he had successfully rescued Dayax. If the oppos
were true, she would know.

The performing act finished their routine, and An
line joined the audience in giving applause. The em
appeared on the opposite corner of the stage, gave

roduction to the next category and then called out the nes of the nominees.

"And the Song of the Year goes to—"

Angeline held her breath, but the emcee had trouble ening the envelope. She nearly passed out from lack of ygen before the song title was announced along with name of the songwriter. Generous applause erupted.

At home, she would do her happy dance in front of the evision. But in the auditorium with a stage and lights l cameras, Angeline froze.

Anonymous for so long, she wasn't as prepared for the otlight as she'd hoped.

"Come on, hon." Taking Angeline's arm, Sandra helped stand.

Clutching a handwritten speech, Angeline made her y to the stage. A young man wearing a tuxedo escorted up the steps and across the stage to the podium where was handed a small statuette of a golden hat.

The bright lights prevented her from seeing the audice, which she decided was a good thing. As applause d down, she opened the note card in her hand.

"Thank you for this wonderful honor. Usually, I'm at me watching the awards ceremony on the television. t it is a privilege to be here with you tonight and, for first time, to share this special moment with my fam, who are somewhere in the audience."

She paused. "Until recently, they didn't know that I was ongwriter. Despite any previous awards or accolades l songs that reached number one on the charts, part of felt that my talent wouldn't measure up in their eyes."

Angeline wished she could see her family's faces right w. Too many opportunities to share her life with them l been lost because of the fear of their rejection. "But lly, I was reflecting my own insecurities onto them.

And I'm so very thankful to Lincoln Adams for com
into my life and teaching me how to have faith in mys
in my loved ones and in him. He's the reason I came
night, because he's out there somewhere, working har
make the world a better place. And before he left, I di
take the opportunity to tell him how much I love him.
I'm doing it now."

She thought of his smile, his larger-than-life presen
but mostly she thought of his unwavering loyalty. "Linc
wherever you are, whatever you are doing, know that I l
you with all of my heart. I believe in you. Thank you
teaching me to believe in myself. I miss you, and I'll le
the light on so you can find your way home."

Tears rolling down her cheeks, Angeline stepped aw
from the podium to the sound of thunderous applau
Though a weight lifted from her shoulders, her heart
mained heavy.

An escort led her backstage, where she walked a gau
let of flashing cameras and big fat microphones bei
shoved in her face for impromptu interviews. Of cour
Sandra steered her safely through them.

When her splotchy vision returned to normal, she s
a young wolfling approaching with a red rose. His
brown eyes, flawless bronze skin and dark, tight, cu
hair cropped close to his head caused an unusual bea
her heart. He flashed a gloriously beautiful smile. "A r
for an angel," he said with an accent.

"Thank you, sweetie." Accepting the flower, she kr
in front of him. Prickly tears threatened to blur her vis
again. "Are you—"

"Dayax Adams," he announced proudly. "Linc
signed papers to be my *aabbe*. The tall man on the pl
said it's not 'ficial, yet. But I can say he is."

"Come here." Angeline hugged him tightly. "I'm so happy to meet you."

"You smell good," he said, sniffing her hair.

"Already taking after your dad." She laughed. "Speaking of Lincoln, where is he?"

Grinning, Dayax took her hand.

Angeline had to step quickly to match his pace. All the while her heart raced as the wolfling led her straight to a man wearing a black tuxedo and surrounded by her entire family.

He turned and stepped from their midst.

Lincoln!

Her heart couldn't decide whether to race, furiously pound or flutter with happiness. She forgot to breathe and her knees threatened to buckle.

"Hello, Angel." Lincoln opened his arms, and she melted into his embrace. "I'm so proud of you."

Her family echoed his words.

"I missed you," she said, pressing her face into the curve of his neck and inhaling his clean, masculine scent.

"I missed you, too." He kissed the crown of her head and a feeling of rightness spread through her body, all the way down to the tips of her freshly polished toes.

"Why didn't you call me after you found Dayax? Or reach out through the mate-bond?"

"I couldn't make any calls. We left Somalia immediately following Dayax's extraction and flew to Germany on a transport. Once we got to HQ, we went through extensive debriefing and then I had to be fitted with a new prosthetic. Since I didn't know when we would get back to the states, I asked Councilman Bartolomew to get word to you. But he cut through the red tape and flew us here in a private jet."

Lincoln grazed her cheek with the back of his hand. "As

for the mate-bond, you don't know how much I wanted to reach out to you. But it's against protocol and I didn't want to risk screwing up the adoption or my retirement plans. It's scary what the Program can do. But that's all behind us now, baby."

Her heart settling comfortably in her chest, Angeline took her first easy breath since Lincoln had left. "Did you see any of the show?"

"Enough." He smiled that wonderful smile of his. "I love you, too, baby."

"Angel?" Dayax tugged her arm, then presented to her a tiny box. Inside, she found a beautiful marquis diamond ring.

"I choose you, Angeline O'Brien, to be mine for now and always." Lincoln slid the ring onto her finger. "And I promise to love you until my last breath, and beyond."

"That's an awfully long time, Dogman. Are you sure you're up to the challenge?"

"Retired Dogman." Lincoln gathered Angeline close and held Dayax's hand. "And I've been preparing for this my whole life."

* * * * *